CHEYENNE ATTACK

All of a sudden a handful of Indians boiled up out of the sagebrush, whooping and shouting and coming angling over toward us. "Get down in the boot," I yelled at Bucky. Then I commenced laying on the whip to make a run for it.

The shooting was pretty fierce, but the men inside the coach were answering the fire now, and from the tail of one eye I saw one Indian go down. I cut a quick look and saw Bucky kneeling behind the mudguard with my shotgun resting on it. "You damned little fool," I yelled, "get down! The men'll take care of the shooting."

Just as I saw she was safely down again, something like a cannonball hit my left arm and knocked me sideways, and the near reins went slack in my hands. I knew I was hit.

Next thing I knew Bucky was up on the seat beside me and reaching. "Give me the reins."

"If you'll just lift up my hand . . ."

"Give me the reins!"

JANICE HOLT GILES
SIX-HORSE HITCH

AVON
PUBLISHERS OF BARD, CAMELOT AND DISCUS BOOKS

AVON BOOKS
A division of
The Hearst Corporation
959 Eighth Avenue
New York, New York 10019

First Avon Printing, November, 1980

AVON TRADEMARK REG. U.S. PAT. OFF. AND IN
OTHER COUNTRIES, MARCA REGISTRADA, HECHO EN
U.S.A.

Printed in the U.S.A.

To my father

JOHN A. HOLT

*who drove an automobile to the day he died
as if it were a team of horses*

Spirit of the Overland Men

Ben Holladay's drivers and stock tenders were the best. No storms, no dangers could daunt them. I wondered at the time, and have often wondered since, what it was that inspired them. They seemed to possess the spirit that any army does in battle. The fight was on: the bridges burned behind them, and the only thought was "Forward!"

Many heroic deeds by agents, drivers and messengers would be recounted—of facing blizzards, plowing through snowbanks, the dangerous snow and landslides; swimming coach and team across swollen streams; ferrying coach or team across torrents of rivers on frail boats; facing Indians on the warpath; drivers and messengers shot from the box by Indians and road agents. I have known coaches to come in to the station with the driver dead in the front boot, the mail soaked with his blood. I recall instances where employees traveling with coaches attacked by Indians have kept up a fight for a whole day and part of a night, and, finally, with their dead and wounded on the front wheels of the coach, abandoning everything else, and, under cover of the night, making their escape to the nearest station.

. . . There was some incentive that induced these men to brave all these dangers, and I can liken it to nothing except the spirit that pervades brave men in battle.

—David Street, *Paymaster and General Agent, Holladay Overland Mail and Express Company*

Author's Note

Only the Fowler family, the Westmoreland
family and the Indian, Popo, are fictional.
All the other characters are real.

Chapter 1

The first time you climb up on the box of a main line stage and thread the reins of a six-horse hitch through your fingers you feel bigger than you'll ever feel again in your whole life. The kingdom and the power and the glory are in those six cool slick leather lines in your hands. It is Genesis but you feel like it's Revelations. You are skin full and ready to bust with pride.

It happened to me when I was nineteen years old. It was the summer of 1859 and I was at Fort Kearney on the first leg of a long freight haul. The agent for the Leavenworth & Pikes Peak Express came looking for me in the Pawnee Bar in Dobytown. "You Joe Fowler's boy?" he said.

"Yes, sir," I said.

"You the wagonmaster of that freight train over at the fort?"

"No, sir. That's my brother Matt. You want him, he's at the fort."

"Didn't know there was two of old Joe's boys with the train," the man said. He was a short, portly man with a lot of high belly up under his vest, out of which his voice came rumbling up easy and quiet and deep, with no hurry in it.

I grinned. "I'm third in the stairsteps. The second one, Dave, is with us, too."

When the man laughed, his belly shook. "You sure old Joe ain't along, too?"

"No, sir, he's not."

"I've not seen him this season. Where's he keeping himself?"

"Where he most generally is when Congress is in session," I said, "Washington."

He laughed again. "More grease for the axles, eh? Army freight contracts take a lot of time in Washington, don't they?"

"Yes, sir."

"So do mail contracts." He got down to business. "I'm looking for Starr Fowler."

"That's me," I said.

"Yes. They tell me you've driven stage some."

"Some."

He nodded. "I guess you know who I am. Agent for the L. & P.P. here. They tell me you can handle six horses."

"Yes, sir." I didn't say so, but I expect I looked surprised. You didn't need sixes around Fort Kearney. You didn't start pulling sand that heavy until you got farther west.

"We use sixes on the mail stage," he said, explaining, "and we got a mail stage coming in at one. I need a relief driver for it. Think you could take it?"

"Westbound?" I said. Not that it mattered. The run either way would take too long with me due to move out with the train as soon as Fort Kearney unloaded.

"Yes," he said. "Plum Creek. Pat Tweedy's run."

I shook my head. "I'd like to oblige you but I can't do it. I don't have the time."

The agent wore a gold watch chain across his vest big enough to drag logs, and like most men who wear a big heavy chain he had a nervous habit of fidgeting with it. He began fingering it now. "You've got plenty of time," he said. "That train of yours is going to be here at least four more days. I just talked to the Quartermaster."

"The Quartermaster wasn't the one to talk to," I said. "My brother Matt says when that train will move."

The agent was dogged. "The Quartermaster told me he was shorthanded. He's got two wood details out. Said it would take him four days."

"I expect," I said, "the Quartermaster is a good friend of yours and he's agreed to stretch that unloading job to help you out. It's a two-day job and Matt won't stand for stretching it. A wagonmaster," I grinned, "don't like to hang around Dobytown too long. Not if he wants to have all his whackers with him when he leaves."

The man laughed. "I've got ten that says half of them

are over at the Dirty Woman's shack right now." He quit laughing.

"It was the Quartermaster told me about you. That's the only way he's trying to be a friend. He's not holding up the train."

"I don't think he could," I said. "What happened to Tweedy?"

"He got boozed up last night and dropped dead over at the stables a couple of hours ago. Heart failure."

"Well," I said, "that's short enough notice. Why don't your Thirty-Two-Mile Creek driver take the stage on for you?"

"There ain't no Thirty-Two-Mile Creek driver. The man bringing that stage in has been on the box since Liberty Farm."

I whistled. "What happened to the other one? He drop dead too?"

"He might as well have. Him and a couple of boys over at the fort sloped off to the gold diggings."

I laughed. "That gold at Pikes Peak is sure drawing them, isn't it?"

"I never saw the beat of it."

"Not even in '49?"

"In '49," he said, "they all had to get to California on their own. There wasn't no public carrying system then. This one is in my lap because I'm running a stage station."

"I can see there'd be some difference," I said. "The boys helped themselves to some Company stock, I reckon."

"Oh, yes. They didn't pass up a thing. They took a horse apiece and a couple of mules for packs. Guns and ammunition. Supplies. They outfitted themselves pretty well. Which wasn't hard to do, seeing the mess the line's been in since we moved up here."

It had been front-page news when the Leavenworth & Pikes Peak Express had moved their line up from Kansas onto the Platte, so he wasn't telling Company secrets when he went on talking. "We had a pretty operation down in Kansas. Had us a daily. Leavenworth to Denver City. Best equipment this country's ever seen. Best string of stations. Best service and accommodations. Everything going like clockwork."

"Everything but a mail contract," I said.

"You're right. No mail. So they buy the Hockaday line to Salt Lake, just for the mail contract. And it sure has messed us up. Postmaster General made us move everything, lock, stock and barrel, up here on the Platte. Close out everything already going so good and come up here and you might say start from scratch. Hockaday was running on a shoestring. Not half enough stations and the ones he had falling down. We haven't got it all straightened out yet. Everybody in the world and all his kinfolks wanting to go to Denver, and my God, Denver ain't even on the line no more. Got to build a short line down. We haven't got the stage stock all moved up here yet. Haven't got tenders for what we've moved. Haven't got the stations lined up. And we got mail twice a month that come hell or high water we've got to get through. We got treasure on the eastbound runs, and then that sonuvabitch driving the Thirty-Two-Mile run slopes off to the gold diggings with a couple of deserters and Pat Tweedy gets boozed up last night and drops dead on me this morning. We got a mail stage coming in with a driver that's been on the box halfway back to the Missouri. *And* the division agent is riding the line."

I whistled again, long and slow. "You're wearing a real tight crupper, aren't you?"

"It's binding," he admitted. He quit twisting his watch chain and shoved his hands in his pockets. "Well, I've got him a relief for the eastbound run and if I get him one for Plum Creek he can maybe shake the bushes and find some regulars."

A division agent on a stage line did all the hiring and firing. When drivers got too sick to work, or took off for Denver City, or got killed by Indians, or dropped dead, a station agent did the best he could with what he could lay hands on until the division agent showed up. It was then his job to get things straightened out again.

An idea began to glimmer in the back of my mind. It was a brassy, proud, green-kid idea, but nineteen is mostly brass and pride and green-kidness. It's a prickly age to be. The trouble with it—or the best thing about it, take your pick—is it doesn't see any obstacles. It will try anything. It will take on a grizzly bear as quick as a housecat.

The agent took his hands out of his pockets and started fidgeting his watch chain again. "Well, what about it?"

I shook my head. "Sorry."

"If it's pay that's bothering you, I'll make it worth your while."

"How much worth my while?"

"Twenty-five dollars. Round trip."

I shook my head.

"Thirty."

"No, sir."

"Thirty-five and that's as high as I'll go."

"Sorry."

He studied me and fidgeted his chain. "Well, how much do you want, for God's sake?"

"Tweedy's job."

He blinked a couple of times. "That's a job for a man, boy. We don't turn a main line stage over to a kid."

I didn't say anything.

"Tweedy, now," he said, "Tweedy was a fine driver. He could drive anything that could be hitched. He was driving stage thirty years. Tweedy drove in New England."

"Tweedy's dead," I said.

He studied me some more, then he hawked his throat and delivered the spit so expertly into a brass spittoon ten feet away it rang like a bell. "Who the hell you think you are trying to hold up the L. & P.P. for a six-horse job?"

"I'm a six-horse man," I said.

"I don't know it," he said. "I've not seen you drive. There's a hell of a lot of difference between driving stage and bullwhacking."

That was so elementary it didn't even deserve a reply.

"I don't know anything about you," he went on, "except what they told me over at the fort, which was that you'd driven for some short lines around Leavenworth and Omaha."

"Which was good enough for you to make me a proposition," I said.

"For a relief. For one short relief run."

"No," I said.

"You're daft," he said. "What about your freight train? You going to run out on your brother?"

"That's for my brother and me to settle," I said.

"I don't hire the drivers," he said.

"The division agent does."

"And he don't need recommendations."

"He'll listen to you."

"What makes you think he would?"

"Listen," I said, shoving away from the bar, "if you've got a cousin or your wife has got a brother-in-law you want to ring in on this job, say so. That'll be all right with me. But don't try to tell me you can't get me this job. All you station agents have got your friends and relations working for the Company, all up and down the line. Anywhere. Any stage line. Now, I'll swallow you got somebody in mind for the job. But I won't swallow you got nothing to do with it. I'm Starr Fowler, remember? I grew up in St. Joe. I'm no greenhorn from the east."

He studied the floor for a minute then he looked up at me from under his bushy eyebrows. "Has old Joe got any money in this line?"

I threw him the truth. "If he has, I don't know it."

"You're playing this hand yourself?"

"Joe Fowler is my father," I said, "but you brought him into this, I didn't."

He threw in and he did it handsomely. He started laughing. "All right. I just didn't want old Joe twisting my tail, too. You want to look at the string?"

"If they're going to be mine," I said.

"They'll be yours."

We walked out of the bar, which was cool and dim the way the inside of all 'dobe houses are, into the full glare and heat of the morning. It was like a sheet of fire waved in your face. I squinted my eyes and bent my hat brim down.

We untied and mounted and the horses shuffled off through six inches of dust. Dobytown was a couple of miles from the fort. It was a gaggle of dobe and log and sod buildings thrown up in a clutter around a short stretch of the road. In a moment of enthusiasm somebody had tagged it Kearney City but it didn't stick. The fort was Kearney, the settlement was Dobytown. The reason for it was the soldiers. A long way from home and bored to hell with soldiering, the soldiers mostly wanted three things—girls, gambling and whisky. Dobytown provided a great plenty of all three, none a hundred proof. It was a dump. A good place to get fleeced, catch the sickness, or die from forty-rod whisky.

The stage station was at the fort, on the west side, a couple of hundred yards away. It was a huddle of buildings, dobe and log with sod roofs—stables, corrals, smithy, carpenter's shop and storehouses. Kearney wasn't stockaded so the stage buildings looked like part of the military installation.

"Where'd you know my father?" I asked the agent as we rode along. Everybody in the west knew who Joe Fowler was, but the agent had talked as if he knew him pretty well.

"Used to teamster for him," the man said.

I tried to place him and couldn't. He wasn't as old as my father, but that didn't signify. Men started young in the west. "Looks like I'd remember," I said. "I've been making these hauls since I was a grasshopper."

"Your father wasn't even married when I worked for him," he said. "It was back when he just had one freight line—St. Joe to Santa Fe. I got a leg broke on a haul when we got jumped one time by a band of Kiowas on the Cimarron. Had to quite driving. Your father," he said, "is a man that's got hair on his chest."

"Thick and bushy," I said.

"What's he going to think of you taking a job driving stage?"

"He'll think, well, the kid finally made it. He don't try to hold us boys close-hitched. He knows it's what I've been wanting to do most of my life and trying to get ready to do." I decided to lay some cards on the table. "I'm not blackmailing you. You don't need to worry you've made a bad bargain. I'm just taking the best chance that's come my way to get the job I've been wanting. I'm good. I'm as good as I said I was. You won't be taking any chances on me."

He laughed and said, "Modesty isn't one of your long suits, is it?"

"Modesty don't get you anywhere," I said, "but there's a difference between being sure of yourself and being a windbag. I'm no windbag. I can back up what I claim."

He laid some cards on the table, too. "That's what I

hear," he said. "They tell me Big John Kenny taught you to drive."

"Yes, sir. He did."

"Yankee style?"

"Yankee style."

"He was a real reinsman," he said, "Big John was. Tweedy drove Yankee style, too. He was from up there some place . . . Connecticut or Massachusetts."

"Big John was from Rhode Island," I said.

"Well, wherever. Tweedy and Big John knew each other. Used to drive for the same line up there. Best stage drivers in the business come out of New England. But we don't get too many of them around here. Most of them went out to California," he said. "You were lucky Big John stopped over in St. Joe long enough to teach you."

"Yes, sir," I said.

We came to the stables. My eyes had to get used to the gloom but the smell was the same as always, and to a horse man good in the nose—strong in the heat with hay, ammonia, manure, leather and horseflesh. And the horseflesh was as handsome as I'd expected it to be.

The Leavenworth & Pikes Peak Express hadn't spared any expense outfitting their line. My father, who heard it in Washington, said they spent a quarter of a million dollars putting it into operation. They spent a hundred thousand on the stagecoaches alone, buying fifty-two brand-new Abbot & Downing Concords. Then they bought nothing but the finest and best Kentucky horses and mules, and to make certain the stage stock was always in top condition they didn't graze them. They were hay and grain fed and kept corraled and stabled.

The tenders were working with the horses, rubbing them down, looking them over. The agent motioned them aside. "This is Starr Fowler," he said. "He's driving the mail stage today."

They stepped back out of the way. Ordinarily a driver doesn't check his string until the stage is brought around to the station and they're already hitched. But ordinarily a driver knows his team like a mother knows her child, and all he's doing when he checks them is making certain the hitch is comfortable and secure. Being strange to the string, the tenders understood I wanted to make the acquaintance of the horses before taking them out.

I moved around among them. They were the prettiest stage stock I'd ever seen. The wheelers were big fellows, running to twelve hundred pounds at least. The swings were a little lighter, and the leaders, always the lightest of a team, were down around eight hundred pounds. They weren't matched. It was several years before staging on the Overland got fancy enough for that. But they were fine horses.

I asked for their names and spoke to each one, calling him by name, and held a little conversation with him so my voice wouldn't be completely strange to him later. I touched and rubbed each one, looked at their mouths for tender, sore places, looked at their legs and feet. "Any of them cold-mouthed?" I asked.

A tender answered, "No, *sir!* Not in Mr. Tweedy's strings."

A horse got a cold mouth when a driver had cold hands . . . that is, he was awkward and clumsy, sawed the lines and had a rough touch. "I wouldn't think it," I said. I slid my hand down the shoulder of a pretty chestnut leader. "All right," I said, "they're beauties, boys."

They grinned, pleased at the praise.

The agent and I went outside. "You'll pick up mules at Platte," he said. "Begin to pull sand pretty heavy there." He laughed. "But I don't guess you need any telling about the road."

"No," I said. "You know how many times I've been up and down this road in my life? At least once a year since I was ten years old, and sometimes twice. I know every damned, blasted, long mile of it. I know every sandtrap, every gully, every creek, every grove of cottonwoods, every spring, every mountain from the Missouri to Fort Boise. No, sir. There's not much anybody can tell me about this road."

I untied my saddlehorse for the short ride over to the barracks. "I'll tend to my business," I said, "but I'll be at the station before the stage pulls in."

He squinted up at me. "You need anything?"

"No."

9

"What about a whip? You got anything better than a bullwhacker's lash? I reckon you can have Tweedy's. He sure as hell won't be needing it any more."

"I have my own whip," I said.

"You come prepared, don't you?"

"That whip has gone wherever I've gone ever since Big John gave it to me," I said.

He looked at his watch. "Forty minutes," he said.

"I'll be there."

I found my brother snoozing in the heat of the four-man pyramidal tent we were sharing. In 1859, a row of tents constituted the enlisted men's barracks at Kearney. I told him my chance for a main line run had come and I wanted to take it. He thought about it awhile. The whole family knew how bad I was hurting to drive stage. They'd been living with it long enough. But I knew Matt had to sort out the train in his mind and figure the changes he'd have to make to let me go. It didn't take him long. "All right, buster," he said, "you just as well get it out of your system."

He might have raised more of a fuss if he'd known that driving stage is like going to sea. It gets in your blood and you don't live except when you're on the box, handling the lines. Neither of us knew we had driven our last freight haul together. I thanked him and said I didn't have much time and I'd better get along with it.

Matt said, "You know where we're going . . . Laramie, Bridger, Salt Lake. You know when we'll be there. If this don't work out to suit you or if you change your mind, you can catch us."

"Sure," I said.

I packed my hand satchel, took my whip down from the peg where it was coiled, got my gun and was ready to go. I felt a little awkward when it was time. Not much to say. "Well, I'll probably meet you coming down. Between here and Plum Creek."

Matt slapped me on the shoulder. "Don't forget whose boy you are."

I grinned. Every time we left home our mother said that to us. It was her way of telling us to behave ourselves. "Tell her I'll get home when I can. Where's Dave?"

"Playing cards."

"Well. I'll wave at him when we pass on the road."

"You keeping your mare?" he asked.

"I sure as hell am," I said. "You've had your eye on her a long time but you're not getting her yet."

He laughed. "All right. Keep your powder dry."

"I'll do it."

That was all the good-bye there was. I was too full of myself to feel anything but excitement. This was my big chance.

I had about ten minutes to wait at the station. The whole settlement and most of the men from the fort had swarmed out to watch the arrival of the stage. The driver brought it in fast, raising a dust so heavy you couldn't see the coach.

The passengers began piling out, looking like they'd been wallowing in mud. Summers are blistering hot on the plains and the inside of a stage was like a baking oven. Cram it full of people of different sizes and shapes, and it wasn't long till they were sweating so hard it was like they had been dunked in the river. Dust turned to mud almost as soon as it settled on them. The more they wiped at it, the more streaked it got. Add to that the natural dirt from several days' traveling without a bath, some whisky fumes and food spills over their clothes, and it was the rare passenger who could emerge from a stage looking or smelling like a human being.

They hustled inside the station to wash up and eat, and the driver threw his lines down. A man wearing a dark wool suit got down from the box. The driver followed and bent his elbows and swung his arms from the shoulders a few times, as if they might be a little stiff. Then he got his belongings from the front boot and turned the stage over to the hostlers. You could tell he was tired, but he was a long way from being beat out and I guessed if he'd had to, he could have turned right around and driven back to Liberty Farm without caving in. He made a beeline for the station, then. He was blown wind-dry, I knew, so dry he wouldn't even want to talk till he had wet his gullet down.

The station agent called me over, then, to meet the division agent, the man in the dark wool suit. His name was Slade—Jack Slade. He was medium height but built tight and wiry. Quiet fellow, that didn't say much. Asked a few questions, let the agent do most of the talking. Then he nodded and he and the agent went inside. I'd never seen him before though I knew who he was. He whacked for Russell, Majors & Waddell a while, then started driving for the Hockaday lines. He'd been a division agent for Hockaday when L. & P.P. bought him out. They'd kept him on. He had a reputation for being a very tough, but good, man.

Kearney was a twenty-minute meal stop and there was about fifteen minutes yet to go. They seemed like a couple of hours. I wasn't scared but I sure wasn't as calm as I tried to appear either. I was nervous and I was excited and I was swearing more than I needed to and my heart was thumping pretty fast. My mouth was dry and my stomach was pulling some queer tricks on me. I knew it would pass. I felt the same way every time we had to corral up and fight off a band of Indians. It was the waiting. When it was time to begin pulling the trigger, I was always as steady as I needed to be. I could depend on it.

And it worked the way I was sure it would. When the agent blew the whistle for the boys to bring the stage around, my insides began quieting down. I set my own things outside on the gallery and stood in the door looking on.

A couple of passengers had been for the fort, but there were nine wanting their places. The agent sorted them out and made room for seven by letting five climb to the roof. Thirty pounds of luggage was all a passenger was allowed and as the agent nodded at the ones he was letting through, his assistant began stowing their bags in the hind boot. The mail agent rearranged the mail sacks on the floor of the stage and somehow made room for two more. I began to understand why six horses were used on mail day.

When the coach was loaded—luggage, mail and passengers, Slade swung up on the box and I went out and stowed my belongings in the front boot. Every eye was watching me now and I knew it. I had done enough of the same kind of watching. This was when the driver took over. I wanted to make a good show of it. The only way I knew to do it was to forget I was Starr Fowler and was a green nineteen-year-old kid that stood five foot eleven in my sock feet and had brown hair and brown eyes and brown skin and didn't yet have much more than enough weight on me to cover my bones. I just put on Big John Kenny, like a loose old comfortable coat. "Do it in style, boy," he was telling me, "do it in style. If it's nothing but a mud wagon and a team of spavined old mules, do it in style."

I made my walk-around the team as slow, as easy, as careful as his, missing nothing, checking every strap and chain, feeling the bridles and collars, checking the bits. The tenders were good boys and I didn't expect to find anything wrong, but it kept tenders on their toes if they knew you had hawk eyes and wouldn't overlook a rough bit or a thin place in a collar that could chafe, or a twisted strap that could rub.

When I had walked around the string I looked over the stage. It was a beautiful thing. They'd washed it down outside and its red paint was gleaming, still new and bright and shiny. The scrollwork and the lettering, "Leavenworth & Pikes Peak Express Co.," showed up as gold as the sun, and the landscape painted on the doors had mountains and high blue skies in the background. The running gear was straw-yellow, and the sides of the coach cambered up as pretty and as graceful as the curves of a woman's hips.

The body rode slung on wide, heavy leather thorough-braces instead of springs. In motion there was very little bounce. Instead there was a rock forward and backward—a little rough on passengers but a lot easier on horses. Hit a chughole or a boulder in a vehicle with springs, and the effect on the teams was as if the brake had been suddenly put on with full force. Hit the same obstruction with a vehicle on thoroughbraces, and the body rocked forward and actually helped it over. Nothing but a clipper ship was ever as graceful as one of Abbot & Downing's Concord coaches. Both had the sheer and the lightness and the curve built in for motion and speed. I could have patted this sweet red beauty, I was so proud of her. I thought of how many times I had cracked my old bullwhip at one of Hockaday's broken-down old mud wagons. It was a custom with freight drivers to salute a stage, meeting or passing, with whip popping. As the stage reached the first wagon, the first whip went off and they followed down the line, one after the other, like firecrackers exploding. Now, I'd be taking that salute and I felt mighty yeasty about it.

I tried the play of the brake, which reached up long and was four inches wide so the driver's foot could reach it easily and use it like another hand. I looked at the sand-boxes. They were full. Then I asked for the dope pot. I didn't know what the custom was here, but Big John was still talking to me. "Grease your own axles, boy. See to 'em yourself, then you'll know you won't ever have a hotbox out some place where there won't be nothing you can do but go ahead and cut a spindle in two. A driver who has a hotbox is a disgrace to his whip."

A tender handed me the dope pot, grinning. By the grin I knew that Tweedy had been another Big John, seeing to his axles himself and I knew the hostlers had been waiting to see if I had the makings of a real stage driver. First test passed, I figured. I handed the boy my whip to hold and out of the corner of my eye saw he never even turned it in his hand he was so scared he'd let the tip fall and drag in the dirt. A driver's whip is a sacred object.

I took pains with every axle, sludging the dope in good and full. Then I gave the pot back to the boy, took the rag he held out and wiped my hands. As I reached for my whip, he said, low so nobody else could hear, "They don't break in a gallop, sir. Tweedy didn't like it."

I nodded. It suited me fine. But the tender's warning showed he had been won over and didn't want me to be embarrassed in any way. A gallop is a showy break, but it's the worst gait a horse has got. Two feet are off the ground all the time and sometimes all four are briefly in the air. They are off balance the whole time and not only your control of them is loose and uneven, their own control of themselves is bad. The only excuse for galloping teams, as far as I was concerned, was a passel of Indians chasing you.

A fine spanking trot is a horse's best natural gait. His balance is perfect because the feet off the ground at one time are alternating—left front and right rear, right front and left rear. It'll eat up the miles and it won't kill the animals. It's pretty and it's smooth.

I climbed up on the box, took the lines from the wheel tender, threaded them, threw the loose ends of the near reins over the back of my left hand, let the ends of the off lines hang loose, settled the whip in the palm of my right hand, tested the brake with my right foot, settled my rump in Tweedy's cushion, and looked over at the station agent. He had his watch out and open, looking at it. He looked up at me and snapped the watch shut. I nodded to the lead tender and began talking to the horses, easy and low, speaking to every horse. The tender turned loose of the off leader's head and stepped back.

My God, they broke pretty! As smooth as butter. If a passenger inside felt the motion it was little more than a tremble. And they broke fast. They were reaching for that easy racking road gait by the time we straightened from the pull-out, me talking them on. When they hit it, I thought I would bust wide open. My skin was too small for me, I was so full inside, so full that my eyes stung with salt for a moment and the road blurred. I needed to have a bigger body. I needed skin that stretched. I wondered why Tweedy needed booze. This was booze enough for me. "Ah, but you're beauties," I said, "you're beauties. Git along, now. Git along."

I never was a shouting, whip-cracking driver. Even leaving and arriving, when most drivers like to do a little showing off with their whips, I didn't. But don't think I didn't do my share of showing off. It was just a little more subtle. Popping a whip around the leaders' heads was a trick anybody could learn. And it could hide a lot of driving sins. I took pride in a fast smooth break and satin handling. I was a driver's driver. The public never knew the difference, but I wanted the drivers' approbation. I wanted them to say, as I have said of so many, "God, he's one of the best."

By the time we had coursed the dusty street of Doby-town and left the Dirty Woman's shack on the left, the running sounds had fallen into place. They are the sounds I love most in this whole world. With a stage whose couplings are well leathered, there is no sound but the chuckling of the sandboxes. With a string of horses trained to move at an easy, rippling road gait, this regular chuckling sound marks the time for them, like a drumbeat setting cadence for them. It's hypnotic and neither the horses nor a reinsman likes for it to be broken. Which is one reason a good driver doesn't talk much to whoever is sitting on the box with him. He is hearing that cadence all the time, the chuckle, the swift even clopping of the horses' feet, the swing and jingle of the chains, and talk from anybody is a nuisance and a bother.

Then, though his hands are resting easy on his knees and you can't tell that his foot on the brake is putting on any pressure, he's working all the time. There's hardly fifty feet of the straightest and easiest road that you aren't climbing or slipping a line, to the off leader, to the near swing, to the near wheel, just a little. Not more than the pull of a thread on the horse's mouth, maybe, such a little it looks as if they were driving themselves. But you're driving them and they know it, and you're helping them with a little brake, or with none.

That's the great beauty of driving Yankee style. You're driving six horses, or four, but you're driving each one separately and you have full control of six horses, separately. It's also why you work every minute of an eight-, ten- or twelve-hour run, and every foot of thirty or forty or fifty miles. You don't have time or thought to spare from the concentration it takes to carry on a conversation. Few people ever seemed to realize that. Passengers riding the box with the driver nearly always wanted to chatter, ask questions, keep up a conversation. They nearly always ended their journey believing, and many times saying it and even writing it, as Mark Twain did, that drivers were truculent, sullen, inarticulate men. We weren't. We were busy men. And tending to our business was what got passengers, and the mail, where they were going.

I was lucky with the division agent that day. He was no talker. He was just riding, and looking. Watching me, the road and the country. Westbound, we were carrying no treasure. Gold dust and silver all traveled east to the banks. There wasn't any danger of a holdup. And, in 1859, Indian trouble for stages was the exception rather than the rule. They swooped down on emigrant or freight trains pretty often, raiding for horses and mules, guns, ammunition and supplies. They hadn't yet connected the stage lines with the settlement of the west, so for the most part the stages weren't worth bothering with. Just the same, and because it never paid to take safety for granted, Jack Slade kept his eyes peeled.

After the first hour the passengers quieted down and I guessed most of them were dozing. With a full stomach and in the heat and with as smooth a ride as a stage could give them, it would be the natural thing to do. Every once in a while a wheel would hit a hole and there would be a big jolt and I'd hear them rouse up and complain a bit. I don't, and I didn't then, pull a team out of the road to avoid chugholes, rocks or other minor obstructions. It not only tired the animals, in time they got cold mouths from too much pulling, and a cold-mouthed horse or mule is double the work to drive. If they get too hard to rein, they're useless as stage stock.

Besides, a stage string gets to know their piece of road as well as the driver. If you're always pulling them out of it to give the passengers an easier ride, it confuses them. Come some dark night when you can't see your hand in front of you, or there's a hard rain blinding you, or a blizzard of snow blowing, you've got to give your horses their heads, trust them to stay in the road, and give thanks you've not bewildered them swerving them out of it all the time. The only thing I pulled out of the road for was something big enough to wreck us, or other traveling vehicles.

It was ten miles to Platte, the first relay station, a three-minute stop for changing teams. About two miles out, Slade reached down under his feet and hauled out an old brass horn. It was a curious-looking object, all battered and beat up and a little lopsided. He handled it delicately and for the first time opened his mouth. "Pat didn't like to yell to announce his arrival, as is the common custom. He thought a stage should arrive with more style. He got this horn off the bugler at the fort."

"I hope it was a gift," I said. "It looks like a mule has been wearing it for a shoe."

"I believe it did get tromped," Slade said. "The bugler bought himself a new one."

"I don't blame him," I said. "I would think it was necessary."

"Yes. Well, the bugler taught Pat to blow several army calls. Reveille and Assembly and Retreat and whatnot." Slade turned the horn up and studied the bell as if trying to memorize its flare. "The call Tweedy liked best," he said, "was Charge."

"I like it myself," I said.

Slade waved the horn at me. "Would you like to give it a try?"

I bunched the lines in one hand and took the horn. "It makes me sad I can't blow Charge," I said. "I don't know it. But I promise to learn. For now, we'll just have to make do with a blast."

I raised the horn to my mouth and blew. There wasn't a sound. Not even a squawk. I took it down from my mouth and looked at it. "I've blown cow horns, bull horns and tin horns," I said, "but this is the first time I ever tried to blow an army horn. You sure it works? Maybe Tweedy didn't iron out enough of the wrinkles."

"Oh, it works," Slade said. "It just takes a considerable amount of air."

I gathered me in all the air both lungs would hold and cut loose. It worked. It went like a bull moose trumpeting for his mate. It not only notified Platte station, but Craig, ten miles beyond, that the stage was arriving. The horses jumped and then streaked out like I'd laid the whip on them. Slade grabbed his hat with one hand and the seat hold with the other. He didn't say a word, though.

I didn't either, for a few minutes. I had to let the team know somebody was still driving. Then I said, "I'll probably get the hang of it."

"I hope so," Slade said. He looked around at the roof passengers. "I think you lost one."

"He's not got far to walk," I said.

Slade looked again and grinned. "He just got flung down on the boot. He's climbing back up, now."

We whirled up to the station with the dust flying. The mule relay was ready and standing. The tenders eyed me curiously until Slade told them the news about Pat Tweedy. It would give them something to talk about for several days and wonder about . . . if I was going to be the new driver or who might be if I wasn't. One or two passengers got off to stretch their legs. Most of them stayed put.

We pulled out of Platte on the dot. The mules were a fine lot, too. But a mule is a critter and the best of them is not a particularly handsome animal. If you've worked with horses and mules all your life you get to where you either hate animals, or come to have a feeling for them almost like they were human beings. A mule has really got more sense than a horse. A horse will kill himself for you. A mule won't, not without a lot of punishment and then sometimes he'll die of the punishment without giving you an extra mile. In Indian country, I wouldn't want to bank on mules running long enough and hard enough to get me out of a scrape. Horses, on the other hand, will go till their hearts quit. But in heavy sand, pulling heavy loads, mules last better.

Eleven miles farther on we wheeled into the Craig station and picked up the next relay. We were almost five hours out of Kearney now and the shadows were beginning to get a little long. The only things to make shadows were the station, the stage and ourselves. The road followed the river and down by the river there were some scrub willows. Up by the station there wasn't even a bush. The tenders looked me over in the same curious way the boys at Platte had done and Slade passed on the same news. He threw them a package of old newspapers and magazines. "They go sky-crazy without something to read," he said.

The tenders at a swing station had a lonesome life. Nothing to do but tend to the stock and watch the road and wait for the stage. Mostly they were drifters. Took the job for a few months then moved on. Few men wanted to make a career of it. Especially in the early days before there was much pride in the organization.

"We'll have the sun under our hat brims the next couple of hours," I said, when I'd swung back up on the box. It was fourteen miles to Plum Creek. Three hours, as near as made no difference. And it was the time of day when driving was a chore instead of a pleasure. Sun in your eyes, dying wind that didn't blow the dust away, and while it maybe wasn't the hottest part of the day it always felt like it with the wind laying down. But the first hour of it would be taken up getting the feel of the fresh mules, and the rest of it would pass a lot faster than our wagon trains ever made it. I wasn't complaining. I wasn't even feeling any strain.

It was dark when we got to Plum Creek. The lights of the home station showed up across the flats several miles out, even before time to blow the horn. The passengers spotted the lights and began to stir around inside the stage, waking up, making ready for the stop. They would have twenty minutes here and supper.

We came in with the mules stretched out and rolled up such a fog of dust the lights of the station were almost hidden. The hostlers ran for the mules and I threw the lines to one of them. Slade got down and the passengers began to unload. As the dust cleared I saw the driver who would take over here standing just outside the door and felt relief to see him. The unsettled way this line was operating, it wouldn't have surprised me if he'd been missing, too, and I'd have had to make the next stage of the run. I could have, but I was glad not to have to.

The station keeper gave the passengers all the necessary information—where they could wash up, where the out-houses were, and that supper was waiting inside. Slade stood and talked to the next driver and the station agent, then he and the agent went inside.

I coiled my whip. When I'd got it to suit me I got down, dusted myself off with my hat and got my things out of the boot. I looked at the beat-up old horn. It was Pat Tweedy's and didn't go with the stage. I liked the idea of arriving blowing Charge. I had inherited Pat Tweedy's job, I didn't think he would mind throwing in the horn. So I took it.

It was a happy thought. In time I blew Charge over the Sierras, across the Great Salt Desert, in the Medicine Bows, and up and down the whole nineteen hundred miles of the Overland line. I think my greatest feat with the horn was the time I blew Charge for six blocks down Larimer Street entering Denver. It took a lot of wind.

When I went inside the station I was so surprised at what I saw I stopped just inside the door to look. In 1859, most stage stations were little more than hovels. If they were serviceable, that was good enough. But this big room was not only clean and the lamps clear and bright, there were curtains at the windows and there was a red-checked tablecloth on the long eating table. There was even a little plant in a pot on the table. You didn't often find a station keeper's wife willing to put a lot of extra work on herself to make things pretty and homelike way out in the middle of nowhere. This was a pleasant place to come into, and I thought how lucky I was that this end of my run would be so comfortable and cheerful.

The woman herself was dishing up the food and a little girl with two fat braids of the blazingest red hair I ever saw was helping her. The woman was bosomy, red-faced and cheerful looking. Her own red braids were wound around her head. She looked at me, started to speak, stopped, looked at her husband, then looked back at me and laughed. "Well," she said, "your whip shows you're a driver, but you sure aren't Mr. Tweedy."

"No, ma'am," I said. I hung up my whip and my hat and set my satchel over by the wall.

The little girl was giving me the once-over but she was sliding it out of the corner of her eyes. Her hands stayed busy and she was too polite or too shy to gawk. I didn't mean to be rude to the woman, but I figured it was Slade's business to pass on the news about Tweedy and say who I was. You never knew but what people were related and sudden death would come as a shock to them.

Slade was passing the news on right then, for before the passengers began trickling in the station agent motioned for his wife and she went over to him and Slade. Her hand went up to her face at the news, and she looked thoughtful and shook her head a time or two. Then she came over to the table where I had sat down. "Mr. Slade has told us about Pat Tweedy," she said. "I'm sorry. I didn't approve of him drinking so much but he was a good man, in his way. We had got used to him and we all liked him. You can put your things in the drivers' room now, if you want, Mr. Fowler. I'll show you. And you'd maybe like to wash before you eat. The wash water for the drivers is in their room."

I said that would be fine and got my things again. Going past, the woman said to the little girl, "I'll be right back, Bucky. You can commence pouring the coffee." To me she said, "They always want a cup of hot coffee first thing. Soon as they get a little of the dirt off."

The drivers' room was through a door to the side. I was prepared for it to be clean, seeing how clean and tidy the station was. There were four cots lined up against the wall. In some home stations the drivers used the same beds, in shifts. I was glad to see I'd have my own bed, nobody but me using it. I'd have built me a bunk if there hadn't been. "Which bed you want me to take?" I said.

"Mr. Tweedy liked that farthest one," she said, "because it was right next to the outside door. He liked to come and go that way. And there's more air stirring on a hot night near the door."

"It'll suit me, too," I said, and I slung my satchel under the cot. There were pegs on the wall for clothes and there was one where the whitewash was rubbed that I figured Tweedy had used for his whip. I hung mine there and it looked like it belonged there.

"Our name is Westmoreland," the woman said, "Ed and Emma Westmoreland. Supper's ready when you are." Then she went out.

I had just finished washing when Slade came in. I sat down on the cot and waited till he washed. There was a mirror over the stand and a comb pocket. He chose a comb with all its teeth and ran it through his hair. When he got through he turned around and looked at the neat beds. He heaved a big sigh. "I sure wish I could stretch out on one of those," he said. "I'm beginning to need a night's sleep."

"You going on?" I said.

"Yes."

"Well," I said, "you won't be having to keep an eye on a new driver now. You can ride inside and maybe catch a little sleep."

"With that crowd?" He laughed. "I'll curl up in the front boot." He settled his gun holster more comfortably. "I hear you can take this run regularly."

"Yes, sir."

"All right," he said, "it's yours. The pay is seventy-five dollars a month and found. No drinking on the job. This will be your regular stage. Commonly you'll lay over at each end for rest, but if you're delayed it'll be your rest that suffers. Even if you haven't shut an eye, you'll take out your regular incoming stage within twenty minutes. And if for any reason the next driver, at either end of the run, isn't able to take the stage on, you'll take it, and keep on taking it as far as you have to, or you fall over dead."

He grinned, and went on. "The schedule is important and is to be kept if possible. That doesn't mean killing the stock to keep it, but it does mean they might have to take some punishment occasionally. I don't have to tell you that the stock and equipment is expensive. Nobody expects you to get killed defending it, but don't hand it over easy, either. Use your gun carefully. Don't fire at Indians or let any of your passengers fire at them except in self-defense. You're responsible for the safety of the passengers. That's what the rule book says. But there are a lot of damn fools riding the stages. A good driver is worth more to us than any damn-fool passenger, so use your judgment if you get in a scrape."

He stopped.

"Anything else?" I said.

"Yes. The most important thing. Don't ever forget it. Nothing on God's earth must ever stop the United States Mail. Nothing. That's all."

He left me with that to chew on and it was a right sobering mouthful. I sat there on the side of the bed and thought about it. I think it was the first time it had occurred to me that driving stage was more than handling horses Yankee style. It was responsibility. If I had a string of horses shot up . . . if me and my passengers had to fort up behind a stage and shoot it out . . . if nobody was left alive but me . . . I had more than my own skin to think about. I had the United States Mail. I wondered what you'd do with ten or twenty sacks of mail, each one weighing around a hundred pounds, if you came up against that kind of scrape? Bury it? Try to lug it out? Build a fort of it? Or sit on it and die?

I stood up. My stomach was telling me I hadn't eaten for eight hours. Well, I thought, you asked for it, buster. Now you've got it. And you'd better be man enough.

Well, that was my first run on the box of a main line stage. It was the beginning of my association with the Overland line. In the next ten years, though the line changed owners three times, I was either driving or riding an Overland stage. They were the happiest years of my life. That's what this story is about.

23

Chapter 2

Well, I wasn't all that good and I knew it. To be perfectly truthful I was a fair driver but I was not yet a good one, although I had the potential to be a good one. I had good hands and good wrists and Big John had taught me style and reinsmanship. But it's a long way from short lines and their scrapped-up teams and broken-down stages to the main line. I was long on hope and confidence and very short on main line experience. It takes years of driving to make a good and wise driver, just as it takes years of living to make you a good and wise man. You've got to go through a few things before you know whether you can or not. Big John couldn't give me those years. I had to get them for myself.

And lack of experience almost wrecked my stagefaring career before it got well under way. I had the Plum Creek run. It was mine, unbound one trip, downbound the next, laying over between first one place then the other.

It sounds monotonous and to some extent it is. That's why stage drivers shift about so much. They get sick and tired of one stretch of road. But for me, in the beginning, it wasn't monotonous. I was learning my trade and I was learning that no two trips are ever exactly alike.

It is to be remembered that the driver of six horses holds three reins in each hand. The near horses of the team are those on the left side of the hitch. The line to the near leader is the top line, the one between your first and middle fingers, in your left hand. The line to the near swing is next, between the middle and third fingers, and the line to the near wheel horse is the bottom line, between your third and little fingers. The same is true in your right hand, with the reins to the off horses. The horses are hitched as a team and they must work as a team, but the lines to each horse, held separately and worked separately, give a driver separate control of each individual animal. Directions are given to any horse in the team by means of slipping, or letting out his line, or by climbing, taking in the line. It is a very fine skill, requiring perfect muscular control of each finger of both hands.

The driver sits on the right side of the box. The brake comes up tall and broad and he drives with his right foot always resting on it, because he drives almost as much with the brake as with the reins. When you use the brake, even a fraction of an inch, it slackens the lines slightly. The horses feel that slight slack before the lines are climbed and they are alerted to the tightening of the reins. They are ready for whatever the driver is going to ask of them.

Well, say you have a leader this trip who's feeling his oats and wants to romp a little. It's a brisk morning and he's full of steam and doesn't want to settle down. The leaders are the spark of the team. They're the lightest of the animals, they're up front and they set the pace. But your near leader this morning keeps breaking out, tossing his head, pulling off. There are several things you can do. You can punish him a little, with the whip. This is really an admission of failure with the reins. If the rest of the team is infected with his high spirits, you can let them out and let them run it off. Most generally, however, it means working patiently with the horse, telling him through his rein who is boss, who is driving, and that while you're in full sympathy with his high spirits you're not going to let him or them get out of hand. That one rein can keep you working most of the time until you've got the horse settled down.

Or maybe one of the wheelers decides he doesn't want to move at a road gait this trip. He's tired of a road gait, he lets you know. He is just going to lag along this time. Every few hundred yards he has to be prodded with the butt of the whip. He perks up, then directly he's bored with it all and he's lagging off again. Drive twenty-five or thirty miles with a lagging wheel horse and I guarantee you'll feel like you had pulled the stage every mile yourself.

Then, even if the whole team is working well, working evenly, keeping the gait, maybe there will be heavier travel on the road than usual. You'll meet or catch up with more freight trains and more emigrant trains. Freight trains have a habit of driving well to one side of the road, if there's room. It takes a long time to pull a mile of bull train out of the road, so they avoid the time and the trouble by leaving most of the road for other vehicles.

Emigrant trains are a horse of a different color. They are usually green and inexperienced and they hog the road. They have no road courtesy, they plod stolidly along smack in the middle, they wouldn't give you an inch, and on a narrow stretch of road they can hold you up for an hour or two. All you can do is poke along behind them, cussing them up one side and down the other. When you meet or catch up an emigrant train one thing is certain. You'll have to go round, and you'll be lucky if you can. Drivers hate them and begin cussing the minute they come in sight. And some drivers, maddened to recklessness, will clip in short and take a wagon wheel off to pay a particularly pestiferous wagoner back. A driver's whip can start a stampede with a loose herd of cattle or horses and even the score with an uppity emigrant, too.

And then, even when all things went well on a trip, the unexpected could happen, the off chance, the accident, which is what happened to me about a month after I began driving the Plum Creek run regularly.

I was bringing the eastbound stage into Fort Kearney, running about an hour late and trying to make as much of it up as I could on a long, level stretch of road. Dark had come on and the side lamps were lit. I had the team in a hard road gait, moving at a very fast clip, when all at once the rein to the near leader went slack in my hand. Something about the rein had been bothering the horse the whole trip. He'd been tucking his head down into it, tugging on it, keeping me working the entire run. I was fretted because we were running late and in my inexperience I had grown impatient with the horse. The last several times I'd had to pull his head up, I'd done it with more of a yank than was needed. Just a green kid, angry over being helplessly late, and angry over what I took to be a fractious animal.

When the rein went slack I knew instantly it had broken and I had no more idea what to do than if I had never driven a team before. I had never had a line break before, I

26

had never heard of anybody driving stage having a line break, and nobody had ever told me what to do if one ever did break. It was a brand-new experience.

A free horse in a team, with absolutely no control from the driver, is dangerous, naturally. He's likely to do any wild thing. What my leader did was leave the road and bolt, taking the rest of the team and the stage with him in a crazy, headlong gallop across the prairie.

The country was flat and level but it was occasionally criss-crossed with shallow gullies, a craze of them running in all directions. If we hit one of them, going full out as we were, the stage would wreck and some passengers would be hurt, maybe killed, and I would almost certainly be thrown from the box and badly hurt.

I was as near panic as I have ever been in my life. I had no idea what to do except hang onto the reins and keep sawing away, and keep riding the brake. But the team was infected with the panic of the loose leader and they had the bits in their mouths. For a change, they were taking us where they wanted to go, and it was anywhere except down the road.

A passenger was riding the box with me. I didn't know him, but by the look of him I knew he was a westerner. He was tan and weathered, he wore a beat-up old wideawake hat and his boots were worn to the softness and easy comfort that only good and expensive leather can reach. He wasn't old, but he was a lot older than I was. He had been slumped in the seat, dozing, when the team bolted. I didn't have any time for him, but at least he showed no signs of alarm. He sat up and hung on and kept quiet. Which was more than the passengers inside the coach were doing. Two women were shrieking and at least one man was doing a hell of a lot of cursing and shouting.

Suddenly the man on the box spoke to me. "Son," he said, "haul on that off line and commence running 'em in a circle."

A circle. Well, sure. I had a line to the off leader. Why hadn't I thought of it? All my driving sense had left me and I'd been treading the brake as hard as I could and sawing the lines like the biggest greenhorn in the business, which I almost was. I let up on the brake some and began climbing the off lines and the off horses began slowly to

27

answer. They veered slightly right, then more right, and we began a large circling movement. "Tighten 'em into it," the stranger said.

I tightened them.

"Keep tightening 'em," he advised. "Keep bringing 'em in till you're so tight they're walking."

It was a beautiful maneuver. Slowly, one round after the other, I brought them into a tighter circle, tighter and tighter, until of their own accord they were so slowed they dropped into a walk, and then a full halt. The run, the bolt, the stampede was over. They stood there, their heads hanging.

The passenger jumped down on his side and made for the leaders' heads and I jumped down on my side. We mended the broken rein. It had frayed in two where it snapped into the bit. I felt ashamed that I hadn't stopped when the horse began his fretfulness to see what was bothering him. That frayed leather right at his mouth had made him nervous. He had been telling me all during the run as best he could. But I had been too green to read his message. I had thought he was being ornery and cussed, and of course in my impatience I had broken the rein myself with the last of my hard, quick yanks.

That experience taught me several things. One, I had been fretted because I had to take the coach out from Plum Creek late. I didn't like being late. So I hadn't made my inspection as thorough as I should have. I should have found that frayed rein when I checked the hitch. But I didn't. I would never again take it for granted that the hitch was in good order. I would see to it, late or not late.

I had learned, also, that sometimes a horse isn't being fractious out of high spirits or meanness or cussedness. Sometimes something is wrong and it will pay you to find out. I would know to make sure what was causing an animal's fretfulness next time.

But perhaps the most important thing I learned is that as long as you have a team broken to harness, accustomed to being driven, you'd better drive them. If you have any lines at all, there is something you can do to keep them under control.

When we were moving again I asked the passenger his name. "Hodge," he said, "Bob Hodge."

I would have liked to go right through the floor of the box. Big John had talked about Bob Hodge and what a reinsman he was. One of the Yankees, of course. I was ashamed to have been caught in such a mess in front of him and worse ashamed to have lost my head. "It's a wonder," I said, "you didn't grab the lines yourself."

"Oh," he said, "it wasn't that bad. A line don't break with a man often and the first time it's pretty startling. You did a better job than I did the first time it happened to me. You did a good job."

"Yes," I said, "after you told me."

"Well," he said, "I've seen some drivers couldn't have done it after they was told."

"Big John has told me about you," I said.

"Big John," he said, musing. "Big John. Yes."

He told me how they used to drive together in Rhode Island. He told me they had both come west as the railroads put staging out of business in the east. He told me he had been driving in Mexico, and then he'd drifted on out to California. Now he was on his way to Atchinson. He was going to drive for the Kansas and Western, a short line just opening up.

"Why don't you put in for a job with the L. & P.P.?" I said.

"It don't look too promising right now," he said, laughing. "You think it's going to last?"

"Yes," I said. "If the L. & P.P. folds somebody else will take it over. There's going to be a stage line on this road."

"Well," he said, "I'll see."

I didn't ask him, but he told me anyhow, that he had got restless in California. Most of the lines were short lines, running back and forth to the gold camps. "Gets tedious," he said. "I thought I'd try something a little longer."

He asked me about myself. I am not usually a garrulous man, but I was still excited, feeling up in the air about the runaway, feeling a kinship with the man because he was a driver and feeling almost like it was talking to Big John again. So I told him, and maybe took longer than I should, about myself and my family and how I'd come to know Big John and how he'd taught me.

29

I told him how my father's family had gone west from Kentucky in the early 1800s when he was just a little boy, and settled in Arkansas Territory. And how my father, Joe Fowler, had pushed on across the plains to the mountains when he was still a youth, in 1821. And how he was a free trapper in the beaver trade and one of the best of the real old mountain men, a tribe that included Jim Bridger, Tom Fitzpatrick, the Sublette brothers, Bill Williams, Jedediah Smith, Kit Carson, and my father's two partners Moses Strong and Big Starr.

I was named for his two partners. My mother gave her consent for me to be named Moses Starr on the condition I should always be called Starr. I have been grateful to her. It is an unwieldy handle which I have been careful to conceal. If I hadn't, nothing in this world could have kept me from becoming known as old Mose Fowler.

My father was always a shrewd man with a good business head on him. He foresaw the end of the beaver trade early. With his uncle, who lived in Santa Fe, he established a freight line between Santa Fe and the Missouri. Thus he had a good business going when the bottom dropped out of the fur trade.

It took him a while to give up his life in the mountains. He made a stab at settling in Oregon, but it didn't take. He drifted on down to California. He said the climate there was so soft and easy it took the sap out of a man. Then he made a trip back to Kentucky to see his grandmother's home—where he was born—and to see his relations still living in the vicinity. He wasn't tempted to stay. "What you've once turned your back on," he said, "you can't turn around and face toward again." But he met my mother there. Her name was Mahaley Cooper and she lived a neighbor to some of his kinfolks. The families were connected in some distant way—they had married into each other occasionally—but my father and my mother were not related.

They married and my father gave up the mountains at last. He brought my mother to St. Joseph and established himself full time in the freighting business. I was born there in 1840. When the government began to build the forts along the emigration route, the Fowler Freight Line branched out and in addition to its regular commercial freighting got its share of army freight contracts. The army made such a hash of trying to freight its own supplies they quit trying about 1848. From then on, the government contracted with various commercial freighters. It was a lucrative business and, as is always the case with government contracts, open to a lot of skulduggery. As far as I know my father always gave value received. I don't know of his ever substituting merchandise of inferior quality, or of his pulling any other kind of chicanery with his contracts. What he did in Washington to get them is another matter. He wouldn't have got them unless he could buy and pay, trade and deal.

My mother didn't waste any time being homesick for Kentucky, though she did sometimes say the dust made housekeeping a lot more work, and she did sometimes wish it didn't get so hot in the summer. My father built a big handsome home and she was busy and cheerful and happy. She was interested in everything that went on around her and well padded with humor against the shocks of the frontier. She laughed quickly and could always make the rest of us laugh.

But what made our home such a special place was that she was always singing. Over all her tasks, and they were endless, she sang—mostly hymns she had sung all her life, but she also learned many of the new rollicking songs of the west. More than anything she wanted an organ, and when my father brought it down from St. Louis finally, she said, "My cup runneth over." She didn't know one note of music, but she could play anything she heard by ear. My father grumbled he didn't have a clean shirt for three weeks after he brought the organ and that he ate so much mush and milk his brains turned soft. "Music is food for the soul," my mother said.

"But it don't do much for a man's stomach," my father said.

We were lucky with our parents.

I don't remember much about the first trip I made with a wagon train and that isn't because I don't have a long memory. It's because I started so young. My mother said that she began letting us boys go so early because she always had such a houseful younger it was a relief to have

31

some of us out of her way. Maybe. It's true there was a houseful of us. Twelve. Six boys and six girls. That summer I got my first job driving stage for the L. & P.P. the youngest was a new baby.

I don't really remember learning to drive. My father says that on my first trip with him I begged to drive and he let me. But I do know that by the time I was eight years old I was driving our supply wagon with a four-mule hitch. Matt and Dave were handling freight teams ahead of me and I joined them before I was twelve. Our lives settled early into the routine of long summers out on the trail and winters at home and in school.

It was Big John Kenny, though, who taught me the difference between a driver and a reinsman. He was a whisky-soaked old wreck who drove a short line run for Hockaday out of St. Joseph. He told me that in New England you began to learn reinsmanship when you are eight or nine years old, out in your father's barn, with a rig. He began that way. "You start," he told me, "with two reins tied to some palings. The palings are fixed to a rack and they'll pull forward. They're weighted so they'll drop back. You string those lines between your first and middle fingers of each hand and you work at climbing 'em and slipping 'em till you can do it so smooth and easy the palings will drop back without a sound."

"How long did it take you?" I asked.

"About a year. Then your pa adds the next two reins and you work with four another year or so. Them extra two are awkward at first," he said, "for you've got your lead reins well in hand, but them two between your middle and third fingers will slide away from you if you give 'em a chance."

I nodded. I was nine years old and I was handling four lines already, but I was mostly bunching them—handling two teams as if they were one. "How long did it take you to learn to handle four?" I said.

"Another year. Maybe a little longer. Then you put on the last two. Now, that's when you find out if you've got the guts to stick with it. That's when it's easy to say you can't do it and quit and give up. Try it, boy. Try holding six reins between your fingers, then try to climb the lead rein in your right hand and slip the swing rein in your left, at the same time holding all the others steady. If you don't have fingers that work like each one had a brain of its own, there's not much use trying it. You're working with a rig, but someday those lines will lead to the bits in the horses' mouths, and you got to know what you want six different horses to do and how to get 'em to do it. It's a fist full of leather, let me tell you, and you're still a little fellow and your hands ain't full-sized yet. I begun to think them blasted little fingers of mine never would get strong enough to hold and slip and climb."

My own hands were working. I could feel those lines in my fingers and I was itching to try six.

"There's many a driver can handle fours," he said, "that can't ever learn to handle sixes. A great many fake it." He picked up my hand and showed me. "You see here. The weakest muscles in the fingers are on the underside of this third finger, here, and on the little fingers. A lot of drivers learn to depend on the strong muscles in their middle and first ones and never learn to strengthen the others. Sometimes they can't. They maybe just haven't got the hands for it."

Scared to death I might not have, I said, "What kind of hands have you got to have?"

"Well," he said, "they're a free gift of nature, I'd say. Big hands, they ought to be, with long, limber fingers or square strong ones. And a good spread of palm. And they got to be hooked to the wrists with no weakness in them. A stagefaring man's wrists have got to be like steel for strength. They've got to have bend built in, but no break."

I spread my hands for him to see. "You reckon I've got stagefaring hands?"

He tested them, one finger at a time, spread them, bent them, felt the bones in the wrists. My heart was pounding in my chest and I felt a pit of sickness in my stomach. Finally he said, "I reckon you have. I just reckon you might have. They're shaped right and they're stronger than most boys' your age. I'd say they were worth giving it a try. But you'll have to unlearn any bad driving habits you've picked up."

"Will you help me put up a rig in the barn so I can practice?" I said, eager to begin right that minute.

"I'll help you," he said. He went further. "I'll coach you,

33

too. I'll teach you everything I know, the way my father taught me."

My father didn't mind as long as I didn't neglect my other work. I spent hours in the barn at that rig. When Big John was at our end of his run, he would come over and watch me, correct errors, sit there beside me and with the reins in his own hands show me. He rested his hands easy on his knees, the lines threaded through his fingers, and I dare anybody to be able to see a finger move as he slipped and climbed the reins. That is real Yankee-style reinsmanship, the prettiest, best, finest driving men ever did.

It was Big John who told me that the best reinsmen came out of New England. "Rhode Island," he said, "where I come from, or Massachusetts or Connecticut, or somewhere up there."

"Why?"

"Well," he said, "that country settled up first, and a lot of the stagefaring families brought good driving over with them from the old country. Why, there are families up there that have been driving from father to son for three or four generations. Comes down in the family, like seafaring. And, boy, if you don't mean business don't commence it. It gets in your blood, the way the sea does in some men, and when you begin driving stage you can't ever get away from it."

"How come you to leave Rhode Island?" I said.

"Well, they got railroads back there nowadays," he said. "Stage lines are beginning to fold up. Most of us drivers have had to come west."

He was my hero for a couple of years. He taught me all I know about driving. When I was eleven years old he decided I was good enough for my whip. He asked my father's permission to give it to me. "A stagefaring father always gives his boy his first whip," he said. "I've got no boy of my own. Starr, here, is as close as I'll ever come. If you don't care, I'd like to give him his whip."

"I'd be proud to have you give him his whip," my father said.

I still have it and still use it and it's the only one I've ever had. It was a few years before I had the chance to break it in good, but after that its silver ferrules and nine-foot rawhide length got to be pretty well worn. A driver's

34

whip is dearer to him than gold in the bank. He keeps the rawhide oiled and the silverwork polished. He never lays it down. He coils it and hangs it. He wouldn't loan it to his best friend. Whips become so identified with their owners that you can walk in a strange bar, see a whip hanging on the wall and know the driver before you ever lay eyes on him.

I made my family miserable with mine for a year or two after Big John gave it to me, allowing nobody to touch it, worrying about it. The hardest licking my father ever gave me was for whacking one of the girls for getting jelly on its silverwork.

About the time Big John gave me my whip he drifted on. My whip was, in a way, his farewell, for he didn't say any other kind of good-bye. He was just gone one day. I was heartbroken for a week or two, for now who would let me ride with him on the short line and sometimes let me drive? And who would tell me the old stagefaring stories? And who would constantly caution and correct me? "I heard," my father said, "he has gone to California. Down at Hockaday's they say staging is mighty big business in California since the gold rush."

I was all for jumping a wagon train and following Big John straight to California myself to get in on the ground floor of staging out there. "Just wait awhile," my father advised. "There will be stages running from here to there by the time you're old enough to be any use to yourself."

"You sure?"

"Dead sure," he said. "California is a state now. One of the United States. The government has got to provide mail and military protection and they mean transportation and people going back and forth. You'll see. The wheels will roll, boy."

My father saw the first wheels roll across the plains. He was there ahead of them, in Taos and Santa Fe, when the first big wagons began to roll on the Santa Fe Trail. He was at the fur trappers' rendezvous in the Tetons the summer the first wagons rolled up the North Platte. He told me about it.

We had a freight haul to Salt Lake one summer. I was sixteen as best I remember. My father got along with the

Mormons and did business with Brigham Young. He was one of the few Gentiles President Young felt friendly toward, but he never forgot that my father had shown his people many kindnesses in the days of their persecution in Missouri. To my father's profit, he never failed to show his gratitude.

We had camped for the night just beyond the Green River crossing. Matt and Dave had gone visiting to a Shoshone village nearby. My father allowed it. "They're young bucks now," he said. "They're older than I was when I had my first squaw."

Ever since he got his first War Department contract and began freighting to the forts, when we'd be at Laramie or Bridger, or camped anywhere in the vicinity on the trail, my father's old compañeros would come visiting around. Matt and Dave and I were old enough that he didn't try to hide from us the fact that he had had, in his day, Indian women of sundry tribes. We had listened to a lot of tall talk and had heard his friends joshing him about a pretty little Shoshone, or a little light-skinned Cheyenne. But the one they teased him most about was a Ute squaw they called Betsy. She must have been his favorite, for he had kept her with him several seasons. Big Starr said one time, "She wasn't no looker, Betsy wasn't. But Joe didn't pick her for looks. She was the workingest squaw this coon ever seen. She was dumpy and had a behind on her like a brood mare, but she cured out the prettiest skins of any woman amongst us. And she taken the best care of Joe. He always had plenty of new clothes and good warm moccasins. He knowed what he was doing when he picked Betsy."

We understood, without asking questions, that in time Betsy went back to her village and understood that was the way of trappers with their Indian women.

That night at Green River crossing I felt sulky because my father said I was too young to go with Matt and Dave and so, more smart-alecky than I had any right to be, I said, "I reckon you're saving me for a Ute woman."

Caught in the right humor it could have got me backhanded so hard I'd have been sprawled fifteen feet, but he didn't riffle. Just grinned. "If I ever think you're man enough," he said, "I'll find you one myself. But it takes a right smart man for a Ute squaw, I warn you."

It took the sting out of having to stay home. I couldn't help laughing at the notion of my father, so foolish about my plump little mother that he hated these trips away from her, had ever been such a stallion.

Nights in that country are chilly and a fire always feels good. We sat by the fire and smoked. A short-stemmed pipe was hardly ever out of my father's mouth and I was beginning to imitate him. He allowed that, too. He was sitting cross-legged, a way of sitting he had picked up from his years in the mountains. As young as I was, I couldn't do it more than half an hour without my legs hurting so bad I had to unlimber. He could sit like that half the night.

It was still. The only sounds were those of a night camp. Oxen and mules grazing, moving about a little. Except for the night guards the men had either gone with Matt and Dave or turned in. We were the only ones awake and our fire was the only one burning brightly. My father began to talk. "When I first came to this country," he said, "there was nothing but buffalo and Indian trails through it. There wasn't even a cart track north of Taos. Nothing with wheels had ever rolled over this land."

I hadn't given it much thought. I was so used to the emigrant trains, the freight trains, the military details coming and going, so used to meeting and passing some outfit every five or ten miles all along the road every summer season, I hadn't thought about how it all got started, or that it hadn't always been a heavily traveled road. "Who brought the first train over the road?" I said.

"It wasn't a train," he said. "It was eight or ten wagons, and a herd of milk cows. Bill Sublette brought them. Summer of 1830. He was carrying for the Rocky Mountain Fur boys. We had rendezvous on the Popo Agie that year. He brought his supplies out in wagons. First time wheels ever rolled up the North Platte."

He took time out to refill his pipe. "Next time was the summer of 1832. Captain Bonneville brought wagons up the Sweetwater, over South Pass, to Horse Creek on the Green. First wagons ever to cross the Pass."

"Who was Captain Bonneville?" I asked.

"He was a regular army man. From Fort Gibson, near where I was raised. He had a leave of absence to do some

37

trapping. That's what he told, anyway. But I went to Oregon with him and learned he was actually spying on the British in these parts for the government. The Oregon line hadn't been settled yet and the government was keeping a pretty close eye on it. Bonneville brought wagons to the Green. He cached them up there on Horse Creek and went exploring around the country horseback. I always figured he was surveying and mapping for the government and maybe recommending places for forts to be built and roads laid out. At that time it wasn't believed wagons could go any farther west than the Green."

"Who was the first one to take them farther?" I said.

"Dr. Whitman," he said. "Marcus Whitman."

I nodded. Everybody knew about the Whitmans.

"You know," he said, "a country settles up pretty much the same way, wherever it is or whoever is doing it. First come the footloose wanderers or the adventurers, like me and the boys trapping beaver. Then comes the Church. The Spanish took the Cross *with* them when they explored into the New World.

"My uncle, Johnny Osage, was one of the first white traders in the Indian Territory on the Arkansas. Before there were a dozen settlements there, here came the missionaries. He married one of them, because there weren't six white women in the country.

"A little later the settlers and the colonists begin. But the missionaries go ahead of the colonists. They help open up the way. In their own way, they are wandering, footloose adventurers, too. You take Whitman, now. There weren't any settlers in Oregon, except the British around the mouth of the Columbia. And there weren't any settlements between the Missouri and the Columbia. And there wasn't any road. He wouldn't have wanted to go if there had been. He wanted to go *ahead*. Break trail."

"When was that?"

"Summer of 1836," he said. "Rendezvous was at Horse Creek. Bonneville's Old Fort we called it, because he'd thrown up some breastworks and a shelter there. Tom Fitzpatrick brought the supplies through that year—by pack train. But traveling with him were these two missionaries and their wives. One of them was Dr. Whitman.

38

The other was Henry Spaulding. They had a light wagon with them. They had left the Missouri with two wagons, a heavy one and the light one. They traveled with Lucien Fontenelle as far as Laramie, where Tom took over. Tom persuaded them to leave the heavy wagon at Laramie. Tom was traveling fast and he told them he wouldn't wait a minute on them and they'd never get that big wagon through the broken country up the Sweetwater and keep up with him. The Blackfeet were troublesome that year and it wasn't safe for them to travel alone. So they abandoned the heavy wagon, but Whitman was bound and determined to get that light wagon all the way to Oregon."

"Did he?"

"No. But he got it as far as Fort Boise before he had to give up."

The Waiilatpu massacre in 1847, in which Dr. Whitman and his wife and thirteen other people were killed by the Cayuse Indians, had made the Whitmans famous, of course. "What kind of people were they?" I said. "Those missionaries."

"Oh, Spaulding and his wife were typical, I'd say. Long-faced, complaining, sick, troublesome, full of their own importance, preachy and mean-mouthed. They couldn't even get along with their own people. Whitman? He puzzled me. Why he wanted to be a missionary I didn't understand. He was a good frontiersman and at heart, I believe, that's mostly what he wanted to be. I believe he mistook the same thing that made me, and a lot of others like me, come west, for a missionary calling. He grew up in a churchy place and to go missionarying was the most respectable way to adventure into new country. But if he mistook his calling he mistook it good and proper. The mission board wasn't sending any single men out and they say Whitman got married, on very short notice, so he could be sent."

"I'd say that was a pretty real calling," I said, "for a man to make that kind of sacrifice."

My father laughed. "You couldn't call being married to Narcissa Whitman a sacrifice," he said.

I looked at him, astonished. "Was she beautiful?"

"Yes."

"Don't tell me you fell for her," I said, jeering. "A missionary's wife? You?"

"I wasn't the only one," he said. "Every last man-jack of us at rendezvous that year fell for her. Head over heels. Why wouldn't we? She and Eliza Spaulding weren't only the first white women ever in this country, or the first white women ever to make the journey over the Trail, they were, by God, the first and only white women ever to attend a fur trappers' rendezvous! Great blowing blizzards, boy! A rendezvous was an orgy. You'd have to see one to believe it. They were the drinkingest, sex-craziest, gamblingest, fightingest, wild and woolly gatherings this country has ever seen. A Roman saturnalia might have been something like them, but it couldn't have been any worse. When Tom Fitzpatrick rode in with the alcohol, everybody was nursing one whale of a big dry. Everybody rides out to meet the train and get the first kegs. And there, riding sidesaddle on a pretty little mare, is a pretty little mare herself . . . Narcissa Whitman."

"I reckon your dry didn't get wet down right then," I said.

"No," he said, "it was postponed until we got over gawking at her. Oh, the women didn't really put a damper on things. We just did our sinning pretty far away from their end of the encampment. A lot of the boys, though, got some religious needs all of a sudden. Enough of them to wander around Mrs. Whitman for advice and help and encouragement."

"Encouragement in what?" I said.

He laughed. "You're growing up. That was just it, Starr. She wasn't just pretty. And she wasn't just the first white woman the boys had seen for a year or two. That woman was the lushest female you ever saw. She was overripe with sex. It just plain oozed from her. I tell you . . . lace her into a pink satin dress, curl that straw-gold hair of hers, put some high-heeled white kid shoes on her feet, set her on the bar at Chugwater Joe's, and she'd have looked right at home. She was built like a floozy.

"And I tell you something else. She knew it. And even when she was singing a hymn or preaching platitudes at you, she acted like one. She used her mouth and her eyes and her body—in the name of the Lord. And every man watching her was lusting. My God, it was a sin just to look at her! The squaws got rich that rendezvous from men worked up over Narcissa Whitman."

He knocked the dottle from his pipe and fingered the bowl, rubbing it around in his hands. "They say the Cayuses mutilated her worse than anybody else in the massacre. After they killed her they worked her over and cut her up. And they smeared blood and mud and dirt in that straw-gold hair." I could hardly hear him his voice dropped so low. "The mountain men at that rendezvous in 1836 would know why."

There wasn't anything I could say to that. It was too much man stuff for me. But when he quit rubbing his pipe bowl and began filling it again, I said, "Who was next?"

"I don't know," he said. "I left the mountains that year. The first big wave of emigration started in 1842. Whitman and Tom Fitzpatrick got the first emigrant train through to Oregon that year. From then on, it was just one emigrant train after another . . . to Oregon or California."

Hardly ever did my father hark back to the old days in so lengthy a way. He talked on and on, as if once begun the memories must pour out. He told about trains he had met or passed, things that happened to them, like the Donners, and ways in which he had come to know some of them. He told of the coming of the army to the west. "In 1848. The government built Kearney and bought the old trading posts at Laramie and Fort Hall and garrisoned them. Then Bridger later."

He told about the first struggling stage lines. The fire burned low and finally he stood up, stretching and yawning. "Wherever the people go," he said, "the United States government must follow with military protection and the mail. Wheels have rolled. Emigrant wheels have rolled. Army wheels have rolled. Freight wheels have rolled. Stage wheels are rolling. And someday, boy, the iron wheels of the railroad will roll right across this country. Nothing is going to keep the wheels from rolling."

I was sleepy and hypnotized by the sound of his voice and staring into the fire. It seemed to me I could suddenly see all those wheels rolling and rolling and rolling. West. A line without beginning and a line without an end. Always moving . . . going west. It made me dizzy to think of them, all of them, rolling on.

My father hit me on the shoulder. "Hit the hay," he said. "We have to roll ourselves in the morning."

I dreamed of wheels all night.

When I had finished my story Bob Hodge chuckled. "I reckon you're still dreaming of wheels rolling, aren't you?"

I nodded. "It's what I want to do. Make 'em roll."

"It gets in your blood," he said. "They say an old sailor can't ever get the sea out of his system and I knew a steamboat man one time said he had river water in his veins instead of blood. Driving stage is the same. It gets to be a religion with a man."

"Big John warned me," I said.

I asked about Big John.

"He's driving for Jim Birch," Hodge said. "Out of San Francisco. He likes California. Says the climate is good for his rheumatism. Says he reckons to stay till he throws down the lines for good."

I was pleased to have such good news of him. I would owe him all my life more than I could ever pay. The least I could do was be as good a driver as it was in me to be, and to wish him well.

Chapter 3

When I laid over in Fort Kearney I lived with the other drivers in a long, low log hut attached to the back of the stage station. I mostly loafed around the stations and stables, with some time spent with the boys at the fort, and some time spent over at Dobytown where a dance-hall girl a cut above the average held some attraction for me. She was a little strawberry blonde called the Omaha Pearl.

She'd been on her way to Denver with a fellow who had promised her the moon but who lost his stake in a poker game at the Pawnee Bar and left her flat, busted and stranded. She went to work at the Pawnee, but she had no intentions of staying permanently in Dobytown. She had high ambitions and she meant to move on as soon as she could.

The Pearl liked nice things and it took most of my extra cash to keep in her favor. She didn't expect diamonds—not from me, but she did expect pretty trinkets, a goodly yardage of satin and lace, a plume or two for her hair and stockings for her pretty legs. She liked the shine of gold, too, and when I ran short of other things, a little pinch of gold dust was sure to put two white arms around my neck with as much love as I had any right to expect.

She wasn't mine and I didn't feel possessive about her. She had other obligations besides me. But she gave me a little preference, probably as much because I was young, tireless and relatively good looking as for any other reason. At least I shaved every day, took a bath fairly often, had all my teeth and hair and didn't get slobbering drunk every time I hit the bar.

I didn't know her real name. She was young yet, about twenty-five, and she was good company whether she was entertaining you alone in her room—and at twenty-five she could make a night memorable for you—or shouting up the trade on the floor, or driving out with you in a rented rig. She had a great, if bawdy, sense of humor. She was gay and sort of sweet and she hadn't yet begun to cry in her whisky, which she didn't guzzle in great quantities, and as far as I knew she didn't take laudanum, that great pain easer for the general run of saloon and parlor girls. Someday, if she didn't hit it rich fairly quick, she would come to it, and maybe as so many others did ease her way right on our of life with it. But the Pearl was young and pretty and she still had high hopes.

She made no bones of the fact that she meant to find herself somebody who had struck it rich in the gold fields who would set her up in style, and if she was lucky, for life. In the meantime, and in Dobytown, we enjoyed each other, were fond of each other and dallied a considerable number of hours away together.

Among the employees, around the station and stables and even over at the fort, there was a lot of talk about the trouble the Company was in. It was everybody's business and everybody wanted to prophesy, and they were mostly gloomy prophecies. Luke Hawkins, the station agent, was one of the gloomiest. "Moving the line up here just took the starch out of it. Why, my God, man, just look at the route now! This long haul to hell and gone up the Platte, up the Sweetwater, over South Pass, down Echo Canyon to Salt Lake. It's a sonuvabitch, and we only got mail for it twice a month. If Russell just hadn't bought old man Hockaday out, we'd be all right now."

"I don't know how you figure that," I said. "You had a good straight route into Denver on the Smoky Hill, but no stage line can pay out without mail and express. Hell, man, you'd go broke in no time flat if you only ran passengers. You know that. What else could Russell do?"

"He could have pulled some wires in Washington and got a mail contract on our own L. & P.P. route, that's what he could have done."

"You think William Russell didn't try that? My God, as much of a hustler as Russell is and as many strings as he's got leading inside, you think he didn't try it? And I figure he would have got it if Aaron Brown hadn't died just as the L. & P.P. commenced operating. I'd be willing to bet a month's pay if the Postmaster General hadn't died when he did, Russell would have got a mail contract to Denver. But just as Russell gets set up and running, Brown turns up his toes and dies, and the new Postmaster General is that old buzzard, Joe Holt. And old Joe Holt is a penny pincher and he decides the Postal Department is playing fast and loose with the government's money and too many mail contracts are being given to too many of Brown's good friends and he's not going to run any Postal Department that way at all. So he commences to cut back on the routes and contracts and first thing we know Hockaday is cut back from a twice weekly to a semiweekly and they whittle sixty thousand dollars off his compensation and Hockaday can't swing it and has to sell. My father says the old man is in a pitiful state over it yet. Says his reason is just about gone."

"I would think it."

"Well, all right. The only thing Russell can do, with this big dream of a million-dollar contract and a daily mail to California, is the best he can—buy Hockaday. How the hell would he know old Joe Holt was going to say no, sir, you can't carry that mail on your L. & P.P. route. The contract calls for the mail to be carried up the Platte and that's where it's going to be carried, come hell or high water, so you can just forget your L. & P.P. route and a contract for Denver. Strain at a gnat and swallow a camel, that's old Joe Holt. Russell just happens to be one of the camels he's swallowing."

"Which I hope gives him a bad case of indigestion," Hawkins growled.

"Oh, a new administration will do that. After the election next year Joe Holt won't be the Postmaster General. I would think Russell will try to hang on till there's a new Postmaster General and hope he's a friend of his."

The history of staging up the Platte was very short as yet. Staging in the west was only nine years old. Not until gold was discovered in California and James Birch, a New England driver out of a job, went there to dig gold and discovered he could put more gold in his pockets running stage lines out of the gold camps than he could pan out of the creeks, did staging of any kind start in the west.

It took gold to open the west. Gold. Since Adam and

Eve men have coveted it. The lure of gold has opened new worlds, sent armies into battle, built empires and destroyed them. It is the one unique and eternal treasure of all men everywhere. And it is so beautiful. The metal of gold stays forever young. It is the color of the sun. It is pure. It will not tarnish. It became the symbol of the west . . . the golden west. Its glitter changed the face of the country, and its wealth changed the whole world. Men stampeded to the gold creeks of California, to the gold mountains of Colorado, the gold hills of Nevada and the gold gulches of Montana.

And wherever men go they set up a yammer for mail and news from home and a road to get to and fro on, and the government has to give it to them.

The mail to California had to go by steamer around the Horn. Then James Birch opened some stage lines and began carrying the steamer mail and express out to the camps. But when California became a state in 1850, the United States government had to take over the mails.

Brigham Young had gathered the Saints in Zion and they were yelling for mail, too. So Aaron Brown, who was the Postmaster General and a dyed-in-the-wool southerner from Memphis, Tennessee, let the first contracts for the United States mail overland. From Sacramento to Salt Lake City the contract went to George Chorpenning and his partner, and from St. Joseph to Salt Lake City, the contract went to Samuel Woodson, who was a good friend of a Missouri congressman. That's the way you got mail contracts. Through your congressman, or if you were lucky enough to stand that high and know him, directly through the Postmaster General. There was a formality of putting in a bid, but there were dozens of ways around awarding a contract to the low bidder and giving it to a friend. Mail contracts were federal subsidies, they were pure patronage and they went the pork barrel route.

Woodson had to give up on his contract between St. Joseph and Salt Lake, and it went through one or two more hands before John Hockaday got it. But George Chorpenning hung on by using muleback, footback and every other means he could devise. The trouble with any mail line overland was winter. And the mountains in winter with deep snows and blizzards. It was a wonder the mail ever got through at all before the government graded out what passed for a road.

But Chorpenning on the California end of the line and Hockaday on the Missouri end were struggling along pretty well by 1859. They had worked Aaron Brown up to a decent compensation and they had a twice-weekly service going. Then came Joe Holt and the cutbacks. He let Chorpenning alone, but he whittled Hockaday back to where the old man had to give up. That was when William Russell stepped in and bought himself a mail contract which old Joe Holt wouldn't let him run on his own stage line.

"But he can't swing it," Hawkins said. "He's losing money every day. He set up all those stations clear into Salt Lake and he stocked them and he bought all that new equipment. Old man Hockaday didn't have a real stage line, and you know it. He just ran when he could with what he could scrape together. Russell has spent a fortune outfitting this line. And mail twice a month ain't going to pay him out. It's too big a debt."

"I tell you," I said, "he's spending money like water now to set up the line and impress the government. He'll make it all back and more if he can ever swing that daily mail to California and a million-dollar contract."

"Well, he'd better look to his flanks. The people he's owing money to now might cut his throat. And he'd better tend to the bird in hand and quit looking for two in the bush. My God, we can't even make a schedule that will work. Twice a week to Denver, because that's what he promised, and twice a month to Salt Lake because we got a contract. It won't work!"

"We *are* doing it," I said.

"We're making a stab at it and a pretty weak one. And the whole line is slack. You can feel it, like a loose wire. And you can't tighten it up because of short cash. Nobody is getting paid regular. You'll have empty pockets yourself this quarter. See if you don't. And you know how the boys are paying themselves? The tenders and some of the station agents? They're taking stock and equipment. They're stealing all up and down the line . . . stock and feed and harness, just being drained off. Them easterners ain't stage people, Starr. There's not a stagefaring man among 'em.

What did they do? They hired a bunch of riffraff and put 'em to work tending stock and keeping the stations. Then they can't pay them regular and when riffraff don't get paid, they know how to take their pay.

"Now, you take that old man, Jules Beni, up at Julesburg. What the hell did they put him in there for? Division point. One of the most important stations on the line. Where the line splits and Salt Lake angles up the North Platte and Denver angles up the South Platte. And they put a scoundrel there to keep the station. Everybody west of the Missouri knows Old Jules and they know he's the evilest old man on the plains. And that's who they pick for a division point."

Jules Beni was a French-Canadian who had been in the west forever, a fur trapper and Indian trader back in my father's days. He was a squaw man. In fact he had several squaws and a whole passel of young ones by Lord knows how many of them. It was true he had a bad reputation. He'd as soon cut your throat as look at you. But I laughed. "Your nose out of joint, Luke? Maybe you thought they ought to have given you that division point."

"I could have handled it," he admitted. "I could have done it a lot better than Old Jules. And not stole the Company blind doing it."

"Oh, well," I said, "I reckon they figured they had to give him something. He was sitting there on that piece of land they wanted, running his little old trading store. And he did give 'em a lot of advice and helped them set up the place. He gave them the benefit of his experience, you might say. Reckon they figured they owed him the job."

"Well, they're paying a pretty price for it," he said. "The boys say he's running a ring right out of that station and right under their noses. Raiding for fifty miles the other side of Julesburg. The joke is, he's stealing the Company's stock and then selling it right back to them. Don't tell me they're so blind they can't see that, either."

"Well," I said, "he's a tough old man. It would take a lot of guts to face him down and get rid of him."

"Which they've not got. Not one of them. But I know one man who has," Hawkins said. "If they'd turn him loose on Old Jules he would clean out that buzzard's nest and make it stick."

"Who?" I said.

"Jack Slade. He's not afraid of the devil himself."

Slade was our division agent, and a good one. He ran a very smooth division, but he had no responsibility at Julesburg. Slade's division began at Kearney, but it ended at the last station this side of Julesburg. The agent on the Julesburg-Denver division had responsibility for Julesburg itself.

We had precious little thieving on our division. Slade wouldn't tolerate it. When stock came up missing at one of our swing stations, which is where stock was usually stolen, Slade moved in fast and if he had any reason at all to suspect a tender was involved he lost no time getting rid of the fellow. And he didn't do it very pleasantly. He usually ran him off at the point of his Colt's Navy revolver, fanning the dust around him and sometimes getting a little high and nicking an arm or leg.

Thieves didn't operate near Fort Kearney much, because of the troops, so I had never seen Slade working a suspected thief over. But I had heard how he did it. The boys said he always collected up his facts ahead of time, before he showed up for business. Then he never said but one word to the thief, and that was, "Git!" Then he commenced shooting.

I didn't know Slade well. Nobody gets very thick with a division agent usually. It wasn't a job that encouraged it. But I liked Slade all right and had respect for him. He treated everybody fair and square. When he rode with me he never said much. I figured he wouldn't as long as I gave satisfaction. He wasn't a man who cut you down for nothing, just because he could. He expected you to do a good job and as long as you did he backed you up. If you didn't, out you went. That's Bible for a good division agent and it was all right with me.

I knew by now that Slade had been a bullwhacker at one time, and then he'd gone to driving for Hockaday. Then Hockaday had put him on a division and when the L. & P.P. bought out Hockaday they had inherited Slade. He had given them their money's worth, too.

I had also heard a little talk about him having killed a couple of men. Nobody seemed to know too much about it. And nobody thought too much about it. There wasn't any law in the west and men did sometimes quarrel and have trouble and somebody wound up getting killed. Men figured it was their own business. Nobody figured Slade was going to make a habit of it.

"Maybe you better write the General Manager a letter," I said to Hawkins, "and advise him to shift Jack Slade to the Julesburg division."

Hawkins gave me a bitter look and told me I'd be better off if I would learn to keep my lip buttoned up.

I had been with the Company about two months when I was very much surprised to see my father get off the westbound stage at Kearney one noon. He saw me and motioned for me to join him while he waited for his luggage. "Do you take this stage on?" he said.

"No, sir," I said, "this is a mail stage. I'm on the passenger run now. I don't go out till tomorrow."

We had got the line pretty well straightened out. We were running twice a week to Denver, four-mule hitches with the regular Concord stages to Julesburg, and six mules from there. And every stage was packed full of passengers. For just about the time the Cherry Creek gold boom at Denver was petering out, rich veins of quartz were found all up Clear Creek behind Denver and the mining camps like Golden, Central City, Blackhawk and others had sprung up. Everybody and his cousin wanted to try their luck in the gold camps, so we packed passengers wherever they could hang on. And we ran with the hind boot packed with excess baggage at seventy-five cents per pound and the front boot crammed with sacks of letters at twenty-five cents each and newspapers at ten cents apiece. There was no mail contract, but we had a private mail service.

But twice a month we had to run to Salt Lake. We had the problem of mail coming into the terminal at St. Joseph and piling up. On Hockaday's old schedule his stages carried anywhere from twelve to seventeen sacks of mail, weighing around a hundred pounds per sack. Most of it was what we called Pub. Docs.—the franked mail from the politicians in Washington to their constituents in the west. Every congressman from the west appeared to want every word he said to reach all the people.

What Russell ran into on the cutback to semiweekly was more weight than a single stage could carry, so twice a month he had to run two mail stages, each with a six-horse string, to Salt Lake. There was so little mail eastbound that one stage had to deadhead back. It was a mail stage I drove my first time on the box for L. & P.P. But I was on the regular passengers run now.

"Good," my father said, "we'll have time to do some talking."

He always stayed with the commandant at the fort when he was in Kearney. I took him there and left him and he asked me to come back in a couple of hours. I felt like a kid waiting for a whipping. I had told Luke Hawkins my father would take it all right, me leaving the train and going to work driving stage, and he would. But he would have a few things to say and I didn't believe they were going to be very pleasant.

He did, and they weren't. He said he thought I had more sense than to become a driving tramp. Said it reflected somewhat on his raising of me and he couldn't take much pride in it and he'd expected better of me. And I said like what, for instance. And he said like staying in the family business. He said if I had had my fill of this nonsense he was ready to give me my own train next season. Make me a wagonmaster. I said no, sir, I didn't have my fill of it. It was a job I liked and meant to stay with. "It's what I always wanted to do," I said. "You know that."

He sighed. "Yes. I remember. But I always figured it was the kid in you and you'd outgrow it. You're sure, are you?"

"Yes, sir."

He cut his losses handsomely, and with no more regrets. That had always been his way. "All right," he said, "if that's the way you see it." He would never try to persuade me out of it again. But more than that, I could count on him to stand behind me like a block of granite. I was glad it was over and with no more unpleasantness. I hated to go against him, but I felt easy with him now.

He gave me the news of home and said he was on his way to Denver. Said he thought he might dabble a little in some gold mining. At least have a good look at what was happening out there. I asked him what was happening in Washington.

"Well," he said, "your big boss, William Russell, is borrowing money from Peter to pay Paul. Ben Holladay has collected a lot of paper on him. Russell has managed to get Russell, Majors & Waddell in a hole with him. They'll be taking over this stage line shortly. In fact, they've already come in to bail him out."

"That's good news," I said. "Maybe we'll get paid once in a while now."

"Don't count on it," he said. "They're not getting any freight contracts next season from the government. They're going to be mighty short of cash."

"That don't make you cry, does it?" I said, grinning.

He grinned back at me. "You're damned right it don't. Their loss is my gain."

"What happened?" I said.

To understand this kind of shorthand talk it is necessary to know something of the background of the men involved and the business they were in and of the way they did business together and the places they were doing business in.

When the great transportation era on the Overland began in 1859, Utah consisted of all that present state, plus Nevada, plus the southern part of Idaho and the western part of Colorado and Wyoming. Kansas had only just succeeded in establishing itself as a territory separate from Nebraska. Dakota Territory included part of Montana and the eastern half of Wyoming. It would need a file of the *Rocky Mountain News* to untangle Colorado which was respectively Arapaho County of Kansas, then Jefferson Territory, then Colorado.

Denver was two mining camps, one on each side of Cherry Creek, and when we said Pikes Peak we meant the whole front range of the Rocky Mountains. Salt Lake was Utah to us, the Carson valley was Nevada, and Santa Fe and Taos were New Mexico.

The Missouri River was the jumping-off place to all the west. In that short piece where the river is the boundary between Kansas and Missouri there was a little group of towns all in a huddle—St. Joseph and Westport (now Kansas City) on the Missouri side of the river, Fort Leavenworth and Atchison on the Kansas side. These were four of the most important towns in the history of the west.

A remarkable breed of men operated out of those towns. Most of them had come to the frontier as very young men, or had been brought by their families while still children. They grew up on the Missouri, they all knew each other, and in many cases were related to each other. They developed the towns, opened banks and stores and land offices, and then they fanned out from those towns into the freighting business, the mining business, the real estate business and the stage business, to open the west.

Not that they had any great intention of doing that. They were simply men of brains, energy, imagination and ruthless and sometimes unscrupulous ambition. They operated on the theory of who gets there first with the most is the winner and each of them meant to be a winner. They knew gold when they saw it, whether it was in land, minerals or freight. Or government contracts. They wanted a pile of it for themselves.

There were William Russell and Alexander Majors and William Waddell who combined to form the huge freight company of Russell, Majors & Waddell. There were dozens of other freight companies, such as my father's, and Stebbins & Porter, Dennison & Brown, Roper & Nesbit, Burr & Co., and Irwin, Jackman & Co. In 1860, there were forty-one traders and freighters doing business out of Atchison alone.

And there was Ben Holladay, who made a pile of money freighting for the army during the Mexican war, and around Salt Lake in the fifties, and who became the stagecoach king of the world. There was Bela Hughes, a lawyer and cousin of Ben Holladay. He was a good man to have when you needed favorable legislation in Kansas, Missouri or Colorado. There was Francis P. Blair, Jr., who served Missouri for years in the Congress of the United States. He was also related to Ben Holladay. F. P. Blair's brother, Montgomery Blair, became Postmaster General in the Lincoln administration, which paralleled Ben Holladay's era as stagecoach king and certainly did not hurt his chances for lucrative mail contracts.

One of the most remarkable things was how many of

these men stemmed originally from Kentucky. I used to wonder sometimes if Kentucky didn't breed mighty good men who didn't do much good till they left Kentucky, so many of them seemed to have left. The Holladays, the Hugheses, the Blairs, the Majorses, my father Joe Fowler, and dozens of others came from there in the beginning. But maybe Kentuckians had just got used to opening frontiers.

These men, serving their own interests primarily, served the west well, also. There has been a lot of argument about how well they served the country. They did a lot of grabbing, sure. But they helped build cities and towns and roads. They influenced—well, make it plain, they bought legislation (which is still an honored custom) which influenced whole territories and states. They built lines of communication and transportation. They made millions for themselves, but give the devil his due, they also opened up the country. How far west would the stay-at-homes be today?

They were the first big business tycoons in the west, and as the station agent at Fort Kearney said about my father, they had hair on their chests. Sometimes they were partners in a business venture. Sometimes they were enemies and cut each other's throats. They were not men of mercy or pity in business. A competitor was to be crushed. They were powerful men with little scrupulosity for the niceties of the law. They pretty much made their own law. They believed totally in the power of money, for they early learned they could buy a whole state legislature, they could elect their own congressmen, they could buy cabinet officials and they could even, sometimes, buy themselves a President.

In the greatest travel decade in the history of our country, 1859 to 1869, in these four towns, therefore, were concentrated all the great freighting companies who every year sent out hundreds and hundreds of ox and mule trains to Denver, to Santa Fe, to Salt Lake, to the mines in Colorado, Nevada, Idaho and Montana; to the forts and military posts. In these towns the great emigrant and pilgrim trains made up and left. And from these towns during that decade the beautiful, graceful Concord coaches of the

Overland Stage Line left for their fast, brisk, lively trip across the plains.

On an old map, those plains just west of these towns will be marked the Great American Desert. It shows up a vast and lonely country. We know now that Lieutenant Long and Lieutenant Pike and Captain Frémont did it an injustice in naming it a desert. They said it wouldn't even graze cattle because the grass was so sparse. And they said an ear of corn would never grow in Colorado. The thousands of fine little towns and flourishing farms and ranches that now grace those prairies prove how wrong their prophecies were.

But in 1859, when public lands in Kansas and Nebraska had just been opened to homestead, the country had only been settled up a hundred miles or so west of the Missouri —in the valleys of the Big Blue and the Little Blue. Away out on the Platte there were a few ranches, mostly Indian trading posts, and along the overland road there were only three military posts, Fort Kearney, Fort Laramie and Fort Bridger. Fort Bridger and Fort Laramie were old fur-trading posts which the government had bought after the War with Mexico in 1846. The end of this war brought all the Spanish possessions south of the Arkansas River, and California, into the United States. Emigration began to increase and military protection along the road was necessary. Fort Kearney was located and built on the Platte in 1848.

From Atchison to Denver was 653 miles of mostly unsettled country. It was 1255 miles to Salt Lake City, the last third of it over mountains. It was 1913 miles to Placerville, California. Vast, vast distances over a vast, vast country.

And yet, nobody who didn't witness it could believe the enormous amount of travel on that Overland road in the decade from 1859 to 1869. In one year, 1860, those forty-one regular traders in Atchison sent out 1328 wagons, with 1549 men and 15,263 oxen. Gold in Denver had only been discovered two years, since 1858, and the population was barely 2500. But of the forty-one trains sent out from Atchison in 1860, thirty-three were bound for Denver.

One of the trains had 125 wagons and carried 750,000

pounds of merchandise. It employed fifty-two men, twenty mules and 1542 oxen. Several of the trains for Denver had as many as fifty wagons. Among the other trains sent out from Atchison that year, one was for Santa Fe, one for Colorado City, two for Green River and four for Salt Lake. In all the trains outfitted at and leaving from Atchison that year, 6,590,875 pounds of merchandise was transported across the plains. This was commercial transportation only. One firm, freighting military supplies for the government to the forts, sent out 2530 wagons, with 650 men, 75 mules and 6240 oxen.

Besides all the freight trains constantly on the road, there were the other travelers—the hopeful ones in prairie schooners heading for the mining camps; there were the emigrant and pilgrim trains; there were people traveling in private equipages, and there were the daily stagecoaches east and west. Vast and long and wide was the country and the road, but lonely it was not. Not during that spectacular decade.

We knew these things as automatically as you know the four directions. When my father said William Russell had got the freighting firm of Russell, Majors & Waddell into trouble, it was like hearing small-town gossip. We knew all the principals, had always known them, were interested in the rumors, knew they would affect us, and could at least partially predict the outcome.

"How in the hell," I said, "did he manage to lose the government contracts?"

"Oh, he and Floyd pulled a fast one that didn't come off," he said. "Floyd had to pull in his horns."

John Floyd was Secretary of War in the Buchanan administration. He was a southerner, naturally, since the Buchanan administration was southern. Floyd's department awarded the government freight contracts, and now that it's all a matter of history it can be said he had a big bottomless pork barrel going for him. He took it just as far as he could and always got a very substantial kickback on the contracts.

"Well," my father said, chuckling, "this summer Floyd gave Russell a contract to pick up 800,000 pounds of flour in St. Louis and deliver it to Camp Floyd, Utah. The government price was seven dollars a hundred. Ben Holladay heard about it and he suggested to Russell that he could make a little on the side if he picked up the flour but took it only as far as Leavenworth and got the army to accept it there. Then buy flour a lot cheaper from Brigham Young and deliver to Camp Floyd. Of course, Floyd had to agree to accept the flour at Leavenworth, which he was willing to do . . . for a price. Then he and Russell and Holladay would buy it at seven dollars a hundred, haul it to Denver and sell it for forty dollars. Holladay had to be cut in because they couldn't make a deal without him. Not with Brigham Young. They had no line to old Brigham except Holladay. Well, it was done, cut, dried and wrapped up." He began laughing. "But there's no honor among thieves. Floyd and Russell don't know it. They got their cut on the profit of the flour sold in Denver. What they don't know is that Holladay bought Utah flour for a dollar a hundred, instead of seven, the government price, and just politely put six dollars a hundred in his own pockets."

"Good enough," I said, laughing too. "He don't miss a thing, does he?"

"Not many. He's a sonuvabitch. But he's made it pay. That's why he's worth millions today and don't have to run a freight line any more. He's buying and selling in New York and Washington. Anyway, the news about the contract got out and there's been quite a scandal about it in Washington. Floyd is beginning to smell to the administration, and pretty high. He don't dare give Russell any more contracts till this dies down."

"Did it hurt Holladay any?"

"How could it? He wasn't out front. He was behind the scenes pulling the rug out from under Russell and Floyd. And I'm not sure Holladay don't have his eye on this stage line."

"Hey," I said, "you think he might call in his paper?"

"Well, that's the surest way I know to take over an outfit. Just collect enough paper on it and bide your time, then move in and take over. Yes. I look for Holladay to move someday. He don't want it now. He'll let Russell go on and lose his shirt. Because nobody can budge that old curmudgeon that's Postmaster General now. But after the election, with a new Postmaster General—and Holladay will have enough money in the campaign to elect a friendly President and can call the turns on who the Postmaster General will be—that's when I figure Holladay will want the stage line and mail contract. I may be all wrong, but that's the way I think he'll operate."

"Russell thinks a new Postmaster General will cinch him, don't he?"

"Maybe. But Russell is a simpleton by the side of Holladay and he's got no money. Holladay's got it and he knows how to use it."

"Whew!" I said. "What goes on in the seats of the mighty!"

"They can cut you up and serve you in little pieces in Washington," he said.

"Just out of curiosity," I said, "have you got any money in this line?"

"Not a dime," he said. "I wouldn't touch anything of Russell's. I haven't got that kind of money to play fast and loose with. But I tell you, if Holladay ever takes it over I'll buy in as fast as I can. *If* there's any stock lying around. Now," he leaned forward, "let me ask you something, just out of curiosity. Why, if you wanted to drive stage so bad, didn't you go down and get a job on the Butterfield line?"

There had been so many squalls from California about an overland mail line that Aaron Brown had known he was going to have to provide one. But he didn't want it crossing any northern states. It stood to reason that railroads were going to expand west in time. It stood to reason the first east-west railroad would follow the route of the first fast mail line east to west. Brown wanted to make sure the railroads followed a southern route. So, in 1858 he had awarded a mail contract to John Butterfield on a route that made a long oxbow down from St. Louis to Fort Smith, Arkansas, across the Choctaw Nation and Texas, to Tucson and Fort Yuma and up the west coast to San Francisco. It was 2795 miles long and the mail contract was for $800,000. Two of the executives of the line were Henry Wells and William Fargo, who had express companies in the east. They ran twice weekly and Aaron Brown had drawn up such an ironclad contract with them that old Joe Holt couldn't break it when he came into office.

"That line can't last," I said. "When the contract runs out in 1864, they'll be through. They're to hell and gone from anywhere. They run across nothing but open country and wasteland. I don't know too much about politics, but I don't believe there'll be another southern administration elected next year. And that may mean war. Everybody says so, anyhow. And comes a war what's going to happen to a southern line. No. It just don't figure. This is the road, and this is the line."

My father grinned big and wide. "I just wanted to hear you say so. I'm relieved you've still got a head on your shoulders. Driving stage hasn't softened it too much. You're right. Just hang on and this line will bail out. And you better buy some stock when it does."

He was having dinner with the commandant and I had promised to see the Pearl, so that ended our talk for the day. I drove him as far as Plum Creek next afternoon and waved him on to Denver when I turned the lines over to the next driver. It had been a profitable visit for me.

Chapter 4

I liked my layovers at Plum Creek. It was a lot like home to me. I had got to know the Westmorelands and to like them. Ed Westmoreland was a big burly man with powerful strength and energy. He was keeping the Plum Creek station just by chance.

He and his wife and little girl had been starting out to California. They joined up with half a dozen other outfits to make a small train. It wasn't much of a train and none of them had known each other before leaving St. Joseph. They just decided to bunch together for protection.

The train got mauled by the Pawnees the other side of the river and Ed lost his teams, both of his wagons and everything that was in them. Everything he had in the world except his gun went up in smoke. The rest of the train pulled itself together and went on to Cottonwood Springs. Nobody offered to help Ed and he didn't expect it. He and his family crossed the river to the Plum Creek station, which at that time was a station on the Hockaday line.

The station had been mauled, too. All the stock had been run off, the station keeper was killed, and Ed found the station burning with a slow fire he was able to put out. The stock tenders had sloped, which was what any sensible man would do when there was nothing left to tend or guard and he was outnumbered. The tenders went down to Fort Kearney and reported the attack and waited there until the division agent showed up. He brought them back, along with enough mules to operate again.

Emma Westmoreland was no more a despairing soul than Ed, and when the division agent got there she had cleaned up the mess inside the station, sorted out the supplies not too fried, broiled or roasted to be used, and she had made a list of them so she could check off what she was borrowing from them to cook. Knowing how Emma kept house, I bet that she had made a tablecloth of something, some old sacking maybe, and that she already had something growing in a pot sitting in the middle of it.

Ed had buried the station keeper and raked over the ashes of the stable for equipment that could be salvaged. The division agent was impressed and he offered Ed the job of keeping the station and Ed took it, there being nothing else handy for him to do.

Ed was worried about the L. & P.P. now. He wanted to keep his job until he had enough of a stake pulled together to move on. "This line is going to fold," he said, "as sure as God made little apples. They're not even making the payroll right now, much less making a profit."

"Oh, lay off it, Ed," I said, "I've got some news for you," and I told him some of the things my father had passed on to me. "He says just hang on. We may not get paid regular, but the line's not going to fold. And you're not going to starve here even if you don't get paid. The Company's got to feed you."

"By Jesus," he said, "I hope your father's right. I would hate to lose the time I've put in here."

"You won't," I said.

Emma Westmoreland treated me like I belonged to her. I didn't mind. She humored my preferences in food, picked up after me, scolded me, tried to ration my whisky, washed and ironed and mended for me. She wasn't obligated to do anything but feed me and make up my bed. That's all the Company paid her and Ed to do for me. But she didn't have a son so she made one of me. She was a natural-born mother, anyway.

The youngster, Mary Buchanan—which they shortened to Bucky—was something of a pest, but in a nice sort of way. She had a bad case of hero worship for stage drivers. All kids did those days. Nowadays they think a railroad engineer sits next door to God, but then it was the stage driver. He was the king of the road—the knight of the reins. If he nodded his head at a kid, it caused a glow that lasted all day. If he cracked his whip for a kid, it sent him into fits. And if he blew a blast on his horn, the kid was transported into delirium. All kids loved the stage driver.

61

I got more of it from Bucky than was comfortable. She pestered the life out of me, wanting to hold my whip, wanting to hold the dope pot, wanting to shine my boots, anything she could think of to be part of a stage driver's work. I fended her off as best I could and put up with her the rest of the time.

I learned she was nine years old. She was small for her age at that, thin and stringy, all elbows and knees, but she managed them pretty well and wasn't overly awkward. Most of her size was in those big fat braids of red hair, which I pulled when I teased her. I guess I teased her too much, but I had too many kid sisters not to be a tormenting big brother. Bucky hated to have her braids pulled. She was finicky about her hair and she would yell like a mountain cat, kick, claw, scratch and sometimes bite if I persisted too long.

Her nose was covered with freckles which spread out over her upper cheeks under her eyes. They didn't fade even in winter because she stayed out in the wind and sun most of the time. More than any little girl I ever knew she wanted to be a boy. She wanted to wear pants, but her mother wouldn't allow it. I couldn't see that her skirts hampered her any. She could ride anything she could get a rope on, with or without a saddle. She would close-haul a mustang in near the fence and with skirts flying be astride before he knew what had happened. Then her heels would dig in and he couldn't get rid of her. I never saw her take a bad fall but one time, and that was from the back of a running horse that stepped in a gopher hole. She and the horse both took a tumble, but Bucky lit rolling and didn't break any bones. The horse had to be shot.

She hung around the stable and corral and knew the stage teams as well as I did and better than the tenders. She had to fill up her time somehow, because she had nobody at all to play with. Once in a while Emma let her go into Fort Kearney with me and stay a few days with the Hawkinses, who had several children. "This is a lonesome life for her," she said. "There's nothing for her to do but run wild."

Without thinking, I said, "You ought to had her a brother or two, Emma."

62

Emma looked so stricken I knew I had put my foot in my mouth. She went in the kitchen and Ed told me. They had had two boys, older than Bucky. They had lost both of them, in Ohio, of the cholera. "That was the main reason Emma was willing to go to California," he said. "She thought maybe it was unhealthy back there. And it seemed like a good time to strike out and make a new start."

"I'm a clumsy-mouthed fool," I said.

"There's no reason you would know," he said.

"I can see why you and Emma wouldn't mention it," I said, "but looks like Bucky would have. She's not ever spoken of them to me, either."

"She hasn't," he said, "from the time they died. That was three years ago. It took us a while to make up our minds and then get ready to leave. Bucky was six when they died. Because it was cholera all their things had to be burned. She watched us burn them. And from that day to this she has never mentioned their names, or acted as if they'd ever lived."

"Except," I said, "to try to be as much boy as she can to make up for it."

"Well, she was pretty much a tomboy with 'em from the start," he said. "But I reckon it explains a little why she's so took up with you."

Well, I didn't particularly mind being stuck with another little sister, especially if she had put me in the place of her dead brothers. I was stuck with her anyhow, so all the difference it made was that I tried to remember and go easier on her and make some allowances.

For instance, she asked so many questions about driving that I finally put her up a rig and began to show her how to handle the reins. She was very quick and good. If she'd been a boy nothing could have stood in her way. I made the mistake of bragging on her. "You've got the hands and you've got the wrists," I said, "it's a pity . . ."

"It's a pity I'm not a boy," she said. I could have cut my tongue out because her eyes were suddenly full and swimming. "Aren't there *any* women driving stage?"

"Not that I ever heard of," I said. I took the reins and hung them up. "That's enough for today. You go be Mary for a while. Bucky's had her turn today."

"I like being Bucky," she said. "I'm going to be the first woman stage driver. You wait and see. I *will* drive stage. I *will!*"

"Oh, be sensible," I said, impatient with her all at once. "Women can't drive stage and that's all there is to it."

"Why? Why can't they? You said yourself I had the hands and you said I had the wrists. I could drive, couldn't I? Couldn't I?"

"Maybe you could handle the team, yes. You could be strong enough. You could have the skill. But for God's sake. You know what the boys are like. We all bunk together. There's drinking and there's cussing and there's . . . well, there's a lot of other things. Where would you sleep and how would you get along with a bunch of men? There just is not any place for a woman and no stage line is ever going to make a place."

"I won't give it up," she said, as stubborn as a mule, "I'm going to drive stage."

It was just as well we didn't know about Charlie Parkhurst then. Charlie was an orphan who ran away and hired out as a stableboy for a stage line in Rhode Island. He was a natural driver and started driving when he was still in his young teens. And he was one of the best. When James Birch started operating his line from Sacramento out to the mines in California, he sent for Charlie to come drive for him. Charlie drove for the Pioneer line for many years, a little sawed-off runt that drank with the best of them, smoked cigars, played a smart game of poker.

Finally Charlie threw down the lines and bought a little ranch up in the foothills and lived alone on it. Some neighbors missed seeing him around one day and went over to see about him. He was dead. The men went to wash him up and lay him out a decent corpse. They were thunderstruck when they undressed him. Charlie was a woman. Totally bewildered they sent for a doctor. After an examination, the doctor said Charlie was not only a bona fide woman, he had been a mother also!

If Bucky had known about Charlie Parkhurst she could have said, "If she could drive stage, so can I."

As it was, I realized I had made a mistake putting up the rig for her and began trying to ease off coaching her. I wasn't getting much of anywhere with it till one day about two months after I'd put the rig up. She had wheedled me into watching her once more. I agreed she was doing fine. Then I said, laughing at her, "Time you're sixteen you'll not even remember you ever wanted to drive stage."

"Oh, yes, I will," she said. "Why? Why won't I?"

"You'll be grown up and you'll get married like every other girl and have a family. And be proud to."

"Oh," she said, breezy as the west wind, "I'm going to marry you someday, but I'm going to drive stage too."

"Well, now," I said, "I'll have something to say about that. I don't know as I'd want my wife driving stage."

"Why?"

"Well, good Lord," I said, "if you're off driving stage who'd keep the house and do the cooking and mind the kids? And be home when I got home? A man don't want his wife off gallivanting around."

"Oh," she said. "Oh . . ."

And be durned if that wasn't the last we heard of driving stage. She took the rig down and quit trailing a couple of lines around with her to practice keeping her fingers limber and we never heard another word about it or saw any indication it interested her in any way.

The days were shorter and the nights were cold now. We shot rattlesnakes and gophers and cut willows and cottonwood for the winter fires. Ed talked about his plans.

"Still going to California?" I asked one night.

"No. We've changed our minds. Since they found gold up Clear Creek, we're going to try Denver. Looks like it's a town that's going to make it."

I hadn't been there yet myself and had a big longing to see it. Eastbound travelers said it was growing so fast it changed almost every day. They said it was soon going to be *the* city of the west. It already had a population of 1500, had every kind of store, even a jewelry store, had a dozen bars, a hotel, the stage station. It had a church, and the *Rocky Mountain News* had issued its first number on April 23.

"Going to try mining?" I asked Ed.

"Well," he said, "I reckon I'll have to. At first. But Emma thinks she could run a rooming house, take in boarders to help out."

I didn't doubt at all that Emma Westmoreland could run

a successful rooming and boarding house. And if Ed would pitch in and help they might even run a good hotel. Emma cooked away and gone the best food I had ever eaten except my mother's. And she didn't have anything to work with but stage station supplies and a little buffalo meat that Ed or me or the tenders brought in.

"Well, if you do go to Denver," I said, "there'll be a school for Bucky by the time you get there. Emma's always worrying about her missing out on some schooling."

"How's that?" Ed said.

"I passed a fellow on the road the other day. He was by himself. Driving a span of oxen. He was wearing a long black frock coat and a high silk hat."

"I don't feel like one of your jokes, Starr," Ed said.

"It ain't a joke. It's the beautiful truth. He was a school-teacher, going to Denver. It was that narrow piece of the road the other side of the creek. He had to pull out to let me by. I had to slow and the passengers had some talk with him. He had 'Pikes Peak or Bust' chalked on the side of his wagon. And he was cussing those blue-tailed ox in Latin and Greek."

"I didn't know you spoke Latin and Greek," Ed said, still disbelieving.

"I don't. But the fellow riding the box with me did. He was a lawyer and a very highly educated man. He translated for me. It was the most high-toned cussing I ever heard. Among other things he called those oxen misbegotten sons of Hebe, bastard offspring of Zeus, he said they were crossed with the wild ox of the Celebes and Balaam's ass, and he threatened them with the worst kind of atrocities, the least of which was drawing and quartering them. Then he promised to leave their bones bleaching in the sand and make moccasins of their hides."

"And he aimed to start a school in Denver? Who would send a kid to learn from a man like that?" Ed said, astonished.

"I would," I said. "That man would have something to teach a kid. It's not every man that's got that much imagination."

Ed shook his head.

"When you get to Denver," I said, "just look for a man

66

still limping with sore feet wrapped in ox-hide moccasins. That'll be him."

"Aw, you've got diarrhea of the vocal chords, boy."

"And I've got a stage to take to Kearney and it's due in ten minutes and I got to eat yet. Emma!" I yelled. "When'll the grub be ready?"

"It was ready and got cold while you was talking Latin and Greek," she said, laughing.

Yes, I liked the Westmorelands. I liked them a lot. They were my family on the road.

Chapter 5

There was a big dance at Fort Kearney during the Christmas holidays. The commandant and his wife gave it and the whole countryside was invited and came. Ranchers and their wives from as far as the Little Blue, station keepers and their wives, the wives of the officers and men of the garrison, everybody was there. There were the Emerys from Thirty-Two-Mile Creek, and the Eubanks from the Narrows. There were the Lemmons from Liberty Farm. And west of Fort Kearney the Westmorelands came down from Plum Creek, and beyond them Dan Trout of Midway brought his sisters, Miss Lizzie and Miss Maggie.

It was the biggest event of the year. The regimental band played for it and, while they were pretty brassy and long on military marches, they blew with goodwill, primed with good whisky, till daylight.

They knew exactly three waltzes. The waltz was a sensation among the womenfolk, who loved to be swung about on the turns to make their long full skirts swirl and they were mad about the new German music in three-four time. It was a pretty thing, a waltz. Smooth and constantly turning. Made for grace. The bass horn player in the band was a German, Sergeant Shultz. He sang one of the waltzes, and the women loved it so much they begged the boys to play it over and over for them. Willie would sing it every time. About the second time he sang it, Bucky had learned it and the next time round her nice clear young voice and Willie's old growl made a fine duet. To this day I know all the words of that waltz-song, *"Ach du lieber Augustin."* Bucky sang it for weeks after the dance and if you hear something around the clock for weeks it gets drummed into your head so hard you will never forget it. But it's a nice little waltz-song.

Jack Slade and his wife, Virginia Dale, were there. She was dumpy and plump, pigeon-breasted, but rather pretty. Gossip had it that she kept Jack on a pretty tight rein. I had heard that they met while he was living in Texas and they were married there. I thought perhaps she knew more about Jack's wild young days than we did and kept her eye on him for that reason. One thing was sure. He was crazy about her. Off duty, he hardly ever went anywhere without her. And he was very courtly with her. He was a good dancer, but he didn't dance with anybody but her and the commandant's wife, and the dance with the commandant's wife was a duty dance.

The hospitality was good that night. The food was good and the whisky was better. The men imbibed it freely, outside naturally. Slade and I were outside cooling down a little and having another drink when I realized he was getting too much. His voice had thickened, though he was still in good control of himself. "The line's getting a new name next week," he said, "did you know that?"

We all knew that Russell, Majors & Waddell owned the line now, but it had never been announced and we still ran as the L. & P.P.

"What's it going to be?" I said.

"The C.O.C. & P.P."

"That ain't a name," I said, laughing, "that's a mispronunciation. You're drunk, Jack."

"I may be," he said, chuckling. "I wouldn't put it past me. But that is what will be painted on the stages that run on this line from now on."

"C.O.C. & P.P.? What's it mean?"

"It means," he said, weaving toward me until I carefully balanced him up again, "it means Central Overland California & Pikes Peak Express Company. That's what it means."

"God," I said, "who thought that one up?"

"The old man," he said, his eyebrows shooting up at me. "The old man himself."

"Well," I said, thinking about it, "you've got to admit he don't quit easy. He's not given up on that California idea, has he?"

"He's not. He's sure not. He's the president of the new line and his boy is the secretary and we're getting a new

General Manager, too. Know who he is?" Slade was weaving again and I propped him up. He wagged his finger in my face. "Old Ben Ficklin, that's who it is. That's who's going to be the new General Manager."

Ben Ficklin was one of the boys in that cluster of Missouri towns. He was a crony and good friend of all the others. He had the name of being pretty rugged. He had some experience staging . . . some place in Texas, down around San Antone.

"That's good news," I said. "We can use some reorganization. Maybe he'll tighten this line up now and run a good stage line."

"Old Ben Ficklin will take care of that," Slade said. "You wait and see. That old bastard's as tough as a sage hen."

There was a disturbance over toward the stage station just then, some loud talking and laughing and shouting and we could hear Hawkins trying to shout it down. Slade broke in that direction in a trot and I followed on his heels. Trouble at the stage station was his job, but it might be mine, too.

It was a bunch of the boys from Dobytown, freighters, teamsters, gambling men, all well liquored up. As usual with men that far gone on the bottle, they had what they believed was a sensible and marvelous idea.

"They want to borrow that old mud wagon we keep extra in the stable," Hawkins explained, "and a team and go for a moonlight ride along the river. Which there ain't no moonlight in the first place and six inches of snow in the second and a horse is liable to get a broken leg for they're too drunk to drive in the third place, and in the fourth it's Company property and they've got no right to it."

They were in high good humor, not actually quarrelsome, but insistent on carrying out their plan, milling around, shouting, laughing, arguing. There were several dance-hall girls with them and to my surprise the Pearl was among them. "Starr!" she caroled at me. "He says the boys are too drunk to drive. *You* can drive us! Come on. Take us for a ride! Starr will drive us, boys. He is a bee-you-ti-ful driver!"

70

I never knew the Pearl to get too much to drink, but she was so high-spirited naturally that one drink could sometimes send her kiting as high as if she'd had five or six. The lanterns made a smoky light and she stood out in the group in her spangled pink satin dress, some sort of dark shawl draped around her shoulders. She edged over to me, laughing, her head thrown back to look up at me. She clutched my arm and clung to me.

"What are you doing here?" I said.

"Going for a ride," she gurgled, "we're going for a ride. If old Demon face here will let us. Didn't you hear? And you are going to drive us."

"You're drunk," I said. "Go home and take the other girls with you. Nobody is going for a ride." The shawl had slipped and her shoulders were bare. I tugged it up and pulled it around her. "You'll freeze to death out in the cold with no more clothes on than that."

"No, I won't," she giggled. "I'll be tucked right beside you. You'll keep me warm. Come on, let's go!"

When she yelled, the boys surged toward the stable.

"No," Slade said, suddenly, the first time he had spoken. "Stay where you are."

He didn't raise his voice at all. It was quiet, clear, deep, maybe too much so, for the boys didn't pay any heed. They brushed him aside and milled noisily on toward the stable. One man, a big bruising teamster, seemed to be the leader. I didn't know him personally, but I knew he drove for Irwin & Jackman and they had a train at the fort. He was yelling directions to the other boys. "Jake, you and Tom and Banjo harness up. Me and the others will roll the stage out."

"I said no!" Slade's voice cut like a whiplash.

"Aw, who are you to be giving orders?"

"He's the division agent, that's who he is," Hawkins put in quickly, "and he's the one has the right to give orders around here."

Slade motioned for him to keep quiet.

"Not to me, he don't," the teamster said, shouldering around the others, "he don't give me no orders. Come on, boys. We're wasting ti-i-i-i- . . ."

He never finished what he was going to say because

71

Slade's gun barked and the last word ended on a long, sliding downnote, which suddenly rose in a high squalling cry as he pitched forward onto his face. Slade pumped another shot into him as he fell, then another after he had fallen. Then he ranged the Colt's around the crowd. Spitting it out, he said, "Git!"

The Pearl had stiffened at the first shot, but she hadn't cried out as some of the other girls did. She stiffened and her fingers dug into my arm.

When the boys began to back off in a dead stillness, Slade's gun holding on them, she turned loose of my arm. She knew Slade, of course. Everybody knew Slade, and Virginia Dale couldn't always keep him out of the bars. The Pearl was standing between me and him. He was not more than two feet beyond her. There was absolute silence except for the shuffling, sliding sound of the men's feet as they backed off. In the silence the Pearl spoke suddenly, her voice as cold as the night and as brittle. "One shot was enough, Slade."

Slade's laugh was a short bark, snuffed off quickly. "But three dunking in sounds better, don't it?"

I thought it was the arrogance of drink, and the excess of drink, but I should have known better right then. I had been surprised when he cut loose. I wouldn't have thought this crowd needed gunplay. They weren't brawling yet and while they were a tough bunch of boys, a little good humor and some firmness could have handled them, I thought. I had expected Slade to be curt with them, maybe, to argue with them a little, in as good a humor as they were in, herd them around and talk them out of their idea and send them along. I believed they would have moved around some and argued and then drifted back to Dobytown.

I might have been wrong, but it seemed to me what had burned Slade was the teamster saying he couldn't give orders to him. I gave Slade the benefit of the doubt. Maybe he knew that particular teamster a lot better than I did and knew his troublemaking capacities. But the man wasn't wearing a gun. Teamsters didn't much, yet. They carried shotguns on their wagons. The day hadn't come in the west when men cut down on each other at the drop of a hat. Those of us who worked for the Company wore the Colt's six-shooters. They were issued to us and were regulation.

But men used their guns for protection against the Indians and to hunt game with. We had to guard treasure and passengers and Company property. Well, Slade had guarded it mighty well.

As the men backed off those behind and on the outside edges began to break up and run for their horses. Slade held his gun steady on the little knot still at the center.

The Pearl suddenly walked out from between us, toward the dead teamster.

"Hey!" Slade yelled at her.

"Shoot me in the back, Slade," she said, "if you want to stop me."

She moved steadily on toward the teamster, reached him and bent over him. I saw her shoulders shudder and in plain kindness went to her. When I reached her she stood up and turned and buried her face in my shoulder. I held her and patted her and said, "You better go home. Come on, I'll take you."

I wasn't aware until then that the shots had brought a bunch of the boys from the dance over to the station to see what was going on. They were suddenly all around us, boiling around, wanting to know what had happened. Slade holstered his gun and spoke to an officer. "Nothing," he said, "just a little matter of protecting Company property. Some Dobytown punks thought they could steal a stage and team. It was my duty to persuade them differently."

The officer glanced down at the teamster. "I take it your persuasion was effective."

The Pearl shifted about to look at the officer but stayed within the circle of my arm. "They weren't going to steal anything. We only meant to borrow the stage. We even asked Luke if we could borrow it. Or rent it. We would have paid for it. Does that sound like stealing?"

But the stage station was off the military reservation and what happened on Company property was Company business. So long as government property was not involved, the officer had no authority over civilians. He shrugged and began trying to herd the crowd off. "Move on out," he said. "It's over and nothing to be excited about. You men, get on back to the fort. This is none of your business."

"Come on," I told the Pearl, "let's get out of here."

Then, out of the corner of my eye, I saw a movement in

the crowd of men, something small and white and wiggling, like a dog, sinuous and insistent between the legs of the men, squirming and urging forward. It couldn't be, I thought wildly, it couldn't be. But it was. Bucky crawled out and stood up and shook her skirts down. She saw me and started toward me, then she checked up quickly, seeing the Pearl.

I dropped my arm from around the Pearl and ran for Bucky. I grabbed her shoulders and shook her. "What the hell are you doing here? You've got no business here. Get on back to the dance, quick, before I whale the tar out of you!"

"There were shots," she stammered, her eyes rounding at the sight of the dead man, "and I was afraid . . . I thought maybe you . . . is he dead, Starr?"

"Yes, he's dead," I said, but I hadn't wanted her to know. I shook her once more, so put out with her I didn't care if I shook the teeth out of her head. "You're going to get in real trouble some of these days, following where your nose leads you. Don't you know curiosity killed the cat?"

"Who shot him?" she said, between shakes.

"That's none of your business. Now, git! Go with the officers. Hurry."

"Did you shoot him?"

"No!" I exploded. "Git out of here, Bucky!"

"What happened? Who shot him? Did Mr. Hawkins?"

"No!"

"Mr. Slade?"

"Bucky!"

Her eyes lifted and followed round and lit on the Pearl, who was walking toward the horses hitched in front of the station. "Who's she?"

"That's none of your business, either. Move!"

"She's from Dobytown, isn't she? She's one of those dancehall girls."

"*Bucky!*"

"I'm going. I'm going. But you had your arm around her. You had your arm around her. Starrrrr!" She was wailing. My God, I thought, Emma will kill me for this!

The Pearl was laughing. She called over to me, "Take care of her yourself, Starr. I'll be all right. I'm going with the girls."

I looked over my shoulder. The Pearl was already on a horse and some of the other girls and a few men were with her. They were beginning to move off. Obviously she would be all right, and obviously I had my hands very full of a weeping little kid. And believe me, it was a temptation to give her something more to weep about. I wished for what my mother called an apple-tree limb. I could have worn one out on the kid.

I waved at the Pearl and gave Bucky a shove that almost knocked her off her feet. "Someday," I said, shoving her again, "I'm going to forget myself and give you a licking you won't forget. You need your bottom blistered for this night's work." And I gave her another shove and herded her as fast as her feet would take her toward the lit-up Quarters where the dance was being held.

She stumbled along for a little piece, then she set her feet and stopped walking. She just quit and stood there, planting her feet wide apart and very firmly. "You quit shoving me!" she said.

"Then keep moving," I said.

"I'll move when I please. You keep your hands off of me, you hear!"

I was so vexed with her that I actually raised my hand to slap her. She ducked and I came to my senses and dropped my hand. "Bucky," I said, "for God's sake, what possessed you to come over here? You could have got hurt. This was a bunch of drunk punks from Dobytown. They were making trouble. Slade shot one of them. Women and little girls can't get mixed up in things like this. Not even . . ."

"She did. That dance-hall girl did," she spat out at me. "The one you had your arm around. Oh, I saw you. I saw you."

"She was crying, too. Didn't you see that? She needed comforting."

"When I cried you just shoved me."

"Well, I was angry with you. You scared me. You didn't have any business here."

"She didn't either."

"No, she didn't. But dance-hall girls . . . well, they're different . . . they sometimes . . ." Oh, hell. How could you explain a dance-hall girl to a nine-year-old kid?

"Is she your girl?"

75

"No," I said, suddenly weary. "I just know her is all."

"Did you feel sorry for her?"

"I guess so."

She came flying, suddenly swarming all over me, her arms tight and hugging about my waist. "I forgive you," she whispered, butting her head against my belt buckle. "I do forgive you, Starr. But you mustn't feel sorry for too many girls. It's dangerous."

I untangled her and set her aside and took her hand. She was the most confusing kid I ever was around. Most of the time she was like any other nine-year-old kid and I thought I knew something about nine-year-old little girls. But Bucky was a little out of joint somewhere. Sometimes she wasn't anything like my kid sisters at all.

"Come on," I said, "your mother will have my head on a platter for this. She's probably called out the guard by now."

"Oh, no," Bucky said, giving a hop and a skip. "I didn't tell her I was coming over here."

"I'm sure you didn't," I said. "I'm very sure you didn't. You just sneaked out."

"Well, good gracious," she said, "mothers worry so."

"You might remember that oftener," I said, "and give her less reason to worry."

She gave my hand a squeeze. "I thought maybe you'd been killed."

"And what would you have done if I had been?"

"Killed whoever killed you," she said, simply.

I had to laugh. "God save me from the innocent."

"What does innocent mean?"

"Bucky," I said, "if you ask me one more question to-night I'm going to turn you over my knee."

She thought it over. "Well," she said, "I've got on six petticoats, I don't *much* think you can hurt me. Why did Slade kill that man? Did they have a fight, or did he just feel like killing somebody?"

"Men don't kill each other because they just feel like it," I said.

She was quiet for a moment. Then she said, "I think Jack Slade would. He's mean, Starr."

"Has he ever been mean to you?"

"No. But he wouldn't be. Not to me. But he looks mean. In the eyes. He's got eyes just like a snake's."

"When did you ever see a snake's eyes?"

"Well, for heaven's sake, Starr. With all the rattlesnakes there are on the prairie, I've seen a million of them."

"That's a lie."

"Well, I've seen a hundred."

"That's a lie, too."

"A dozen? Ten? Five?"

"One."

"No. Three. Real close. Papa killed them."

"You see their eyes before he killed them, or after?"

"Weeell, after. But not long after."

"See. You don't know what you're talking about."

"All right." She was put out with me. "I don't know what I'm talking about. But Jack Slade is a mean man and someday you'll find out."

"You better start thinking what you're going to tell your mother if she's going around like a chicken with its head off when you go inside."

"Oh," she said airily, "I just went outside for a breath of air . . . like the other ladies. And of course you were with me all the time . . . like the other gentlemen. What do they do when they go out for a breath of air, Starr?"

She flabbergasted me, absolutely flabbergasted me. Nothing escaped her. "They take a breath of air," I said lamely.

"Hoo!" she hooted. "Tell that to the horse marines. I bet they kiss. Kiss me, Starr." She held up her face.

I shoved her in the door instead. "You find your mother, and you stick with her the rest of the evening, hear?"

"Where you going?"

"None of your business."

She stuck her tongue out at me.

I fled, thinking what a wonderful relief it would be to spend an hour or two with the Pearl.

Chapter 6

Slade's stock with the Company went up over his protection of Company property. You could see it in men's eyes when they looked at him, and you could hear it in their voices when they talked about him. "He shot the damned sonuvabitch," they said. "Just pumped him full of lead. That'll teach 'em to leave L. & P.P. property alone. They got a fast gun up against 'em now."

All the old stories of how fast he was were hauled out and told again. "He can draw and fire before I can even get a gun out," men agreed. And I myself knew it was true. I had seen him, shooting target, and it was like a good driver climbing six reins—you wouldn't much more than see his hand move till the gun was blazing. He had always warned us, "Don't ever dare me to shoot. Not anything or anybody. I don't take dares."

After seeing him shoot, nobody ever tried.

He was built a little on the short side, about five foot eight or nine, and I don't suppose he ever weighed more than 150 pounds. When I first knew him he was wiry and physically hard. He could endure as much punishment from weather and weariness as any man I ever saw.

He had smooth dark hair and small eyes, set close together and deep. They were gray, and a little heavy-lidded, hooded, and in spite of me I remembered Bucky's saying they were like snake's eyes. They were.

His face was shaped like a shield, broad across the brow and eyes, then tapering down to a narrow chin. He had a thin-lipped mouth. When not drinking he was a gentleman, a perfect gentleman, with a quiet courteous manner and a soft easy voice. When he was drinking he became wild and reckless. Virginia Dale was the only one who could do anything with him when he was drinking. Fortunately he didn't drink much and mostly when he did it was at Kearney and somebody would send for Virginia Dale to come get him. As if she had been his mother, he always went with her without quarrel. He was a strange, strange man.

After he killed the teamster, whose named turned out to be Ham Johnson, the boys on the line brought up the other killings. There was more knowledge of them by then, or maybe men just felt freer to talk about them. It was said that he killed the first man when he was just a kid, twelve or thirteen years old. He and another boy had been playing some kind of game and the fellow had come along and stopped them—interfered somehow. In a blind rage Slade had picked up a fence rail and clubbed the man to death. "They say he just pounded the feller to a pulp," a driver told me. "That was when his folks sent him to Texas to get him away from the law. He got the rest of his raising in Texas, with some of his relations. Met Virginia Dale down there and got married. Then come to Missouri."

The next killing had been up on the North Platte, somewhere in that vast loneliness near Scott's Bluffs. It was said Slade had been drinking with another bullwhacker and got to shooting target and made his warning about never taking a dare. The fellow taunted him and dared him to shoot *him*. "Slade hauled out his gun and shot him right between the eyes," I was told. "I reckon he's made a believer out of everybody on that daring business."

I agreed he probably had. I wouldn't have been willing to dare him, myself.

It was certain that Slade's readiness with his gun had earned him the admiration and respect of nearly everybody. I suppose it was the beginning of the era when a tough man with a fast gun was highly esteemed. It hadn't been so, but I saw it happen with Slade. The talk I heard was all bragging talk. "We got a division agent that don't fool around. He shoots first, then talks." And men began to draw around him in loyal, admiring knots.

About the middle of January the new organization of the Company was announced in all the newspapers, with great flourish and fanfare, and a man with a pot of paint made the rounds and painted the new name on all the stagecoaches. He couldn't get the full name on, it was so long, but he scrolled a brightly gilded legend across each coach, *C.O.C. & P.P. Express Co.*

"Same horse," Luke Hawkins chuckled, "with a new set of harness."

William Russell, who had never set foot west of the Missouri until he opened the old L. & P.P., made one of his rare journeys to Denver in one of the newly painted coaches, reinforcing his position as president of the line. It was an empty office, as we all knew. The freight company owned the line, but it was mortgaged to the last set of harness and bale of hay to Ben Holladay.

"Maybe we'll get paid once in a while now," said one of the drivers.

"I'm not counting any chickens before they hatch," said another. "I ain't sure but what *we* own the Company, much as they owe us."

And Bill Trotter, one of the veteran drivers, coined a phrase. He said he was afraid the initials of the Company stood for Clean Out of Cash and Poor Pay.

I found myself in a strange situation. I had been hired within one month after the L. & P.P. moved up onto the Platte. Some of their drivers didn't make the move. They drifted on down to Butterfield's line, or out to California, or onto the short lines in Missouri, Kansas and Nebraska. In the general lack of faith in the line's future only a dozen or so made the move up onto the Platte, and all but six of them had quit by now. The Company had to hire a lot of new drivers as they expanded their facilities, opened the branch line to Denver, stocked new stations and put new equipment on the Salt Lake Division. They reached out and brought in drivers from all over. They advertised in the newspapers back east and in California.

But a man's seniority dates from the time he is employed on a line and it grows with time, if he has no break in his service. It has nothing to do with the total time he has been driving stage. So I found myself with a hell of a lot of seniority. I ranked men who were twice my age and had three or four times my driving time. That cut no ice. I had gone to work for the L. & P.P. among the first, and there was no break in my service. I was a veteran on the line, even if I wasn't yet a veteran driver.

With the exception of six men who ranked me, the whole line was mine. I could move around where I pleased, bump anybody but those six men for any stage of the line I wanted to drive. It was a curious position for a kid barely twenty years old. I give myself a little credit for not abusing it. I knew my limits as a driver and didn't fool myself about them. There were some sections of the line I had no business driving on yet. I might have the seniority, but I still didn't have the experience for them.

But I was learning all the time. It had pleased me immensely to find Bob Hodge in the drivers' room at Kearney when I came in one evening. He had decided the line had a future, after all, he said. He was driving the Thirty-Two-Mile Creek run and since we weren't yet running daily I had enough time between my own runs that I sometimes rode out with him as far as Hook's, eight miles east of Kearney, just to watch him handle the lines.

He was a real reinsman, as much of a reinsman as Big John. You had to watch closely to see any movement as he climbed and slipped the lines. I had trouble with the third line in my left hand, the line to the near wheel horse. The line goes between the third and little finger. My little finger on that hand was pretty weak. Bob showed me how to use it better and he showed me some exercises to take. Then he laughed and said, "Take up playing guitar, Fowler. Fingering a guitar will make that left hand as strong as steel strings."

I took him seriously and before long found that I actually liked playing guitar. He was right about the little finger. Putting pressure on guitar strings with it made it much stronger. And more limber. But he led me into one of the great pleasures of my life, also. Making music.

But Bob didn't like the plains. He didn't like the sand and the dust and the heat and the insects and he shortly said to hell with it and worked back onto the Little Blue. "I like country to look like God had made it for people," he said. "This bastardly country out here was made for buffalo and rattlesnakes."

Another fine driver took his place on the Thirty-Two-Mile Creek run, Enoch Cummings. That man was the finest driver I ever saw. He was even better than Bob Hodge. He drove with a skill and grace no other driver I ever saw possessed. I had to work to be a good driver. So did most men. But Enoch's skill was purely a gift of God which he never even had to think about. He must have had to learn, sometime. But he said he took to it like a duck to water and his hands had their own knowledge from the beginning. But then he had never been a bullwhacker. He had never had a lot of bad driving habits to unlearn.

One grand thing about the brotherhood of stage drivers. They are always willing to help a young driver. Enoch didn't know how to tell me what he did, but by watching him I could catch on. And by watching me, he could tell how good I was becoming. It was Enoch who finally persuaded me I was ready to drive the Devil's Dive. I was scared to death of it. "Are you going to duck it all your life?" he said. "The sooner you drive it, the better. Go on. Get that first time behind you."

Way up on the Platte, between Cottonwood Springs and Julesburg, the broken country of the plains begins. It is the first wrinkling of the earth's crust, crazing out from the foothills of the Rockies. The road ran along a canyon for a long stretch, a deep and in places a very wide canyon. At two places the road crossed the canyon. The first place the canyon was wide but its walls sloped down so that a passable road could be angled down. Then the road, flat and level, stretched out on the canyon floor for half a mile before it climbed out. This wasn't too bad.

The next crossing was near the head of the canyon. The road went straight down on the steepest incline vehicles could travel and stay on their wheels. It was literally a pitchdown. Then it climbed immediately out on the other side just as steeply. The old drivers all said there was only one way to take it. Flat out. Go down hard and fast, hell-bent-for-election, because the team had to have the momentum gained by speed to pull up the steep opposite wall. This was the Devil's Dive.

Well, I had to drive it sometime because if I didn't get over cold feet about it I wasn't going to be much good to myself or the Company. So, putting my toes in the water by degrees—I sure didn't want to drive it regular yet—I deadheaded out to Diamond Springs and made the driver a proposition. I would relieve him for one run and back. He could spend the time soaking up some forty-rod whisky I had brought along.

He was glad to accommodate me. He was a long, lanky fellow called Arkansaw. He was an old Butterfield driver but he was fairly new on our line. He didn't yet have much say about where he drove. I didn't see why anybody in their right senses would drive that piece of road regular, but Arkansaw said he liked it. "You'll see," he said. "Just let 'em rip, bub. You may not hit bottom, for it's as close to flying as man can ever get, but I guarantee you'll get the thrill of your life. When your stomach clunks down back where it ought to be, you'll know you've topped out the other side."

If it hadn't been too late I might have backed out, but I put on as bold a face as I could. "Well," I said, "if I take up my abode in some heavenly mansion, don't waste any tears. Just try to keep some other fool from following after me."

"Aw, it ain't that bad," he said. "There ain't ever been a wreck there, has there? Just drive 'em. Drive 'em like hell."

The Dive was between Diamond Springs and the swing station. Your first warning was when you began to run along the lip of the canyon. For about a mile the road ran along the rim then swung away as the canyon made a wide bend. This was my warning that I was almost there. "Move 'em out when you make that swing," Arkansaw had said. "It's not more'n a quarter of a mile till you pitch down."

I had two passengers, both men. I didn't try to put on any side with them. As we had loaded in Diamond Springs I had told them this was my first time over the Dive. They could knock on the side of the coach if they wanted to and I'd haul up and let them walk if they didn't want to risk it. One of them grinned and said, "We've ridden it. We'll ride it again."

I make no bones about it. My heart was in my throat as we came to the bend in the canyon and it was pounding like a triphammer. I was scared out of my mind. But I moved the team out, with a few pops of the whip and a lot of shouting. We were going flat out when we tipped over the rim, and my God it was straight down! I hadn't ever even ridden it before, much less driven it, and nothing

I'd ever heard could begin to describe it. Driving freight we always went a hell of a long way around it.

But I suddenly found myself exhilarated and on my feet, whooping and hollering, the wind flattening my mouth and zinging in my ears, the team bellied down and their feet pounding like thunder on the hard road. Down and down and down, with a falling feeling in your stomach and no more fear, just crazy, wild jubilation. And the passengers were whooping and hollering. "Let 'em rip, boy! Let 'em rip!"

They ripped. That team mortally did rip. They ripped a hole right through the air, so that the sounds of the stage, and their feet pounding, and all the shouting and hollering was too late to catch up with us. They strung out behind us like echoes. They ripped like a prairie fire so you could almost smell the smoke. They ripped like lightning streaking through the sky. Down and down, faster than you'd believe sixteen legs could go, and faster than you'd think sixteen feet could keep up. Pounding like blood in your veins, like a hammer on an anvil, like a fall of water going over a cliff. Pounding and echoing and reverberating from the hollow canyon so that the noise was all broken and dissonant and jagged and all around you.

Down and down, and then we hit bottom, and then there was a level patch, not more than a hundred feet wide, then still the pounding going up and up and up, the feet slowly slowing, the pounding slowly ceasing, not flat out now, but trotting, and then the hard, hard heaviness of the slow walk with all the weight of the coach and the pull, and the team was bellied down now but not from speed, from pulling. It took everything they had. They heaved into it and strained, their feet slipping, the coach almost halting. And the jubilation was still riding in me, I was talking to them, hoarse from shouting, but talking now, talking heart into them, talking help to them, talking pull to them, talking them on.

Then we topped out and it was over and I went as flat as a biscuit without any soda. Flat and limp, the jubilation and wild excitement blown out. I felt weak and soft-boned and jelly-shaky. But I had done it. I had driven the Devil's Dive. One of the passengers stuck his head out and yelled, "Well, you been initiated, boy. You done good!"

I tipped my whip at him and slipped the reins to pick up the team into the road gait. I felt like I had been initiated ... the way an Indian boy going through his puberty rites must feel. Sweated and hungry and weak, but tall and proud and full of manhood. I could drive it now, any time. I never would be afraid of it again. And it might, in time, grow on me. But I thought for a while I'd just save it for the times I was feeling a gray world all around me and needed a little picking up. I was certain it would never fail to do that for me.

Chapter 7

It was about two weeks after the reorganization of the Company had been announced that the new General Manager, Ben Ficklin, came riding into Kearney on his way to Denver to take over. He was a little fellow, short, thin, wiry, with a moustache bigger than his face. But he was a tough little man, with a hot quick temper. And he knew stagecoaching and he knew how to run a stage line. He had the name of being absolutely fearless, and it was said he knew how to put the fear of God into men. It was expected he would make short shrift of the stealing and thieving going on.

I was sitting at the table in Oliver Wiggins's eating place at Fort Kearney with Slade the day Ben Ficklin walked in, swung a chair around and started talking. "I'm moving you to the Julesburg section," he said to Slade.

"When?" Slade said.

"Now. You'll go with me. I want you to clean out that nest of robbers. Clean it up. Get as much of our property back as you can, and fire Old Jules."

Few men would have tackled Old Jules. He was mean. Pure mean. Just as soon kill you as look at you. But Slade just grinned and said, "Any specific way you want it done?"

"No. Just get rid of him. I'm going on to Denver. When I come back through I want him and his gang off the premises. I'll bring a new station keeper with me."

Slade turned to me. "I want you along. I want you to take the Mud Springs run. I'll make some more shifts later. I want my own boys with me around Julesburg the next couple of months till things settle down again."

It didn't take me long to get ready. It was a twenty-four-hour run to Julesburg and we pulled in around one o'clock the next day. Ficklin headed straight for Old Jules and said, "Slade is your new division agent. You'll take your orders from him."

Jules was a dirty hairy old man, long-bearded, shaggy-headed. He combed his fingers through his beard and grinned. "So?"

"So." That was all Ficklin said. He wheeled around and walked out and left with the stage.

When the stage had gone, Jules came back inside and looked at Slade. "So," he said again. Then he laughed. "Slade . . . you be nice with me, I be nice with you."

In his quiet, soft-spoken way Slade said, "You know Starr Fowler, Jules? He'll be driving Mud Springs now."

I had crossed trails with Old Jules once or twice, freighting, but they were brief encounters. The old man eyed me and nodded. "I know him. Joe Fowler's boy, ain't you?"

I said I was.

"I know your father. Long time. Way back."

"He has been around a long time," I said.

"Good man," he said. "You ain't so big as him."

"Not many men are," I said.

I went on to find the drivers' bunkhouse, but I didn't miss any action, for Slade didn't make his move that day. He just loafed around, looking, watching, seeing everything that went on. He talked with some of the boys, felt his way till he knew the ones he could count in, knew the ones that would have to go with Jules.

We weren't running a through stage but twice a month, so I had time on my hands and Slade made use of me to help him with his poking around. One of the things he learned was where Old Jules corralled the stock when he drove it off. It was up Lodgepole Creek in a little canyon. A tender, loyal to the Company or ratting on Jules—it made little difference which as far as the information went —told Slade about it. We saddled up the next day and rode out there. The tender guided us.

From a high brushy point overlooking the canyon we counted twelve mules and some oxen that belonged to the Company, and the tender said there were several sets of harness cached away in a skin lodge up in the cedar neck of the canyon. The man was very nervous. He was running a big risk telling Slade about the corral. "That old man will cut my throat if he finds out," he said.

"He's not going to be around here long enough to cut anybody's throat," Slade said. "Let's go."

We walked into the station with guns drawn. The old man looked at us, looked at the guns, and said, "You got a complaint, Slade?"

"Twelve of them," Slade said, "with long ears out in that corral in Paint Creek canyon, besides twenty head of cattle. We'll drive them in, Jules."

The old man was caught red-handed and he made no trouble. He rode out with us. When we got to the canyon Slade made the old man call the guards and tell them to round up the stock and bring it in. One of them started to argue and Slade put a bullet through his leg and that ended any tendency to argue in the other one. We drove the stock in and penned it. Then Slade said, "You've got one hour to get yourself and all that belongs to you off the premises. That includes your squaws and all your kids."

The old man didn't argue about that, either. He just slitted his eyes and said, "You better never ride a foot of line alone again, Slade. I will kill you for this."

"Unless I kill you first," Slade said. "You're wasting time. Get moving, old man," and he motioned him out the door with his gun barrel.

It was quiet when the old man and his people had gone. Only six stage employees were left at the station. Three of them were drivers, none of whom had been involved. Three were tenders. The other tenders were part of the gang and had rustled out while we were out at the canyon. We made out. Slade handled the station and I helped the hostlers with the stock. I made one run to Mud Springs and back. When I got back to Julesburg, Ficklin had come through bringing new tenders and the new station agent.

We set up guards for the station corral and stables, for we figured Old Jules would pull a raid as soon as he got himself squared around. But a couple of weeks went by with everything as quiet and peaceful as could be. So Slade started riding the line again.

He made one trip up to Fort Laramie, the other end of his section, and came back. He rode in with me from Mud Springs. We had two passengers. We pulled up in front of the station at Julesburg and Slade got down from the box.

He let the two passengers out and they ran for the station. It was December and colder than Christmas and they were undoubtedly feeling numb from the chill. I threw the lines to the hostler and got down, Slade waiting for me. I felt stiff myself from the long cold drive and Slade beat his arms and said, "We'll get snow by tomorrow."

I agreed we might. He was ahead of me and he opened the station door and flung it back and went on through, me on his heels. Just as I stepped inside Old Jules stepped from behind the door and fired a blast from his shotgun into Slade's back. Slade dropped like poleaxed steer. Then I saw that the station keeper and the two passengers were covered by two of Jules's boys. They were also covering me. There isn't much you can do under such circumstances.

Slade was lying in a pool of blood and he hadn't moved since going down. I thought he was dead. I didn't see how he could help but be, blasted that close. Old Jules walked over and looked at him, then he kicked him in the side. "If he's not dead he soon will be," he said. "You can start digging his grave, Fowler."

He motioned to his boys and they backed around toward him, keeping all of us covered. They went out the door ahead of Jules and made a break around the corner of the station. Old Jules had drawn his revolver now and it was in his hand as he backed out the door. As he reached the door, Slade stirred and moaned a little, then he said, thick and husky but plain, "You needn't be in any hurry about digging that grave, Starr. I'll live long enough to cut that sonuvabitch's ears off and wear 'em on my watch chain."

Old Jules fired, but I jumped and knocked his wrist up and the shot went wide. The old man ran then, for I had my own gun out. Jules was shooting, very wide, and I was fanning the dirt around him, nearly everybody else behind cover, when right in the middle of the shooting scrape the stage for Denver pulled in. The driver dropped his reins and pulled his gun and started blazing away. Ben Ficklin poured out of the coach with his gun going. With Old Jules's boys potshotting at us from behind cover, Old Jules himself chinking lead all around, and the three of us blazing away, it was right warm for a few seconds until one of us got lucky and hit Old Jules in the leg. That ended the battle, for when he dropped his boys ran.

Ficklin didn't waste any time. He called for a rope and we strung Old Jules up behind the stable and left him swinging. Then we moved Slade to a bunk and did the best we could for him. None of us thought any more of Old Jules and nobody hung around to watch him die. We had two stages to hitch up and move out and the tenders were busy. Ficklin had the mail sacks to sort and the record to write up. Somebody had to tend Slade, who was still bleeding pretty bad. By the time things had quieted down a little and we could quit hustling about, a half hour or so had passed. Then, curious, one of the tenders went around behind the stable to take a look at Old Jules. He came dusting into the station. "He's gone! He ain't there! He's been cut down!"

Ficklin swore a few rounds and then shrugged it off. "Well, I reckon they got to him in time. If he'd been dead they wouldn't have bothered to cut him down. Slade'll have to get him after all."

Slade was fully conscious now and we all heard him make his vow. "I will kill him on sight."

Slade carried some of the buckshot from Old Jules's blast all his life. When he recovered enough to make the trip he went to St. Louis to a surgeon who picked out seven pieces, but those he couldn't reach stayed in Slade's back to the day he died.

Now that he didn't have to maintain even a semblance of decency, Old Jules organized a formidable band of real outlaws and criminals. With a hideout in the foothills up near Platte Bridge he led this gang in one foray after another all along the line between Fort Laramie and the Sweetwater. He had a band of about twenty of the toughest ruffians in the country and they would appear suddenly, out of nowhere, and descend swiftly on a station, run the stock off and set it afire and be gone again as swiftly as they came. Tracking them was very difficult in that country, for they knew every draw and gulch and canyon and could disappear as if swallowed up, leaving no trace. They managed to disorganize that section of line, while Slade was sick and away at St. Louis, so badly that the Company had trouble running over it at all.

Slade came back from St. Louis in the summer of 1860.

Two things were observable in him immediately. He was drinking heavily, and he had an obsession about Old Jules. Virginia Dale told us that he had begun leaning on whisky for relief because he was hardly ever out of pain and it was the only thing that would give him any relief. It was too bad. Slade wasn't a man who could handle much whisky. As high-tempered as he naturally was, it made him even more hot-tempered and it made him unpredictable. The obsession with Old Jules was understandable. The man had shot him in the back. One or the other was going to have to die.

So he could more easily hunt Old Jules down, Slade asked for a transfer to the Platte Bridge section and he made Horseshoe Station his headquarters. He was no longer my boss and he didn't have the authority to move me onto that section with him, but he asked me to go. I was young enough to like excitement, I had a little personal interest in seeing Old Jules brought to taw, and I felt some loyalty to Slade. So I went. I moved up onto the section and I took the Platte Bridge run.

We were still running the mail through only twice a month, but the mines in Virginia City were attracting so many people we were running twice weekly to carry the passengers. Slade put me on the passenger run so I could cover the stretch regularly. He himself rode constantly. He never laid over. He never rested. Day after day he went up and down the section. But he never rode the box any more. Partly, this was because he didn't want to be ambushed; partly it was because he was trying to keep Old Jules from learning he had transferred. Up and down the line the standing orders were that Old Jules was to be taken alive if possible, and if taken he was to be kept for Slade. Nobody else was to touch him.

Slade was drinking more than ever and gradually he began to grow sullen and mean and ugly with everybody except a few of us he liked and trusted. He was short-spoken and tetchy with the employees, riding them hard over the least fault, and because he was hardly ever entirely sober any more he became high-handed with his orders. Men who had liked him and respected him began to hate him. Though they understood what was itching him, he made things too miserable for them and a good many of the best men transferred off his section. I began to be afraid for him, and afraid *of* him, those months I was hauling him back and forth and watching him slowly going to pieces and falling apart right in front of my eyes.

To this day I don't know whether or not Old Jules ever learned Slade had transferred to his bailiwick. Maybe he didn't learn it and that accounted for his carelessness. Or maybe he felt so sure of himself his carelessness expressed contempt. But one thing is certain. Old Jules did slowly grow less cautious and begin to take more risks. He came down out of the foothills oftener and took to being sociable again with some of the ranchers, most of them French-Canadian like himself, along the line. They were all old friends of his and just about the same caliber.

Word came up the line one day that fall that Jules was at Bordeaux's ranch. Was staying with him for a while. Slade was at Pacific Springs when the news reached him. He took over the stage there, laying the passengers over, and filled it with a bunch of the boys. They came down the line hell-bent for leather. I was at Platte Bridge, laying over. When they came through I was ordered to join the party. In the old days, Slade would not have ordered me to do anything. It wasn't his way then. It was an evidence of how much he had deteriorated that he would give me, his friend, a flat order, and so coolly that there was no mistaking the intention. He was beginning to enforce his will at the point of a gun, nowadays. A habit of keeping his hand lightly resting on the butt of his gun in its holster was growing on him. He hadn't yet got to the place where he could play with a man, like a cat with a mouse, before shooting him between the eyes, but it wasn't far off. I went.

For quite a while Slade had been accompanied everywhere he went by two tough, fast-drawing, drinking cronies of his. They were with him now, one on each side of him on the back seat of the stage. When we got to Bordeaux's, Old Jules wasn't there. Slade's toughs roughed the old man up until he told where he was—at Chanseau's ranch. We got to Chanseau's about the middle of the afternoon. Slade had a bottle and was drinking steadily, and he had got quieter and quieter. He wasn't drunk, but he was a long way from being cold sober.

Some of the boys wanted to leave the stage this side of the shack that passed for a ranchhouse and surround it. Slade wouldn't have it. "Hell, no," he said, "we're not going to pussy-foot around." And he ordered the driver to go in flat out. Which he did, and we pulled up in a cloud of dust that made a good cover. We piled out and scattered around the shack while Slade and his two guards hit the door and walked right in, guns blazing. Jules and old Chanseau were alone in the shack and they were taken by surprise and caught flatfooted. They winged Old Jules and it wasn't much trouble to tie him up. Slade had him taken out and tied to a post in the corral. The old man knew his time had come, but he didn't open his mouth. He didn't say a word.

Slade took over, then, as cold as a fish. First he went to the stagecoach and got his bottle. He came back and set it on the ground. Then he paced off his distance and drew his gun. "I'll take another wing, boys," he said, calling his shot. He took his time, aimed, fired, and the shot went right through the Frenchman's good shoulder. The impact jolted the old man against the rope, but he didn't say anything. Didn't cry out or moan or beg. On his own two feet he stood there and took it. Slade walked over and took a swig from his bottle and then he took his distance again. I began to feel sick at my stomach.

Slade called his shot again. The right leg this time and it thudded home. Old Jules was hanging on the rope now, but he was still conscious and still not begging. Slade had another drink and took his distance again. The left leg, the right knee, the left knee, the right side, the left side . . . Slade kept calling his shots until he had sunk seven of them in the Frenchman, one for each piece of lead the surgeon had taken out of his back. Between every shot he had a drink. It took a long time. Along toward the last the old man passed out. This was no fun, so Slade had the boys drench him with water and bring him around. Then he plunked the last bullet right square between the old man's eyes, calling the shot beforehand. And right to the last the old man never once begged. Not once.

It was the most brutal, cold-blooded thing I ever saw in my life. I was twenty years old but I added ten years watching it. I was as cold as if a blizzard had been blowing and shaking so hard I had to clench my teeth together. I was so sick I had to keep swallowing the bile that rose in my mouth. I knew I would never be able, no matter how long I lived, to put this scene out of my mind. It would live with me and haunt me all the days of my life. I had believed I was pretty tough. I thought my raising had made me as tough as the next man. But this wasn't toughness. This wasn't even execution. This was the kind of merciless inhumanity the Indians practiced. And as evil as the old man was, he came out of it a better man than Slade. He knew how to die.

When it was over and the old man was dead and all the fizz was gone for Slade, he told the boys to cut Old Jules down. They did and laid him out flat. Slade then holstered his gun and pulled his knife from his boot-top. He walked over and cut off both the old man's ears. Bloody and raw, he stuck them in his pocket. He nudged the body with his toe and laughed. "All right," he said, "let's go."

It wasn't courage that made me speak up. Slade or one of his boys could have gunned me down in two seconds, but I was sick of my part in the whole thing. "Aren't you going to bury him?" I said.

"Hell, no," he said. "He'll make good buzzard bait."

He walked on to the stagecoach. If anybody else had made a stand with me, there might have been gunplay. But nobody did. Everybody else followed him. When he got to the stage he looked around. "You going with me?" he said.

I had such a knot in my throat it hurt, but I shook my head and said, "No. I'm not going with you."

One of his guards laughed and said, "Want me to take him for you, Jack?"

Slade knocked his hand down. He didn't say anything. He just looked at me, straight and steady and for a long time. I didn't say anything either. Just looked back at him, as straight and steady as I could manage. He had crossed a line I couldn't follow and I wasn't one of his boys any more. He knew it and a kind of sad expression came over his face. I didn't know then and don't know now why he didn't kill me. Maybe it was a good impulse . . . one of the last ones he ever had. Or maybe he'd had enough of killing for one day. For whatever reason he didn't draw. Just looked at me, then suddenly wiped his hand across his face, turned on his heel, crawled in the stage and went wheeling off.

I lost what was in my stomach and felt better. Then I buried Old Jules. Not that it did him any good or white-washed me, but it was a thing I wanted to do. I saw old Chanseau watching out the window and was glad I didn't have to dig another grave. He had been hit, too, but if he was able to stand at a window he wasn't hurt too bad. I called to him I was going to borrow a horse and he motioned toward the corral as if inviting me to take my pick. I suppose he was hoping to see the last of me as soon as possible and glad to get off that light. I suppose, also, he thought he would never see the horse again, but I returned it later in better condition than I took it.

I rode into Julesburg and took the stage to Kearney. I knew I would never drive for Slade again. There would always be a wall of sadness and guilt between us.

My old stage to Plum Creek wasn't open to me. A man who ranked me was driving it. I settled for a run on the Little Blue. I went to see the Westmorelands, who appeared to be no nearer having enough money saved to move to Denver. Ed was still fussing about not being paid regularly. Still planning to make the move someday, but I didn't much think he ever would. Even a station keeper can get stage fever and never get over it. I believed that was happening to Ed.

I got the rough edge of Emma's tongue for leaving so abruptly and Bucky refused to speak to me at all for a full hour. Then she relented and wanted to hear the whole story of Old Jules. I told her I only had one day to spend with them and I wanted to spend it pleasantly if she didn't mind. She said she thought I was mean and maybe she would just cut me off her list of nice people. I said let's go for a ride and she said where, and that was that.

In a way I hated to tell the Westmorelands good-bye, but that was a stage driver's life. Always moving on.

My last sight of Bucky was out in the corral with a rope in her hand trying to lasso a colt. She refused to see me off. "You'll be back," she said. "You won't like it on the Little Blue. I'll just wait."

She didn't even turn around and wave as the stage departed.

Chapter 8

It wasn't too much trouble to keep some distance between me and Slade. I never drove on his section again and he never moved east of Denver. All I had to do was leave his two hundred miles of line alone and I could work west of him or east. The outlaw in Slade liked the raw violent country in Wyoming. He had found his environment, with its violent winds and storms and blizzards and wild loneliness and he could be its king. He stayed on the Platte Bridge section until the line was moved farther south, then he took over the Bitter Creek section. It ran through country that was an alkali waste and a hell on earth. Slade made it more hellish.

He kept his word and wore one of Old Jules's ears as a watch charm. Men who saw it said it was shriveled like a piece of tanned leather. He carried the other in his pocket and took a gleeful delight in throwing it on a bar to scare bartenders into free drinks for him and his crowd. He gradually worked his own special gang of toughs into the Bitter Creek section, but he rode them as roughshod as he did his stage employees. He wanted them around. He had to have adulation and admiration, but he treated them like dirt under his feet. In the mood, he let them pick fights, shoot up bars, commandeer stages and scare passengers to death with wild rides. Not in the mood, he kept them heeled like well-trained dogs.

For a long time he was satisfied with the sport of intimidation. He liked to make a greenhorn dance by dusting his feet. He liked to ride his horse into a saloon and take his pick of the bottles on the shelves, then slowly, one by one, crack them all except the one he wanted to drink from. Rolling drunk he liked to swagger into a bar and shoot out the lights, overturn the gaming tables, send everybody scattering with a few pinked shoulders or arms.

But little by little this all became too tame for him. He had to kill. He always had one good excuse for killing. The man was a thief. And it was a fact that on Slade's section Company property was safer than on any division of the line. There was no stealing, none, on Slade's section. But there weren't enough thieves, so to satisfy his senses, his lust for power and excitement, it was just one step farther to killing because he felt like killing that day.

Little Taw, a new driver unfortunate enough to draw a run on Slade's section, told me about seeing one of Slade's killings. It still made him shake to remember and tell it. He brought the eastbound stage into Elk Mountain, the end of his run. He threw his lines down and went toward the station. Slade and his boys were standing outside. The passenger load was miners and businessmen from Virginia City mostly. Little Taw was making his way around Slade and his gang when he saw Slade draw his gun. "The third button from the top," he said, quiet and soft and slow, "on the shirt of that gentleman standing beside the hind boot. He forgot to button it this morning. I think I must teach him we like our passengers to be neat."

He squeezed the trigger and the man dropped, shot precisely through the third buttonhole from the top. "He never even saw the man before," Little Taw said. "The poor fellow hadn't done nothing to him. He just drew and shot him, like he was a target."

That easy, that remorseless, a life snuffed out, as if it were worth no more than a bug squashed under the heel. For the brief flaming pulse of excitement—to sight, to watch this man, alive and unaware of his intent and his power, to exert that slight pressure needed to use the power, to see the enlarged buttonhole precisely where he meant it to widen, to see the living man quit living because he, Jack Slade, could make him quit living and decided he should quit living. He needed no more reason than that. And in the three years in which he killed twenty-six men, many were killed with no more reason than that.

Mark Twain wrote about Slade. When he went to Nevada with his brother in 1863 he had breakfast with him. His count was twenty-six then and Mark Twain, humorously, feared he might be twenty-seven. He should have felt more fear with less humor. It happened to be a day when Slade felt like acting the part of a gentleman and instead of shooting Mark Twain he poured him a second cup of coffee. He could just as easily have shot him between the eyes.

I suppose he was the first, the original bad man of the west, the example and the model for all the others. He was such a legend on his section that everybody in the west took to calling any rough troublesome character a sonuvabitch from Bitter Creek.

William Russell was hand in hand with Senator Gwin of California, who was very eager for a daily mail over the central route. In January of 1860, Russell, without conferring with his partners, plunged the firm into the disastrous operation of the Pony Express, which was said to be Senator Gwin's idea to publicize the central route. It cost $75,000 to stock and equip, though they used the stage stations for relays, before a rider ever left either end. It could carry only a tiny percent of the mail, and though the riders flashed across the land and captured the imagination of the public, as a business venture it just about put the finish to the Company as a solvent outfit.

With the help of Senator Gwin again, in May of that same year, 1860, the mail contract of poor faithful old George Chorpenning on the Salt Lake-Placerville route was canceled and a new one was awarded the C.O.C. & P.P. The compensation for the new mail contract was pretty puny—a meager $33,000 per year. But it did give the C.O.C. & P.P. the whole line from Missouri to California. We heard Russell had hocked everything he owned to get the money to beef up the line and finance the Pony Express. It was said he now owed Ben Holladay in the neighborhood of $400,000. You had a feeling of a spider waiting in his web for a fly to quit struggling.

During most of the time all this was happening you couldn't have told it from the way the employees behaved. The stages ran, the tenders stayed on the job, the equipment looked good and the service was regular. Few of us quit, even when we didn't get paid. We grumbled but we kept right on driving.

There was a lot of war talk, and after Lincoln was elected that fall war looked to be just around the corner. Somehow, in the west, it seemed pretty remote from us. Almost as if things were boiling up and stewing about in Europe. We read about it, we talked about it, but it felt like a long way off.

But in February of that year the Texas Rangers moved in on the Butterfield line down south, and in a series of raids across Texas confiscated a lot of its equipment and most of its stores of hay and grain. The first shot of the Civil War was fired in Texas two months before Fort Sumter heard a shot.

Congress acted in a hurry, within a matter of a few days, to move the Butterfield line up on the central route. They couldn't do a thing about that ironclad contract old Postmaster General Aaron Brown had made with the Butterfield people, and yet communications with California *had* to be kept open. With war imminent, the line of communications became vastly more important. It was absolutely imperative to keep them open. The Butterfield line still had three years to run—till 1864. So they decided to save it from the Confederates.

Well, the same thing had been happening on the Butterfield line that had been happening on the C.O.C. & P.P. Butterfield himself had long since got out of the company. It had been steadily losing money. In 1860 when Congress made no appropriations of any kind for paying any of the postal contracts, the line had to borrow heavily. Wells, Fargo & Company kept them in business. So by 1861, to all intents and purposes, Wells, Fargo & Company owned the Butterfield line—and on the central route the shadowy man in the background keeping us alive was Ben Holladay.

What Congress did very quickly that spring of 1861, with war on their hands and the absolute necessity of maintaining communications with the west, was to ante up the million-dollar daily mail contract everybody had been howling for. But it went to the Butterfield people because of that beautiful contract which could not be broken. Senator Gwin took up the cudgels for the C.O.C. & P.P. and he did well enough for them to keep us in business.

The million-dollar contract went to Butterfield as the main contractor. But they didn't actually have the stock and equipment to run the whole line now. So they would only run the western end, Salt Lake to Placerville. The eastern end, Atchison to Salt Lake, would be sublet to C.O.C & P.P. for $470,000 per year. It was better than nothing, but it ended William Russell's million-dollar dream.

Butterfield moved what was left of its equipment up to the central route, and daily stages, with daily mail, began running for the first time in history across the continent, on July 1, 1861. I drove the first daily mail from Cottonwood Springs to Fremont Springs, which was my piece of run at that time. It was a proud day.

Now, Ben Holladay, who was holding such a lot of paper on William Russell, began to make his play to take over the line. He put his cousin, Bela Hughes, in as president of the C.O.C. & P.P. Butterfield people, or Wells, Fargo & Co., whichever you wanted to call it, had a contract only to 1864. Holladay's cousin, Montogomery Blair, was Abe Lincoln's new Postmaster General. Holladay began to get set for every mail contract in the west.

As time passed that year of 1860 and early 1861, I began to get a bee in my bonnet which included the Westmorelands. Ed hadn't made a move and he was never going to. He would always be some place on the line. All stage drivers are like grasshoppers, moving up and down the line, this direction and that, as they grow tired of different stretches of the road. I worked various stages of the line for a couple of years, and me and my battered old brass bugle got to be pretty well known. I blew Charge into Atchison and out of it, all up the Little Blue and the Platte and, in time, clear to Placerville.

I was struck by the fact that especially on the eastern end of the line half the stations were owned and run by drivers who had taken up land, were running the station with the help of their families, and were farming, operating a profitable store and station, and at the same time following their own profession of driving. I didn't see why I couldn't do the same.

I didn't want a farm, however. Plowing and planting was strictly not my line of business and it could never interest me. My whole life had been on the road. What I wanted was a ranch. Driving freight, I had firsthand knowledge of how good the bunch grass in the west was for all kinds of stock. I didn't see why a man couldn't raise trail and beef cattle on it to his profit. If, in addition, he picked a section of land along the road at some good junction point, he could put in a good store, carry the kind of merchandise the freighters and traders needed, and do a lively business. If he also had good connections with the Indians, he could pick up a nice business in buffalo robes. If he also had a contract with the stage company to operate a home station, he could do still better for himself.

I didn't have a family to pull in with me, but I did have the Westmorelands. Ed said he'd just as soon work for me as the stage line, if I could swing it. I thought Emma might object. In country without trees there is wind and dust and heat and an awful lot of sky. Some people go sky-crazy. Women especially missed the coziness of the east and had trouble getting used to the big, vast land. But Emma was young and strong and healthy and it didn't seem to bother her much. "Just pick a place with water," she said. "If I've got plenty of water, I'll get along."

That was going to take some doing in a generally water-less land, but I kept my eyes open as I drove first on one piece of the line then on the other. There was one likely spot, about thirty miles beyond Cottonwood Springs. It wasn't very likely looking, I'll admit. It was sandhill country, but it was broken up enough that the monotony of the wide level plains was eased. It was near the O'Fallon's Bluffs and the location was exactly right. It was downriver from the forks of the Platte, from the old Lower California Crossing, so that every freight train, every emigrant train, every traveler going west, to Denver or the forts, or Salt Lake or California, would have to pass it. There was no turnoff before you got to it. It was in the heart of the Indian country, with Sioux, Arapahoes and Cheyennes working all around in every direction. In the freighting business, through my father's old connections, the Fowlers had stood in well with most of the tribes. Only occasionally did we have a little fracas with a small band of Arapahoes or Comanches or Kiowas. We had never had any big trouble with the Sioux or Cheyennes. I believed I could count on a brisk trade with them.

The Company had a miserable little log and sod station there at which they couldn't keep a family for any length of time. Half the time we would pull in with hungry passengers and there would be nothing prepared because the station keeper and his wife had hauled out of the place and only a couple of tenders were left to change the team.

There was good water in some cold springs in a canyon nearby and the land was available. I went in to Denver to talk to the General Manager and he said, "Hell, yes. If you can put in a station there and run it with halfway decent service the Company will owe you a vote of thanks. We'll be glad to give you a contract."

I warned him I wanted to take the Westmorelands with me. "That doesn't matter," he said. "We can get plenty of station keepers for Plum Creek. It's that sandhill country that causes us the most trouble."

So, in April of 1861, I took a couple of weeks off and went to St. Joseph for a talk with my father. From the time he put us boys to work he had coolly taken 80 percent of our wages back from us and invested in the Fowler Freight Line for us. We continued to work for wages when we drove for him, but we also had money in the outfit working for us. I wanted to draw some of that money out now.

My father liked the idea. He nodded his head over it. "Good business sense," he said, "I don't see how you could go wrong. It's a short-term proposition, say six to ten years, as far as the stage line and the freighting is concerned. But you've picked a good location for it. You'll draw trade from everything traveling the road. When that's played out, you'll still have a good ranch and the Indian trade is going to last a good long while. If you watch all the angles, you'll do fine."

We were in the dining room, which was such a big room that my mother had fixed up one end of it for a sitting room. In front of the big fireplace she had put couches and comfortable chairs and it was the favorite place in the whole house for all the family. My father got a decanter from the sideboard and poured each of us a drink. Swirling it around and watching it, he went on talking. "About the Indian trade. That ought to be all right. You'll have a little of everything drifting up and down the road, but the Sioux and Arapaho and Cheyennes will be your mainstay.

You ought to get all the skins you can handle from them. How good is this man you're going to put in charge . . . with Indians?"

"He's got no name with them yet, one way or the other," I said.

"That can be good or bad," my father said. "He'll have the Fowler name to guarantee him till he proves up. I hope you've picked a man who'll prove up."

"If I didn't think so," I said, "I wouldn't have picked him. One thing I know. He'll do what he's told. He'll follow orders."

"That ought to be good enough," my father said. "Keep him on a tight rein, Starr. Don't let him ever get slack. And you build strong. Use dobe. If you ever have to fort up then you can't be burned out and you can stand off an army of Indians if you have to."

"Yes, sir," I said, "I had that in mind."

My father eyed his drink thoughtfully. "I hear Charlie Bent has gone wild. Living with his mother's band. A half-breed with a white man's education can stir up a lot of trouble. Keep that in mind with those Southern Cheyennes, Starr."

Charlie Bent was old man William Bent's boy by his Cheyenne wife. William Bent and his brother Charles had had the finest trading post and fort in the west during the fur-trapping days. It was on the Arkansas in what is now southeastern Colorado. Charles had lived in New Mexico and was the first territorial governor. He was murdered at Taos. William had run the fort. He had married a Cheyenne woman, then when she died married her sister. It was mostly through his influence that the Cheyennes had split into two bands, about half of them coming down from the north to live along the Arkansas and Smoky Hill rivers. For a good many years he had had a monopoly on the trade with this band. He had several children by the two Cheyenne women. He had them all educated in the east. It took with some of them, notably the girls, but two of the boys, Charlie and George, had given him considerable trouble.

"I heard that, too," I said. "Reckon why he wanted to go Indian?"

"Oh, hell," my father said, "he was raised Indian till he was big enough to be sent east to school. Why wouldn't he? Living Indian is a lot easier than living white. Especially if you're just half white. You can imagine what his life was like trying to be white. Everybody looking down on him, sneering at him. A whole hell of a lot easier to go back amongst his mother's people where his Bent name meant something. When he got old enough to think about it, likely he studied on it and got to feeling bitter against the old man . . . for breeding him and putting him in such a halfway position. In my opinion, what Charlie Bent would like to do is drain out every drop of white blood in him. Since he can't do that, he can hate all whites. He can go wild and live Indian. The old man made a mistake with that one, trying to make him white."

"You think it's better if these half-bloods stay Indian?"

"Generally," he said. "There's not much of a place for them among whites. But old man Bent was proud. These were, by God, his kids. They were Bents and they were as good as anybody. You can't force that down the kids and you can't force it down the whites. It's not much of a kindness to try. Among the mother's people they can live the way that's natural to them. If a man don't aim to stay in the mountains and raise up the kids himself, the best thing he can do is cut it clean when he leaves. Then they'll never know anything but the easiest, most natural life for them . . . they won't be pulled and hauled around. And it's the kindest thing he can do. Leave them alone. Maybe," he said, getting up to fill his glass again, "maybe it even shows more love than pampering his conscience and guilty feelings. What he does when he does that is ease his own feelings and ruin the kid. I don't know as a man has got a right to do it."

My mother came in and set the table for supper. When she left my father went back to the trading venture. "You'll do all right there. You'll be running so many skins back east before long you'll have to go in the freight business yourself."

"I figured you might do the hauling for us," I said. "You're already set up for it."

"We can," he said, "if that's the way you want it. But I'll

charge you exactly what I do everybody else. No favors because you're my boy."

"I wouldn't expect any," I said, laughing. "Now. How much have I got in the outfit?"

"In round figures," he said, "ten thousand dollars."

"I won't need that much," I said. "I can do it for five." I grinned at him. "Can I keep on banking with you with the other five?"

"Sure," he said. "But if I was you I'd start buying some real estate in Denver. That's a town that's going to stay there and grow."

He had already put in a good store there which my brother Matt was running for the firm. Matt was married now and he had been anxious to get off the road. Running the store suited him fine. "All right," I said, "I'll look into it next time I'm there."

He sat there, easy, not looking his age at all, almost as lean and lank as I was for all his fifty-seven years. He said, "If it suits you, I'll match you dollar for dollar and pick up some lots for us I've had my eye on."

"It would suit," I said. I never knew him to lose a dollar on anything. He never overreached himself and his judgment was always sound.

We drew up a contract in which I agreed to buy the merchandise for my store and ranch at Fremont Springs from him and he would do the hauling. He would also buy and haul buffalo hides for me. He would buy cattle for me and drive them out that summer with his trains. He didn't give me a single thing. He nailed down a tight contract advantageous to him, but one which would also be advantageous to me. I think he was pretty proud of me for showing as much of a business head as I did. It didn't make him forget to take care of Joe Fowler, too, however.

It was while I was at home that the war broke out. Fort Sumter was fired on and all at once the country was at war. For a few days I didn't know what to do. I thought maybe I ought to enlist. I even went over to Leavenworth and talked to the commandant. He said, "I wouldn't if I was you, Starr. Stick with your stage. You boys will have to keep communications open to California. Your job will be as important as fighting in the line. The country is going to need the gold and the mines must be kept open. Communications must be kept open. If all of you quit and enlist where'll we be?"

I talked to my father. "I think the colonel is right," he said. "If it's a long war they'll likely pull the regulars out of the forts in the west and garrison them with the militia and volunteers. A lot of the officers in the west are southern. They'll be leaving. Don't think you won't be doing your duty. I predict a lot of Indian trouble when the regulars are pulled out. You don't need to go hunting a fight. There's going to be plenty of it out here before it's over."

I thought about it several days and then decided that my talents as a soldier were as yet undiscovered and I might turn out to have very damned few. As a stage driver I knew I had more than most and if the country needed the mail line to California kept open, I could guarantee to do the best job that could be done on my piece of run. So I didn't enlist. I went ahead with my plans for opening the station and ranch.

As soon as I got back to Plum Creek, Ed and Emma and the youngster shifted out to the new location and camped in the old building until something more solid could be put up. We hired Indians and some Mexicans out of Denver to put the buildings up. I didn't miss a day of driving but I transferred to the Cottonwood Springs-Fowler Ranch stage so I could oversee the construction on my layovers at the ranch. We put up a big store with a nice, roomy, four-room dwelling connected. We put up a good big barn with stables and blacksmith shop. We fenced a big corral. And before fall that year we were in business and doing fine.

We hired a bunch of hands and I started my herd with some loose cattle that had been stampeded and never rounded up. It was almost impossible for trains to find every head after a stampede. A few would invariably be lost and just wander around on the range. Stampedes occurred from many natural reasons, but mostly they were a part of the general harassment by Indians. I bought *some* cattle from the Indians I knew had been purposely stampeded. If I hadn't, Jack Morrow's ranch up the road, or Beauvais over at Ash Hollow, would have. It was part of the price of traveling . . . to lose a few cattle. But I didn't incite any stampeding and we added to the herd with the good stock which my father drove out for us that summer.

We also picked up a lot of wild mustangs the Indians had caught and we broke them for the stage line. We kept a fairly good-sized bunch of extra horses and mules on hand from which the Company could buy.

By the time the stage line began to run daily, on the first of July, we were operating. Ed got along fine with the Indians and we did a brisk business in skins and robes. The freighters and other travelers began to patronize us and we had good markets for every head of cattle we could handle. We got off to a very fine start.

But the daily stages created a problem for Emma. Twice-weekly stages hadn't made too much kitchen and dining room work for her. Dailies were more than she had bargained for single-handed. And because her food was so good and the place was clean and attractive, it drew many of the other road travelers as well.

Now, kitchen help way out on the Platte was something you either furnished with your own family or did without. There wasn't enough money in the world to hire good kitchen help. It would have been a rare combination of circumstances that would have made a good, reliable, clean white woman willing to live at Fowler Ranch and work for us. Besides, there just weren't that many women. In the first census taken in Colorado, in 1860, there were 18,000 white males, 4000 white females. Almost five to one. There weren't a dozen Negroes, and an Indian woman's notion of kitchen work was so primitive as to be worse than useless. So Emma had to go it alone, with Bucky's skimpy help.

Bucky was on the young side, I admit, but I thought she could be more help than she was. She just plain didn't like inside work. When she was needed she was always out of pocket, outside with the hands and the horses. "You ought to keep her to her tasks more," I said.

"She's only eleven," Emma said. "I hate to put too much on her so young."

It always surprised me the kid was adding on years. She stayed nine years old to me.

Bucky blew in about that time with a half-grown pup I had brought her on my last run. He was all feet and already as big as a young calf and Emma had groaned when I unloaded him. But somebody had left him behind on the road to stray and starve and make a target for some gun-happy Indian or stage passenger. I thought he'd be company for Bucky.

They tore around the room until they began knocking over the chairs. Then the pup darted between my legs and before I could get my balance Bucky butted into my belt buckle and knocked the wind out of me. I grabbed the table to keep from falling and Bucky reeled around and collapsed under it. She crawled back up my leg onto her feet and hung on, as winded as I was. I was mad enough to shake her teeth out and I shoved her away. "Why don't you look where you're going? I'm not a piece of furniture."

"Then get out of the way," she yelled, "stay out of the way!"

She had on my hat and it was way too big for her and had slid down on her nose till she was half blind. I snatched it off. "I've told you to leave my hat alone. You're going to lose it."

She snatched it back and jammed it down to her ears. "I don't lose things." She brandished a short rope at me. "I'm trying to rope that dog and tie him up. And you got in the way and . . ."

We heard the back door bang. "You're too late," I said.

She glared at me. "Now see what you've done! Now he's got away! He's got out the back. Oh!" She ripped the hat off and slammed it on the floor and flung the rope across the room.

"Oh, *damn, hellfire and shoot!*"

Emma was galvanized. She grabbed the kid and began hustling her out the door. "That's enough out of you, young lady. Soap and water will wash swear words out of your mouth. Then you'll stay in your bed for a while!"

Bucky was struggling. "Starr says it!" she yelled. "Starr says those words all the time! Wash his mouth out, too!"

Emma strong-armed her through the side door into their quarters, and from the sound of it Bucky gave her a real tussle with the mouth-washing. The way she screamed and carried on you'd have thought Emma was killing her.

Ed was laughing. "She's pretty outrageous lately."

"She needs a good dose of hickory tea now and then," I said.

"She gets it. Emma don't put up with much foolishness from her."

I picked up my hat and dusted it off and picked up the rope and coiled it. Ed and I turned the chairs up and set them straight. Emma came back, flushed up and her eyes snapping. She tackled me head on. "That child," she said, "has not only commenced talking like you, she tries to walk like you, she's learned to pull her ear like you, she's taken to wearing that old hat of yours whenever you've not got it on, she's sewed pockets on her skirts so she can put her hands in her side pockets like you, and she's even forgot all her table manners eating the way you do."

"Has she commenced drinking whisky and smoking a pipe yet?" I said.

"You think it's funny, don't you?"

"Don't you?"

"No, I don't," she snapped. "I don't think it's funny at all. The least you can do is watch your language and mind your manners around her."

"I'm not the only one that cusses around here," I said, "and as far as my manners are concerned I've got a lot better table manners than most of the people who eat here. She sees a lot of people eating besides me."

"But she doesn't copy them," Emma said. "She doesn't pay them any mind. It's you. Anything you say and anything you do is the gospel according to Matthew to her. If Starr does it, it's fine. If Starr doesn't do it or Starr doesn't like it, she won't touch it with a ten-foot pole."

"Well, what do you want me to do about it?" I said, feeling more than a little put out about it.

"All I ask you to do is watch your language and mind your manners a little," Emma said.

"All right. All *right*," I said. "I'll try to remember not to cuss around her. And I'll try to remember not to put my elbows on the table or talk with my mouth full or hold my fork like a shovel. I wish to God she'd pick herself another hero."

"Like who?" Emma said. She wiped her face with her apron tail and sighed. "Oh, it'll pass." She laughed. "I remember when I was about her age we had a revival in our church and I just worshiped the young visiting evangelist. I went to the mourner's bench every night of that revival. I thought I'd die when he left and the revival was over. In two years' time I couldn't even remember his name."

"Well, Bucky's revival just as well be soon over, too," I said. "I'm putting in for another run pretty soon."

Emma started cooking dinner. The stage from Denver, which I would take on, would be in at noon and a meal for the passengers had to be ready. I was oiling my whip when Emma went out and brought Bucky back. The kid made a face at me as she passed and I stuck out my tongue at her. Emma said, "Don't start anything. Bucky, set the plates around."

She rattled the crockery around and then said, "I'm going to Cottonwood this trip with you."

"No, you're not," Emma said.

"But I *need* to go," the kid wailed, "and you said I could go soon. You said I could go and get me some new shoes. I haven't been for a month and you promised I could go."

"I didn't promise you could go this trip," Emma said. "Here. Put the silver around."

Bucky slapped it around the table. I stole a look at her and saw tears running down her cheeks. Hell, I thought, she's just a little kid doing the best she can in a godawful place for a kid to live. "Why don't you both go next week?" I said. "I hear they're going to have a dance next Friday night. Get one of the boys to keep the station and Ed can go, too."

We had dances every once in a while down at Cottonwood Springs or over at Julesburg. For fifty miles on either side, everybody would go—the ranch people and hands, the stage employees, any of the troops happening by, all went, sometimes riding horseback, sometimes riding the stage up one day, going back the next, sometimes even chartering a stage and taking up a collection to pay for it.

The dances were about the only social life we had in that part of the country in those days. The women caught up on news and gossip, discussed the latest fashions in the east, traded recipes, floated rumors about who was going to have a baby and how soon, who was courting whom, who was passing on the road, who had stopped, what had happened, which of the drivers was working where.

Nearly every man could play some kind of a musical instrument—and the music for the dances was strictly local, a few fiddles, a couple of mouth organs, sometimes a flute or piccolo, guitars and banjos. A lot of the drivers played fiddle and carried them with them in the front boot. Nearly everybody played a mouth organ. I, myself, picked a pretty good guitar. There were dances every few months and always a big one on the Fourth of July and during the Christmas holidays.

If a stage came in while a dance was in progress passengers were always astonished and wondered *where* that many women came from. They came from every ranch and station for miles around. In their homemade dresses and with their brown, windburned faces maybe they looked pretty rough to easterners, but we thought they were beautiful—and they were. That pretty dark-haired woman in the flowered calico dress doing a do-si-do to the center with the big awkward man held a band of ten Sioux off at her station until her husband could bring the stage in, flat out, and he and the passengers could add their artillery to hers.

And that older woman, caging the bird with such a flourish, was riding the box with her man one time, coming home from a trip to Denver. She was wearing a brand-new bonnet, covered with roses, and they were spanking along down the South Platte when all of a sudden an arrow went right through her rose garden and her husband had a race on his hands with half a dozen Arapahoes. They made it to the station and not a passenger was injured, but when the stage pulled up at the station, that woman's husband was lying dead in the front boot and she was handling the reins.

They were mostly young women, in their late twenties or early thirties, with young and growing families. And they were strong and they were brave and they were beautiful.

Emma looked at Ed. "Can we? I could use a change for a couple of days."

"I don't know," he said. "Maybe. We'll see."

Bucky did half a dozen hopskips around the room, then stopped in front of me. "Will you dance with me, Starr? Will you?"

"Hey," I said, "that's for the gentleman to ask."

"But will you? I can dance. Watch." She started waltzing about the room. "See?"

She was little and thin and scrawny, but waltzing she was as graceful as a flower in the wind. I got up and waltzed her around and around until we were spinning and whirling and her braids were flying. When I let her go she still went spinning around dizzily. "We're going to the ball . . . we're going to the ball . . . and I'll dance and I'll dance and I'll dance. And I'll be so beautiful in my ball gown . . ." She stopped and stared at her mother, both hands flying to her mouth. "What'll I wear? Oh, my goodness, what'll I wear? Mama? Your white muslin? We can cut it down for me. Or the ruffled taffeta? Oh, I haven't got a thing!" She went flying out of the room.

I looked at Emma, who was staring at the calico curtains that hung in the doorway and were still swinging as if a tornado had just passed through. "Who," I said, "did you say she wanted to be just like and was copying after? *I* don't wear white muslin or ruffled taffeta."

"Oh, shut up," Emma said.

Chapter 9

Ben Holladay made his final move to take over the line in December of 1861. Without any fuss or bother he just suddenly foreclosed on the C.O.C. & P.P. and he forced a sale of its assets in March of 1862 and got the outfit for an additional $100,000.

Other debtors squalled like scalded cats but Ben Holladay brushed them off. He painted a new name on the stages, Overland Stage Company, got the eastern terminal changed from St. Joseph to Atchison, and was ready to roll. You could feel new life all up and down the line. We all knew the fooling around was over now. This had been coming a long time. It was here, and this man meant business. This man would make the Overland roll on greased wheels.

My father bought some stock in the Overland, but my money was all tied up. I had to let it pass.

Ben Holladay took over a sick line. If William Russell had been able to get along with Ben Ficklin, Ficklin was tough enough to keep the line in shape. But he and Russell had quarrreled before the end of his first year as General Manager and Russell had fired him. The line went slack again. Everywhere except on Slade's section the outlawry became almost as bad as ever and the morale of the men as slack.

Holladay inherited Slade. He kept him on and a lot of people, including the *Rocky Mountain News*, thought he turned his head the other way to encourage a general toughness, in a milder form than Slade's, along the entire line. It may be that Holladay let Slade go too long, but it is to be remembered he took over an ailing and sick stage line and no doubt it was a great relief to have at least one section which functioned without losses.

What Ben Holladay had to do was what the general of an army corps has to do with his command. He had to take this ailing, limping, spiritless stage line and whip it into a tight, disciplined, healthy outfit. He had to give it spirit and morale. He had to make it respect him and respect itself. He had to make it a proud outfit. And he had to make it pay.

You don't do that by letting ruffians steal you blind. And when thugs and outlaws are stealing you blind you don't stop them by going to see them and saying, "Please stop." There was no trial, no judge, no jury yet. So you stopped them by making it too expensive for them to keep on stealing. You hunted them down, you hung them or you shot them. Ben Holladay let every division agent on the line know that he would not tolerate losing Company property to thieves and outlaws. A division agent who could not put a stop to the stealing could expect to lose his job. I don't know of a single man who tried to emulate Slade, but they did get tough and they did stop the stealing. They tightened up the line by teaching the robber bands that every raid was going to cost them in men lost. There was some violence. There was some killing. But guns were blazing from the other side, too.

Ben Holladay was a booger, no two ways about it. He was ruthless and he was hard and he was unscrupulous. His friends loved him, his enemies hated him and called him a scoundrel and a rogue and said he was so crooked he could hide behind a corkscrew. His enemies were the men he beat. He operated on a high, wide and handsome scale. When somebody tried to open another stage line, even a short line, he let them have a little rope, then he tightened it around their necks, bought them and buried them. Then he usually hiked the express charges and the fares and made the public pay him back. He bought a dozen short lines that way, and he made hundreds of envious defeated enemies.

He lived in a princely palace on the Hudson, and his associates were other millionaires and senators and cabinet members in Washington. His two daughters married European noblemen. His brother-in-law said he lived only for the excitement of beating out his competition and accumulating wealth. It was typical of the age and it was the bread of life to him.

But on the Overland line we liked him, we respected him and we admired him. He was one of the boys who had gone up the hard way. When he called a turn he could make it stick. We were proud of him. And before he was through he ran the damnedest best stage line ever seen in this country or anywhere else on the face of the globe. There was never anything like the Overland Stage Company before, or since.

When he rode the line it was in his own special coach, in luxury. But he could handle sixes on any stretch of the road with as much skill as any driver he employed, and we knew it. He could have lived by his gun had he been a violent man, and we knew that. There wasn't anything we had to do he couldn't do himself and do it as well.

With a man like that at the top, we became an army, tight and trim and disciplined and proud. There wasn't anything we wouldn't do for him. There wasn't anything we wouldn't go through for the line. Under Ben Holladay, a driver really became a "king of the road." He believed in his men, he respected us and he backed us to the hilt. He took care of us and be damned to the whining, complaining newspapers and general public.

We had a station agent at Denver for a time who was something of a poet. He wrote a poem called "The Song of the Overland Stage Driver," and one stanza of it said pretty much how we felt about Ben Holladay:

> *You ask me for our leader; I'll soon inform you, then;*
> *It's Holladay they call him, and often only Ben.*
> *If you can read the papers, it's easy work to scan;*
> *He beats the world on staging now, or any other man.*

We sang it to the tune of "The High Salary Driver on the Denver City Line." To be an Overlander during the five years Ben Holladay owned the Company was about as proud a thing as a man could ever hope to be.

Unlike William Russell, who had the dream of a daily mail line across the continent but lost it through foolish management, Holladay was a practical man. He didn't lose money on a stage line through foolish management. William Russell never set foot across the Missouri until he had lost the line. Ben Holladay knew every inch of the west, he knew the men of the west, he knew what men and animals in the west could do together. He made them do it.

By 1863, he owned nearly five thousand miles of stage lines. He not only operated the Overland from Atchison to Placerville, he had branch lines up to the gold camps in Colorado, and he ran a daily stage from Salt Lake to Bannock, Virginia City and Helena in Montana after gold was discovered up there. After gold was discovered in the Owyhee, Idaho City and Boise mines, he got a contract for carrying the mails from Salt Lake to The Dalles, in Oregon, via Fort Hall and Boise City. He built an immense staging empire.

Few people have any idea, then or now, how a stage line was organized or what a big operation it was. For this big staging empire of his, Holladay needed five hundred stagecoaches and about the same number of freight wagons. He had five thousand horses, mules and oxen, the latter being used for freighting in his forage and supplies and to provision the stations. He very early quit using commercial freight lines and did his own freighting.

There was an army of about 150 drivers, and about three hundred hostlers and stock tenders. There were fifty stations between Atchison and Denver, fifty-one between Denver and Salt Lake, and fifty-five between Salt Lake and Placerville. I don't know how many stations there were on the various branch lines. I never drove the branch lines.

At the top of the organization there was a General Superintendent. He was Mr. George K. Otis and he lived in New York. Four times a year he made the trip over the entire network of lines. And he always accompanied Ben Holladay when he rode the lines.

There was an attorney, who was Ben Holladay's cousin, Bela Hughes. He was called General Hughes. He was strictly a militia general, but that made no difference. The courtesy title went well with his fine and portly appearance. He lived in Denver and became an important and respected citizen in Colorado. What impressed us on the line more, probably, was his marksmanship. He was a dead shot. A bunch of us were fooling around the station at Latham one time, shooting target. General Hughes was waiting for the Denver stage. Seeing us shooting he came over and said, "Give me a turn, boys." We tacked the ace of spades to a post and the General squared away, emptied his six-shooter and hit the pip with all six shots. There wasn't a one of us who could duplicate it.

The Company also employed an auditor and paymaster. He lived in Denver, too. For most of my time with the Company he was David Street. He went to work for the old C.O.C. & P.P. and stayed right on through every change till the railroad came. Mr. Street was one of the most respected men with the Company. We were paid every quarter, and until the Civil War made gold scarce and greenbacks began to be used we were paid in gold. David Street rode the whole line each quarter and met the payroll at every station.

The terminology of staging is a little confusing. For instance, the Overland was divided into three main Divisions. Officially they were the Eastern, the Salt Lake and the Western. We rarely used those terms. We said the Atchison, the Denver and the California Divisions. Each Division was about six hundred miles and each Division had a Division Superintendent responsible for his six hundred miles.

But each Division was divided into divisions, or sections, of about two hundred miles, which came under the supervision of a division agent. A Division Superintendent rode his six-hundred-mile line fairly often, but he had a lot of paper work in his office to do. A division agent was riding his two hundred miles constantly. He had full charge of all the property belonging to the stages, kept an eye on the stations and their keepers. He bought the hay and grain, he hired all the employees—drivers, stock tenders, station agents, blacksmiths, harnessmakers, carpenters—everybody that worked on his section. He was paid a hundred dollars a month and board. In every case he was an experienced driver, a levelheaded man who could be trusted with all the thousands of dollars' worth of property and the immense business of the Company.

Passengers often became confused hearing us speak, because the Division had a Superintendent, while under him were three divisions, each with agents. We always knew what we meant. There was no confusion with us.

It was also true of driving that the terminology was a little bewildering. There were stations every ten to fifteen miles, some being swing stations, some home stations, some meal stations. The home stations were twenty-five to thirty-five miles apart and a station agent as employed. They marked the end of a driver's run and the station was his "home" at each end. Sometimes meals were served, mostly in fact, but occasionally the schedule found meal-time falling between home stations and a meal station was set up. The intervening stations were swing stations and were usually manned by a couple of stock tenders. Stops at swing stations were only two or three minutes. Just long enough to change teams.

The stretch of road a driver drove back and forth was called his stage. But he also drove a stage. And while he was driving he was staging. Passengers shook their heads over it. "How do you keep it all straight?" they asked. It was like breathing. You didn't even have to think about it.

One of the things about which there has been great misunderstanding in the public mind was the use of messengers, or guards. It has been assumed that somebody rode shotgun, or guard, on every stagecoach. That is not true. In fact, on the Overland there were only nine messengers, three to each Division. On Monday of each week no mail was carried. Instead a special express coach went out from all terminals loaded with the valuable express packages. On these special express coaches the treasure box was bolted to the floor inside. If a regular Concord was used, the treasure box rode in the front boot.

Usually there was room for two or three passengers; but occasionally the stage was packed so full of express no passengers could be carried. A messenger rode this express coach. One messenger would be going west and one east on each Division all the time, while the third was laying over a week at Atchison, Denver, Salt Lake or Placerville. He was resting after a full round trip over his Division.

The messenger rode the box with the driver and he rode

six days and nights without undressing. He had twenty-four hours at the end of the run for sleep before starting back the six days and nights of his return trip. Then he had a week of layover. These messengers did sleep, however. No man can go six days and nights without sleep. They all learned to curl up in the front boot and sleep as soundly as if in a bed. It was a job nobody much wanted and they never stayed long. They got paid the least of anybody on the line and had the meanest job. Their pay was $62.50 per month. Even the stock tenders made more.

The highest paid men, outside the officials, were the blacksmiths. In a special wagon they moved up and down the line constantly shoeing the animals. They were paid $125 a month.

The Overland mail route was officially, on Postal Department records, No. 10773. The mail was put up in pouches weighing about one hundred pounds each. After we began running daily, the distribution was as follows: San Francisco, two pouches; Sacramento, one or two; Virginia City, one; Carson City, one; Salt Lake, one or two; Denver, two to three. And there was one way-pouch which was opened at the post offices along the route—Daniel's Ranch, Valley City, Fort Kearney, Cottonwood Springs, Fremont's Orchard, Latham and Fort Bridger.

The letter mail was sacred to us. Men would have died, and did die, to get it through. When a coach was lost, they hauled it on their backs, dragged it, carried it, swam flooded streams with it, to get it through. I, myself, never lost a sack and I know of few others who did. We never forgot that though the passengers were important, nothing on God's earth must stop the United States Mail.

After Ben Holladay took over the line everything ran more smoothly and efficiently. The entire line showed the effects of tighter organization and better discipline. Employees were weeded out for efficiency and more carefully hired. Because a lot of the old, veteran drivers were pretty whisky-soaked and the public frequently complained, a new regulation went into effect—no drinking on the box. This was purely to satisfy the public. The old topers went right on nipping at their bottles. If passengers reported a driver, there was a token investigation. Theoretically, a driver was to have a fine deducted from his pay the first two times he was reported. He was to be fired and blacklisted on the third time. Naturally we protected each other. I never knew one man to have so much as a nickel deducted from his pay and certainly nobody was ever fired or blacklisted. But it looked good to the public.

Holladay wanted the line to give the appearance of uniformity and elegance and quality. This extended to uniforms for the drivers. They weren't issued to us. We had to buy them, but he bought them in New York and sold them to us at cost plus freight. It wasn't mandatory to wear them. If you didn't want to, you didn't have to. But we took so much pride in the line by that time it was a rare driver who didn't buy the long, navy blue overcoat, with short cape over the shoulders, and the high, fine, shiny leather boots. A broadbrimmed, flat-crowned "wide-awake" hat was already uniform in the west. Holladay, himself, wore one.

We had the finest sets of harness money could buy, made by Hill Brothers in New Hampshire. A set cost $150. Many of us cared for our own sets, oiling and polishing them and keeping them in such good condition that after years of service they were still as good as new. Some of us, and I was one, put special decorations on them. One driver strung small ivory rings on his. Another put scarlet rosettes on his bridles. I had some Cheyenne beaded work done on mine and sank Spanish silver pieces on the bridles. We came to think almost as much of our harnesses as we did of our whips. Old drivers, like me, had special privileges. When we moved along the line, our harness went with us.

The stages were all Concords, beautiful and sheer and graceful. Holladay quit using mules except in certain hard-pulling places. He wanted speed and, while mules were fine for pulling, horses were much better for brisk, lively work.

Under him, we began to get the beautiful matched teams. My Lord, but they were beautiful. Perfectly built, perfectly matched, they could make you choke with pride. We had strings of perfectly matched bays and sorrels, blacks, chestnuts, grays, even creams and whites. There were roans and buckskins. There was one string of paints, and there was a team called the catfish grays. They were almost steel-colored and very lightly dappled. They were all so handsome that often passengers tried to buy a horse out of a string. One man offered six hundred dollars for a perfect little jet-black leader. There wasn't money enough to buy a good Overland horse. The Company was never interested in selling a good horse. Holladay took pains to buy only the best. His stock buyers were the soundest and most knowledgeable men he could find. Mostly they bought in St. Louis, where nearly all the breeders in Kentucky and Missouri took their stock to sell. He didn't care what they paid for stock as long as they got their money's worth.

The beautiful matching of teams was pride. Their speed and performance wasn't. The old Butterfield contract would run out in 1864. Holladay figured Wells, Fargo, who now owned it, would bid on the new contract. He didn't mean for them to get it. He meant to put that new million-dollar contract in his own pocket. He wanted the line to prove to the Postal Department it could run the mail faster and more efficiently than Wells, Fargo or anybody else. So we kept a very fast schedule, the maximum speed at which decent care of horses could be performed.

When Holladay rode the line, he killed horses and mules to get speed. But when he rode the line it was news. Every newspaper in the country reported it. He wanted them to. He saw to it they knew he was riding the line. Reporters met him at Denver or Salt Lake or Placerville and interviewed him. For good publicity for the line, he had to be able to say he had cut ten hours off the regular run, say, or twelve or sixteen. The implication was always that the through time could eventually be cut to his own time. He didn't have to say, and didn't say, how many teams had been killed to achieve his record time.

Californians were especially eager to keep whittling on the time. They wanted their mail so fast that only flight on a crow's line could really have satisfied them. So they invariably headlined any record run, any cut in the through time.

I remember the time Holladay made his fastest run. He was in California and he was going home. Orders came down the line from Placerville to every Division Superintendent, and from them to every division agent and the hostlers and tenders at the swing stations: "Lay your stock so as to catch him with your best teams."

This threw the whole line out of gear, upset all normal arrangements, inconvenienced everybody, passengers included, but the whole line reacted as if lightning had run down the wires. He was going all the way through, Placerville to Atchison, without a layover. And when he got home if he hadn't made a new record a few heads would be certain to roll.

I was driving out of my own station at the time, but I got a telegram from my division agent telling me to shift over to Julesburg and catch Holladay there and stay with him to Cottonwood Springs. It was 104 miles and twenty-four hours of steady driving. Division agents weren't risking anybody but the best drivers, however. Good drivers weren't good enough. Only the best would do. So a few of us were tabbed.

Bob Spotswood was division agent between Julesburg and Denver. He was at Big Bend, about fifty miles out of Denver, when he was notified to report in to Denver and bring his fastest team with him. There were some fine drivers on that section, but Spotswood decided to handle the reins himself. He laid out his stock for the run. Because of heavy sand in several places this was one of the sections that still used some mules. Spotswood took a team called the Benham mules into Denver with him. Alex Benham had matched them up when he was agent on that section, and they were not only fast for mules, they were faster than any any other team on the entire line.

When Holladay arrived at the stage office in Denver, General P. E. Connor, commander of the Department of Utah, was with him, having joined him at Salt Lake. General Connor's black servant was also along. Bob Spotswood said Holladay lived up to his expectations. He was big and handsome and burly looking, was dressed finely, was smoking a big cigar and was wearing the western wideawake hat he had never given up and had made famous in the east.

He stayed two hours in the office, smoking, having a few drinks, although he was a man who never took but a few.

He sent for Bob, who was twenty-three years old at the time, when he learned who would be driving him. "Everything ready?" he said.

"Yes, sir," Bob said.

"Fine. I'll be out in five minutes."

He didn't quite make it. It was half an hour and Bob was sweating it out with the Benham mules getting more nervy and restless every minute. When Holladay appeared finally he stopped before climbing in the stage and took out his watch. "All right," he said, "let 'em fly. I'll give you an hour and a half to make the first station."

It was fifteen miles to Pierson's and Bob said it curled his hair to think of it. The Benhams were trotters, fast trotters, and it was Bob's lucky day. The road was clear and the team didn't break the whole fifteen miles. Bob pulled them up in one hour and a quarter. That was a mile every four minutes.

The next team was the catfish grays. They had been brought over from the mountain short line, where they had been known to do the Denver-Golden run in one hour sometimes. Bob clipped them eleven miles to the next station in exactly fifty-three minutes.

That was the way it went the whole two hundred miles to Julesburg. Every relay was a picked team. Every stage was clipped off at flying speeds. Spotswood brought him into Julesburg in twenty hours, handling the leathers every second and every mile. Holladay was highly pleased. He said to Bob, "Boy, you've done a fine job." Then he lit his cigar. "How many mules do you suppose I've killed?"

It sounded heartless and maybe it was. It earned him the reputation of being heartless, at any rate, for unfortunately the remark was overheard and passed around until it reached the ears of a newspaperman in Denver and was quoted in the *Rocky Mountain News*. From there it was flashed east and the record run Holladay made had to bear the stigma of being a horse and mule killer. The irony was that Bob Spotswood's driving, as fast as it was, had been so skilled that he didn't lose an animal.

I was ready and waiting on the box to handle the next section. I had brought my own best team, the Gray Ghosts, to Julesburg. Don't ask me why grays are so fast. I don't know. But a good many of our best and fastest teams were grays. General Connor's black man was to ride the box with me. He looked sick when he crawled up beside me. "You don't look like you feel too good," I said.

"I ain't feeling my dead level best," he said. He rolled his eyes at me. "Is it your intentions to take us flying along as fast as that other gentleman?"

"It is," I said. "Those are my orders."

"Then I just as well commence praying again," he said.

"Why?" I said. "You scared?"

"Man," he said fervently, "I been so skeered since we left Salt Lake I've done run out of anything to be *skeered with!* I ain't ever rode so fast. Not in my *entire* life. It's a wonder my hair ain't turned white and my skin bleached out. If I live to Atchison, I aim to depart from the Gineral. I ain't coming back this way. The Lord didn't mean human beings to take wing and fly."

It was fourteen miles to South Platte and my grays did it in an hour and ten minutes. Charlie Haynes was the division agent on my section at that time and he had ridden the line and warned all the freighters and emigrant trains to keep the road clear. They cooperated and we had a clear road. It punished the team but it didn't kill them.

Fifteen miles to Diamond Springs and the chestnut team I picked up at South Platte flew over it in one hour and twenty minutes. Eleven to Sand Hill with a team of bays that clipped it off in fifty-two minutes. Twelve to Alkali Lake and a sand drag that hurt the buckskins that relayed at Sand Hill. I knew when we rolled into Alkali Lake we'd lose some of them and we did. They pulled their hearts out and they never broke, but we lost two of them.

So on down the line. I took the short cut over the Devil's Dive. We were coursing along the edge of the bluff and the black man was moaning. "Don't git too close to the edge, man. You getting powerful near this jump-off."

"We're going to jump off in a minute," I said.

"Lord God," the Negro groaned, "hold this child in the holler of your hand, these here stage drivers is crazy men."

We went down flat out and I heard Ben Holladay whoop. He was prepared for it. I'd heard he liked the thrill of it. I liked it myself, but we had drivers it scared and who wouldn't take a team over the Dive. Down and down and down, so fast that one stumble, one wheel blocked, and we'd go rolling, wrecked stage, dead passengers, maimed horses, to the bottom of the canyon. Down and down, then haul out, the momentum carrying the coach three-fourths of the way up—then the horses heaving into the dreadful pull.

When we pulled out at the top the Negro was down in the front boot hiding and he wouldn't get back up until we got to Cottonwood Springs. "I ain't going to look no more," he said. "If we going to do another one of them dives, I don't want to see it."

When we pulled into Cottonwood Springs we had made the run, 104 miles, in ten hours and ten minutes. I never did it before, and never did it again. I never even wanted to. I was stove up, but not beat clear out. Charlie took over at Cottonwood himself and ran the great man on to Fort Kearney.

Crossing Nevada and the mountains drivers had driven ten or twelve animals to death. In our section, Bob Spotswood lost none and I lost two. We all wondered if it was worth it and we waited to hear the final time. It came by telegraph when they reached Atchison. Two thousand miles—twelve days, two hours. That was 166 miles every twenty-four hours, for a line average of fourteen miles every hour. It was a record that stood for the whole stage-coaching era and it cost Holladay twenty thousand dollars. But maybe it helped him get the million-dollar contract.

Chapter 10

I wanted some time farther west, so I moved along and drove that winter in the Mountain Division—Fort Bridger, Bear River, Echo Canyon—into and around Salt Lake. It was a change from the plains and mountain driving tested all your skills.

In April of 1862, what my father had predicted began to come true. On a very small scale, but it began. Many of the officers did resign their commissions and leave. Some of the enlisted men and non-commissioned officers were also pulled out and sent into the battle lines in Missouri and Tennesee and Virginia. Volunteers and militiamen took their places and the garrisons at the forts grew very thin.

The Indians hit the stage line that spring along the Sweetwater. The telegraph line to the Pacific had been completed in the fall of 1861, and the Shoshoni and Utes had begun to put two and two together. The telegraph line and the stage line were dangerous to them. They would make war upon them.

They ran off a lot of stage stock, chopped down some telegraph poles and tore up some line, scared the wits out of some stage passengers and played havoc with the schedule for a while. The government brought General P. E. Connor, a fighting Irishman, into the area with his California volunteers. He took up headquarters at Salt Lake as head of the Department of Utah, built Camp Douglas there and he very shortly quelled the Utes and Shoshonis.

General Connor was one of the foremost proponents of the school of thought that the only good Indian was a dead Indian. Seek and kill was the way he operated and he quickly brought the Utes and Shoshonis to taw. All except a little band of Southern Utes, headed by a half-breed called Popo, who refused to smoke the peace pipe and accept the government's presents. Instead, he took his little band down onto the Platte and joined them with Charlie and George Bent's Cheyennes. Here, for a year or so, they made a nuisance of themselves and that was about all. They stampeded the stock of the freight and emigrant trains along the road and once in a while they caught a small, disorganized train of emigrants and butchered it. Occasionally they ran off some stage stock, but not often. They all just sort of drifted here and there, harassing, being a nuisance. At the ranch we got along with them pretty well.

I bought some of the stock they ran off myself. Sometimes the troopers could help a train recover at least part of their stock. Sometimes they couldn't. It would be too well hidden out. But once a train had moved on, the stock went to the market. I bought some from the breed, Popo. He was a bigger Indian than most Utes, who were usually squatty and low-slung. He was a fine-looking Indian except he had the Ute flat nose and mouth and he was very dark. But he was tall and built well. It's impossible to guess at an Indian's age, but he was still young. He didn't like white people and it was plain to see. He bore himself haughtily. He had clear cold gray eyes and he would look you straight in the eye with them, level and steady and unflinching. He appeared to understand English pretty well, but he spoke it only well enough to conduct business.

For an Indian he had a lot of business sense. He could hold his own in a trade. He knew what buffalo hides were worth and he wouldn't bargain. He brought in clean skins and he got his price—at least from me, which may be one reason he traded with me more than the other ranchers and traders. When he brought in stock, he knew what the market was for mules and horses and cattle and got the price.

He didn't buy much in the way of fripperies. And he didn't drink, which was so unusual in an Indian as to be a curiosity. He had a plain dumpy little squaw who was always with him following at his heels. I never heard him speak to her except in a grunt which always sent her running to obey him. I judged she was responsible for the good condition of his furs and skins. He didn't buy her much in the way of finery either. I guessed he did the trading for his whole band, for he bought a lot of general supplies. He wanted guns and ammunition, but we weren't allowed to sell them to Indians and I wouldn't have if we had been. The fewer of them had guns and ammunition the safer our lives would be.

I didn't like him. He was an outlaw from his own tribe and that is always bad medicine. When a man's roots are cut he's more dangerous. When I was at the ranch and he came along I was always glad to see that he tended to his business and left, didn't spend any time hanging around. "That one," I told Ed, "will bear watching. He's a renegade and could make trouble."

"He don't ever," Ed said. "Comes in, like you see, trades and gets out. Don't say much. Don't linger."

"But he don't miss a trick," I said. "If you don't take care, you'll wake up some morning and every head of stock we've got will be gone."

The rampaging along the Sweetwater that spring was enough to make Ben Holladay pull some wires in Washington and get the stage route changed. From Julesburg, the through stage had always followed up Lodgepole Creek, up to Fort Laramie, Horseshoe Station, Platte Bridge, Devil's Gate, Pacific Springs, South Pass, Green River, Fort Bridger. Late that summer Holladay quit running up that route. Instead he angled the whole line southwest from Julesburg, along the Denver route. But at Latham, he left the Denver route and crossed the South Platte and ran thirty-five miles west to Laporte, then began to angle back up northwest across the Medicine Bows and Bitter Creek to pick up the old route at Fort Bridger. That was called the Cherokee Trail. A bunch of Cherokees from Three Forks had traveled up the Arkansas heading for the mines in Nevada. They had used that trail and found it could be traveled. It was longer, but Holladay's argument was that it was much safer. And for a while it was.

When we closed up the stations along the old route, all the stock and the stages being used there were taken to the Devil's Gate station to be moved down to the new route. I was driving out of Fort Bridger at the time and I was sent to help with the changeover. It was so beautifully organized and so well carried out that we didn't miss a trip or a mail. The stations and equipment on the new route went into operation the day the changeover was made. We made quite a caravan the morning we left out of Devil's Gate. We had all the rolling stock for five hundred miles of line, plus all the supplies and provisions for the stations being abandoned, plus all the hay and grain being shifted, plus all the stage stock and extra cattle, horses and mules. We made a sizable train, but besides ourselves we had other traveling companions. A couple of emigrant trains were scared to go it alone on the old route so they tied onto our tail. And we had a military escort with its train of baggage and supply wagons.

After the raids in March the government decided to reinforce the weak garrisons at the forts with some more volunteer outfits. The Fourth Iowa Cavalry was the first sent out. Then came the regiment that did so many years of western duty that they sort of took root. When U. S. troops were mentioned, everybody in the west automatically thought of the Eleventh Ohio. They arrived at Fort Laramie in May of 1862, under the command of Colonel Collins. Our escort for the changeover was Company A of the Eleventh Ohio, with Major O'Farrell commanding. They had another duty besides escorting us down to the new route. They were to locate and build a fort to protect the new route.

We began moving out of Devil's Gate at four o'clock in the morning, heading due south into the mountains. It was a well-organized line of march, with the military in the lead, on the flanks, and bringing up the rear. We'd been on the road about four hours when a trooper rode up alongside my stage and offered me a drink from his canteen. I said I had my own.

"Oh," he said, winking at me, "try mine."

I did. It was whisky. "Where'd you get it?" I said.

"One of the emigrants," he said, grinning. "He's got four kegs full. Selling it cheap, too. One greenback and he'll fill your canteen. Want some?"

I said I didn't believe so.

I never had let myself get into the habit of needing

whisky, but I never was without a bottle of *good* whisky. In case I wanted a drink, or needed one, I didn't want to risk being blinded with somebody's forty-rod.

Well, it didn't take long for the word to make the rounds, and the tedium of the hot, dusty march was considerably eased for the troopers and stage employees, too, for the rest of the day. Some of the boys in blue had a little trouble staying in the saddle by the middle of the afternoon. Most of the drivers were pretty well oiled, also, but I never saw a stage driver who couldn't handle his string even when he was so drunk if you put him afoot he'd fall down.

We made camp eleven miles out from Devil's Gate. There was a gap in the mountains there where there was a good supply of wood for cooking fuel and a nice cold spring of water.

The major hadn't noticed a thing until we halted to camp. As soon as his boys dismounted and tried to proceed on their own feet, they started to collapse all over the place. They fell about, sprawled, crawled, staggered and reeled, one happy, heedless, hilarious drunken company of cavalrymen. He was right dismayed. He sent for the officer of the day, a young lieutenant named Brown, and said, "These men are drunk. Drunk and disorderly!"

"Yes, sir," the lieutenant said.

"Where did they get the whisky?"

"I don't know, sir."

The major gave it some thought. "There's some whisky in some of the wagons," he said.

"Yes, sir."

"Obviously it is not in the military wagons."

"No, sir."

If I hadn't known where it was, I wouldn't have bet on it. Nobody was ever cleverer at finding the component parts required to make whisky than United States soldiers, and they were never without it if they could help it. It was, they said, what made the wheels go round. It was what made western duty bearable. It was what put a little life into a living death. Whatever it was, they had a capacity for it that was little short of phenomenal. Their barracks at Fort Laramie wasn't called Bedlam for nothing.

"Very well," the major said. "You will search every wagon in the entire train. When you find the whisky, pour it out."

The lieutenant, who doubtless hadn't had a drink yet, gulped. "All of it sir?"

"All of it."

"Yes, sir."

Lieutenant Brown collected the four soberest men he could find and set to work making the search. As stage drivers, it wasn't any of our business. Half a dozen of us went ahead making our own camp. But we discussed it among ourselves. Bill Trotter was of the opinion it was a shame to pour all that good whisky out and waste it. "A pure shame," he said. "There ought to be some way of saving a little of it."

"What would you recommend?" I said. "I don't think we could get very far trying to stop the lieutenant."

Bill was morose. "What's the penalty for attacking the U. S. Cavalry?"

"I don't know," I said. "I've not ever attacked them . . . and count me out now if that's the way your mind is running. They're bad enough shots cold sober. As drunk as lords and shooting wild, somebody could get killed and probably would."

I picked up a camp kettle and went to the spring to fill it. When I came back I set the kettle down and said, "There's a big crack in the rock just over that spring."

"Do tell," Bill said. "How noticing you are. There usually is a crack in the rock where there's a spring . . ." He caught on. He chuckled. "Now, ain't that interesting? You *are* a noticing man, Fowler." He lowered his voice. "How'll we manage it?"

We gave it some thought, worked Lem Flowers and Alex Benham in on it, and they agreed to distract the lieutenant when he got ready to pour out the whisky. Bill and I would see to the rest.

The whisky was found in the emigrant wagon. One keg was empty, three kegs were full and they were duly confiscated. Lem and Alex went to work to create the diversion. They went to meet the detail and stopped the lieutenant. They believed they'd found some Indian sign back up the trail a piece, they told him. Would he come take a look? Immediately alert, the lieutenant would. "Sergeant," he said, "knock the heads of these kegs out and pour out the whisky. Pour out every drop. That's an order."

"Yes, sir,".the sergeant said.

When Lem and Alex had led the lieutenant off, Bill Trotter and I approached the sergeant. "Where you going to pour it out?" I asked.

"Dunno," he said. "One place is as good as another, I reckon." He looked sad.

"Ain't it a shame," Bill said, "all that good whisky wasted?"

"It's plain inhuman," the sergeant said.

"The lieutenant didn't say anything about where to pour it out, did he?" I said.

"No. Just said pour it out."

"We know a place," Bill said. "Come with us."

We led him to the spring and pointed to the crack. He grinned from one ear to the other. "Now, ain't that the prettiest little crack in a rock you ever saw? Boys, roll them kegs over here."

Never was a spring contaminated so fast. In half an hour it was flowing practically a hundred proof alcohol. The detail passed the word around and the stampede was on. Every canteen, camp kettle, mug and skillet was soon filled with that good old mountain water. Men who couldn't find containers stamped their heels in the mud around the spring and drank from the fillup. Before long men who had been half sober were full drunk, and men who had been drunk were paralyzed. It was the biggest run on spring water I ever saw and the most total drinking spree I ever witnessed. It was also the happiest camp the United States Cavalry probably ever made.

The major was furious. He stomped around trying to find the whisky, fuming, cussing and stewing. "These men are so drunk," he stormed, "if three Indians jumped from behind a bush they could make a successful raid on the whole camp."

"Yes, sir," the sergeant of the whisky detail said, saluting. He could barely get his hand to his head. "Report the whisky poured out, sir. Every drop . . . hic . . . every last drop, sir . . . hic . . . poured out." He felt so good he was beaming. "But we sure got the best goddamned spring water you ever tasted in your life, sir. Have a swig of it, sir!" And damned if he didn't offer the major a drink from his canteen.

The lieutenant had a hard time mounting a guard that night. There weren't enough sober men in camp. He finally made do with any who could lean against a tree without sliding down. After six fist fights, three knife fights and one head-butting duel, the camp finally settled down. But when it came time for Tattoo the bugler was out cold. He couldn't be roused. "I never played Tattoo in my life," I protested when I was sent for and told to bring my bugle, "and I'm in no shape to begin now."

The major was worn out. He said, wearily, "What *can* you play?"

"I blow Charge right good, sir," I said.

"Don't tempt me," he said. "If I thought it would do any good I'd have you sound it. Can't you play anything else?"

"I don't do too bad on 'The Old Gray Mare,'" I said, "and I can get through 'Camptown Races.'"

"Well," the major said, rubbing his hand over his face, "this is still a troop of United States Cavalry and the horn is going to goddamned well blow when it's supposed to. The shape this outfit is in, I guess it had better be 'The Old Gray Mare.'"

Even though she wasn't what she used to be, Company A of the Eleventh Ohio bedded down that night to the mild and mellow strains of "The Old Gray Mare"—more mellow than mild, because I was so unsteady I was weaving and only met the horn every few notes. But I don't know as they ever had a more appropriate Tattoo. There wasn't a man in the outfit what he used to be.

That gap in the mountains has been known as Whisky Gap from that time on.

When we had got the stage stock and equipment lined out along the new route, our military escort left us and went on about their duty of finding a good location for a new fort. They decided on a site in the Medicine Bows near Elk Mountain. Lieutenant Brown was in charge of the construction. When it was finished it was named Fort Halleck, in honor of Major General Halleck who was Chief of Staff of the United States Army at that time, and for years it was garrisoned by troops of the Eleventh Ohio. Little did I know what the very name, Fort Halleck, would someday mean to me.

Chapter 11

The autumn of 1862, with the Indians quieted down again, I was driving a stage of the line I always enjoyed—out of Denver to Pierson's. The road was the best on the line, as hard as if it had been paved and wide enough you could meet and pass without breaking road gait.

It was a fine run for some high-style reinsmanship, which I always loved the opportunity to do. I had a beautiful string of fours, perfectly matched, perfectly built dappled grays. I liked to bring them in fast. The Concord was always shining. Holladay would never allow a dirty coach to go into the city. There were two extra boys at Pierson's just to shine up the stage for the run into Denver.

We made a beautiful sight, stage and team so elegant and fine and, if I do say so myself, a good driver handling the leathers. I never brought that team in that I didn't feel like a million dollars when I threw down the lines. They did your driving justice. They showed it off for you in the prettiest way and finest style.

We arrived at nine o'clock in the morning. You enter Denver from the east and proceed West on Larimer Street to Sixteenth, then turn north for two squares, across Market to the southeast corner of Blake Street where the station is located.

Watch me, or Bill Trotter, or Alex Benham, or any other good reinsman make that turn, barely slowing. A full square before you reach the corner, you begin climbing and slipping the reins. Nobody watching can see your fingers move, but there is the smallest hair touch in the horses' mouths. You reach out your right foot and rest it on the pedal of the brake shaft. You let the leaders reach the center of the turn, then at the exact and precise moment you brake lightly. The brake takes the slack out of the reins and the slack out of the traces. Now you signal the leaders, just as their tails reach the intersection, to turn, and they swing into the corner. You hold the swing horses, if you're driving sides, straight on a bit, for if they follow into the turn too soon the stage will cut too sharply. With any speed it can overset.

As the swings reach the center of the turn, they get a little tug on the lines to make the turn, but the wheelers, still feeling nothing, are straight. Finally, leaders and swings turned, the wheelers make their turn. Riding the box with a fine driver you'll swear the horses made the turn on their own, for you've seen so little guidance the driver seems to have done nothing at all. But it is a pretty thing to execute and to do it perfectly takes precise timing and precise control.

We draw up the station which is in the Planter's House on Blake Street. Blake is the principal street of the city. Inside of five minutes of a stage arrival a huge crowd has gathered. They are people of all classes and kinds—lawyers, politicans, abolitionists, bankers, freighters, merchants, clerks, teamsters, miners, ranchmen, prospectors, preachers, and a good percentage of gamblers, saloon-keepers, criminals and fugitives from justice. All sorts and kinds, good, bad and indifferent. If you think the arrival and departure of trains in your town creates interest and excitement nowadays, you should have seen what the arrival of the daily stage from the east did in Denver. The Civil War was going on. Everybody was eager for news, wanted their mail, the express and especially the newspapers. "How's the battle going?" This was the battle at the place called Antietam, fought in September of that year.

We had plenty of secessionists in the west. Especially after the tinned ranks of the regular troops in the forts were partially filled in by Confederate prisoners of war. We called them "Galvanized Yankees." Prisoners didn't have to come west and help garrison these forts, but many preferred to, especially since they were not called on to bear arms against their southern brethren, rather than languish in the northern prisons. For some, it was life when they might have perished. But they could and did spread a considerable amount of disaffection and not many of them were held in esteem or respect. They had a hard time of it in the west, those who stayed on, for years after the war ended.

Denver had only a few brick buildings in 1862, and none of them was more than two stories tall. Most of the business buildings were on Blake Street. My father had bought some lots for us on that street and built several frame buildings. The store my brother Matt managed for him was in one of them. I owned a half interest in the others, which we rented to saloon-keepers. There were three, side by side, in a row.

Over on Fifteenth Street were some banking houses, and the mint was on Market. There was a theater on Sixteenth. But along Blake was where the city pulsed and stirred with most of its activity. There were more gambling houses and saloons than anything else and they ran twenty-four hours a day, seven days a week. They never closed. There were many Mexican houses in Denver. Some of them ran gambling houses and if you want the wildest gambling in the world, just get into a monte game in a Mexican house! You could also get Taos lightning in any of the Mexican places fairly cheap. It'll burn your insides out in time, but you can get drunk mighty fast. Sunday was the busiest day of the week for all business houses, gambling halls, dives and bars. The miners were in town that day.

The post office was one of the few brick buildings and it was on the north side of Larimer between Fifteenth and Sixteenth streets. D. H. Moffat had a news and stationery shop in the same building.

The Elephant Corral was where freighters and teamsters hung out—on Blake between Fourteenth and Fifteenth. All the grocery stores and trading establishments were on Blake—Brown Bros.; Stebbins & Porter; the Cornforths', and Fowler's. They were all Atchison men.

The *Rocky Mountain News* office was in a building in the bed of Cherry Creek which until 1864 had never been known to have a drop of water in it. Then a waterspout, cloudburst and terrible flood rushed down the creek and washed most of Denver away.

I liked Denver. It was a wild, wide-open, wicked, wonderful town. The excitement was like dynamite, so explosive it shocked against your skin and rippled it. And the air

. . . so clean, so crisp, you breathed and thought you'd swallowed diamonds. I saw my father from time to time when he would be in town, and I often spent a night with my brother, Matt, and his wife. It was living the way I liked to live. It pleased me that the Pearl had come to Denver. She was working at the Dutchman's and we took up right where we left off in Dobytown.

It must have been October that I decided I'd better move out and see what was going on at the ranch. I worked back to that run every so often to keep an eye on things. Ed was good and he could be trusted with your life, but there's nothing that takes the place of the man who has the money invested to keep things tightened up.

Emma had been struggling along with the eating station. Twice she had found help for a short time. A stranded emigrant and his family had stayed a couple of months and his wife had helped in the kitchen. I sent her a Mexican woman once, a widow who needed work. She stayed about three months. They always got tired of the loneliness and the hard work and moved on.

It had been over six months since I had been home. I had helped move the line down from the Sweetwater, and I had been driving out of Denver ever since. I bumped the driver off the run to Cottonwood Springs from my place and deadheaded in with a few days' grace before going back to work. I walked into the dining room and a strange girl was waiting on the tables. I stopped in my tracks. She was the prettiest thing my already seasoned eyes had ever seen. She wasn't ripe-fruit lush like the Pearl, she was just pretty and fresh looking and so young and so slim and so graceful.

I stood just inside the door and watched her. She had on a plain sprigged calico dress but it was almost all covered up with a blue-checked pinafore apron, which was starchy and ruffled and tied in a wide bow in the back. If she saw me, she took no notice. She was busy with the hungry passengers.

She was fair, but not fair in that white, blue-veined, thin-skinned way. Her skin was like good dairy cream, a little touched with honey. Her face was flushed up from the heat of the stove and a dust of light freckles stood out against the pink. Her mouth was wide enough to be generous, but not too wide, and the lips were pink and a little full. Her hair was heavy and curly and it was a warm, rich dark brown that looked springy and full of life. She had it piled on top her head with some curls loose from the knot.

I don't know if she knew that her way of doing her hair left her neck so beautiful. It takes all of a woman to make a beautiful woman and to each man one thing may be more appealing than others about her. To me, the back of a woman's neck can be the sweetest, youngest thing about her, especially if she doesn't clutter it with a knot of hair— if she sweeps her hair up and away from it. It can make me ache with its tender curving line. Watching this girl, I had the strongest wish, so strong I had to make fists of my hands, to touch that lovely young neck.

She came to the end of the table nearest me finally and glanced quickly at me. Not more than a glance. She met my eyes for a second, then moved on around to serve the back side of the table. But there was time enough for me to see that her eyes were brown, a light goldy brown.

I fell in love with her that moment . . . without even knowing who she was. I fell right down to the bottom of the cellar in love and I knew this girl was for me and there never would be another and that I had to have her, and it was the worst feeling in the world and it made me sick. I didn't want to be in love. A stage driver has got no business being in love. He has got no business marrying until he's ready to throw down the lines for good. I had seen too many good drivers ruined by marrying. Women don't want their men off all the time and it's a rare one that can keep from nagging about it. Even if a woman couldn't make a man quit his work, she could keep him in such turmoil it affected his driving. So most good drivers didn't give marriage a serious thought, though they all dallied with any pretty girl they found. Driving is love enough for a man. I didn't want my emotions tangled up with this girl or any other. But I didn't have any say about it. There she was, and there I was, and it happened.

I went into the kitchen where Emma was cutting pies. "Who is the girl?" I said.

"The girl?" she said, looking blank for a moment. "Oh . . . that's Bernie. That's my sister, Bernie." She slid a fourth of a pie off on a plate for me and shoved it across the table. "I had to have somebody. I was at my wit's end. It suddenly came over me that Bernie was eighteen now and could be a big help if she was willing to come. So I just wrote and sent her the money for the trip. You remember . . . I've mentioned her to you."

"The way you mentioned her I thought she was just a kid . . . about Bucky's age," I said.

She laughed. "Well, time passes, Starr. She's grown up since I first named her to you."

"That is the beautiful truth," I said, "she is certainly grown up."

"Now, don't go getting any ideas in your head," she said. "She don't much care for stage drivers."

"What does she know about them?"

"Not much," Emma admitted. She wiped her hands on her apron and grinned. "She caught Bob Hodge, Uncle Charley Manville and Jim Douglas, all, on the trip out."

"So she thinks we all tipple," I said.

"That's close to it. She quit riding the box after Jim. Said if she was going to be killed by a drunk driver she'd rather be inside and not know it was coming."

"Oh, Lord," I said, "three of the best drivers on the line and because she saw a bottle she decides her life is in danger!"

"Well, Jim Douglas gave her the ride of her life," Emma said. "She said he had the team flat out when the right front wheel came off. Said they were going so fast the axle didn't even touch the ground for a quarter of a mile."

"No harm?" I said quickly.

"Well . . . no."

"So all right," I said. "He had the team flat out. So a wheel ran off. It took a real expert to handle the team and stop the stage without wrecking it. Didn't she understand that?"

Emma balanced plates of pie all the way up her arm to the elbow. "You explain it to her," she said, "you're another expert."

"How long is she going to stay?" I said.

"A good long time I hope," she said. "She's the best help a body could have. It's like me being two people. She hadn't been here a week till she'd got the hang of things. Just caught right on and took over the dining room. She's a good cook, too. It's been the biggest relief to me." Easing toward the door she stopped and looked at me. "Why? You bring somebody out from Denver? If you did, just put them on the next stage back. I don't need anybody else now."

"No, I didn't bring anybody." I started on the pie. "How long has she been here?"

"Oh, a month . . . little over."

"How much you paying her?"

"Forty a month and her board."

"It's not enough," I said. "Make it fifty."

Emma laughed. "Well, here we go. You're taken with her or you wouldn't be putting up ten dollars more than you have to. But I warn you, Starr—this is not the kind of life for her, permanent."

"You brought her out here," I said, "she'll be the one to say how permanent it is."

She was just the right size to drop your arm around and bend your head to kiss. Whatever her thoughts about stage drivers in general we got along fine until I tried that. She slapped my face and I never tried it again. She wouldn't allow any freshness of any kind, but Lord you everlastingly wanted to and kept sizing up the fit.

Emma was right about how much help she was. She was like Emma in all her ways, just as neat and clean and quick. They worked together the way Lizzie and Maggie Trout over at Midway did, putting a meal together and serving it to fifteen or twenty people, fast, never keeping the customers waiting, always watchful of empty cups and glasses and plates. Nobody ever had any reason to complain of the food or service at our station.

Like Emma, she loved pretty things, color in her dresses, pretty flowers and plants in the house, pretty curtains at the windows. She brought some plant cuttings when she came and the big dining room at the station was full of pots and plants that always surprised the passengers. It was astonishing to find good food, good service and a pleasant dining room away up on the Platte.

I stayed on the run into Cottonwood Springs that year a lot longer than I had meant to. It wasn't an inspiring stretch of road and I usually lingered just long enough to set some things straight and take an inventory and order in fresh supplies, and then I was ready to move on.

But Bernie was so pretty—so pretty, and so womanly. When you looked at a woman like Pearl you put her immediately in the only place she belonged—a bedroom. You might do it with excitement and lust and great enjoyment, but women like Pearl belonged with the fever of a pair back-to-back, the glass of whisky, the piano beat in the dance hall, the smoke and smell and the sound of men and men's women.

When you looked at Bernie, you saw a home and a black range in the kitchen and a table where three times a day you sat down opposite this girl and your grace forever included her presence. You saw in time a rocking chair and babies in her arms and you saw the body of life and the breast of life and you saw your own immortality. You even saw the end of life, as I saw it in my own father and mother when I was at home, comfortable and packed with memories and jokes and habits, and steps taken together.

It had come too soon and I knew it. I wasn't ready for it yet. I didn't really want it yet. But I wanted it someday, and I wanted it with Bernie, and Bernie might not sit and wait. There were nights when I laid over at the ranch when we were all sitting together in the big room with the lamps lit and Bernie was piecing on a quilt, or braiding rags for another rug, or patching or mending, or helping Bucky with her lessons, when I yearned for her so much that I was not only willing but eager to make it right now . . . no matter what.

I proposed to her within two months. She set me right back on my heels. Under all that prettiness and softness there was bone and iron. She didn't want a stagefaring man and said so. "When I marry," she said, "it won't be to any stage driver. You're a reckless lot. All of you drink too much and you gamble too much and you're on the road too much. What kind of husband would you be, I'd like to know!"

"The best kind," I said. "Gone enough you wouldn't get tired of me. Home enough for the new to last."

"How would you be home enough?" she said. "You aiming to drive this piece of the road the rest of your life, so you'll be home every other night?"

She had me there. It would have driven me crazy. No, there would be times when I would be away for three or four months. Even if I could stand it, I would go stale on one stretch too long.

I did some pondering about it. The only thing I came up with for certain was that I couldn't quit driving. I'd be only half a man if I did. Not even for Bernie could I do it. But, my God, I wanted Bernie. It was pure misery to think of giving her up.

I thought maybe a higher-sounding job and a little more money would appeal to her. "I could take a division," I said. "I been offered this division more times than I've got fingers. Would you settle for that?"

"What good would it do?" she said. "You'd still be gone all the time. Besides, you wouldn't stay with it. You have to be blowing Charge and handling the reins yourself. You wouldn't be satisfied to ride when you could be driving. I know you *that* well by now, anyway."

"If you know me that well," I stormed at her, "you ought to know I *can't* quit driving."

"Then just put me out of your mind," she said, and went switching into the house.

Yes, I thought, just *try* putting you out of my mind. You know damned good and well I can't.

We quarreled and made up and quarreled and made up till Emma said she was sorry she ever brought Bernie out to the ranch and if we didn't quit making so much trouble she was going to send her home. Bernie flared up then and said, "I've got something to say about that, Emma Westmoreland. You try sending me home and I'll move down to Cottonwood Springs and cook for them. Or I'll go to Fort Kearney and work for Oliver Wiggins. I don't mean to go back to Ohio till I'm good and ready."

"See," I told Emma, "she's a westerner already. She'll never go back east now. She just as well to marry me."

Bernie flounced out of the room and Emma lit in on me. "I don't see why," she said, "you can't be satisfied with your floozies in Dobytown or Denver. I don't know why you have to make so much trouble with Bernie."

Emma had never approved of my trifling ways with dance-hall and saloon girls and she tried to regulate them for me, along with my drinking. She was a good Methodist and didn't like my sinfulness. I came right back at her. "Maybe I will. Maybe I will be satisfied with them. Maybe I'll just marry one of them and bring her to the ranch."

"You do," she said, so mad she was spitting, "and we'll be leaving. I won't have any dance-hall hussy in the same house with Bernie and Bucky."

"Why don't you talk some sense into Bernie, then?" I said and stalked out.

I worked on that piece of line until I hated it. I stayed on it longer than I had ever stayed on one stretch of road and took a lot of ribbing from the boys. It was worth it when Bernie and I were getting along well. But we only got along well when I kept quiet about marrying. She was wonderful fun as long as I kept my mouth shut about that.

For a girl from Ohio, it surprised me how quickly and how well she learned to handle herself in the west. She liked to ride and we had many a fine ride together. She learned to shoot and could bring down an antelope as handily as I. She was sparkly and gay and quick to laugh, hardly ever tired, never ill, so sweet and interested in everything, and good, till I forgot and began nagging again. Then her temper flared and we were like a cat and dog in no time.

It was hopeless. She wouldn't say she didn't love me, but she would not say she did, either. She just stood out for something I couldn't give.

We had ridden over to the Bluffs late one evening. It was a favorite ride of hers and she found the broken country of the canyons and bluffs interesting. She had brought a basket supper and it was a wonderful, beautiful time. She was in high spirits. Everything pleased her. We went down to the bottom of the canyon and shot target. I told her how, until the bypass road was made, we drove stage over the Devil's Dive and how it scared all the passengers. "One look at where the road went," I said, "and they refused to ride. We always had to stop and let them out to walk."

"Weren't you ever scared of it yourself?" she asked.

"Yes, until I drove it. Then I learned it's nothing to scare a good driver. What I was *most* scared of, and what every other driver was scared of, was an Indian ambush at the bottom of the canyon. A whole tribe of Indians could hide in these canyons and this broken country, all unbeknownst to travelers."

"Did they ever?"

"Sure. More than one freighter along here has seen a band of Indians come boiling over the rim of these canyons. One minute, nothing but the road and long lonesomeness. Next minute, a skyline full of galloping Indians."

She was thoughtful. "When that happens, what does one do?"

"A stage driver has to try to outrun them, and usually can. That's one reason we have the finest horseflesh money can buy. A freight train will corral up and stand them off."

"When you think of all the hazards," she said, "it's a wonder there's so much travel."

"When you think of all the travel," I said, laughing, "there's remarkably little happens."

We clambered back up to the top and had a quarter-mile race with our horses. On my fine mare, she easily won. Then we had our supper. The sun set, one of those magnificent sunsets so gaudy it looks as if it had been painted on a calendar. She watched it and then it was time to go. "I love this country," she said as we moved toward the horses. "I love it. I don't ever want to go back east. I would stifle there, now. I couldn't breathe."

With deliberate intention I did what I had been longing to do. I pulled her, perhaps more roughly than I meant to, into hard-locked arms and kissed her, endlessly, longingly. She didn't fight me off, but she was not stirred to any great response, either. She simply allowed it. When I let her go, what she did was smooth her hair and rearrange the band of her skirts. I thought, my God, why does a man want to marry a good woman! When you kissed the Pearl she let you know there was a lusty woman inside. There was as much fever in her as there was in you, a hot, excited, impatient fever. Whatever a good woman felt, she was careful to conceal. It wasn't nice to show it. But it was this woman, and not the Pearl, I wanted. "Why won't you marry me?" I said.

"Why won't you quit driving stage?" she said.

"I can't," I said.

"And I can't marry you until you do. I won't even think about it till you quit. Till you get clear out of the stage business."

I caught her hand and swung her around. "If you can tell me you don't love me, I'll never bother you again."

She looked at me quietly, an intent, absorbing look. "Starr, why must you drive? You don't have to. You have the ranch. You have that property in Denver. You don't have to drive stage. Why do you? What is there about it?"

"It's my life," I said.

"It doesn't *have* to be your life," she said, and then she jabbed with a needle. "And it is certainly nothing to be proud of."

"I'm prouder of being a fine reinsman than of anything else in the world," I said. "You don't know, Bernie, you just don't know . . . I can't tell you. You just don't understand."

"I certainly don't," she said, "and I don't intend to, so you can just save your breath. But I can tell you one thing, Starr Fowler. I will *not* marry a road tramp. I won't even consider marrying you till you quit the whole staging business."

I lost my temper and yelled at her. "Which will not likely be till I'm too old to make *any* kind of husband!"

"Don't yell at me," she snapped. "And I don't know as I care one way or the other. *I* don't have to wait all that long. You're not the only husband I can get."

Which was certainly, my Lord, all too true. For every woman in the west there were a dozen men. Bernie was surrounded by men and they weren't all ranch hands and stage drivers. Men of every type and class stopped at our place, freighters, judges, lawyers, businessmen, miners, cavalry officers and men, newspapermen. I could have named half a dozen offhand she would only have had to crook her finger at. It wasn't much consolation to me she didn't, for there was always the threat she would.

We had an unspeaking ride back home and when we went in Emma looked at us and groaned. "I would like," she said, "to take each one of you over my knee. I never saw two more stubborn idiots in my life."

It was the miserable, aching, unholy truth. Bernie thought if I loved her as much as I said I did, I should be willing to give up driving. I thought if she loved me at all she wouldn't ask me to. Her shoulders drooped as she went to her room and when I went outside to put up the horses my feet dragged with lead.

The Christmas dance that year was way down the line at Midway, where Dan Trout kept the station and his sisters ran the dining room. It was a long way to go for a dance, but we all went. Nothing but a blizzard or an Indian war could have kept the women from going.

The officers from Fort Kearney were there, all the ranchers and Overland people, even some businessmen from Denver, and Bernie was so surrounded with men that I only danced one set with her. I made out with Bucky, who was as pretty a dancer as any girl there but a little on the young side for romantic interest. "All the time you're dancing with me," she accused me late in the evening, "you're looking at Bernie and thinking about her."

It was true. She looked like an angel right off the Christmas tree, in a blue silk dress that floated and ruffled about her ankles as she danced. She had taken some blue flowers off a bonnet and made a coronet of them for her hair. She was so pretty and so gay and, needing me not at all for her happiness, so happy as she danced. But I denied watching her to Bucky. "No, I'm not," I said. "This is a pretty tricky step we're doing. I have to keep my mind on it."

"Someday," Bucky said, "I'm going to be as big as Bernie. Then you'll wish you'd paid more attention to me."

"I can't wait," I told her, swinging her wide and looking down at her. "You'll probably be as pretty as Bernie, too."

"I'll be prettier," she said flatly. "Bernie's hair is just old-carpet brown. Mine is red."

"Nobody can argue about that," I said. "It's the reddest hair I ever saw."

"Do you think it's pretty, Starr?"

My mind was already wandering. "The prettiest hair any little girl ever had," I said.

It made her mad. "I'm *not* a little girl! I'm almost thirteen years old!"

I just didn't have any luck with my women at the ranch. All I could do was make all of them mad at me.

It was that night I thought the hell with it. Nothing is ever going to come of it. We're deadlocked. She won't give in and I can't. I'll just keep rubbing myself raw if I hang around any longer. I'm going to move on and put Bernie Buchanan out of my mind and out of my life where I had no business letting her in in the first place.

That decision taken I proceeded to get drunk which didn't help the cause the least little bit. Dan Trout told me the next day I picked three fights handrunning, taking on a ranch man first, moving right on to a lieutenant in B Company, and winding up with him, himself. It sounded likely.

I didn't even stop overnight when we got back to the ranch. Went straight on into Denver and told the General Agent if he had anything open I was ready to try being a division agent. It had been a long time since I had seen much more than one stage of the road at a time. I thought if I widened my world a little, I could get out of myself better and get Bernie out of my mind easier.

He said Tom Audley was getting fiddlefooted and if I wanted it I could have the Atchison division. I said that suited me fine.

Going east I went through the ranch like any other passenger, with one difference. While they ate I gathered my belongings together. Ed and I talked a few minutes. We had long since put an assistant station keeper in because Ed was so busy with the store and the ranch. The Indian, Popo, was there with a load of buffalo hides and Ed didn't have much time. There wasn't much to say anyway. We had a very smooth operation, but if I was needed he knew he could reach me anywhere along the line simply by starting the word with the next eastbound driver.

I noticed the bales of buffalo robes stacked around on the floor. "Looks like he brought more this time," I said.

"About double what he usually brings," Ed said.

"What's he trading for?"

"He wanted guns, ammunition, as usual. So when I don't have 'em, he wants to be paid outright. Money."

"He's got a connection," I said. "He knows where he can buy them."

"Probably."

Bucky stuck her head in the door and said, "They're bringing the stage round, Starr."

"All right," and I told Ed to take care.

Bucky swung on my arm out to the stage. "When will you be back?"

"I don't ever stay away very long, do I?"

"But this time you might," she said. "You're mad at Bernie. You might *never* come back."

"Oh, don't be silly," I said, "this is my home, isn't it?"

"No," she said, quick as a flash, "your home is a stage-coach."

I laughed. "Well, those wheels always roll me this way in time. I won't be gone too long."

Emma came out and cautioned me about not letting my laundry go too long; it made the shirts hard to get clean. And she warned me about drinking too much and she was just ready to advise me again to read my Bible oftener when the driver came out.

I didn't mean to look, but I did, at the dining room door. Bernie was standing in it. She had one hand against her cheek, looking serious and a little sad until she saw me looking at her. Then she smiled and waved me good-bye. I swore at myself for looking because now I would always remember her, framed in the doorway, smiling and waving at me.

Then Bucky wound her little-kid arms around my neck and almost choked my breath off. "Don't forget me," she whispered.

"Good Lord," I said, pulling free, "how could anybody forget you!"

Emma got a handful of skirt and hauled her off. "Bucky, stop that foolishness. You act like he never left before."

The kid was a born actress. She put on a pathetic left-behind look and gazed mournfully at me. "He never did," she said, "not since I've been grown up."

Emma swatted her on the bottom. "You've got some more growing to do before that happens. Get in the house."

The kid's tragic pose broke and she grinned at me as I

climbed up into the seat to the left of the driver. "Don't forget to bring me a present when you come," she yelled.

The hostler turned loose of the off leader's head and we began to roll. We had a young whip-cracking driver, but over the noise of the departure I heard Bucky yell once more, "I want a white rooster! Starrrr! I want a white rooster!"

A white rooster! My God!

Chapter 12

It was a good year, 1863. It was a year of fairly smooth sweet operation for the Overland. In some ways, it was perhaps the best year the line ever had, with less Indian trouble, high efficiency, good service and maybe the peak of financial return. It was a year when the wheels rolled swiftly and well oiled.

In the east, the Union armies were beginning to win the war. That was the summer of Gettysburg and Vicksburg, Chancellorsville and Chickamauga. We kept the gold flowing east and the lines of communication open to California.

It got off to a bad start for me personally. I felt clawed and bruised and wrung out, and for several weeks I took no pleasure in my life. But breaking in on the new job gave me ten thousand things to think about besides Bernie Buchanan, all of them pressing, all of them important, all of them necessary if my division was to operate smoothly.

I rode the line constantly. I rarely took more than a two-day layover at either end, Atchison or Fort Kearney. I had driven various stages of the line before, but I got to know the entire division from a different point of view. I got to know the drivers differently. They were all my friends and I was one of the boys, but as their division agent I learned the individual quirks, characteristics, strengths and faults which had never been important to me before. I had whooped it up with them, liked or disliked them, and that was as far as it went. But now the fact that a man had a weakness for the bottle had to be kept in mind and watched. Maybe he could handle it, maybe he couldn't.

Another man's liking for pretty girls on the box with him had to be considered. Pretty girls, insulted, could make trouble for the Company. This man wasn't as good a driver as I had believed him. His teams constantly had sore mouths. Another man was a better driver than I had realized. This man had lost a lot of weight and had fallen into the habit of dozing along at night. Did he have lung trouble? How long would he be safe as a driver?

Little by little I slowly learned that it isn't true that absence makes the heart grow fonder. Instead, absence deliberate and purposeful blurs images and eases hurts. There came to be whole days when Bernie Buchanan didn't cross my mind oftener than half a dozen times, then several days at a stretch, then a week or two when only passingly, and a little wonderingly, I remembered her and winced again. This was usually when I heard from the ranch.

There was a business note from Ed now and then, usually in Emma's handwriting, with a personal word or two from Emma herself stuck in. It was Bucky who called up the images. She deluged me with letters. Big thick letters in a sprawly handwriting that covered page after page, the lines seesawing up or down and very rarely even. If she went up one line, she went down the next and she crosswrote so that I had to stand on my head to read them. They were full of the smallest details about the family and inevitably there was a lot of news about Bernie. For half a day after getting a letter from Bucky I was irritable and hard to get along with.

I didn't write to anybody. I didn't have time and it wasn't necessary. If I needed to tell Ed something I sent word by the stage drivers. As far as writing Bernie was concerned, I felt that if this break was going to work it had to be a clean break. It wouldn't do any good to fool around with a half break.

Laying over in Atchison, I sometimes rode over to St. Joe and had a visit with my folks. Not often, for once a man goes out on his own, home is never the same again. For one thing, he loses his place in it and it can never be recovered. Life has gone on in the home, the kids have grown, the mother has added a few pounds and some gray hairs, the rooms have been changed about or papered and painted new colors, there's a new piece of furniture that didn't use to be in that place in the hall, the lilac bushes are three feet taller, and the yard which once looked as vast as the prairies has narrowed behind its white paling fence. The family are loving and thoughtful and kind, but more strange than familiar. A lot has been going on with them you weren't there to see or feel with them. There are new jokes you don't know, and new teasings, and new habits and new friends and loves. The place that was yours has been filled and sealed over and it won't ever quite open for you again. It is nothing to be sad about. That's the way it has to be.

At first I wondered why my visits weren't as satisfying as I had expected them to be and why I became restless so soon and ready to leave so early. It took me a while to understand that while I had been working and living *my* life, life here at home hadn't been standing still. It had been going on as busy and as purposeful as my own. We just didn't walk in step any longer. And that wasn't tragic either. Unless you are touched in the head and want to be greedy about everything you ever had, as well as everything that can possibly come to you, it is natural and a pretty good thing. Cutting the leading strings works both ways. If it frees the colt, it also frees the sire.

Freighting was increasingly important in those days. The mines were opening up fast and towns were growing up around them. Every blessed thing people needed, from tools and mine machinery to salt and flour and canned milk, had to be freighted out to them; and as is always the case when people are almost entirely dependent on imported supplies, prices were as high as the mountains themselves. My father's freight business alone was making him a very wealthy man.

But he foresaw the end of freighting. "When the war is over," he said, "the big push will be for railroads west. Wagon trains will be a thing of the past then." He was making the most of the good freighting days but he was planning ahead and he not only knew where he was going and what he would do next, he was looking forward to it. "Freighting has provided for my family," he said. "It has given me a good business reputation and it has earned me a sound base." He grinned. "But a man don't want to be a bullwhacker *all* his life." More and more his interests were centered in Colorado. He had acquired considerable property in and around Denver. He was going back to the mountains.

"I just want to know one thing," I said. "How are you going to get Mama out there?"

When my father brought my mother from Kentucky to St. Joseph, she said that was as far west as she was going. In fact, she thought St. Joe *was* the Far West. And the jumping-off place to nowhere. She wasn't, she always said briskly, going to let Joe Fowler inch her out across those prairies to some heathen place in the mountains. She would like him to know she wasn't born with four hoofs for jumping from rock to rock.

He grinned, a big, slow, happy grin. "We swapped out. She's tired of me being gone all the time. I told her I'd sell out in three more years if she would move to Denver." He broke into laughter. "Don't tell her, but she don't know I've been meaning to sell by then anyway. I don't want to hang on too long. I want to get out before the railroads come . . . while there's still a few years of freighting left and I can still get a top price for the outfit."

"I hope you've not misfigured," I said.

"Don't think I have. The war is a long way from being over yet. Then it will take the country a year or two to recover enough to begin building. I think I have it worked out about right." We were in the dining room, where we usually were when we talked together. We each had a drink. He reached out and set his glass on a table and hooked his hands behind his head. "Timing is one of the most important things in life. The time you make your moves. I got out of the beaver trade and went into freighting at the right time. It'll soon be time to get out of freighting. But my clock tells me I can head for the mountains again pretty soon."

"You'll be glad, won't you?"

"Yes." It was a simple, flat admission.

I added another dollop of whisky to my glass. "You ever been sorry you left them?"

"No. No, not really." He said it slow. "Not really. They pull at you, when you've spent a lot of time in them. If I hadn't married and had such a whopping big family, I might not have left. I might have stayed on and become an old mountain tramp . . . like Jim Bridger. But you can't actually squeeze that much juice out of one way of living. You'll run out unless you keep filling yourself up."

I laughed. "Well, you're a long way from running dry yet."

He chuckled, too. "I know it. I've still got enough old horse left in me to go back . . . make something pretty good of the years left to me." He became thoughtful. "You know, I took gold out of those mountains behind Denver when I wasn't as old as you are. Beaver gold. Queer. Men are taking the pure stuff out of them now. The gold camps are just about where South Park pinches out. I've spent *so* many seasons trapping those streams up through there.

"Why, just over the Rabbit Ears from the camps we had to cut Pete Smith's leg off. And we buried Pierre Driant there. Pete was one of my boys. We were heading up for the Wind Rivers and we guided Driant's outfit for him."

He brooded for a while over his memories, then shook them off. "I've got a number of things going in Denver and up at Golden, but what really gets me excited is something else." He made a shallow cup of his hands. "There's a section in the lower end of the Park that lies about like this—like a saucer in the mountains. I've taken up some of that land and I want to run some cattle on it and build me a little cabin up there. I'd like for Mahaley and me to spend summers up there. Buffalo used to like that hole. We made meat there many a time. Cattle will like it, too." He eased his big shoulders on the cushions and laughed. "I've spent so many years making money that I can't abide throwing it away. That piece of land will have to pay for itself or it will bother me. But cattle ought to do it."

That piece of land paid for itself all right. As foresighted as he was, my father didn't foresee that his land up there was right on top of one of the biggest money mountains in the world and that long after he and my mother were dead and gone, Cripple Creek gold would line the pockets of every one of his children. All he wanted was a log cabin in a place where the ghosts of his old friends still walked. In his lifetime that's all he had out of it.

I've never known whether to be glad or sorry he didn't live to see it ravaged for the glittering stuff buried underneath the land. He would have exulted in the wealth. He was a man of his times, a practical man. A successful man, to him, was a man who made a lot of money. He didn't quarrel with the measuring stick. But I think he would have grieved inside at what happened to the peace of South Park.

After taking over the division I missed driving. I knew I would, but I worked like a dog to be as good a division agent as it was in me to be. I rode the line steadily, daily, and riding for much longer periods than I ever had before, I got a very good feeling of what it was like for the passengers, and their comfort became more important to me. I began to keep a close eye on the eating stations and on the occasional stops where they could lay over and rest a night. I could see the entire line differently, the whole long road stretched out and covered, day after day after day—not the patchwork pieces of the drivers' runs, but the whole long snake-length uncoiling forever ahead of you.

Come ride it with me.

Chapter 13

Come ride it with me.

Ride it to Denver. Choose May for your journey if possible, for it is the pleasantest month of the year and on the Overland it offers you a wider variety of pleasure than any other. The trees will be fully leafed out, the prairies will be tender and green with new grass and brilliant with wild flowers. Halfway to Fort Kearney you'll breathe air that not only smells like sweet perfume but tastes like it. And when you come to the plains May is kinder to you, with less heat than full summer brings. So, choose May if you can.

You will arrive on the Missouri River by railroad and then cross the river on a steam ferry to Atchison. The stage office is in the Planter's Hotel, so you will buy your ticket there. Until 1863, it would have cost you seventy-five dollars to Denver, with thirty pounds of luggage free, all over that costing you one dollar per pound. In 1863 the fare went up to one hundred dollars to Denver.

At eight o'clock in the morning, any day of the week except occasionally Monday when there may be too much express for the stage to carry passengers, you can take your departure.

Try to pick Tuesday, Thursday or Saturday to depart and catch Bob Hodge as your driver. This is my old friend who rode out the runaway with me when a line broke and who by his wise counsel saved me from a possible disaster.

He is a big heavyset man who looks a little like an Indian and stands as straight as one. I have already said that he was one of the New England drivers who went to California around 1850 and drove for James Birch, who later came with us about the time the L. & P.P. became the C.O.C. & P.P. He found his driving home on this run out of Atchison. "Here's where I stay," he said, and he has never again moved.

He will be driving four perfectly matched sorrels. This team is known as the Arkansaws. Bob often lets them out on the ten-mile stretch to Lancaster and they do it without any trouble in forty minutes. Notice the harness. It is hung all over with little ivory rings. This is a fancy of Bob's. When he comes out to take the reins, Bob will be dressed in a fine buckskin suit. He dislikes the Overland look and fancies looking wild western.

Once aboard, much of your enjoyment in your journey depends on the luck of the draw in your companions. I hope there will be no big fat woman who insists on the right-hand corner of the back seat and takes up far more than her third of it. But if there is, don't argue with her. Just console yourself with the fact that nothing makes a better cushion against the jolts and the bumps of the journey than a big fat woman.

There are three seats in the stage, to hold nine passengers. The back seat is considered the choice because it faces forward. The front seat, facing back, is the next most comfortable. The middle seat is to be avoided if possible. It has no back except a broad strap which is detachable. The seat itself folds up to allow passengers to get in and out. Many people, however, like the middle seat. There's considerably more headroom over it, if you happen to be tall. And if the stage isn't crowded, a single riding the middle seat can stretch out and sleep.

There will be more men than women riding with you and they will be all sorts and kinds. I hope there won't be, but in all likelihood there will be at least one long-winded, loudmouthed parson, politician or lawyer. An orator in the narrow confines of a stagecoach can be mighty tedious. But you'll learn to sleep to the tune of his chin music.

I like kids well enough, but kids traveling are the greatest nuisance you'll find. They eat all the time, tend to have motion sickness and don't always make the window before spewing. They whine and cry and wiggle. Many a time I've taken a kid on the box with me so not only the mother could have some relief but the other passengers could keep their sanity.

After the first day there's likely to be a poker game going on, day and night. It's a way to pass time some people like. Don't get involved unless you're pretty sharp. We can't control the professional gamblers who ride the line and make a business of fleecing the passengers. At one time we had so many complaints that Holladay made a rule against card playing on the stages. It was unenforceable. So get into a game at your own risk.

At least one passenger is invited to ride the box with the driver, and it is the driver who decides who it will be. Unless, that is, some very important person, or one of the stage officials, is traveling with you. Company policy gives such people the box seat, if they want it. Otherwise, it's the driver's choice. It may be a pretty girl, some fellow he knows, or just somebody his eye lights on and likes the cut of his jib. Or it may be you, if you're lucky.

Some of the stages have an extra seat on the top to carry two more passengers, three in a pinch. And even without the seat, men in a hurry to get to the mines will often ride the roof rather than wait over another day.

Bob will be the last person to board. He's a showman and he makes a big show of his walk-around and mounting the box. This is his moment. Give it to him. Once he's settled on the box, however, no time is wasted and he will take you out at a brisk, lively pace. If it's one of his lucky days the gait won't be broken for ten miles. But he may not be lucky. The travel on the road may be troublesome, or one of the horses may be feeling lazy, or playful, or frisky. It isn't likely with the Arkansaws, but it has been known to happen. If it does, Bob's day is ruined.

If you're riding the box you'll notice that Bob takes a nip from the bottle he keeps under his cushion from time to time. Drink is his only weakness. He has always been a hard drinker and he can't go more than thirty minutes without a nip now. But don't let it worry you. He never gets drunk and he can handle that string with more liquor in him than most men can carry and walk.

You will head slightly northwest out of Atchison and about a half hour out you will meet the inbound stage. It is due to arrive at Atchison at nine o'clock. This early in your journey you will probably pay very little attention to it. At eight-thirty tonight, however, when you catch the glimmer of lights approaching, you will likely ask the driver what they are. "Eastbound stage," he will tell you.

You may accept it, for the moment, as the side lamps of the coach come nearer and nearer. Then, having pondered it a little, you may remember the stage service is daily. You can only take a stage out of Atchison each morning. You know one coach each day is also leaving the western terminal. Now, it is six days to Denver. You do a quick mental calculation and come up with six stages meeting. But you met an eastbound coach this morning at eight-thirty. How can you be meeting another eastbound stage this soon?

I have yet to meet a passenger, no matter how clever or shrewd or smart, who isn't momentarily confused and who doesn't have to have it explained. When you left Atchison, six stages were already on the road from Denver. Six more will leave, one each day you travel, so you will actually meet twelve coaches in the six days. The last one you meet will be half an hour out of Denver, leaving as you arrive.

It worries some people to the point they get out pencil and paper and begin figuring. One distinguished gentleman who rode the box with me spent the entire time of my run drawing little boxes to represent stages, trying to work out their precise meeting points. All he had to do was ask, but he wanted to calculate it for himself.

Probably not until you reach the Platte valley will you begin to anticipate the meeting. Till you reach the head-waters of the Little Blue you are traveling in fairly settled country. There are farms occasionally, and there are even little towns. There are people coming and going in private vehicles. It is timbered country and looks very much like the country you are accustomed to. And the stage seems part of the picture.

But when you get out on the plains and there is no more timber, in fact very little vegetation of any kind, when there are fewer and fewer people and settlements, when all around you there is that vast spread of strange-looking land, like nothing you ever saw before, and over you that immense tent of sky, if there is a long piece of road without travelers you will begin to long to see something else moving. Even a freight train, which means you must eat dust till you're past, is welcome.

And long before you know another stage is due, you will begin watching, first for the tiny cloud of dust, far, far ahead. You can't calculate precisely, to the minute or even the hour, when you'll meet the next stage. It may be ahead of schedule, or it may be a little late. But you'll be peering ahead, watching—waiting for it. Then there's the little cloud of dust. It could be only a whirlwind. It could be a small band of Indians. You keep watching. Then, "It is! It's the stage. I can make it out now!"

Slowly it looms up, each horse becoming distinct, and you can see the rocking motion of the stage itself. It seems to be traveling very fast, much faster than your own vehicle. Dust billows from the wheels. Now you pick up the first sounds, the crack of the driver's whip, maybe, which is like a revolver shot and carries a long way. Then, over the jangle and creak of your own coach, you can hear the other. Your driver has hauled to his side of the road by now. If he has a message for the other driver, the team is slowing. If not, and the other teams slows, your own team will begin to slow. The conversation between the drivers is cryptic. It may even sound meaningless. "Pete's drunk."

"Son-of-a-gun! That's twice this month."

One may offer the other a chew of tobacco. "How's the crossing?"

"Floor deep."

The halt is very brief, then on you go. What information have they exchanged? Well, one driver has told the other that he'll have to double today. The next driver is drunk and can't take his stage. The other has learned that the water in the next creek crossing is high—floor deep on the stage.

You and the passengers in the other stage have perhaps exchanged a few words. You have, at any rate, had that strange, uncanny feeling that these people have been where you're going, and are going where you've been, neither of you can communicate this to the other, for truly that is all you have in common. Meet, nod and pass on. But the next hour, maybe, is lighter for you because of a different human contact. There are some people in the world besides those rubbing shoulders with you inside the stage.

But all of this is ahead of you yet. At the moment you are leaving Atchison, and Bob Hodge is driving you rapidly

through what most of you will think is very beautiful country. The land is rich and good, the fields already plowed
and planted, the homes neat and painted. If you are an
easterner you approve of all this and you comment on
it.

It isn't important that I don't agree with you, but I don't.
I call it pretty country, not beautiful country. It is fast
settling up and it is cozy and snug and fruitful. It has its
merits. But to me this is chained country—country where
work is sweat behind a plow. Where you plod along prod-
ding the blue-tailed ox.

Beauty has to have more scope than this. It has to be
wider and go deeper. For me it has to be flung as wide as
the plains and peeled down of timber to the bare rind of
the land, stark and structured and uncluttered. Too many
years on the Platte road make me feel smothered in grassed
and timbered and hilled country. I want to push it all out
of the way and let the wind through and see a long way
ahead.

Lancaster, ten miles out, is your first stop. This is a
swing station. You can get out and stretch your legs if you
like while the team is being changed, but you aren't really
needing it yet. The team is quickly hitched in, and inside of
three minutes the stage is rolling again.

I will not henceforth tell you about all the swing stations. They may change slightly in appearance, but their
function is the same the entire distance. They furnish no
facilities for passengers and have only one purpose—to
furnish the next team for the stage. Two men usually man
the station.

It is fourteen miles from Lancaster to Kennekuk, the
first home station out of Atchison. There are half a dozen
frame houses at Kennekuk, a store and a blacksmith shop.
The old stone building of the Kickapoo Indian agency is
one of the landmarks of the settlement. You will arrive at
1:00 P.M. and there is a twenty-minute stop. You will have
dinner here and it will cost you fifty cents. There will be
every good thing to eat. Tom Perry is the station keeper
and his wife is a fine cook. She makes the best coffee on
the line, so take a second or third cup. You'll have coffee all
the way. Even in the middle of the night you can get a
cup of hot coffee. Drivers and stage people drink it by the

gallon, and a pot is always brewing at every station. I can't promise you it is all delicious, however. Some make it strong, some make it weak, and the quality of the water makes a big difference, too. But coffee you can get when you want it.

You'll tell Bob Hodge good-bye here. He'll appreciate it if you tell him it was a good ride. He knows it was, probably the smoothest, finest twenty-five miles you'll have the whole journey, but it would be nice if you said so. Bob lays over here and takes the eastbound stage into Atchison tomorrow.

Uncle Charley Mannville will probably be your next driver. He's a little shrimpy fellow with a beard and a cud of tobacco in his jaw. He'll look old to you, and for a stage driver he is. He's fifty. He's driven a lot of stage. Used to drive for the Hockaday lines.

Shortly after you leave Kennekuk the road enters the Kickapoo Indian reservation. Some say this is the richest land in Kansas. It may be. It is rolling, with small streams crossing it, and a lot of fine timber, walnut, elm, oak and cottonwood. It is twelve miles to the Kickapoo station, which is on the reservation. You will arrive at 3:00 P.M. Kickapoo is a swing station.

Thirteen miles farther on is Log Chain. This station is kept by a stage driver, Bob Ridley. He took up a quarter section of land here and is doing well with his farm. Log Chain is a home station and you arrive at 5:15. Bob will take over the lines here. If you're riding the box see if you can get him to tell you about the time he was taking a new and empty express coach to Denver, all alone. Way up on the Platte he was chased by a band of Indians. Ask him how he escaped. He will say, "It was a picnic. My mules could outrun any of them Indian scrubs. I just whipped 'em up, tied the lines around my waist, hauled out my artillery and commenced blazing away."

"And luck?"

"A little." His voice will drawl deceptively. "Wounded four and killed three of the rascals."

Sixty miles out of Atchison and twelve hours of riding for you, you reach the town of Seneca just a little before dark. This is your supper stop. The station is kept by a man from New Hampshire named John E. Smith. If you're tired or ailing you can lay over and take a room, for he keeps a good hotel. He has fed and slept more famous people crossing the plains by Overland than any other hotelkeeper on the line. And it is a good hotel, a two-story frame building painted white, and kept fresh-painted all the time. Mrs. Smith is a wonderful cook and you will enjoy your supper here. Her hot biscuits are extra light and you'll probably eat more than you should with her good fresh butter and grape jelly.

When you leave, the stage lamps will be lit, for it is full dark now and you will ride all night without seeing much of the country unless there's a moon.

Tommy Ryan may be your next driver. He began driving stage on the old Butterfield line. He drove out of Fort Smith, Arkansas, down the old Choctaw road, all across Texas. He moved up to the central route with the line in 1861. Tommy talks to his team a lot. If you're tired, now, and riding inside, Tommy's voice will be a part of the night sound, talking his horses along.

You'll pass through Frogtown and never know it, except there'll be a new team.

Next is Guittard's. Guittard is French and he settled at this station in 1857 with his big family of sons and daughters. The oldest son, Xavier, conducts all the stage business. He is the only one who speaks English. This is a home station for drivers and, although it isn't a meal stop, a couple of old man Guittard's daughters are usually on hand and can give you a piece of pie and hot coffee if you want it.

Until 1862, your next stop would have been Marysville, where you would have crossed the Big Blue River and followed on through Hollenberg and Rock Creek. Marysville is a pretty little town, but Ben Holladay had some kind of trouble with the businessmen there and decided to shift the line to the north and leave them off.

So in 1863, you won't go through Marysville. You will go on north to Oketo and cross the Big Blue at the place on a rope ferry.

Next, just as daylight is coming, is Pawnee. This is a home station kept by George Hulbert, a driver. George's wife will have a good breakfast ready for you and after the long night her biscuits, fried ham or chicken, and eggs will taste mighty good. George will take the lines here.

Grayson's is fourteen miles.

Then comes Big Sandy, another home station. You have left Kansas now and are in Nebraska, and you'll be in Nebraska a long, long way. Ed Farrell, another driver, keeps the station, but the most important thing about Big Sandy is that Daniel Jenkins keeps a store here and there is a post office in it, the first on the line. Dan is the postmaster, or as we used to say the local Nasby. Petroleum V. Nasby, the newspaper writer, had made all postmasters notorious, so that for a good many years they were spoken of as Nasbys.

So, if you have discovered you need something this is your opportunity to buy it, and if you want your people back home to have news of you, you can mail a letter here.

Ed takes the lines here and will swing you up one of the finest roads you ever saw. You don't yet really appreciate these roads along here, though. They are no more than you are used to back home. If you were going the other direction, however, coming to the end of the long trip across the plains, this road would seem as smooth as a kitchen floor after what you'd ridden over. Drivers going east can always make up lost time along here.

I once drove the fourteen miles between Big Sandy and Thompson's, with twelve passengers and all the mail and luggage, in fifty-eight minutes. It held the record for a number of years. I had a team to do it with, though—the Red Rovers. They were all pony express horses. The off leader was a little black horse named Hunter. He carried the first pouch of pony letters that crossed the Missouri out of St. Joseph on April 3, 1860. He could travel twenty-five miles in two hours and not even work up a lather. He was the finest stage horse I ever held a rein on.

Kiowa is another fourteen miles and another home station. It is kept by Jim Douglas, a stage driver who will take the lines here. Jim Douglas is the driver who lost a wheel on this stretch when Bernie was riding with him. He is also the driver who had the hotbox on this stretch that has become so famous. I've heard that story about Jim's hotbox almost as many times as I've heard the one about Horace Greeley's famous ride with Hank Monk down the last mountain stretch to Placerville. It will do to repeat, however.

Jim had a hotbox and had nothing to dope the axle with. He was madder than a short-tailed cow in fly season at the last driver who'd neglected to dope the wheels, but that didn't help matters any. He was about to cut a spindle in two, so he had to think of something to use for padding. He grabbed a handful of grass and began wadding it up. A passenger suddenly spoke up. "What you need is grease, isn't it?"

"Yes, sir," Jim said, "what I need is grease and mighty bad, but we are fresh out of that commodity."

"Reckon cheese parings would do? I've got a rind of cheese in my satchel."

"We'll give it a try," Jim said. "Cheese is sure greasy enough."

Jim pared the chunk of cheese into small shavings and filled the axle chock full of them. He said dope itself wouldn't have worked any better. They rolled right on into the next station without so much as another squeak. When Jim tells the story, and he will if you ask him, he always winds up by saying, "I've not been caught without a hunk of cheese in the front boot since then. I wouldn't pick up my lines without knowing I had my cheese along. You never know when a handful of cheese parings are going to come in handy."

Little Blue is twelve miles, then comes Liberty Farm, on the north bank of the river. You are now 193 miles out of Atchison and it is night again. Liberty Farm is kept by a Mormon family named Lemmon. It is a home station and supper is served here. I don't know what a Mormon is doing keeping a station here—whether he got this far on the journey to Zion and played out, whether Brigham Young set him up here, or whether he just liked the place and settled here. But he keeps a good station, farms a good farm, makes a good living. You won't get so much as the use of his outhouse free, for Mormons are above all else shrewd about money, but you'll get your money's worth. The outhouse is clean.

Lew Hill will climb up on the box here. Lew has a good

voice and likes to sing to his horses. Many drivers do, especially at night when it's lonesome on the box and when a team could spook easily. It soothes them as they rock along. All through his run you'll hear him singing, soft, easy, sort of crooning his team on. It's a nice sound at night, when you're riding inside and you're tired and sleepy but too crowded to sleep soundly. Nice to know there's a man on the box singing you through the miles and the dark.

Just a short distance west of Liberty Farm the road leaves the valley of the Little Blue and begins to angle across the divide toward the Platte. Fifteen miles out comes the Lone Tree swing station. You have left timber behind now. If you could see it, the lone tree perched on top of the bare round mound might look tall and lonesome to you. Shuddering lonesome. It is something of a landmark since it can be seen for miles in all directions. Most daytime travelers remark on how bare the country looks. It does, for it is bare. From here on you will not see any timber except the scattered cottonwoods now and then and the willows along the Platte. From here on I breathe better. From here on it begins to be my kind of country.

Ten miles from Lone Tree is Thirty-Two-Mile Creek, a home station. This is your breakfast stop. It is a long, one-story log building kept by Charlie Emery, another driver. This is a busy stop, for the eastbound stage is either already here or will be shortly, and two stages and two sets of passengers make quite a lively crowd. But you'll never eat a better meal. In fact, until you get to Fort Kearney the food is uniformly good. There is plenty of fresh milk and butter, cream, eggs, ham, bacon, grouse, prairie chicken, wild turkey and fruit.

Charlie may take the lines here himself, but if it's a layover day for him, Enoch Cummings will be your driver. I hope he will be.

Enoch is the driver who looked at a green kid and knew he was funking out of facing up to his next big driving test and put iron in his guts to make him do it. He is the driver who made me drive the Devil's Dive.

He is a tall, handsome man who comes from Virginia. There is still a lot of Virginia courtliness in his manner. He came west when he was around sixteen and began driving for the Kansas Stage Company on the Kaw. He's been with the Overland since the old L. & P.P. days and is one of the few drivers who is senior to me. He is the finest reinsman with the Company. He may be the finest natural reinsman God ever made. I wouldn't quarrel with anybody who said so.

Women passengers eye Enoch with considerable favor and like to be asked to ride the box with him. He has an eye for a pretty girl, but that's as far as it goes. He's in love with a wonderful girl in Seneca.

Enoch's team is one of the prettiest on the road—matched, beautiful blacks. With the red Concord washed down, the gold scrollwork glittering, and the blacks hitched ready to go it's something to see—you'd like a picture in color, or a painting of it.

He'll move you along briskly and you'll be glad he does because you are now coming to a desolate stretch of road among sandhills, all broken and crisscrossed with a lot of ravines and gullies. There is no vegetation of any kind, not even a bush, and to you it will seem a lonesome, dreary land. It weighs heavily on you and you begin to remember the map and that part of it marked the "Great American Desert." This is the divide. You are crossing from the Little Blue, which rises not far away, over to the Platte valley. Here you will slowly climb to an elevation of two thousand feet and at Summit, the next swing station, you will be at the highest point between the Missouri and the Platte.

Summit will look very dismal to you. There is nothing here at all but the land and God and two wind-crazy stock tenders. Nobody likes to work here and we can't keep tenders stationed here very long. They say it drives them crazy. We are constantly having to replace the men here. The Company didn't want to put a swing station here, but it is twenty-five miles from Thirty-Two-Mile Creek to the Platte River, and that is too far for a single stage. Like it or not, a relay had to be located here.

Now you come swinging down into the Platte valley and the whole country changes. Before you is the wide shallow river. Its course is marked by cottonwood trees and the river is full of islands covered with low brushy willows. There are so many islands that before Fort Kearney was built the spot was known as "Thousand Islands." The bottoms along the river are covered with tall rank grass. The road is sandy but hard and Enoch will bowl you right along.

You'll pass through and stop briefly at a place with three names. On your schedule it is listed as Hook's. It is named for the man who owns the store and is the postmaster here. The Postal Department in Washington lists the place as Valley City. Stage people call it Dogtown because of the hundreds of prairie dog villages all about. This is the second post office on the route and the stop here is merely to leave and pick up way mail.

It is only seven miles on into Fort Kearney from here, thirty-two miles from Thirty-Two-Mile Creek. Enoch will let the team out now. He knows you are eager to arrive. Because there is no timber except along the river, you can see the fort five or six miles out and the first sight of it excites you and lifts your spirits. It is a green oasis in the wide flat land and it looks cool and beautiful and restful. For you have begun to feel the heat a little more and you are beginning to be more than a little road-weary.

The first commandant of the fort, which was built in 1848, couldn't bear the flat and empty land, so he had his boys move a lot of cottonwood saplings up from the river and set them out all around the buildings and the square. They are big trees now, almost twenty years old, and they give a fine shade.

Close up, Fort Kearney isn't as handsome as it looks five miles out. No military installation is. The buildings are pretty old and the wind and sand are hard on paint. Most of the buildings are log and sod, but they are slowly being replaced by the regulation frame barracks. But it's good to see the flag flying and it's good to see the men in uniform. It's comforting to know that way out here in the middle of nowhere is this piece of land owned by the United States government, and that its purpose here is to protect you as you travel, to protect the emigrants moving farther west, and protect the United States Mail.

You'll arrive at 1:00 P.M. A crowd of people will be gathered for the arrival. Troops from the fort will be here, officers, and townspeople from Dobytown. You are now

253 miles from Atchison, you are fifty-three hours out and you are in your third day of travel. You probably feel like it's been three weeks.

Fort Kearney is the end of the Atchison division. It is also a junction point for the short lines from Omaha and Nebraska City to make connection with the Overland. But you needn't worry. Traveling Overland, your seat is safe.

The eating station here is one of the best on the line. Oliver Wiggins runs it. The food here is almost as fancy and good as you'll get at the Planter's House in Denver. I never ate mountain trout here, which is a favorite with Colonel McNassar at the Planter's, but Oliver's cooks can do wonders with buffalo, elk, antelope, wild turkey, chicken, duck and grouse.

Major Wiggins is getting on in years now. He is a Canadian by birth and an old fur trapper. He worked for the Hudson's Bay Company when my father was a free trapper out of Taos. He served as a guide for Frémont on one of his expeditions in the forties and he often scouted with Kit Carson. It is your privilege to meet him.

There is a post office at Fort Kearney. The postmaster is Moses Sydenham, an Englishman who has become an American citizen. He has lately brought his mother and sisters over from England and bought a ranch not far away for their home. He calls it Hopeville.

You will have the usual twenty minutes in which to eat and stretch your legs and maybe mail another letter back home.

Your next driver may very well be a young fellow who rode Pony Express for a while, Billy Cody. He got a very early start in the west. When he was only twelve years old he began working for the big freighting outfit, Russell, Majors & Waddell, as messenger. They frequently had such long wagon trains they broke them into sections. Billy carried messages between sections on several journeys across the plains.

Then he rode Pony Express on a section along the Sweetwater in Wyoming. He drove Overland about a year. Later, he worked as a meat hunter for the Union Pacific when they were laying track. He got his nickname, Buffalo

Bill, from the fact that he killed so many buffalo to feed the construction crews. In eighteen months he is said to have killed over four thousand. It averaged eight buffalo a day.

Billy is a show-off and *not* a very skilled driver, which is the main reason he only lasted a year on the Overland. He's a whip-cracker and the ladies fancy him because, given him his due, he's a right handsome lad with his long greased curls. None of the boys who knew him in his younger days was surprised when he took to circus driving. It was just about all he could do. What did surprise us was how that hard-drinking peacock had the business sense to make three months on the Pony Express and a year on the Overland pay off so well. My! My!

Well, when you leave Fort Kearney you begin that long pull up the water grade of the Platte. It looks level but it isn't. It is all uphill and all dead pull, but the pull is so gradual that only the teams and the drivers know it.

From here on the road follows along the south bank of the river and is hardly ever out of sight of the broad, shallow stream. For the most part the road is very wide. There is room for a dozen normal roads to lie parallel, and the hundreds of thousands of wagons and other wheeled vehicles traveling it have beaten it out hard and level.

The river is always there and it is always interesting. It is almost a mile wide, but that doesn't mean there is a mile of water. The channel of water may be quite narrow, the rest of the riverbed taken up with sandbars and willow islands. There are thousands of these bars and islands grown over with low, thickety, scrubby little willow bushes.

The river is muddy and sluggish looking, very shallow except when flooding, and it is forever shifting its course. When it is low, you can wade across at any point, but in flood there is a dangerously fast current. And it is a treacherous river because of the quicksand bed. Old-timers say the reason it doesn't have any banks is because they are quicksand and they rise and fall with the river. That may be. But it is true that it seems to flow right along on top the ground, bankless, as if it were too old or too tired to cut itself a bed.

On his first sight of the Platte, Artemus Ward said if it was stood on edge it might make a pretty good river.

Farther back in time some wit said of it that it was too thin to plow and too thick to drink.

Farther west, on the opposite bank, the land occasionally rises to form low bluffs which are topped with black scrub cedar. Farther west also, on this side of the river, there is a crisscrossing of canyons and gulches and ravines, at the bottom of which little creeks rush down to join the river. This is the broken land, way out on the plains yet from the mountains, but it is the first wrinkling of the earth's skin which is thrust up from those giant upheaved peaks and deep, deep canyons of the Rockies.

If you saw any Indians before you got to Fort Kearney they were very likely Pawnees. Once this tribe was very numerous on the plains, but they have been greatly reduced by smallpox and cholera. Don't be misled by their begging ways around the stations into believing they are spiritless and tame, though. They can still give a good accounting of themselves, such a good accounting that even the warlike Sioux treat them with great respect.

From Fort Kearney on, however, you'll be seeing Indians much more often. They will be the Cheyennes, Sioux, Arapahoes, even the Kiowas and Comanches. You will see them in small bands usually, drifting up and down the valley, going to and from the various ranches and trading stores where they trade their buffalo, elk and antelope skins for the trinkets, food and tools they need.

If you have never seen wild Indians before you will find them a little scary, very colorful and sometimes pretty ridiculous looking. Those who drift up and down the valley have been around white men a long, long time. They have adopted a good many of the white man's tools and utensils and in some cases the white man's clothing. But they are like children playing dressup with the clothing. They keep what is comfortable of their own costume and add on what takes their fancy of the white man's.

You'll see a Cheyenne warrior, maybe, with a high silk hat sitting atop his eagle feathers, a black frock coat buttoned around his bare torso and nothing but a breechclout below. Or you'll see one with U. S. Cavalry breeches below, a cavalry hat above, and a woman's gorgeous red satin opera cape floating about his shoulders. Mostly these garments they take a fancy to are presents or are bought in trade, but you never know, and if they could talk they might have a grim story of attack and massacre and rifled trunks to tell.

Indians have a strong instinct for clowning and they have a wild ribald sense of humor. This doesn't mean they are simple-minded, or that they aren't as dangerous as wild animals when feeling roiled or otherwise prodded into an ugly mood. You can't take it for granted that any band you meet is wholly friendly. If the circumstances are right, and their mood is angry, your driver may suddenly have to lay on the whip and make a run for it. And the men passengers may have to haul out their artillery and commence using it. The fact that so few passengers ever lost their lives in Indian attacks is mostly due to the fine stock the Company used. Even pulling a heavy coach most Overland horses could outrun Indian ponies, and Indians, not liking to take casualties, usually gave over the chase when the next station appeared in view.

The home of the Southern Cheyennes is between the Platte and the Arkansas, but this time of the year, May, the Northern Cheyennes and the Sioux and the Northern Arapahoes come down onto the Platte to hunt buffalo. Watch for their encampments. A Sioux encampment is an especially beautiful sight. Their tepees are decorated beautifully, painted in bright blue and dark red and black and they are so big that some of them easily measure twenty or thirty feet in diameter. A whole village of these gorgeous bleached and painted skin tepees is a magnificent sight.

You can tell a Cheyenne encampment because they set up their lodges in a circle. You can even tell which way they are going, because they leave the circle open in the direction they are moving.

When you leave Fort Kearney you go through Platte station and Craig and then you reach Plum Creek, the next home station. In 1861 a telegraph office was put there and there is also now a store. The ranchman who took over the station when Ed Westmoreland left runs the store.

Now, this is the heart of the buffalo country. You will see your first ones along here. When I first began driving stage there were so many that often I had to stop the stage and wait for a herd to cross the road. You will eat a lot of buffalo meat from now on. And the price of your meals goes up here. You've been paying fifty cents. Until 1863, the increase was to seventy-five cents. But now you'll pay one dollar and the food is not quite so good. There is no longer any fresh milk and cream. You'll take condensed milk now. You'll get very little bacon or ham. It will be buffalo, elk or antelope meat. There is no fresh fruit, either. It's all dried.

You get a new driver at Plum Creek. Along here on this stretch of road I hope you aren't traveling in the dark of the moon, for while the Platte is a muddy, sluggish, shallow river and you can weary of its monotony in the daytime, in bright, waxing moonlight it is magical. Its siltiness and its shallowness refuse the moon any depth and they turn the light back into blazing silver glory, which at times is a broad sheet like hammered steel, at other times a narrow silvered sword blade. And there are always the dark and patched shadows of the willows. You will forgive the Platte most of its sins when you ride its course by moonlight.

Willow Island is the swing stop, then fourteen miles west of Willow Island you reach Midway. This station is called Midway because it is almost exactly midway between Atchison and Denver. Dan Trout keeps this station, and his sisters, Lizzie and Maggie, live with him and manage the dining room. Going west, you get to Midway at a time not scheduled for a meal, between midnight and morning, but it is a twenty-minute stop for drivers to change, and take my word for it and ask for your breakfast. Lizzie and Maggie Trout are two of the best cooks on the line and they can cook your meal from scratch before you must leave.

They are past first youth but still young enough to be full of zip and fire and to attract their share of male attention. Don't try getting fresh with them. Either of them can handle you by herself. Together they are formidable, and as if that weren't enough, half a dozen stage drivers will climb right down your throat in their defense. They are two of the most admired, respected and loved women on the line.

Charlie Haynes will take you out of Midway. Every driver on the Overland is competent. An incompetent driver doesn't last long. Many Overland drivers are good.

175

Some are very good. Then there are a dozen, perhaps, who are superb reinsmen. You have ridden behind one already, Enoch Cummings. You will ride behind another now.

Charlie is around thirty years old and he has been driving stage since he was sixteen. He is from Ohio.

Charlie has a long stage to drive—thirty-two miles to Cottonwood Springs. As daylight comes you will look out upon the vastest land you have yet seen . . . wide, level, long ahead of you and long behind. There is very little vegetation and almost no water except the river. The road is heavy for the team, but it isn't yet a deep sand drag. Your time begins to drop down here, however. Though Charlie moves the team along it isn't the briskest or liveliest pace. About four miles an hour is the best that can be done, unless you want to kill a team. We only do that for Ben Holladay.

So you'll be eight hours reaching Cottonwood Springs and you'll be ready for the meal that's waiting. Cottonwood Springs is an oasis in the desert. The country breaks a little here, into canyons and gulches, and there are a number of fine springs in the vicinity. Where there is water there is timber and the settlement is shaded by a stand of cottonwood trees.

This is an important station on the line. You are one hundred miles from Fort Kearney and 353 miles out of Atchison. Cottonwood Springs is a supply depot and the Company has built a number of buildings here in addition to the station. They are all built of logs. There is a blacksmith shop, several warehouses and a telegraph station. You may have noticed as you came along that most of the stations were built of logs. They came from here. Not far from the settlement is a canyon whose floor is heavily timbered with cedar. The logs for Fort Kearney were cut here, and for all the stage buildings a hundred miles east and west of here. It is a long way to haul logs but this is the only source of timber in the area. In time the cedar here will play out, for emigrants and freighters stop at the canyon and cut the trees, too.

The stations are nearly all built the same way, whether one, two or three rooms. They are flat-roofed. Poles are laid across the tops of the logs, then grass or hay is piled on. Finally dirt or sod is laid over and tamped down, with gravel from the river mixed in to hold it. This makes a leaky roof, and a muddy leak, but shingles are far too expensive and too hard to come by.

The one-room stations are usually divided by calico or muslin curtains into public station, living quarters for the keeper, and kitchen-dining room. Stations owned by ranchers, with trading stores attached, run to several rooms, and at various points on the line, such as Cottonwood Springs, where supplies are kept and more employees must live, the Company builds several structures.

You'll have twenty minutes, as usual, for eating and tidying up and resting a little. Sandy Sterling will take you out of here. He's been with the line since 1860 and while he is an unspectacular driver he is a veteran and very good.

A few miles out of Cottonwood Springs the South Platte runs into the main river. Here is where, in the old days, most wagons going west crossed, then proceeded on up between the two forks of the river. This was called the Lower California Crossing. It is still used some, but most trains going west nowadays go on up the South Platte to Julesburg, cross there at the old Upper California Crossing, then proceed up Lodgepole Creek, heading over gradually to the main Platte again. The stage route follows up the South Platte.

Cold Springs is fifteen miles, then comes my own ranch at Fremont Springs, fourteen miles beyond Cold Springs. My buildings are dobe and if I do say so myself the place is neat and attractive. The station building is the biggest, with the store attached at one end and four rooms of living quarters behind. The other buildings include the drivers' bunkhouse, stables, a blacksmith shop, and there is a cedar pole corral.

When you walk into the dining room you'll notice the calico curtains at the windows and the geraniums and other pot plants on the sills. There are Indian rugs on the floor. The tables are cedar and Emma keeps them beeswaxed to a high polish. The pretty girl who passes you hot bread and pours your coffee is my Bernie. She is pleasant-mannered and quick to smile at you, but you won't find her very talky. For two reasons. She's too busy for one thing, but she's also learned it's the best way to keep men passengers from getting fresh with her. So just save your breath. And don't think you can make an impression by being a loudmouth and bragging and showing off. She knows chin music when she hears it and the impression you'll make will be the wrong kind.

We have to charge you a dollar and seventy-five cents for your meal here. Except for the meat the boys kill, every bite you eat has to be brought on. I can guarantee you it will be as good as any food you ever ate and I don't believe you'll mind paying the bill.

This is broken country with a lot of sandhills and bluffs. I like it for that reason. You have a long view, a very wide view, but it isn't monotonous and flat. You have been traveling slightly north of west all across the plains. Here at my place, or just a little beyond, you reach the farthest north of this angling. You will begin to make a southing then. And here at my place, and a little beyond, on a very clear day when the atmosphere is exactly right, you can see Chimney Rock, on the old wagon road fifty miles north of us. This is the only place on the line it may be seen. But when the conditions are right it is very plain and the white sides and the dome are easily recognized.

Though I chose this location mostly for business reasons, it doesn't hurt to have as much beauty as you can. You might disagree with me that this is a beautiful place. You may think it ugly, with its sparse growth, its bareness, its distances. But ugly can be magnificently beautiful. Pretty never can be.

Your driver out of my station is a very interesting person, though you will not know it. He goes by the name of Jim Harvard but that is not his real name and none of us know what his real name is. He is twenty-three years old, he is from Boston, and he wanted to drive stage so bad that he ran away from home, ran away from Harvard College, where he would have taken his degree in one more year, and came west to drive for the Overland. He is a superb driver, one of the best. We all believe he comes from a wealthy family and learned to drive British style four-in-hand when he was growing up.

He doesn't say. He lives in daily fear his family will find him. So, if he looks you over pretty carefully it is only because he looks over all the passengers carefully, and afraid each time there will be somebody who will recognize him.

Nobody has ever told him, because we like him too much, but he gives himself away on the box. He spouts Shakespeare to the team. He is partial to the King's speech from *Henry the Fifth*. It is plain hair-raising to ride up the South Platte with that boy with the golden locks and the thin droopy golden moustache and the pure mellow golden voice as he gives tongue to perhaps the most deathless lines ever written in English:

> *If we are mark'd to die, we are enow*
> *To do our country loss, and if to live,*
> *The fewer men, the greater share of honour.*
>
> . . . .
>
> *This story shall the good man teach his son;*
> *And Crispin Crispian shall ne'er go by,*
> *From this day to the ending of the world,*
> *But we in it shall be remembered . . .*
> *We few, we happy few, we band of brothers;*

Some of us learned the whole speech ourselves and dipped our whips at each other in passing and cried, "We few, we happy few, we band of brothers."

I would be jealous of this man with Bernie except for the fact that he shares with me the fault of being a stage driver and therefore falls beneath her notice. She also considers him a flibbertygibbet and a lightweight. She sells him short but since that is to my advantage, I don't quarrel with it.

Jim never stays on any run long, since he's always running from his people. You'll be lucky if you catch him before he moves on.

Elkhorn is eleven miles and you get a new team. Then brace yourself for some thrills. A few miles out of Elkhorn you come to O'Fallon's Bluffs. These are steep sandhill bluffs, a natural Gibraltar. The road follows along the rim of the bluffs for several miles. It has a clay and sand base which travel has bonded into the hardness of cement. Jim takes this road with one set of wheels practically hanging over the rim and flat out, with a great clatter of drumming hoofs. Men swear and women scream and sometimes

swoon. It won't do any good for me to tell you, but I will
... you're perfectly safe.

But that really isn't the worst. Suddenly the road begins
to angle down and very quickly it has reached a pitch of
forty-five degrees. There is no way to take this downpitch
except fast. Full brake will chock the wheels to a slide but
it can't slow the team. You just have to go—with wings.
Since nothing can slow the team, Jim lets them go. Just
take a deep breath and hang on. Count the new gray hairs
next time you look in the mirror.

The road follows the floor of the canyon then for a little
way, and while you're glad to be down the driver is wanting to get back up. This is a good ambush spot. It doesn't
pay to loiter so you'll go through pretty fast.

Alkali Lake is next, fourteen miles from Elkhorn, and I
will agree with you that this a dreary, desolate spot. The
earth is dusty, flat and absolutely white with alkali. The
soil is so strong with soda that the Indians scoop it up and
use it in their bread.

To add to the bleakness, thousands of buffalo skulls are
scattered all over the plain. Shot for their hides, the car-
casses have been left to be picked over by coyotes and
buzzards, then the rib cases and skulls lie there, forever
bleaching in the hard glaze of the sun.

Jack Gilmer will be your next driver. He used to whack
mules for Russell, Majors & Waddell. Went to work for the
Overland in '61. Sand Hill is twelve miles, then comes
Diamond Springs. This is deep drag sand through here and
the going is so heavy and so slow that Diamond Springs is
another home station, after only twenty-three miles. This
part of the road is wearisome for you, and the heat, even in
May, is bad. It is also wearisome for the team. The best
they can do through here is a slow trot and time seems to
stand still.

The worst stretch of road in the sandhills is just before
you now. Just outside Diamond Springs is the deep, deep
canyon again and the Devil's Dive. You are spared it in
1863, however. The new road goes the long way round,
and it will seem endless to you but at least you needn't
make that dreadful downpitch.

It is fifteen miles to South Platte. You will be almost
certain to see a mirage along this fifteen miles. The road is

long and straight. You may see fairy castles, or a large lake, or a fantastically big herd of buffalo. Whatever you see it will look so real you won't believe it isn't. Only as you cover the distance and it shifts and changes do you believe the driver isn't pulling your leg.

Just beyond South Platte lives the only doctor between Fort Kearney and Denver. He calls himself John Lewis and says Ohio used to be his home. Nobody knows if that is his real name or if Ohio was his real home.

I remember when he came. He rode the box with me out of Diamond Springs. He was so tall, around six foot four, that riding inside was mighty uncomfortable for him and the drivers had been kind to him all along the way. He was a nice-looking man, about thirty-five or so. Quiet. Hardly said a word. And there was something sad and melancholy about him. He didn't volunteer any information beyond his name, where he was from, and that he was a doctor by profession. He didn't say where he was going nor what he meant to do. He had a ticket for Denver.

When we pulled into the swing station at South Platte, he walked off toward the river alone and paced up and down the bank. I had to call him that we were ready to leave. He hurried up to the stage and asked me to hand him down his medical satchel. "I'm going to stay here awhile," he said.

"Well," I said, "this is just a swing station and the boys aren't fixed up to accommodate travelers very comfortably, but I reckon they can feed and sleep you till you're ready to move on."

"I'll manage," he said.

He didn't ask for his luggage out of the hind boot, but I delayed a few minutes to hunt it out for him. I drove off and left him standing there, luggage piled around his feet, staring off into the distance.

Next day when I came back through, blessed if he hadn't bought himself a tepee from some Sioux camped nearby and put it up about a mile below the station. Little by little he kept adding to the place. Got a bigger and handsomer tepee, put up a corral, bought a couple of horses. Then one day he added a Sioux wife. He never did build a house of any kind. That fine big white tepee that easily measures twenty-five feet in diameter down by the river amongst that little stand of cottonwoods is his. And if you went inside you wouldn't find a neater or cleaner house in the east. He married himself a "princess." She was the daughter of a Sioux chieftain and she's a very pretty Indian. He calls her Mrs. Lewis and everybody else had better, by George, do the same.

He practices his profession out here on the plains. He is in great demand up and down the line and he never turns a call down. Day or night if he's needed he hauls out and climbs on his horse and starts out, little black bag tied to the saddle horn. His wife is usually riding behind him. She helps him when he has to operate, and the two of them have been known to stay by the bedside of a patient three or four days, nursing and seeing him through. Mothers along the line are greatly comforted by the doctor's presence. He is especially good and kind with children.

You wonder. You wonder what sent him west. If maybe he lost his wife back east, or if some great loss in the war caused him to cut his ties and start wandering. Men travel for such a variety of reasons. And why did he pick South Platte? Whatever his reasons, he is greatly respected and admired, and though his Sioux wife caused some talk at first, she is now accepted with good grace. Not in any sense of the word is the doctor a "squaw man."

You now come to Julesburg. This is a division point, the end of the Fort Kearney division, the beginning of the Denver division. You are 456 miles out of Atchison and at the end of your fourth day of travel. Say good-bye to Nebraska. You are now, but a few feet maybe, in Colorado.

This is the Upper California Crossing of the South Platte. The Company has built quite a sizable little town here. There are a dozen buildings, including the stage station, three stores, a blacksmith shop, several grain warehouses, a livery stable and a saloon. Don't quench your thirst here. It is forty-rod whisky at two bits a glass and it's pure poison. I saw a man walk straight into a campfire when he was drunk on the stuff and burn all the skin off his feet without feeling a thing. He was numb all over. This is the place that was named for Old Jules Beni, whose ears Jack Slade cut off. You will have heard that story as you rode along from South Platte. It has become part of the legend of the Overland. You will also have heard, likely, that Slade still works for the Company, over on the Bitter Creek division, and that he is as mean as a rattlesnake. You will have heard that he has killed twenty-six men. You don't know whether to believe this or not. You may think it's another tall tale. You can believe it. It's true. He has become a mean, hard-drinking, cold-blooded killer. He began by killing outlaws on the line. Now he has a blood lust for killing. His score goes up each year. The company can't tolerate him much longer, but what everybody wonders is *who* will have the guts to fire him and make it stick. Nobody wants to walk up to Jack Slade and say, "You're through." He's likely to be a dead man before the words are out of his mouth.

But you needn't worry. You're only going as far as Denver. Slade's division is beyond Denver. He comes down as far as Laporte, north of Denver, and he likes Fort Halleck, but he rarely comes into the city itself.

Julesburg is no longer a hideout for outlaws, but it is a tough frontier settlement. It is wide open and red hot, and more men per square foot have been killed in it than any other one settlement along the line. Not until the railroad went through Wyoming, and Cheyenne and Laramie were built did a place any hotter spring to life.

Julesburg used to be a junction point. Through stages for Salt Lake and California used to go straight on west here, cross the river and proceed up Lodgepole Creek. The Denver stage angled southwest up the South Platte. Since Holladay got the line changed, however, all stages move on up the South Platte as far as Latham, where the through stages head due west over to Laporte.

There is a telegraph office here, if you want to wire your people that you're still on the face of the earth. You, yourself, may be doubting it. And this is a meal stop. It will fill you up but it won't be anything fancy.

Bill Trotter will likely be your next driver. He is another of the very fine drivers. He's from Pennsylvania and was brought west to Iowa when still a boy. He began driving stage at sixteen in Kansas. He went with the Company when it was the C.O.C. & P.P. He likes a good run, but gets restless and moves around a lot.

A short way out of Julesburg, about five miles, if you

were making this journey a couple of years from now, you would see the new Fort Sedgewick. It was built in the fall of 1864.

But in 1863 there is no fort yet. There is only the wide, sandy plain and over near the site where the fort was later built a high point of land called Pilot's Knob. It sticks up out of the plains alone and singular and is a landmark for miles around. My father says that in the old days Indians built their signal fires on its top. After the fort was built it was used as an observation point. The county in all directions can be seen and scanned.

Antelope is twelve miles from Julesburg. You'll see sagebrush for the first time along this dry, sandy, monotonous stretch. If it is the first time you have seen it, you will notice the smell immediately. It's a little like camphor and turpentine mixed. I like it. It may be my imagination but it seems to clear the head and clear the lungs. It's a high altitude bush and you're beginning to come into the foothills of the mountains. Shortly you'll see the whole plain covered with the bush, low, rounded over, a dull gray-green in color. Sage makes a very hot but quick-burning fire. Only by feeding constantly can you keep a fire going long enough to take the chill off your food. You'd have to have a wagonload of it to cook a meal from scratch.

Spring Hill is thirteen miles from Antelope. It was here at Spring Hill that a farmer from the Little Blue had a terrible mishap one time. Since there wasn't even a square inch of a vegetable garden the entire length of the Platte, nor in all of Colorado, nor any fowl or domestic stock raised, every blessed thing the people ate or wore or used had to be brought in to them. Prices in Denver were therefore as high as the mountains.

A farmer down along the Little Blue had a fine crop of turkeys one year and he thought to sell them to the best advantage to him. That could only be in Denver. So he built a superstructure of coops on his big wagon, covered and sheltered them with canvas and set out on the long five-hundred-mile journey. All went well until he reached Spring Hill, on almost the last lap of his long trip.

He camped alongside of the station that night. Along in the night there was a wild squawking and clamor in his camp. The farmer rose up shouting and yelling, "My turkeys! My turkeys! My turkeys are loose!"

There were four drivers sleeping that night at the station. To a man we turned out to help round up the turkeys. There were four stock tenders at the station. To a man they also roused up and ran to help. The scene was wild, with turkeys squawking and flying about, men running around flapping their arms and shooing and shouting, the poor farmer diving here and there, distractedly clutching at a wing or leg and never once ceasing his yelling.

For some reason the more we chased, the more we flapped and yelled and ran, the wider the turkeys circled, the crazier they became, the farther they scattered. After a frantic hour, when no more could be found, the farmer counted those retrieved. Then he sat down and put his head in his hands and moaned in his grief. Out of two hundred turkeys, he had only forty left. "It's ruination," he wept, "pure ruination! All this expense! All this long journey! And it comes to naught! It's ruination!"

We felt for him in his misery, but we had done our best to be helpful. No men could have done more than we did. Next morning the farmer sadly drove on up the road to Denver.

It was a strange thing, but every station clear back to Midway had baked turkey on the table for a week after the farmer's mishap. A hundred and sixty turkeys parceled out among twenty stations makes quite a few for each.

A man we always called Rattlesnake Pete will take the reins here at Spring Hill. He has a last name, but nobody ever knew it. He had a passion for killing rattlesnakes, of which there are a great many on the plains. He always kept a handful of buttons to rattle around in his pocket.

Next comes Dennison, then Valley station, the latter being a home station. Ed Kilburn takes the reins at Valley station. He is one of the oldest drivers on the line, both in years and in service. He was killed by Indians in 1867, right along this same stretch of road.

But in 1863, Ed is alive and driving you up the South Platte. At Kelly's, which used to be called the American Ranch, there is a brief stop to change the team and if you look closely, and if the air is clear, you will get your first glimpse of the Rocky Mountains. They are a hundred miles away but on a fine day they loom up well, dark timber at the base, heads white with snow.

That big fellow to the right is Long's Peak. The one down to the left is Pikes Peak. All in between, blocked and massive, are the Ramparts—the blue-soldier mountains. They look like ramparts. No fortress wall ever looked more impregnable. But there are gates in them. The Indians knew the gates and the beaver trappers knew them. My father used to come down out of South Park through one called Ute Pass. There are many such passes. None of them is easy, but mountains have never yet stopped men.

After Kelly's station comes Beaver Creek. This is a home station. Get ready for a little bit of hell now. It is twenty miles to the next station, Bijou, and every foot of it is the deepest drag sand on the whole line. "Bishop" West will drive you and not once will the team go out of a slow walk. Flat, featureless, dreadful and monotonous country is ahead of you, which even in May is hot and brassy.

You may notice as the "Bishop" mounts the box and moves you out that another team is following. One of the hands is riding one horse and leading three. No team can make this stage in one haul and there is no place to put a relay station. So the relay team goes along, following the coach. About halfway to Bijou it will be hitched in, and the tired team will water in the river and rest awhile, then be led back to Beaver Creek.

West is called Bishop because he is a very religious man. He sings hymns to his horses and he likes to preach. He isn't ordained or licensed so he can't perform weddings but he can and does hold funerals, and at the drop of a hat will preach as fine a sermon as you ever heard.

We had a passenger to die of a heart attack on the stage along this piece of the road one time. The "Bishop" stopped the stage and while he didn't exactly administer the last rites to the man, he did do his best to comfort his dying moments. And at Bijou, when the man was buried the next morning on the bank of Bijou Creek, the "Bishop" laid him to rest in moving and charitable terms. He never once referred to the fact that the man had been dog drunk every mile of the way since Fort Kearney.

Bijou is another home station, of course. The next stretch, sixteen miles to Fremont's Orchard, is just as grueling as what you've been through. The only thing better about it is that it's four miles shorter. A spare team doesn't follow along on this stretch, however. We use a spike team of mules and they make the whole stage. This is five mules, two on the wheel, two swinging, and a single in the lead. It's a fine team and will pull you slow but sure right along. Your driver is Gassy Keane. He is a big talker. Chatters to the team every minute.

These two men, one who sings hymns to his team, the other who never stops chattering, may strike you as crazy men. You may wish they would shut up and let you suffer in peace and quiet. But these men are exceptionally good men for these two mean stages of the road, for teams react to the road, too. There is not one thing along these two stages to give teams any heart in working well. There isn't a tree or a bush or a rock. There isn't a hard stretch where they can let out a little. There's just deep sand and hard drag and pull. They won't do it well, not even mules, without some help. So the "Bishop" and old Gassy put heart in the teams with their hymns and chatter. Listen and be thankful.

You will rejoice when Fremont's Orchard looms up ahead of you. There is a nice little grove of cottonwoods here and the way they are clumped together does look a little like an orchard of fruit trees back home. There is good water here, too. This is a home station and there is a post office.

"Pap" Russell, a wrinkled, leather-hided, tobacco-chewing older man, will take the reins now. He will tell you he's been driving stage since time began, and he just about has. He's a real old-timer, going back to the fur-trapping days. On his off days he hunts and he keeps the station in plenty of meat.

The drag is over now and, although there is still a lot of sand, you can move along. Eagle's Nest is eleven miles, then twelve miles farther is Latham. Coming into Latham is like coming back into civilization after crossing the desert. It's a home station, with a post office and a junction point. There is usually a lot of activity here. Through coaches to Salt Lake and Placerville cross the South Platte here and proceed straight west to Laporte before beginning their long angle north again. Denver stages keep on up the South Platte.

You'll often see four coaches here at one time, east- and westbound through stages, and east- and westbound Denver stages, meeting and connecting and changing passengers. If you have been riding a through stage to this point, your luggage will be shifted now and you'll board a different stage for Denver. Perhaps you'll be glad to say goodbye to some of the people who have been your companions for so long. Perhaps, though, you've made a friend or two you'll never forget.

Anything that can happen to humanity can happen on a long stage journey. People have died, babies have been born, romances have ripened, and marriages have ended. We even had a man go crazy, wave a gun around, slash up a couple of passengers with his knife, and we took him into Denver in chains.

Latham. On a modern map you won't find it now. It has become Greeley.

The most embarrassing thing that ever happened to me in all the years I drove stage occurred here at Latham. Because the station was situated with a lot of space around it and the road was flat and level for miles, we sometimes broke in new teams here. It sometimes happened that the Company bought horses from the Mexicans in this part of the country. They were nearly always wild horses, or mustangs, which the Mexicans caught and broke. When first hitched they would invariably cut up considerably, bucking and plunging about, causing a lot of sport and fun. A driver had his hands full and it took a lot of whip to straighten them out. Then they would run like hell for three or four miles before settling down to a good road pace. This was why Latham was used to hitch in those teams for the first time. With all that room no real harm could come of a runaway.

I was driving the Latham-Fort Lupton run and one morning the station agent asked me if I would take out a new team and break them in. I was always game. In fact, I liked the tussle and fight and the fun of the runaway, and I had never got hold of a team yet I couldn't handle. I said I'd be glad to.

It was a hitch of sixes and they were really wild. It took a man at the head of each horse to hold them while the boys hitched them in, and then a couple of boys to each pair had to hang on to keep them standing. The passengers were all men, happily. They loaded on, most of them a little leery of the whole operation, but game. I climbed up on the box, got myself settled and braced, whip ready, and yelled, "Let 'em go!"

What happened you wouldn't believe. The off leader jumped straight up in the air and came down astraddle of the near leader. The near leader bucked him off and jumped right back over him. The off swing jumped over the near swing, and the near wheeler jumped over the off wheeler. In less time than you could say Jenny cracked corn I had six horses in the biggest mess you ever saw, every one of them down, kicking, squealing and plunging, the lines and traces tangled over and under and around mustangs, tongue and singletrees. Not a horse could get up, though all six were trying and making the mess worse and worse.

Over on the sidelines, standing there looking on and laughing fit to split a gusset, was the station agent and half a dozen drivers, passengers off the through coach, hostlers and tenders. I was so mad I was strangling, as red-faced as I ever hope to be, humiliated to the point of wanting to sink right down through the ground. Me . . . one of the oldest and best drivers on the line, with a fistful of tangled lines and a useless whip and six down horses. There wasn't one thing I could do but yell for help, which I did in a hurry. "Goddammit, quit your guffawing and come work 'em loose!"

I didn't much believe we'd ever get them up from there and untangled without at least one of them being killed. It took every hand on the place to do it—even the mail agent and some of the passengers fell to and helped. I at least had the satisfaction of being able to sit on the box and hang onto the reins while they worked. It restored my temper considerably, as well as my dignity. Straightened out again, I threw in a good measure of lash and let 'em rip. But most of the rip had been ripped out of them and they settled down to a fine road gait fairly soon.

They made a good team. We used them for several years

in the heavy sand near Bijou. But they almighty sure did get off to a bad start.

You are 592 miles out of Atchison and only sixty miles from Denver now. Lou Huff will drive the next stage with you.

Don't let the name fool you. This is my old friend Arkansaw, who swapped me his Devil's Dive run for a bottle of forty-rod whisky and who told me how to drive it. "Let 'em rip, bub," he said. "Drive 'em and let 'em rip." He's a good driver but without a notion of style. He keeps the biggest cud of tobacco in his jaw I ever saw a man handle and when the wheelers take a notion to lag a little he sprays them expertly with a stinging spurt of spit. It acts exactly like a whip on them.

This is a long stage, thirty-two miles, broken at Big Bend before you reach the next home station at Fort Lupton. You'll make it at night, but you'll know old Arkansaw is taking you along at a good clip.

Fort Lupton is a ruin. But inside the walls of the old fort the Company found a few buildings which they repaired and make use of for a stage station and storehouse.

Teddy Nichols takes the reins here for the last stage into Denver. He is round and fat and jolly, bighearted, big-souled, generous, happy, full of quips and jokes. He's from New York, but he's been driving Overland since the old L. & P.P. days.

It is thirteen miles to Pierson's. Daylight will come during that stretch and if you don't lose your breath when you look out and see the mountains again, and now so near, you are a hard case indeed. They are dazzling in the clean air and they stretch 150 miles north and south ahead of you. Beautiful, spectacular, magnificent—the Snowy Range.

From Pierson's it is fifteen miles to the end of your journey. The road is wonderful. It is a hard smooth bed of gravel and no paved street could be better. Teddy will let the team, four matched grays, out and you'll fly along at the most beautiful gait known to animals. On this piece of road if a driver don't make a perfect run it's his own fault. It is expected of him.

The minute you leave Pierson's with this fresh team you sense that this is going to be grand. Teddy lets the team go at once. They move immediately into that beautiful racking gait and you fly down that hard, level road, the coach swaying on its leathers, the feet of the beautiful grays drumming the road hard, fast and in perfect time, Teddy singing and laughing and talking them on. It's a lovely way to finish your long wearisome journey.

Don't let them down. You're tired and you've been letting your back hair down somewhat, but brace up and go in yourself in comparable style and class. Dust yourself off. Powder your nose. Straighten your cravat. Stiffen your back and when Teddy pulls you into the station at nine o'clock this morning with all that incomparable beauty and flourish, step down out of that stage with pride.

We had it—all along the line. Every man who drove you, everybody who served you, every team that pulled you had at least that one thing in common—pride. We are the Great Overland State Line, the greatest staging outfit that ever rolled on wheels. You paid for your ride with us, but by God, you couldn't find enough money to pay for what you got in skill and style and wonder and beauty and class and pride. That is our private and dedicated life. You are simply the beneficiary of it.

End of the line for you now. Denver. The Planter's House. The mountains and the diamond air. Gold in your pocket, maybe. Or empty pockets. Whatever, six days and nights from Atchison, you are here. If you don't make it, the eastbound stage leaves at eight each morning. And, my friend, *vaya con Dios*, now.

Chapter 14

I had to make several trips out to the ranch. Not many, but occasionally something came up that made it necessary. No matter how able the man you employ is, things come up he can't decide and shouldn't have to. It is your risk and your responsibility and you have to see to it.

From time to time I had given some thought to giving Ed a chance to buy into the ranch, but the longer we were associated the more I realized it wouldn't work. There wasn't a harder-working, more honest, more dependable man in the world than Ed Westmoreland and within limits his judgment was sound. But Ed was one of those men who make a faithful, loyal, reliable employee. He wasn't cut out for the big decisions or the big risks. To put more on him than he could carry would have been to make the whole venture go sour. He seemed to know this himself and appeared to be very well satisfied working for me. He had considerable freedom with me gone so much of the time, his pay was good, and between the ranch, the store and the stage station the work was so varied it never became monotonous. He had a good home for his family and except for schooling for Bucky, Emma was well satisfied with it.

Let it be known I took young Bucky her white rooster the first time I went out. That crowing, wing-flapping, high-legged bird rode every mile in the front boot and the driver on every stage took one look, flapped his own wings, and refused to talk anything but rooster talk with me henceforth. I was heartily sick of the fowl by the time I got him to the ranch and threatened to make stew and dumplings of him if Bucky didn't keep him where he belonged.

"Oh, I will," she promised, "I will."

Where he belonged turned out to be the end of a string

led around by Bucky. "His name," she announced, "is Julius Caesar. And you see! He's no bother to anybody!"

He was. He was a bother to everybody, including the stage passengers. He was forever underfoot, squawking, ruffling his feathers, pecking at crumbs on the floor and feet on the floor and flogging everybody but Bucky. You couldn't pass within three feet of him without having him launch himself, furious and screeching and gouging with his sharp spurs, at your face or your belt buckle. He was the illest bird I ever saw. Bucky said we didn't understand him. "He knows you don't like him," she said. "If you'd just be kind to him he would quit flogging you."

"How do you be kind to a fool rooster?" I said.

"Oh, pick him up and smooth his feathers and talk to him," she said.

"And he'll sheathe his spurs and coo right back at me, I suppose," I said. "Nope. I'd lose an eye if I tried it. I don't trust him. But I'll tell you what's going to happen if he don't watch out. The noblest Roman of them all is going to get his neck wrung. If he flogs me one more time I aim to separate his head from his body."

"You touch one feather," she warned me hotly, "and I'll fill you full of buckshot."

Emma said he was so ill because a rooster wasn't meant to live alone. "He needs a flock of hens," she said, "or at least another rooster to crow back at him. He's lonesome and don't know what to make of having no others of his kind around. I am afraid it's going to make a nervous wreck of him."

"It would make one of me if I had to stay around him long," I said. And I didn't take the hint to bring any more chickens out. Julius Caesar was half a dozen too many.

It would not be true to say that I was over Bernie enough that it didn't give me a sad heartache to see her again. I wasn't and it did. It was worse than sad because it was so hopeless. I knew she was still there when I started on the trip. And I knew she wasn't married yet. Bucky's letters would have been full of either happening. She would have filled pages with Bernie's leaving, if she had gone home, and one letter wouldn't have held all she would have found to say if Bernie had got married. It would have taken at least half a dozen. There would have had to be a full description of the courtship, the decision, the wedding, the works.

I knew who had been coming to see her, and knew also that she hadn't leaned seriously toward anybody. Bucky was pretty clever at sizing up people and their emotions. "Mr. Long has been to see Bernie," she would write, "but he might as well stay in Denver. Bernie don't admire him much. She says his nose is too long and he pokes it in her business too much. And besides, he's too old. Bernie don't say that, but I do. He must be at least *thirty*. One foot in the grave, practically."

Another letter told me a rancher had been. "He ought to have known better than to come to see Bernie without shaving. She can't abide a man that needs a shave. Says she'd just as soon brush a porcupine as a man with a bristly face. Now, if he'd grow a full beard that would be different. A beard makes a man handsome. Bernie didn't say so, but I know, for I think so myself. Why don't you grow a beard, Starr? Can't you? Won't it grow? Or are you too young?"

Too young. My Lord! I wondered sometimes if I had put on a year to Bucky. Maybe she thought I was still nineteen, as I was when she first knew me.

A lot of what young Bucky wrote me went in one ear and out the other. It shouldn't have. For the child was a wonderful letter writer. She chattered along in a happy gossipy way for page after page and told me, in great detail, everything that was happening. I appreciated the news of the ranch but I could have done without a new recipe Mama had tried, and Julius Caesar's sore foot where a clumsy stage driver had stepped on it.

So I knew without any doubt I would find Bernie still free and unattached when I went back. I behaved admirably, if I do say so myself. I vowed I would not pester her, and I didn't. I set myself to be friendly, not to seek chances to be alone with her, and to treat her as near as I could the way I treated Emma and Bucky.

I stayed three days and I spent them mostly with Ed. We rode out on the range the last day to look at the cattle. Bucky went along but nobody asked Bernie. Before, I would have begged her to go and would have made every

opporunity to ride a lot of the way alone with her. I think
it puzzled her a little. She was used to a lot of pestering
from me. She sort of slapped the crockery around at
supper that night. But I ignored that, too. Until she
brought up how quick some men could change. In front of
Ed and Emma and Bucky, she said it. "Out of sight, out of
mind, I guess," she said, "and of course with dozens of
girls in Atchison all around."

"A man don't need dozens," I said, "one will do."

It was a mean thing to say. It implied a narrowed and
serious interest which wasn't true. But I didn't like being
needled in front of the Westmorelands. Women take an
awful advantage of a man that way, boxing him in in front
of people so if he opens his mouth at all he's in a poor
light—either defending himself or picking a quarrel.

Bucky picked it up straight away. "You got a girl in
Atchison, Starr?"

"Of course he has a girl in Atchison," Bernie said,
"didn't you just hear him say?"

Bucky laughed. "It will do her no good. She'll just get
her heart broken."

"Now, how do you figure that?" I said. "How do you
know so much about it?"

She spread her bread with jam and said serenely, "You
oughtn't to trifle with women's affections, Starr, when
you're already engaged."

"Engaged!" Bernie yelled. "He's not engaged. It's the last
thing . . . I've never given him the least . . ."

Bucky looked at her over the bread and jam. "Who said
anything about you?"

"Well . . . for heaven's sake . . . who . . . what do you
mean?" Bernie was sputtering.

"He's been engaged to me since I was nine years old,"
Bucky said, biting a big chunk out of her bread and
chewing solidly, eyeing all of us triumphantly.

Bernie slapped her napkin down on the table and shoved
her chair back and fled to her room.

"Now see what you've done with your silliness," Emma
said. "You've got Bernie upset and hurt her feelings."

"She just as well know," the child said. "Starr promised
to marry me and I gave up stage driving."

"Now, see here . . ." I said.

She drained the last of her milk and made a face over it being canned milk, then shoved her own chair back. "I have to feed Julius Caesar now."

Ed and Emma and I looked at each other. "Starr," Emma said, "surely you didn't . . ."

"No, I didn't," I said. But I felt mighty uncomfortable as I explained the teasing that day Bucky had announced she was going to marry me. "God," I said, "that kid is worse than a woodtick to get burrowed in and stuck with a notion."

"Well, that settles it," Emma said.

"Settles what?" Ed asked. "Looks to me like this is the most *unsettled* bunch of ideas I ever saw."

Emma began clearing off the table. "Bucky has to go away to school. She's growing up a little heathen. I'm going to write Mama and see if she'll keep her a few years."

But even as she said it her hands got still and she dropped a plate on the table. She sat down again, her eyes filled with tears. "I can't. I can't let her go that far away. I couldn't bear not to see her that long."

"Then don't do it," I said. "It's not called for. She'll grow out of this notion. I'm not here much. . . ."

I declare to God, women are the most unpredictable creatures on earth. Emma rounded on me and said, "If you'd just get married. Why don't you get *married!* You've got both of them worked up . . . Bernie and now Bucky! Just get married and they'd get over it."

"Well, I'll be damned," I said. "So I got to get married so your stubborn sister won't be put out, and so your kid daughter will get over the notion I'm waiting for her!" I shoved *my* chair back. One way or another we were sure shoving a lot of chairs around. I looked at Ed, who was shaking his head. "Man, I feel sorry for you. Married to Emma. Got Bernie for a sister-in-law and got a kid like Bucky. And she wants me to stick my head in the same kind of noose! No, thank you. You've told me before to let you handle Bucky. Well, *handle* her. She's all yours. I'm going to keep my hands strictly out of this business."

It was a good thing that the westbound stage arrived

about that time and the driver said the river was out all over the valley down below Cottonwood, and he'd probably be the last stage through and passengers and mail were already piling up. I thought I could do more good down there than here at the ranch. I saddled up a horse and left.

The next time I went home the first thing I noticed was that Julius Caesar wasn't pecking around on the floor. "You had chicken and dumplings, I see," I said to Ed.

"No," Ed said, laughing, "there wasn't enough left of him for that."

"Some passenger tore him limb from limb."

"No, but he came to a very sad end. Bucky got tired of leading him around and one of the boys built him a coop. He got out of it one day and wandered off into the stables. A couple of the mules didn't take kindly to him invading their quarters."

"Trompled on him?"

"Not exactly," Ed said. "The way Browning told it to me was, they maneuvered old Julius Caesar into the alleyway and then both of them took up a good kicking stance. When they'd got him between 'em just right, one of 'em let fly and lofted the old booger over toward the other one. He caught him on the bounce and lofted him right back. They played ball with the old bird, backward and forward, till all that was left of him was a few tail feathers, two yellow legs and a battered beak. The alleyway looked like a flock of geese had been picked and Julius Caesar was the biggest mess you ever saw."

"You're lying," I said.

"My word and honor," he said.

I pondered it. It was downright awesome to consider, the cunning and good sense of those two mules. "They deserve to be decorated," I said.

"That's not what Bucky thought," Ed said.

"She had a fit, I reckon."

"Six or seven, handrunning. I had to take my gun away from her three different times. She was going to kill a couple of mules. It was right busy around here till Bernie got her calmed down a little."

"By what method? A hand applied to her bottom?"

"No. By promising her a fine funeral for the bird. I tell you, Starr, that Roman emperor she named him for didn't have no finer funeral than that rooster had. Toga and all. And they didn't have any Ute half-breeds in Rome to shake a medicine stick and sing over the emperor. That rooster was buried with real pomp and ceremony. Bucky don't know whether he's gone to be with Jove and the other Roman gods, or whether he's in some Cheyenne happy hunting grounds, but she's satisfied he's in some heavenly place, parading around, clucking and flogging everybody. And no mules. Bucky says only here on earth where human beings get things sadly misfitted are mules and roosters ever mixed."

I could see and relish all the ceremonial and humor, but when I'd had my laugh, one thing made me a little sober. "How did Popo get mixed up in it?"

"Oh, he was here, trading, when Bucky came storming in. She'd scooped what was left of the rooster up into a box and she came flying into the store, yelling and carrying on. She flung the box on the counter and made for my gun. It was the Ute who took it away from her. Then Bernie came in and began trying to calm her down.

"The Ute understands a hell of a lot more English than I ever gave him credit for, because he understood right off what had happened and what was going on. I wouldn't be surprised if he couldn't speak it, too, more than he does. But anyway, Bernie and Bucky have both picked up sign pretty good, so when Bernie finally got the kid calmed down and began to talk about a funeral, they understood when the Ute offered to give the rooster a chief's funeral.

"Bucky thought that was fine. 'Just like a warrior,' she said. 'He was a warrior, too. He fought everybody. He wasn't afraid of anybody. He was a fine, brave warrior.'

"Well, Bernie made him a shroud and they put it on him, and they lined a box with some calico and Bernie picked some geraniums off one of her plants and they dug him a grave. Then, would you believe it? He, the Ute, dressed up in his finery for the ceremony and he painted himself for it, and he went through a whole rigmarole over the grave . . . drew signs in the sand, sprinkled cornmeal and some stuff out of his medicine bag through the whole business, and as far as I could tell he did it as serious as if it had been a man. It pleased Bucky mightily."

"Probably put a curse on the lot of us," I said.

"Don't say that around Bernie and Bucky," Ed said. "Bucky now admires him next to you, and being a good Methodist Bernie's sort of a missionary. She's inclined to think she's found at least one noble redskin."

"Oh, my God," I said, "I thought she'd been out here long enough to learn a little something about what Indians are really like. She's still reading the eastern newspapers?"

"I reckon," Ed said. "They're doing a lot of preaching about the noble child of nature and how he's being wronged by white men."

"Yes," I said, "from where they sit it's safe to preach, even those who have money working for them out here. Noble! If there's anything less noble than an Indian I haven't seen it. I'd like to take Bernie over to One-Eyed Jack's ranch and let her visit that camp over there. Let her get lice and fleas and sore eyes and the itch. And let her eat pup. Let her live a few days like a squaw—peg out hides and scrape 'em. Haul wood and water. Wait on their lords and masters while they sit around and play Hand and make eyes at themselves in their mirrors and comb their hair and shine their bracelets and medals.

"Let her work alongside old Bear Walker's squaw and wonder why she limps so bad when she walks. Old Bear Walker broke her leg with a lodgepole one day when he was beating her. But it was real noble of him that he didn't gouge out one eye or cut off one of her hands. He just didn't happen to be that mad.

"Let her go out and drive in his horses for him and see the sores on their backs big enough you can put your fist in and working with maggots, and see if she can put a pack saddle on it without puking. Her noble redskin can, and does, and then he can quirt the horse to death if he's hurting so bad he falters. Why does she think they steal so many? Because they kill 'em fast.

"Maybe one of the young bucks will bring in a white man while she's there. Some emigrant and his woman, like you and Emma. She can watch them skin him, one inch at a time. Or instead of skinning him maybe they'll stake him out and put hot coals all over him. Stick him full of splinters and set them afire. And she can watch the squaws squat over him and fill his face with piss and cut off his privates and shit on 'em and stuff 'em in his mouth.

"Then maybe she'd like to watch those noble redskins work over a white woman . . . put her on the prairie and see what she looks like after twenty or thirty of 'em get through using her."

Ed was making faces at me and funny noises. I whirled around. Bernie was standing in the door. She was pale and one hand was at her throat, but she was almighty angry, too. "You've seen these things with your own eyes, I suppose," she said, "or have you been reading too many Denver newspapers?"

"How long have you been standing there?" I said.

"Long enough to hear your whole sermon," she said. "Your language is vivid but vulgar, Mr. Fowler."

"People who eavesdrop," I said, "have to take the language they hear. I apologize, however, for the vulgarity. If I had known you were listening I would have put it more delicately. It all happens to be true, however, and yes, I've seen it myself. Or what was left to be seen. If I had actually been present I wouldn't be standing here to tell about it. My bones would have been bleaching on the prairie a long time ago."

"All the more reason," she said, suddenly passionate about it, "for them to be Christianized and civilized. All the more reason for them to be treated with pity and compassion. Instead of being driven off their lands and being hunted down. If they were treated with some kindness and compassion . . ."

"The day you treat an Indian with kindness and compassion," I said, "that day you earn his contempt. He doesn't believe in them. Those are woman's things. They are not for men to feel. Men, to be true men, are to live for war and revenge and for a warrior's honor. Men are to show no mercy. To be merciful is to be weak, womanish.

"If an Indian strikes at you and you do not immediately strike back, he spits on you. You are not even a worthy enemy any longer. The only things they understand are the things they live by among themselves—war and raiding and revenge and retribution and treachery and cruelty and barbarism."

"But they are human beings!"

"Barely," I said. "Just barely. Just enough above animals to have a little human intelligence, and just enough intelligence to know how to be savage in a more refined way."

"They can be taught," she said. "They can be civilized."

"In four or five hundred years, maybe. But we can't wait that long here on the Platte River. This is right now and we live here and they are still savages and are a hostile enemy to white men."

"And we have no right here," she said. "This was their land first and we have moved in and shoved them aside."

"Maybe you don't have any right here," I said, "but I do. I have exactly as much right here as any Indian. Who gave it to him? He took it. He came in here and shoved some other Indian tribe over to get it. He decided the game was good, so he would kill them off and take it for himself. They've been fighting amongst themselves for good hunting grounds since time began. But they scream their heads off when white men claim a piece of land."

"The government had no right to take this land. . . ."

"Oh, sugar," I said, "you don't know what you're talking about. You're just bleeding. Men have been fighting over land since they came out of caves . . . who's going to possess it, who's going to rule it. We didn't invent it. And neither did the Indian. But as long as there's a piece of land left to fight over, it looks likely fighting will be the way it's settled. That's the nature of human beings, and I didn't invent human nature."

"You think like everybody else out here that the only good Indian is a dead Indian, don't you?" she said.

Ed put in, "Well, that's about the way it works, Bernie. I don't know how you can stand there and take up for them, when your own . . . you know what happened to me and Emma. Attacked on the trail—wagons burned—lost everything we had. Set afoot and had to walk into the stage station. If they hadn't happened to be Pawnees and not set on killing, we would have lost our scalps. We hadn't done nothing to them."

"You keep out of this," she snapped at him. "Let Starr answer for himself."

I had begun angrily, talking a little heedlessly, in heat. I set myself to be reasonable. "The cold fact is that when one country invades another, and that is what colonization is all about, the natives can be handled in two ways. Either they can be exterminated at once and got rid of, or they can be subdued and ruled. As I see it, the first settlers in our country were too weak to exterminate the Indians. So, little by little, as fast as they ran into them and met up with them, they tried to subdue and rule. That's the way the government is still trying to work it. Subdue and rule."

"If the government would only honor its treaties," she said, "and keep the white men off the Indian lands . . . and if they would find honorable men to deal with them. . . ."

"That works two ways," I said. "Both sides make these treaties with their tongues in their cheeks. The government sometimes means to try to make a treaty work. Sometimes it gets hold of good men, though mostly it doesn't, I'll admit. But the Indian don't ever mean to honor a treaty. A treaty to an Indian is something temporary, to get something he wants. They skirmish around and cause a lot of trouble on purpose, so they'll get another treaty, because another treaty means presents and food and supplies to get them through another lazy winter. Right now the government is feeding nearly a thousand Cheyennes through the winter over near Fort Laramie. Come spring every last one of them will scatter and make war on the trail. But they'll get through the winter without much trouble, in pretty good shape, and that's what they wanted when they turned friendly. Friendlies always use the government that way."

"They learned it from the white man," she said.

"Oh, God," I said. "You think white men invented treaties? Indians have always dealt with each other that way. They didn't sign papers, but they smoked a pipe together. They got together and talked and parleyed and smoked and lined up with each other, or against each other. And this year's ally may be next year's enemy. It's just for one battle. And the tribe that can outparley and outsmart another gets the best of it. The difference now is they're all out to outsmart the whites.

"The United States government has got a lot to give away. And it's pretty free with presents. All the good things they've learned to like and want for themselves they can get as presents. And they mean to get all of them they can. They make a little war, then sign another treaty and get more presents. They can keep this up a hundred years."

"Just the same," she said, "there's a lot to be said on their side. Popo says . . ." She stopped suddenly and her face got red.

There was a long silence. I felt as if a cold hand had touched my neck. The hairs on it rose, creepy and ripply. "Well," I said, when Ed had broken the silence with a long sucked-in breath, "what does Popo say? And how does he say it? He doesn't seem to speak much English."

Her chin went up. "He speaks English perfectly well and far more politely than you do."

I thought I had felt anger in my lifetime, thought I knew what it was like to have it boil up and sweep through me and churn and seethe and shake my insides. But nothing I had ever felt before was like what happened to me when Bernie said that. A man really does see red if he's mad enough . . . everything turns dark and reddish and whirled about. And he has to hang on hard to where he is and what he is and what he's doing. He has to tie himself with a leather strap to keep from going wild. What I wanted to do was get my hands on Bernie—shake her and choke her and hit her, do anything to shut that cool mouth up. I could have killed her for giving that gray-eyed half-breed a second of her time, for letting him near enough to speak to her, for all the implications of nearness and the times they had walked or ridden or stood or sat and talked . . . and maybe touched.

It was Ed who lashed out at her and gave me time to get hold of myself. "He's kept it mighty well hidden," he stormed at her. "He won't speak when he's trading. I never heard him say one word anybody could understand. Just grunts and makes sign. And when did you know him well enough he spoke to you?" He walked around the end of the counter toward her. "Answer me! When have you seen him? Where? What's he doing talking to you?"

She had gone pale and she looked scared, but she stood her ground. "Is there a law against being courteous around here? I have seen him exactly three times. Once he caught my horse for me . . . at the corral. And saddled him for me. I thanked him and he replied in English. I was so astonished . . . and I was pleased. . . . Well, is it a sin to talk to an Indian?"

"No sin," Ed said, "but if you're a woman and alone it's damned risky. So you had a little chat with him out at the corral."

"There was no harm in it," she said. "I asked him where he learned English. He said he worked with white men in Taos for many years. They trapped beaver, he said, and he trapped beaver with them. He grew up in the mountains where they wanted to trap and he was their guide. He speaks French and Spanish, too."

"That's not unique," I said. "Every trader in the west speaks French . . . a little. And everybody in Taos *is* Spanish."

"When was the next time you talked with him?" Ed said.

"Right here in the store," she said, with some spirit. "Not more than a month ago. You were out on the range. It was the day of that bad storm. He brought some hides in. Emma told me to trade with him. When he got through, it was still storming and he waited till the worst of it was over before leaving."

"I reckon he sent his squaw out in the storm to see to his horses," I said.

"She wasn't with him," she said.

"You were alone in the store with him?" Ed said.

"And perfectly safe," she snapped at him. "A lot safer than I would have been under the same circumstances with a lot of the white men who come here."

"That's not true," Ed said. "There's not a white man in the country who would touch you or Emma."

"I don't know about Emma," she said, "but plenty of them have tried with me. Including your boss!"

"Who happened at that time," I said, "to be in love with you and wanting to marry you."

"I'm glad you put it in the past tense," she said. "It's a big relief to me."

"Oh, hell!" I said. "You can sure twist a man's words around. I reckon waiting out the storm was when he gave you that set piece about how mistreated the Indians are."

"No," she said, smiling sweetly, "that came the third time we talked together. That was when he gave me the set piece about mistreatment."

"When was that? And where?"

"Is this an inquisition?" she said. "Well, I don't mind. I haven't got anything to hide. I haven't met him secretly out on the range, if that's what you're trying to find out. It was here. In the store again. Three days ago. Ask Ed where *he* was that day."

With that she swept out of the store and I do mean swept. She whirled about and moved so fast that her skirts fanned up a breeze that set the dust on the floor to flying.

I stared at Ed. "Where *were* you?"

He grinned sheepishly. "I was up at the Doe's. It wasn't *where* I was she was hinting at. It was the condition I come home in. It was like this, Starr. He bought a yoke of steers from us about a month ago and said when it was handy have one of the boys drive 'em up to him. It just never did come handy till the other day."

"How come you to drive them up instead of one of the boys?"

He fidgeted. "Well, goddammit, Starr, I stay stuck in here so much I get to feeling caged up. I got to get out. So I drove them up for him that day."

"And he had a bottle."

"He had a bottle. The best old bourbon I ever drank. And I drank too much of it." He chuckled. "I hadn't tasted any for so long, it sort of went to my head."

"And Emma and Bernie didn't approve."

"I wouldn't put it that mild. Between 'em they stirred up something more like active real violent disapproval. I thought Emma was going to throw a hot pie at me for a minute or two. She might have, but she don't like waste." He pulled at his chin, thinking. "But I left Brownie in the store. Wonder where he'd got to that Bernie was minding it?"

I had begun to cool off and think a little. "Twice he's come when you've been gone. Strike you there's anything funny about that?"

"Well, it could be just a coincidence. That storm come up fast that day and I sure didn't post any notice I was going out on the range," he said.

"You didn't have to. He could have seen you leave. And take the boys with you."

"Yeah. He could have. And seen me leave with them steers for the Doc. But I know I left Brownie in the store that day."

"See Brownie and find out what happened."

"Sure."

Ed went out and I paced around in the store thinking about it. Aside from Bernie's connection with it, I didn't like it—the Ute coming in to trade when Ed was away. And if an Indian, any Indian, could come in and find nobody but women on the premises, Ed was getting too careless. It was always easy to let your guard down when month after month went by and there was no reason for alarm. This laxness, especially in easterners coming to the west, nearly always lay back of swift, sudden, unexpected attack. Ed had to be jacked up.

I was beginning to wish the Ute would take his little band of people and move some place else with them. But he had thrown in with the Cheyennes, the Southern Cheyennes, and their traditional home was between the Smoky Hill and the Platte. As long as he stayed with them, he would be around.

Though the Indians all along the line were fairly quiet in '63, there was considerable uneasiness about them. General Connor, over at Salt Lake, kept insisting that they were confederating and massing together and sooner or later all hell was going to bust loose. The *Rocky Mountain News*, the Denver paper, was always agitating about the Cheyennes.

We didn't see much evidence of trouble along the Platte. The Indians just drifted up and down the river and trailed around the way they always did. Which of course meant to any knowledgeable person that they knew every single thing that was happening the whole length of the road. Not one thing ever escaped an Indian's eye. But as long as you could see them, loose and drifting, it didn't bother you too much.

Ed came back. "Brownie says the Ute brought one of the stage ponies in. He was lame. Said the Ute told him he'd seen it limping down the road and herded it back to the station. Brownie took it to the corral. Said all that was wrong was a loose shoe. He took it off and put a new one one."

"How'd the horse get out?"

"Somebody left the bars down."

"Yes." I studied it over. "I don't know why he would, but suppose the Ute wanted Brownie out of the store. He could have let the bars down himself, driven a horse down the road and loosened the shoe himself."

"Hell, he could have picked a better way than that," Ed said. "He could have driven the whole herd out and started a stampede. He'd have had every man on the place riding after 'em."

I shook my head. "You can't read an Indian's mind. Maybe he didn't want that much of a fuss. But I don't like it, Ed." Then I laid the law down to him. None of the women was ever to come in the store again when Indians were trading unless he or Brownie or some responsible man was present. The store was never to be left without *two* men in it, so that should one be called out the store wouldn't be left unattended. The women were never to ride out on the range without adequate protection and that meant not one man, but two or more. Both Bernie and Bucky had got into the habit of riding out with only one hand along. "Tighten this place up," I said, "and keep it tight. I'd like to send the Ute packing—tell him to trade over at One-Eyed Jack's or at Morrow's—but I'd probably start a war. But I've told you before and I tell you again, watch that one. Watch 'em all, for that matter. Because just when you feel easiest they'll hit. And they'll hit a man who has befriended them just as quick as any other. Another thing. Out on the ranch work in threes instead of pairs and don't put all your faith in your revolvers. Keep a shotgun on your saddles."

Ed had the wind up now and believed me. "We'll take no chances," he promised. "I won't let things get slack again."

Of course I stormed away still madder than a hornet at Bernie. Nothing makes a man madder than a proud, independent, high-spirited, stubborn woman who stands up to him, won't listen to him, won't do to suit him. He runs out of words, it doesn't do any good to grit his teeth, and what he wants most to do is smash something physically. I think the only thing that I could have got any satisfaction out of the day I left would have been to turn Bernie Buchanan over my knee and beat the daylights out of her. Since I couldn't do that, I left vowing to put her completely out of my mind. Never to think of her again. Never to care what she said or did or what happened to her. Just bury her beyond digging up again.

It's only in books that there's any neat, clean ending to things. In life, you just keep going along doing the best you can. To the day you die. Nothing really ends, neatly, cleanly, or even messily, as long as you keep breathing. You just sort of keep sliding from one thing into another. It wasn't possible not to think of Bernie. She was part of the ranch, and the ranch was part of my life. If I thought of it, I thought of her. On a long night ride I often found all my thoughts centered on the place, and the people, and inevitably her.

In August that year I suddenly came to the end of my tether with the division job. I had to get back to driving. I knew I had now learned precisely what driving meant to me. It meant my life, exactly as I had said. Work is the wrong word for what a man devotes his whole life to doing, but I don't know a better one. Or maybe work is the right word for what most men devote their lives to doing, stumbling into it and having to stick with it gray day after gray day. Maybe Thoreau was right when he said that most men lead lives of quiet desperation. Maybe only the lucky ones, the ones who know very early what they most want to do and do it, or the ones who stumble luckily into something they love, ever know work can be the opposite of gray and can be every shimmering color in the rainbow. But to see the colors, it must be work that is life itself.

I was one of the lucky ones and this stint as division agent made me know it for certain. Practically, the purpose of my work driving stage was to carry passengers and the United States Mail twenty-five to fifty miles farther along the road. This was the job and this was what I was paid to do.

But the true purpose of my work was something entirely different. It was the dare that the road, the team, the coach and my own skill handed me daily. The dare of the possible perfect. It is possible, and it can be done, that I can so

208

command my will and my skill that a perfect, absolute harmony of the four parts is achieved. That not once does the team break the beautiful rhythm of their road gait. That not once do my eyes misgauge or my hands err. That not once is the following balance of the coach strained. The purpose, the reason, the dare, is the perfect run.

It it's done, if I bring it off, there is no feeling on earth like it. It's flags flying and bugles blowing and the shivering stars splintered in the sky. It's the first morning of the Seven Days. And that's what work ought to be, at least once in a while, for every man. I was lucky, I knew it, and I knew I must keep my luck.

The agent in Atchison put a man on, I turned over the job and went to St. Joe for one more short visit with my folks. When I started driving again there wouldn't be much chance to see them very often.

I found the place in an uproar, the curtains down, the rugs rolled up, most of the furniture crated and the house buzzing with busy people. "What in the name of God is going on here?" I asked, when I found my mother after picking my way around boxes and cartons and hay and straw. "You moving?"

"You can wrap those plates in newspaper for me, Starr," my mother said, "and pack them in this barrel of straw. Yes, we're moving." She was hot and the sweat was pouring down her face, but her hands stayed busy.

I started on the plates. "Where? You bought another house?"

"I wouldn't be packing all this thoroughly to move into another house. We're moving to Denver."

I almost dropped a plate. "Now? This summer? I thought that was a couple of years off yet."

"So did I," she said, "but your father is out there now. He is building a house."

"Will you stop a minute," I said. "Just sit down and tell me what's happened."

She did. She drew up a chair and let herself down into it with a sigh. Of late years she had put on a lot of weight and was just about as broad as she was tall. She wiped her face and looked at me and started laughing. "It seems sudden, doesn't it? It isn't, really. I knew last year I must begin preparing for it pretty soon. He couldn't wait. He's

209

been restless ever since we decided. Wanting to get on out there. And I don't mind, Starr. Not a bit. It doesn't matter to me when we go. I just want him to be happy about it. In fact," and she chuckled, "I was the one who just happened to wonder, aloud, one day why we had to stay in St. Joe until he sold the freight line. Why he couldn't run it just about as well from Denver as here."

"You set him off like a rocket, didn't you?" I said.

"I thought it best," she said. "He was beginning to fret. He has Dave and Tom ready to take over the business at this end. We drew up plans for the house and figured out what he would need . . . windows, doors, finished lumber and so forth. He took it with him and went out on the first train this spring. The house is nearly finished. He'll be home next week and then he'll drive all this stuff out."

"You going to drive out with him? You and the kids?"

"He says not. He says we'll take the stage. But we aren't." She looked at me, her eyes twinkly and mischievous. "I've always wanted to make just one trip with a train across that country. I've heard nothing but wagon trains for twenty-five years. I mean to do it now. I'll never have another chance."

I laughed. "Good. You'll enjoy it. Why, sick people make the trip for their health. Every season there are dozens of private carriages and camping outfits cross the prairies. People traveling to restore their health."

"Does it?"

"I don't really know, Mama. I just see them along the way. It may kill them for all I know. But most of them I've had any talk with insist they're feeling better for the trip. They travel in pretty fancy outfits. All the comforts of home, usually. And take their time so as not to get played out. Papa can fix you up so comfortably in one of the wagons you'll never know you left home."

"That," she said firmly, "is not my idea of traveling. I want to *know* I've left home." She bestirred herself again. "I can't waste any more time sitting here. I've rested long enough. Oh," she swung around, "I almost forgot. Fanny and Nellie mean to start a school when we get settled. For young ladies. Are there enough young ladies in Denver for a school to do well, Starr?"

"Yes, ma'am," I said. "Denver is bigger than St. Joe, Mama. And growing bigger every day."

"Roll that other barrel over here for me, please. Well, that's a relief. They have set their hearts on it."

"They'll have their hearts set on something else before they've been there very long," I said, laughing. "They'll be marrying. There are a dozen men for every woman in Denver yet. They'll be besieged."

She was bent over a barrel, laying the bottom row of dishes. She was so short she was bent double and I had the irreverent wish to give her a little spank, which you may be sure I did not. She raised up, her face beet red. She looked at me thoughtfully. "It gives me a peculiar feeling . . . to think of my girls marrying in Denver. I've always supposed they would marry here, in St. Joseph. Somebody we knew. Somebody they grew up with. Why, they're liable to marry anybody, aren't they? Some man from St. Louis, or Boston, or New York. Good gracious, Starr! I'm not sure I like that idea at all."

"They're just as liable to marry some man from Atchison or St. Joe," I said. "There are more Atchison and St. Joe men out there than any others. There are even a few," I said, teasing her, "from Kentucky."

"Now, I would approve of that," she said, laughing. "Well, we'll cross those bridges when we get to them. In the meantime, I'm glad to hear they will do well with a school."

I suddenly remembered Bucky. "Mama, could you take on one more little girl?"

"Friend of yours?" she said. "Easily. Mine are growing up. The baby is five now."

"Well, this one is a little older than that." I told her about Bucky. "Emma wants to get her away from the station for a while. Wants her to have more schooling. Emma's taught her the best she could, and her sister has taught her, too. But for nearly five years all she's known is a stage station, and Emma wants her to have a change."

My mother nodded. "She's very wise. How old is the child?"

"I don't know . . . eleven, twelve, something like that." I counted up on my fingers. "Let's see, she was nine when I

211

first went to work for the Company . . . that's four years. My Lord, she's thirteen."

Mama laughed and shook her head. "Time don't stand still, Starr."

"That's the beautiful truth," I said. "It's hard to realize the kid is growing up. She's pretty much of a tomboy, and little and scrawny."

"You sure?"

"Sure about what?"

"Sure she's little and scrawny. They aren't usually—at thirteen and fourteen. Fanny is seventeen, Nellie is fifteen. Take a good look at them sometime."

"Yes, but Bucky's not . . ."

Mama shook her head and I began wrapping dishes pretty fast. So that was what was different about her the last time I was home. She wasn't as little and scrawny as she had been. In fact, come to think of it, and I did, she had looked pretty chesty. I'd heard her fussing at Emma one day. "I need some new dresses. They're all getting too tight."

And Emma had laughed and said, "We'll have to let out some seams, won't we?"

I handed Mama a stack of dishes. She said, "As soon as we're settled, Starr, we'll let you know and Emma can send her to us."

"Maybe you better look her over first," I said. "You'll be stopping at the ranch as you go out. She's a handful, I warn you. You might decide she's too much for you."

"They don't come too much for me," she said. "I've had twelve. No two alike. Each one a different child with different problems. All any child needs is a firm hand and a lot of love."

"She's had them both," I said, "and she's a good kid. But she's just bouncing full of life. Will the other kids mind, you think?"

"No. They'll just tuck her in and she'll be one of them. Probably be a good thing for her to have some brothers and sisters."

"The best thing in the world," I said. "Well, I'll probably bring her over myself. I'm going back to driving."

"You are? That's nice. Where? Which run?"

There was that about my mother. Once her children were grown she never quarreled with what they wanted to do. It was a kind of pride in her and maybe a little smugness. Because they were *her* children, whatever they wanted to do was fine, for her children could do no wrong. They would just naturally choose to do honorable, good things. It was the obverse of laying down the law and it worked a whole lot better. "I'll be driving into Denver," I said. I didn't tell her, for she didn't understand the system, that I would be bumping a good driver for the run. But I was senior and that was the way things worked. I wanted a good stage for a while.

"Now, that *is* nice," she said. "We'll be seeing you much oftener."

I agreed it would be very nice, and went for a hammer to nail up the barrelheads.

Chapter 15

I stopped over a day at Fort Kearney on my way home. Closing out as division agent there were some details at the Kearney end of the division I wanted to check over personally. The chore was almost finished when the eastbound stage arrived. No stagefaring man can ever ignore the arrival or departure of a stage. I stopped work to watch it come in.

Billy Cody brought the grays in at a rough, showy gallop, then sawed the lines and used his brake too hard to pull them up. Rough on the team. If that boy, I thought to myself, was on my division he would quit that kind of stuff or be out of a job very shortly. The passengers began to unload. Two men got out and then, handed down by them most gallantly, came a slender pretty young woman. I didn't notice who else got off, because the young woman was Bernie. I stiffened, taken by surprise. Where was she going? Why was she traveling?

She thanked the gentlemen prettily, with ladylike courtesy but no marked enthusiasm, and quickly walked away from them toward the dining room. She had the most graceful walk, light and easy and natural, swift without being hurried. The gentlemen looked startled at her quick dismissal of them and I felt a touch of glee. You've met your match, I thought, a real expert at handling men like you. She'll let you be courteous, but don't presume on it. She's like silk, smooth but tough.

She was as neat and trim as she must have been when she left home, but that wasn't surprising. By now, having seen all the untidiness and blowsiness and loose-endedness that overtakes most women travelers, she had learned how to travel comfortably and cleanly. For instance, she wasn't wearing crinolines, to crush and take up room. Her dress was a plain dark stuff that wouldn't wrinkle or show soil. It was sleeved to the wrist, both for modesty and to protect her arms from windburn. She wore no jewelry or trinkets of any kind except the pin to close the throat of her dress. There was nothing to jingle or be bothersome. She wore a small hat and over it and her face was pinned a light, sheer veil as protection against dust and insects. If she had been going to New York, she would have arrived looking decent, clean and unruffled.

I went through the office door into the dining room and saw her standing there, hesitating a little at taking a seat at the common table. I went forward. She saw me and a glad, welcoming smile broke over her face. "Starr! What a nice surprise to see you."

"And what a nice surprise to see you," I said. "Look. Oliver keeps a table over here in the corner, for friends and stage people. Wouldn't you rather eat there?"

"Much rather," she admitted. "I've had a great plenty of watching stage passengers eat this past year."

I pulled a chair out for her and she sank into it with a little sigh. "Tired?" I said.

"A little," she said. "It's so hot."

She unpinned her veil and threw it back and I saw that she looked tireder than she admitted. She was pale and there were dark smears under her eyes. "It's nice you're at this end of the division," she said.

I felt uncomfortable, but decided I might as well get it over with. "I'm on my home," I said. "I've given up the division. Going back to driving."

I expected a storm and braced myself for it, but she only studied me quietly, then smiled. "That isn't very astonishing."

"No," I said, "I don't suppose it is. I gave it a good try, though."

She nodded. "Longer than I thought you would." She picked up a newspaper lying on the table and folded it, fanned herself with it. "This heat . . . I don't have much appetite."

"Just take some soup and ask for an omelette. Eat something, but not much. The heat and the motion won't bother you so much."

"I know," she said.

I tried to be offhand about it, but it had to be asked. "Where are you going—in this heat?"

"Home," she said, putting the newspaper down. She began rearranging the silverware. "Back to Ohio."

There was a spasm of pain in my chest. So she was going home. Giving up on the west. "You didn't ever want to go back east, remember?"

"Yes," she said, not looking at me, "well, now I do." The silverware suited her finally and she quit fidgeting with it. "Now I do want to go back."

There is a feeling when something hurts and shocks and betrays you suddenly which I can only describe as all-gone —a sinking, empty feeling, breathy and squeezed tight inside. It was an effort to talk around it. I wanted a big slug of whisky more than anything, to belt down and loosen my insides. "Any special reason?" I said. "Anything happened?"

"No," she said, "I just don't like it out here any more. I want to go home."

A girl came and put water on the table and I told her what to bring us. When she went away, I said, "What did Emma think of it?"

"She understands." She met my eyes finally, levelly and quietly. "And you'd better understand, Starr. I don't belong out here. I never have belonged out here. I never will belong out here. It's best for me to go home."

"I could understand that if it was true," I said. "But you loved this country. And you fitted right in. You learned everything you needed to know. I've not seen many women who belonged more quickly. Something's happened."

She shook her head. "Nothing's happened except that I *don't* like it out here any more." She was suddenly vehement. "It's more than that. I hate it out here. Hate everything about it . . . the country, the people, the ways . . ." and she made a fist of one hand, "I hate all of it." But her eyes filled with tears.

"You been sick?" I said.

She was trying to find a handkerchief in her reticule. She shook her head. She found the handkerchief and wiped her eyes, then smiled weakly. "I detest women who cry. No, I've not been sick. Why?"

"You don't look very well. You're not happy about this, for some reason. If you were as glad to be going out of the country as you want me to believe you are, you'd be looking more joyful. You've been brooding about this a long time, haven't you? Long enough to make dark circles under your eyes. . . ."

"Oh, Lord," she said, "can't you just leave it alone? Do you have to pry into everything? I'm going home and that's all there is to it."

"Has it got anything to do with me?"

"The vanity of the man! No." And she said it so unhesitatingly and so firmly I knew it was the truth. "It has nothing at all to do with you."

The girl brought the soup. Bernie sampled it and said it was good. Neither of us said anything more until we had finished and the plates had been taken away. "You sure nothing has happened?" I said then.

There was a little color in her face now. "Of course I'm sure. What *could* happen?"

"Oh, I don't know. You and Emma could quarrel. . . ."

"I would never quarrel with my sister," she said.

I laughed. "She's about the only one you wouldn't quarrel with. You had many a one with me."

"I know," she said. "I'm sorry. I don't want to quarrel with you any more, Starr. I'm going to miss all of you— Emma and Bucky. And you too. I *will* miss you, Starr."

"Then don't go. Stay here and . . ."

"Don't say it. Please don't say it. I'm going home. It's final. This is the last time I'll see you. Don't spoil it."

The girl brought the omelette and the strong sulphur smell of the eggs was repulsive to me. I couldn't have eaten a bite of it without choking. "You aren't ever coming back?"

"No," she said. "No. Not ever. It's best that way."

She picked up a fork and began eating. She asked for the bread and I passed it to her. It was such a mystery to me. I couldn't make heads or tails of it, and from my knowledge of her, it wasn't like her to throw in the sponge this way. But one thing was certain. Her mind was made up, definitely, positively, she was sure of what she was doing.

"I was a little worried about leaving Emma," she said.

"In fact, I didn't leave until we found somebody to help her." She looked at me brightly. "Did you know Dickson had got married?"

Dickson was one of the ranch hands. "No. Where'd he find somebody to marry him?"

"Down at Cottonwood. The Company put on a new blacksmith last month and he has a daughter just the right age. Her name is Bonnie."

"He talked her into marrying him mighty fast, didn't he?" I said. "A month's acquaintance."

"Oh, it's a time and place to move fast, out here. He went courting four times was all. Then he brought her home with him. But she was the perfect answer for us. I helped Emma train her before I left and she's going to do fine. And she'll be permanent, since he don't work for the Company. Won't always be shifting around."

"You being sarcastic?" I said.

"No," she said, and she laughed. "I'm not being sarcastic at all. That's all over. But it is nice that he works on the ranch and not for the Company, isn't it?"

"Yes," I said, "it's nice."

She ate all of the omelette and drank a glass of condensed milk. The girl urged a piece of peach pie on her but she didn't want it. She did ask for a cup of coffee. "Nothing else, thank you. The omelette," she said to the girl, "was so good. Do you put a little milk in when you're beating the eggs?"

The girl beamed at the praise. "I don't do none of the cooking, ma'am, but I believe they do. In the kitchen. I believe they do put a little milk in the eggs."

"I thought so. It's the only way to make them light." She turned to me. "How much time is there?"

I looked at my watch. "Five minutes."

"Then I must say this fast," she said. "I want to tell you, Starr, that if I've hurt you, I'm sorry. . . ."

"You don't have to . . ."

"I know I don't, but I want to." She smiled at me so winsomely that I thought I'd die. "A girl like me, high-spirited and high-tempered, can be thoughtless and quarrel easily and say ugly things, mean things, without even trying. I know I have and I wish I hadn't. I didn't have to be

218

so hateful. I wish you could remember me . . . remember just the best things."

I just looked at her. I couldn't say anything. The way I would remember her was the way she was right now, so pretty, tired, with dark-circled dark eyes, soft sweet voice talking and hurting me in the talking more than she had ever done. For the things she was saying now told me with absolute finality that she didn't care for me.

In a whole long year nothing she had said or done had convinced me of that. She had raged at me and stormed at me the way a woman who deeply cares does rage and storm at a man, because she not only cares what a man makes of himself, for himself, she cares what he makes of himself for her. She cares about the kind of life they will have together. But this quiet, sweet reasonableness was the opposite of caring. It was possible only if she no longer cared.

In anguish I understood that . . . that it no longer mattered to her. Once, because she did care, at least a little, it did matter. Her own life was involved. She had a big say in what I did, for it would affect her. No more. Now, it didn't touch her. It wasn't important any longer. Somewhere, somehow, sometime, she had said good-bye to Starr Fowler, the man who loved her and who, I would swear it, she had loved. It was over and done with, totally finished. That's what she was saying, and that's what I would remember, and forever the crying grief and loss.

"Who is he?" I said, almost choking on the words.

She stared at me.

"Who *is* he?" I repeated.

She reached for her veil and began to pull it down. "How like you to believe there must be another man. That only a man could make me go home." She dropped the veil, like a final curtain between us, and pinned it neatly. "You are even more vain than I believed you." She reached for her reticule and took out her gloves. "I expect the stage will be around by the time I get outside."

I stood to allow her to pass. She pulled on her gloves and buttoned the wrists carefully. Then she looked up at me and smiled. "I'm sorry, Starr."

I paid for her dinner and walked outside with her and

we waited for the stage to be brought round without saying anything more. When it came, I walked her out to it. I had my hand under her elbow ready to help her onto the step when she turned and put her hands on either side of my face. She kissed me, full on the mouth, but as cool, as untroubled, as lightly as if I were a distant relative. She might have been saying good-bye to a nice young cousin.

I put her on the coach, told her to have a good journey, heard her say take care, then walked away . . . blind and aching and churning and full of loss. Inside the station, its dim gloom suited me. I wondered, bitterly, at the unreason of a man that he could so waste a year of his life, so fix his feelings on one person that he could while the days and weeks and months away, and end the time far more empty than when it began. For if I had fooled myself for a whole long year, I couldn't fool myself now. If there was nobody else, there still wasn't me, either. Say it now, I told myself, say it and believe it and be done with it. I said it, but God, what an empty hole it left.

Two days later I was at the ranch. I didn't want to hear anything about Bernie but I had to listen to Emma's chatter and to Bucky's until it was all told. How she had decided about two months ago to go home. How quiet and sensible about it she had been. How she had carefully trained Bonnie Dickson to take her place. How she had made her preparations, sorting out her clothes, giving some to Bucky and helping Emma make them over for her, then packing her trunk and shipping it home ahead of her. How she had fixed a day to leave and how she had left exactly on the day she planned. "She just made up her mind and that was it," Emma said. "At first I tried to talk her out of it, but when I saw she had her head set on it, I quit."

"She didn't look well to me," I said, finally. "I thought maybe she had been sick."

"No. She hadn't been sick." Emma was thoughtful. "I think it worried her, making up her mind. She didn't say anything to me about it, but I think until she made up her mind it bothered her. In some ways, I believe she hated to go. But it was plain she wasn't very happy here any longer. I guess the new wore off and she could see things for what they are out here. Bernie is a lot better educated than I am, and she thinks straighter about things, maybe."

"That's a big maybe," I said. "For my money, you think a whole hell of a lot straighter than she does. Something hackles Bernie most of the time. But—if she decided she didn't like it and didn't want any more of the west, that's it. That just finishes it."

"That's what I told Ed. I said if she wasn't going to be happy here it was best for her to go back. Though I'll miss her like my right arm." She slid a look at me. "I hope it didn't upset you too much, Starr."

"No," I said, "her going home didn't upset me at all."

"Well, that's a big relief," she said. "I'm glad you got over her enough it didn't bother you. I do hope now we can have some peace around here. If I had known what was going to happen, I never would have sent for her in the first place."

"Put it out of your mind," I said. "Let's start from here, right now." And I told her about the school my sisters were going to open in Denver.

Emma seized onto the idea of sending Bucky with great enthusiasm. "Why, it's no piece to Denver. She can come home for holidays. And with your mother seeing to her . . . why, it couldn't be better, Starr. It's the best thing that could have happened. It takes care of everything for Bucky right now, doesn't it?"

"I thought it might," I said.

Bucky went into delirium immediately. How soon were my father and mother going to move? When were Fanny and Nellie going to open the school? How soon could she go? What was Denver like? Would she like it? What would school be like? Oh, and clothes . . . she had to have lots of new clothes. She mustn't be a shame to me and my sisters and my mother! And would my little sisters like her? Would Fanny and Nellie like her?

She nearly sent Emma into distraction, finickying around about the kind of clothes she had to have. "Bucky, you'll make do with what I can make for you. Stop telling me what you must have!"

"Send one change for her," I said, "and let Mama or Fanny and Nellie get what she needs at the store. For all I know they may want all the little girls to wear some kind of uniform."

Bucky was appalled. "A uniform! What kind of uniform, for heaven's sake? Uniforms are ugly. I don't want to wear a uniform."

"My God," I said, "I didn't say you'd have to. I said that might be their idea. In some girls' schools they do wear 'em. And if all the other girls wear one, you will too, and like it."

"No, I won't. Orphans wear uniforms. In Orphans' Homes they wear uniforms. I wouldn't be caught dead looking like an orphan!"

I groaned and Emma pushed her hair back off her forehead. "Why don't you just keep your mouth shut, Starr? I'll take care of Bucky's clothes."

Bucky immediately shifted to my side. "Mama, he's just trying to be helpful. Don't be cross with him."

"You," I said, "quit pestering your mother. You simmer down and be as helpful as you can. Or, I warn you, I won't take you to Denver at all."

"Oh, fiddle," she said, laughing, "who needs you? I can go to Denver by myself."

As it turned out, I didn't take Bucky to Denver. By the time my people came through on their way, I was working. I met their train between Pierson's and Fort Lupton and, though I only waved in passing, I rode out to their camp that night. Bucky was with them. "She was ready to go," my mother said, "so I just tucked her into the wagon and brought her along. She's a lovely child, Starr."

"I wouldn't go that far," I said, "but she's a good kid."

She poured me a cup of coffee and said, serenely, "That's what I said."

"How'd she take leaving Ed and Emma?"

"Tragically."

I laughed. "Daughter leaving her dear home, huh? Going far, far away, perhaps never to return."

"A little," my mother admitted. "She's young for her age. Still likes to play-act. But she was too excited to keep it up for long. She played and laughed and sang all that day with the children."

"Been homesick any?"

"Oh, she was a little subdued the first night. But I put

222

her to bed between two of the girls and they giggled and whispered and chattered till they drifted off to sleep. When I went to see about them she was as sound asleep as the other two girls."

My mother's last chore at night was to make the rounds of her children, straighten and tuck the covers, feel for feverish foreheads, and brush a light kiss across tousled heads. You didn't get too big for Mama to tuck you in. Which was sometimes embarrassing after you were a full-grown man with maybe a whiff of whisky on your breath, and maybe barely in your bed from a little carousing and Mama came wandering in, tucked your covers, felt for your forehead, gave your shoulder a light pat and brushed you with a butterfly kiss. You sometimes held your breath longer than was comfortable. But you were still Mahaley Fowler's child and Mahaley Fowler was going to see to you. It was very comforting, though—a little like having the Lord himself brush a long wing over your head and whisper a little grace for your sins.

When I got ready to leave the family that night Bucky followed me to my horse. "Starr," she said, "I love your family."

"That's good," I said, "they like you, too."

"Yes."

I hugged her and she wound her arms around my neck. "When we get to Denver you'll come to see us often, won't you?"

"You couldn't keep me away," I promised.

She sighed and dropped her head on my shoulder. "I won't miss Mama so much if you're there."

"You're going to be too busy to miss anybody," I said and kissed the top of her head, then yanked gently on one of her braids. "You take care, now. Mind your manners and study hard and be a credit to all of us."

She gave one little sob and clutched me frantically, then let go and took in a deep breath and braced back. "You'll never have any cause to be ashamed of *Bucky Westmoreland*," she said. "You see that North Star up there in the sky? I'll be faithful and true as that star!"

Her emphasis was fierce and amused me. She meant me to know she wasn't any Bernie Buchanan, blowing with the wind. "That's about as faithful as you can get," I said.

223

"I mean it!"

"I know you do. I believe you. Now, you write your mother often, hear? Don't get so busy you forget to write. She'll worry."

Riding back to Fort Lupton I had a satisfied feeling about young Bucky. She was going to be in good hands and everything was going to be fine for her. My eyes looked at the North Star more than once and I chuckled over her avowal of loyalty. She wasn't far wrong, I thought. Her loyalties hadn't been much tested yet, except to Ed and Emma, and me and a white rooster, but as far as they had been tested they had always proven up. I didn't doubt they would always stand steady if the time for further testing ever came.

Chapter 16

It was in September that we got Bucky settled in Denver.

The first week in October I came into the city at the end of the run one morning and after I had checked in found the whole office buzzing like a swarm of bees. Drivers off the mountains runs, stock tenders, the station agent, a lot of bystanders, were clustering and talking, parting, then coming together in clusters again, and the agent kept going in and out of the General Agent's office. "What's happened?" I asked a driver. "Somebody get killed?"

"No," he said, "but somebody's likely to. It's something about Jack Slade. The major up at Fort Halleck is raising a ruckus about him."

The station agent came out of Mr. Street's office just then. "Oh, Fowler," he said, "Mr. Street wants to see you."

I went into David Street's office. He saw me and began shooing everybody else out. "Everybody please get out. We'll handle this. I want to talk to Fowler."

With one hand he shut the door behind them and I saw that his other arm was bandaged and in a sling. "How'd you hurt your arm?" I said.

"Oh, I got nicked," he said. "Don't amount to much. Sit down, Fowler. Jack Slade came into the city last week. First time he's been in town for over a year. Got on a big, blind, tearing drunk of course, went roaring into the bar across the street and started shooting up the place. They sent for me and I went over to try to calm him down."

"He surely didn't shoot you," I said.

"No. Not on purpose. I ran into a wild shot was all."

"Have any luck quieting him down?"

"It took several of us," he admitted. "We had to get a rope on him. We hauled him out finally and got him sobered up. Sent for his wife and she took him home." He was suddenly very serious. "Then he went on another big drunk and went over to the fort . . . Fort Halleck. Shot up the sutler's store, wrecked the place, ruined a couple of thousand dollars' worth of merchandise and nearly killed the sutler before they overpowered him. The major has telegraphed us that they aren't going to let this one get by. They've got him in the guardhouse up there and they mean to keep him there. And if we don't fire him and get him out of the country, they will go clear to Washington with it."

I whistled. "Got us by the short hairs, haven't they?"

"Yes. Well, I don't blame them. This isn't the first time he's raised hell at the fort." He sat down at his big desk and eased his arm carefully up on it. He grunted at the pain of the movement.

"That arm is hurt worse than you said," I told him.

"No, it's just a flesh wound. The bullet went through the thick part of the upper arm. It's stiff and sore is all. Moving it hurts a little. The thing is . . ." he motioned with his good hand, "pour us a drink, will you?"

I did, and handed him his.

He sipped at it. "The thing is," he said, "Slade is absolutely no good to us any more."

"You're a little late deciding that, aren't you?" I said. "He's been hurting the Company more than he's been helping it for a couple of years."

"Well, that's been my opinion, too. That division of his has been a disgrace to us lately. But I'm not the General Manager. Orders have been to let him alone. Mr. Holladay's orders."

"The orders changed now?"

"The commandant at Fort Halleck has changed them," he said, grinning. Then he grew serious again. "Yes. Holladay says he has to go. We've got to fire him and make it stick. And he's got to get out of the country. You used to know him pretty well, didn't you?"

"Yes, sir," I said, "I knew him too well."

"Used to be a friend of his."

"Yes, sir. Pretty good friends. But we parted ways several years ago."

"Yes. So I've heard."

I thought I knew where this was leading, but neither of us said anything for a few minutes. It is times such as that when being a pipe smoker comes in handy. Nothing can take up a long silence as comfortably as filling and tamping and lighting a pipe, and you can string it out as long as necessary. It gives a man time to think without calling attention to it. And it gives the other man time to think without being too obvious about it.

While I was getting my pipe going, Mr. Street was watching out the window, tapping a pencil absently. When I scratched the match, he swiveled around and looked at me. "Slade has got to go. He has to be fired."

"That's liable to take Ben Holladay himself," I said.

"No," he said quietly, "it will only take me. But I'd like somebody he's known a long time to go along, somebody maybe he trusts. . . ."

"What makes you think he trusts me?" I said quickly. "We parted company three years ago. He's made a lot better friends than me in that time."

"I don't think so," he said, tapping the pencil against his chin. "I don't think so. As paymaster, four times a year I've worked Slade's division, same as all the others. He makes the division with me every time I make the payroll. Do you know what he always finds some way to ask before I move on? Never fails to ask? 'Heard any news of Fowler lately?' I didn't pay much attention to it the first few times, but then I got to expecting it."

"Well," I said, "he could have been wanting to keep tabs on me so he'd know where to find me when he decided my time had come."

"No, I don't think that either. There was a link there, one that he once valued and one that he couldn't quite break. With all that gang around him, he still harked back to a man he knew and liked and trusted. You know as well as I do he couldn't trust any of those outlaws of his. A man who lives by his gun knows he is going to die by it. And maybe at the hand of somebody pretty close to him. No. You tell me if he ever played cat and mouse with you."

"No, sir," I admitted, "he never gave me any reason to believe he was laying for me. He went his way and I went mine and we both let each other alone."

"Yes, that's what I thought. Well, here's what I want you to do. I'm going to fire him, but I want you with me. I have the authority of the Company behind me. I could give you that authority and send you up there alone, but I'll do my own dirty jobs. But you faced him down once and the only authority you had was guts and your conscience. He respected them then. He will again. You never lied to him and he knows you won't. I want you to tell him that this is the way it's going to be. He's through. He has no job with the Overland and he never will again. And tell him that unless he leaves the country the hand of every employee of the Company will be against him, every last damned hand. Does that go against the grain with you?"

"No, sir," I said. "I don't have any friendly feelings toward Jack Slade. I saw him kill Old Jules."

"All right, then," he stood up, closing the conversation. "We'll leave on the next stage."

I don't now remember the name of the commandant at Fort Halleck that year, but I remember what he looked like—short, stout, cigar-smoking, rough and tough talking. "Your man is in the guardhouse," he told us when we went into his office. "He's been climbing the walls since he sobered up. Yelling for his wife. Wants to see his wife. In my opinion, his wife is behind a lot of his meanness. Puts him up to a lot of it."

"Have you let her see him yet?" Mr. Street said.

"Not on your life. We let her in to see him when we had him behind bars once before. She smuggled a gun in to him and they came out together, two guns blazing. Nobody has seen him this time but the guard who takes him his meals."

"His gang been threatening?"

"Oh, they've stormed around some. Said they were going to take the jail down . . . said they'd get him out. Whisky talk. They've done nothing. Now, we've put up with this hoodlum of yours as long as we're going to, sir. He goes, or the word goes straight to Washington and we'll find out how big the Overland State Company is. We'll learn once and for all if the United States Army has to be intimidated by a cheap outlaw. I want this man fired and want it done immediately. And then I want him to get out of the country. We're not going to put up with him any longer."

I felt like asking if the United States Cavalry would help keep Slade out of the country, but thought better of it.

Mr. Street kept his temper, stayed quiet-spoken and courteous. "That's why I'm here, sir. We don't justify this man. He is no longer an employee of the Company."

"Good," the major said. "I don't want to have trouble with you people. Part of the reason we're here is to protect your stage line and the people who travel it. But this man Slade is worse than a whole band of hostile Indians. It's got so the passengers need protection from him."

"Yes. Well, if you'll excuse us, sir . . ."

"Not yet. The sutler is going to put in a claim for damages, sir. Almost his entire stock was ruined. Slade was a Company employee at the time. The sutler feels the Company should pay damages to him."

"I'll talk with him," Mr. Street said. "We'll see Mr. Slade now, if you please."

A guard detail, two men, one on either side of us, escorted us across the parade ground to the guardhouse. We found Slade lying on a pallet on the floor in a little cell not more than six by eight feet. There was one small, barred window set so high in the wall he'd have had to have a ladder to reach it. It was gloomy in the cell and it stank of vomit and urine and stale whisky-soaked flesh. Mr. Street turned to the sergeant of the guard. "I'll see this man in the outside room, please."

"He's not to be moved, sir," the sergeant said. "Major's orders."

"Tell the major I'll be responsible," Mr. Street said.

Slade heard us and roused up. "Is that you, Street? God, I'm glad you're here. I'm going crazy! Give me a drink, quick! Gimme a drink!"

"I don't have any whisky, Jack," Mr. Street said. "You'll have to wait awhile."

Slade groaned. "Why the hell didn't you bring some? You ought to know a man in the clink would be dry as a bone." He was in bad shape, frowsty and dirty and stinking, and he had the shakes. He rubbed his hands over his face and licked his lips and peered at me. "Is that Starr Fowler?"

"It's me," I said.

He clawed up the wall and stood, weaving and weak.

"Come to crow over me, did you? By God, if I had my gun ... gimme a gun and we'll see who does the crowing!"

We waited for the messenger from the major and Slade raved on, begging for a drink, begging for his gun, begging for Virginia Dale. Begging, begging, begging. Crying and weaving around, ranting and slobbering, clawing at the walls, clawing at his face and his clothes, gibbering and raving. This was a man? He was the revolting absence of manhood, a husk and a begging voice, a skin full of emptiness.

The sergeant came and said it was all right and the two guards took Slade by the arms to lead him out. He tried to throw them off and they roughed him up a little until he cried and begged them not to hit him again. "There's two of you!" he screamed. "You don't give a man a fair chance!"

There had been five of us in the corral at Chanseau's and Old Jules had been tied to a post.

In the outer room the guards put him in a chair and he sat there and shook, his hair hanging in his eyes, his clothes fouled and filthy.

Mr. Street stood in front of him and gave him time to get hold of himself. "Slade," he said then, quietly, "this is your last spree as an employee of the Company. You're out of a job now."

"No, Mr. Street, no, no. You don't mean that." He began gibbering. "Why, think of all I've done for the Company. Think of all I've saved 'em! Why, there's not been any trouble on my division for three years! I run a good tight division. You know that! Mr. Street, you take me off and inside a month there won't be a team left on the division. The thieving will begin again. Jack Slade's the one who stopped it. Jack Slade's the only one who can keep it stopped. I won't get in any more trouble. I give you my word, I won't. I promise I won't. I'll keep my nose clean from now on. I know I oughtn't to raised hell here at the fort. I know it. But it's the last time, I promise. . . ."

"You've promised a hundred times before when we've bailed you out of trouble," Mr. Street said. "No. You're through, Slade."

Slade looked ugly. "Who says so? I'll go to Holladay about this!"

"Holladay says so," Mr. Street said. "And you're not only through with the Company, you're through in this country. The people of the country are fed up with you and your gang. You'll have to get out."

"It's my country! By God, I helped make it. I'll decide if I leave or not!"

Mr. Street turned on his heel. "Fowler, I'm going to see the sutler. Bring Slade over to the station in time to make the next westbound."

"Yes, sir."

As Mr. Street went through the door, Slade made a lunge for my gun. I knocked him down. The guards started toward him and I motioned them back. "This is between me and him," I said.

He picked himself up and came at me windmilling. It wasn't an equal fight, the condition he was in, but he had the strength of blind fury on his side and he took a bloody hard licking before he stayed down. The guards doused him with water and picked him up and set him in the chair and he sat there, half drowned, strangling on his own breath, his nose still running blood. I handed him my bandanna. He slapped it to his nose and glared at me over it.

"This is the way it's going to be from now on, Slade," I said. "Get out of the country, or this is just the first beating you'll take. From one end of the line to the other, from every ranch, from every town, there won't be a man that's your friend. Every hand will be turned against you. You've been a big Company man and your word has been law. You've terrorized the country, you've gunned people down and you've made a hell of a lot of enemies. But without the Company behind you, you're nothing. And from here on, the Company will be on your neck, too. And somebody, someday, will gun you down, or hang you by that scruffy neck of yours. That's the way it's going to be from now on. Not one living soul on your side but Virginia Dale."

The bandanna muffled his voice. "I got my boys. They won't go back on me."

"They'll be the first ones to go back on you. Why do you think they've followed you? Because you were a big Company man and had some power. They'll desert you like rats desert a sinking ship. They'll run over each other getting

231

away from you. You'll be poison to them. You're through. All you've got left is Virginia Dale. Take her and get out while you can. Get as far from Colorado as you can, and don't come back."

"Well, just look who's telling it," he sneered. "Tell 'em to give me my gun and we'll see who does the telling."

"That's the only way you can talk isn't it?" I said. "Behind a gun, and with a man tied to a post."

"That still sticking in your craw?" he said, wiping his nose and smearing more blood over his face.

"It will to the day I die," I said.

"Lily-livered," he said. "Old man Beni had it coming to him."

"Maybe," I said, "but I remember one thing about him. *He didn't beg*. You couldn't make him beg. He didn't open his mouth and beg one time. He was an evil old man. But he was a better man than you. He died without begging."

He made another howling lunge at me and I knocked him down again. He lay where he fell and beat the floor with his fists and cried and gibbered. Without a gun, he was a bowl of jelly.

"Take him back to the cell till time for the stage," I told the guards and was glad to walk out of the place into the clean air.

It was a couple of hours to wait and I passed the time in a poker game with some non-coms. Nobody mentioned Slade. Nobody mentioned my swollen right hand and skinned knuckles. It was a quiet game. When the stage came in I had won a few worthless greenbacks. I went to get Slade. Mr. Street wasn't in sight anywhere.

The guards walked Slade over to the station and hung onto him while I went to find the driver to make arrangements to haul him out of there. When I got back outside, Mr. Street and the major were there. "The army will escort him, Fowler," Mr. Street said.

The major grinned. "We want to be sure he's off the military reservation."

"Yes, sir."

It was a relief. I'd thought I was going to have to guard him into Medicine Bow.

Mr. Street arranged to lay the passengers over so Slade

and his escort would have the coach to themselves. Then two fresh husky young lads in blue arrived and took over the detail. The stage left immediately and that was the last I ever saw of Jack Slade.

The Company paid a whopping big bill for damages to the sutler's store, but if there was any grumbling about it higher up I never heard of it. I think everybody from Ben Holladay to the least stock tender was glad to be rid of the man.

What he told his wife was between them, but it must have been enough to impress her. They hung around awhile and made a little trouble. She couldn't believe Jack's important job with the Company was over. But then they left. Hauled out of Wyoming and Colorado. For a while nobody knew where they had gone, then we heard they were in Montana.

Little by little we learned a few other things. We learned that all the time he was an Overland man, running such a clean line on his own division, Slade and Virginia Dale were at the head of an outlaw gang that was stealing from the Company on the other divisions. "My God," Mr. Street said, "he had a perfect setup. His own piece of line was clean as a dog's tooth. And he was stealing the other divisions blind."

Then we noticed there were far fewer road agents working over the line. When the Slades had left, six months went by without a holdup. The Company could put two and two together. Not only had Slade and his gang been running off stock and stealing equipment on the other divisions, he and Virginia Dale and their gang had been holding up stages on his piece of line. He was in a position to know every time there would be a big shipment of gold or silver coming through. Sometimes he would catch the treasure before it hit his division, sometimes he would let it go through and grab it in the next division. But sometimes he took it from his own drivers.

I think it was hindsight but one of the drivers he took a very rich treasure off of told me, "I knew it was Jack and Virginia Dale at the time."

"How'd you know it?" I said.

"Hell, she was short and dumpy. She had on pants but pants don't hide a woman's figure. A woman with a broad

233

bottom has still got a broad bottom in pants. I knowed her when she walked over to get on her horse. You couldn't mistake her."

"You knew it was a woman, but how'd you figure it was Slade's wife?"

"Well, damn, I knowed Slade! He didn't get off his horse. He just set there and looked on. He had a glove on his left hand but you remember he never would wear a glove on his gun hand. And he never could keep his hand off his gun. Always had to be moving that hand over his gun butt. They was both disguised. Had on Mexican pants and jackets and hats. And bandannas over their faces. But she got off her horse and come over where the boys had the box on the ground, trying to get it open. And there *he* set, on his horse, that hand playing with his gun in its holster. Sure, I knowed it was Slade. And I knowed the woman was Virginia Dale."

"You never told it, though, did you?"

"Hell, no! More than one driver knowed they was holding up the stages, but if you wanted to live you kept your trap shut. Slade would have drilled you first, then asked questions."

"You think any of the drivers on that section were in cahoots with him?"

"Yes, there was one or two, but don't ask me to name 'em. They've done and left, anyhow."

And that was that.

But there is an ending to Jack Slade's story that will curl your hair. They settled in Virginia City and for a while Slade swaggered around shooting up bars and winging a few people and getting into drunken brawls. But up in Virginia City they had a vigilante committee that didn't fool around with toughs like Slade very long. They caught him and tried him and condemned him all inside of one midnight hour.

He begged like a dog. "My God, my God, you can't hang me. You can't do this to me. Not to Jack Slade. Don't do it, boys. I'll never get in another brawl again. I give you my word, I won't. But don't hang me, boys. Don't do it!"

Some who had never heard him beg wouldn't credit it.

234

"Jack Slade beg? Never. Why, he was as cold-blooded as a snake. And too proud. Slade would never beg."

But I believed it, every word of it, and knew only the half had been told. He would have been on his knees, crying, pleading, promising, groveling. And watching for a chance to grab a gun.

They hung him. Virginia Dale was out of town at the time, and it was said some of the boys sent for her in a hurry but she got there too late. All she could do for him was help cut him down and turn on the boys with curses and hate for letting him down. "You let him die like a dog!" she stormed at them. "Jack Slade, the fastest gun in the west! To die like a dog!"

They said she wouldn't let him be buried in Montana. She wouldn't desecrate his body by putting it in that hated soil. So she had a coffin made and had it lined with lead. Then she poured it full of alcohol and laid Jack to rest in it. Pickled him in alcohol. They said she kept the coffin under her bed to keep the body from being stolen.

The next spring she brought him out, when the snows in the passes had melted, and still pickled in alcohol she took him home to Texas.

Chapter 17

The winter passed.

Men don't die of love, though they may think they will and sometimes, about two o'clock in the morning of a long white night, wish they could. To love somebody who doesn't love you is such a long yearning anguish I wouldn't wish it on my worst enemy. It's a sore in the flesh that won't heal, which bleeds again each time you touch it, and you touch it with a thousand memories.

Though you determine not to brood, riding toward Denver as the sun comes up and is bounced in a thousand mirrors of light off the mountains, she is suddenly there, coming out of her room this same time of day, the skin of her face still warm with sleep, pearly with a little flush, eyes a little dreamy yet and it's a cross you hang on that she goes into and comes out of that room alone. That all you may do is look at the flesh. Forbidden. The memories catch you when you least expect them and pull the scab off the old sore again.

But time does go by and with it goes a little more and a little more of the pain of renunciation. You lived through it before, I told myself, you can live through it again. But I knew I hadn't really lived through it before. No matter what I told myself, as long as she was in the west there had been a secret hope. I had only given myself a rest from the daily hurt. She was always there. I could always go back. Now it was really over. She had put two thousand road miles between us in the flesh, and a million star miles between us in hope. Nothing to do now but let it stab and get it over with.

In 1864, Colarado Territory was in the middle of an election year, split right down the middle with a pro-statehood party and an anti-statehood party. Governor Evans was head of the statehood party, running hard for the U.S. Senate. Right beside him, running for the House, was the head of the Colorado militia, Colonel John T. Chivington. They took the stand that the Indians had no rights in the Territory and it wouldn't be safe until they were all expelled, or even exterminated. Their screeching voice was the *Rocky Mountain News* and every Indian incident was magnified and headlined to keep the people in a panic and make them vote right.

Judge Armour was head of the anti-statehood party. He had often rendered decisions that much of the land in Colorado legally belonged to the Indians and that many of the whites coming into the Territory were no more than squatters. His voice was the *Blackhawk Journal*. The two parties and the two papers kept a constant wrangle going on.

As far back as 1851, the federal government had promised the Cheyennes and Arapahoes a $50,000 annuity if they would stay between the Platte and Arkansas rivers, consider that area home and live and hunt there. They agreed and signed a treaty. Mostly they stuck by it, but the government couldn't make good on its promises to keep the whites out. Hide hunters and gold-rushers stampeded across it, used up the grazing, killed off the buffalo and staked out their ranches.

In 1861, the government negotiated another treaty, at Fort Lyon, or thought they did, to put the Cheyennes on a reservation along the Arkansas. The Cheyennes never accepted the treaty or recognized it because their principal chiefs were not present. They continued to rove about in their chosen area, between the rivers, more and more unhappy and more and more belligerent. And to make it worse they were now allied with the Sioux.

"I remember when the Sioux started coming down onto the Platte," my father said. "It was after Bill Sublette sold Fort Laramie to the American Fur Company—about 1836. Astor's men persuaded the Sioux to move down off the Missouri and trade at Laramie. Up till then you never saw the Sioux on the Platte. They were all up in the north country."

We were sitting on the side porch of the big, handsome house my father had built out on the south edge of Denver.

All of his business was conducted downtown. He had his office in one of the bank buildings. But he wasn't about to let the town get between him and the mountains. He built his home in the outskirts and every morning he drove a fine team of sorrels in to his office. I was told, when the family got settled, there was plenty of room for me, but my ways had been my own ways too long. It suited me best to continue to live with the other drivers in the Company quarters. But I visited in the new home fairly often, say, once or twice a month, usually after supper for an hour or two.

It was June, now—early June, 1864. There had been a brush between the Colorado militia and a little band of Cheyennes up on the Bijou. My father and I had been talking about it and he harked back to the whole Indian situation and told how gradually the picture had changed.

"Everybody's scared to death of the Sioux now," he said, "because there's so many of them and they're all over the place and they're banded with the Cheyennes and Arapahoes. And they massacred all those people last year up in Minnesota. But we never saw the Sioux in the old days.

"You had the Delawares and Shawnees right across the river from Westport—they call it Kansas City now—and around Leavenworth. But they hunted across the plains and trapped in the mountains and you ran into them all the time. The Delawares are the smartest, scrappiest Indians I ever saw. They'll stand fast any time and shoot it out when almost any other Indians will cut and run after they get a few killed. And you can rely on their word. That's why the army uses so many of them as scouts. They won't betray you.

"Next came the Pawnees, all along the Platte and the Arkansas and Smoky Hill. They roamed the whole plains between the Missouri and the mountains. Up north of them were the Cheyennes and the Sioux. Over around the Black Hills you had the Cheyennes and the Arapahoes. Up in the Wind Rivers and the Big Horns were the Crows. Down here in the mountains were the Utes, and farther west you had the Shoshoni and the Flatheads and Nez Perces. The Blackfeet were up in Montana, around the Three Forks. Down on the Red River and the Cimarron and Canadian, on down into Texas you had the Kiowas and Comanches and the Prairie Apaches.

"Those days there were only a few of us whites . . . hunters and trappers, and we pretty much knew everybody in the country, white or Indian, and with a little scrapping now and then we got along pretty well together. There was room for everybody who wanted to use the country. Of course the Indians scrapped around among themselves a lot, but we got to know which ones were linked up together. Cheyennes and Arapahoes are kin and you could take it for granted they would always side together. And both of them got along well with the Sioux. I never heard of a war between them.

"The Pawnees were everybody's enemy, and they were a tribe to respect, now, let me tell you. Tough and mean and not afraid of the devil himself. The Sioux to this day are scared of them. Being along the Platte and Arkansas roads they got hurt bad with the cholera and smallpox which they caught from the whites. There's just a handful of them now compared to what there used to be.

"Well, when the Sioux and Cheyennes began to move over toward the Black Hills and began to drift down farther south, they liked the Crow country and started fighting them for it. And they've mostly taken it over from them now."

"What caused the Cheyennes to divide?" I asked. "We've get the Northern Cheyennes and the Southern Cheyennes. Ever since I can remember."

"Yes," he said. "Well, they aren't divided, really, except where they live. The Bent brothers did that. Way back in the early thirties when Charles and William Bent built their fort on the Upper Arkansas. The Bents first had a stockade for trading in furs about where Pueblo is now and Yellow Wolf's band of Cheyennes drifted a little farther south than usual that year, to hunt. They wandered up to the Bents' stockade."

"You knew both the Bents, didn't you?" I said.

"Yes. I knew Charles best. He handled their business in Taos. Well, Yellow Wolf told them they wouldn't do any good that close to the mountains. They'd better build a stockade farther out, because the buffalo didn't range that far and there wouldn't be any Indians hunting in their neighborhood. According to Charles, he told them if they would build a fort down around the Big Timbers on the Arkansas he would bring his band and maybe another one down and live along the Arkansas and hunt and trade with them. It proved out that way. The Bents built the fort and two bands of the Cheyennes moved down there."

"And William Bent married a Cheyenne," I said.

"Yes. And that tied the knot between the Bents and the Cheyennes good and tight. They got practically all the trade from them after that. But they're all Cheyennes, north or south."

He stuffed his pipe and lit it. "Few people understand the way Indian societies are organized. Mostly it's just us old-timers who have lived with them and we don't know the whole of it. We just know the structure. Nobody but an Indian knows why this thing is so, and that thing is so, and this must be done this way and that must be done that way. Now, take you, for instance," he pointed my way with his pipe, "you know enough about 'em to know that inside every Indian tribe there is a setup, well, like the nation. The country is the United States, but it's divided into states and territories and each state and territory has its own legislative and governing body, its own organization.

"Same way with the Indians, say the Cheyennes. Nobody but them knows how they divided their bands to start with, or exactly why, or exactly who does what in each band. But each band has its own chief, or council of chiefs, and it has its own four or five different warrior societies. Why one Cheyenne belongs to Black Kettle's band, another to Yellow Wolf's band, another to White Antelope's band, and so on, is something only they know. Usually they are born into a clan, the mother's clan, though they may be adopted into a clan. Then, breaking it down finer, why one man is in the Bowstring warrior society, another in the Kit-Fox society, another in the Crazy Dog society, and another in the Dog Soldiers . . . Lord, you'd have to know all the mysteries before that would be clear, and believe me, nobody not born into it can ever know all the mysteries. They will never tell them to white men. If an Indian was ever foolish enough to tell any of the mysteries to a white man,

240

he'd better be ready to leave his band. He would be exiled, if he didn't.

"But each of these hundreds of different little units has its own identity and can 'move the Arrows' into war if they like, or decide when and where to hunt, or decide where the grazing and the wood and the water is best for them to live during any season.

"The military, however, and the government commissioners think of a tribe as a whole unit and they tend to act as if there is one big Chief. Make peace with the Cheyennes, they say. My God, you can't make peace with the Cheyennes, or the Sioux, or the Arapahoes. You would have to make peace with every band in every tribe. And this band will sign a treaty and that band won't, and this band decides to 'move the Arrows' and make war, and that band doesn't. You're dealing with something like wind and water. You can't glue it together and make it stick.

"Now, sometimes a band decides to 'move the Arrows' and make war, say, against a certain band of Crows. They decide they need some help. They send the pipe around to the other bands. Maybe all the bands will smoke the pipe. Then you have, say, all the Southern Cheyennes committed to make war against that band of Crows.

"Then they get together some place and have a big ceremonial. They have to make a very big medicine. One of the warrior societies in the band that originated the idea is named to conduct the war. This society takes over and makes all the plans, decides the route to take, the form of attack, what each society is to do in the attack, the part each is to take."

My father chuckled. "White men make a lot of fun of the way Indians paint themselves and all the ceremony they go through. To them, the painting is like kids daubing themselves, all hit or miss. It isn't. Every streak, every daub, every color used means something—usually some kind of protection, some propitiation. Every part of the body must be considered, every weapon must be, well, we'd call it blessed—lances, bows and arrows, guns, ammunition, shields, horses, clothing. If one little thing is overlooked, it may cause defeat. Or if one man, say a leader, a great warrior entitled to wear the dog rope, is killed, the whole battle is called off. Something is wrong. Something wasn't done right. There is no use fighting any longer because the medicine isn't right. They don't quit and run away because they are cowards, afraid of an enemy. Mostly they're as brave as anybody with their enemies. But what they are scared of, scared to death of, is if their mysteries don't work for them. They quit right then. They have to go and make medicine all over again. If they don't they might anger still more spirits and if the anger is big enough and enough spirits are angered, the whole tribe might be wiped out.

"You know, white men think Indians are wild, free people . . . free to rove about, free to live the way they like to live. That's the most false notion whites have about Indians. There aren't any men anywhere less free than Indians. They are roped and hogtied with their own societies and social organizations and their rituals and ceremonials and most of all with their mysteries—their religion. They can't make a move without a big consultation and all the appropriate ceremonies and propitiations. They live the most fear-haunted lives of any people I know. Not of their enemies. Lord, no. But of all the spirits that live in everything on earth. You try living with the idea there's a spirit even in your saddle blanket you must always appease and propitiate, and see how free you are!"

"I've not been around them that much," I said.

"No," he said, "you have to live with them awhile before you can even begin to understand it."

He told me then about a six-pole dance he had gone through one time to pacify the Utes traveling with him and his hunters. "We'd lost a man. And the reason we lost him, they said, was because he had lost his prayer sticks. So the spirits were angry. And the only way to appease the spirits was to have a dance. They wanted a big, powerful twelve-pole dance, but we didn't have enough men. So we had to settle for a six-pole dance. We lost another man. In fact, we had a disastrous winter, and it was all because one man lost his prayer sticks and we didn't have a full twelve-pole dance to offset it. The six-pole dance just wasn't powerful enough."

"You believe that?"

"No. We had a bad winter through general mismanagement. But if you're an Indian you believe it. And it dictates much of what you do. There isn't any *use* going against bad medicine. You just as well quit right now and try to offset the bad powers. It's what makes them so chancy as allies, or even as enemies. You never know what their medicine is going to tell them to do. When they'd made their medicine and done every least little thing precisely the right way, and they go into battle believing they can't be killed, and then a man *is* killed, something more powerful than their medicine is at work and there isn't any use going on. Or they forgot to do something. Or they didn't do something exactly right. They just call everything off and go home to try to discover what's wrong, and make it right."

"They don't go through all that when they work the road over, do they? Chase a stage, or attack a little emigrant train?"

"It's not as much chance as it appears to be. There's usually been a council. Horses are needed, or ammunition is running low, or they could do with some hardware, or sugar and flour, and so forth. It's decided to make a few raids on the road. Chance enters then as to where the men will raid. They hit whatever comes along.

"But you take this little fracas up on the Bijou the other day. That was a little bunch of Dog Soldiers—from Black Kettle's band, I think. Some Crows killed a man from one of the bands in the Northern Cheyennes last summer. They decided to 'move the Arrows' against this band of Crows. They thought they would need some help, so they sent the pipe down here to the Southern Cheyennes and this little bunch of Dog Soldiers smoked it. Nobody else, now, remember, in all the bands of the Southern Cheyennes, and no other warrior society in Black Kettle's band, smoked the pipe. Just this one society, the Dog Soldiers. But they smoke the pipe, have their ceremonials, and start for the Powder River country to take part in the war. They get as far as the Bijou. They run up on some mules loose on the range. What was it, four? Well, they round 'em up and herd 'em into their camp."

"That's the way *they* told it," I said.

"All right. So maybe they didn't find them. Maybe they cut 'em out of a herd. But they've got four mules that belong to that rancher, what was his name?"

"Ripley."

"Ripley. So next day Ripley goes over to the camp and says they're his mules and he'll take them back, thank you. The Indians say not so fast there. We had a lot of trouble rounding those mules up and herding 'em into our camp and taking care of them for you and we'd like a little present for our trouble.

"Now, an old-timer would have paid his presents, got his mules and stayed on good terms. We didn't have any militia to call on and it was up to every man to take care of himself and see to it he kept his relations with the Indians good. But times have changed. We've got a lot of Johnny-come-latelies in the west nowadays, and we've got the militia, and the policy with the Indians is to crack a bullwhip over them."

"The policy is to exterminate them, isn't it?" I said.

"To put it plain, yes," my father said. "Neither the government nor the military admit it, but that's the policy. They're a nuisance, they're in the way, they are becoming expensive, and the quickest, most practical thing to do is get rid of them. So it's becoming shoot on sight, shoot to kill, any Indian, anywhere, any time. Or as much as they can get by with, with the preachers and philanthropists in the east screaming their heads off.

"Well, Ripley goes out and cusses the Indians out and goes hightailing it over to the nearest militia camp. And Lieutenant Eayre, acting on orders, goes out with guns blazing. He loses his sergeant and he kills two Indians. Over four mules, mind you, he makes bad blood with the whole bunch of Southern Cheyennes. They have to avenge those two men killed, now.

"Then there's the other fracas up there over those oxen Irwin & Jackman were wintering in the basin. Major Downing goes out to punish the Indians who ran off a dozen or so, he has a shoot-out with a little bunch of mixed Sioux and Cheyennes up Cedar Canyon, he burns their lodges and runs off their pony herd and divides the loot among his boys. Then Eayre goes over and plunders a village near Fort Larned in western Kansas. One way or another Colonel Chivington is going to have himself an Indian war."

My father, of course, was not a member of the state-hood party. He believed Colorado Territory ought to hold its horses for a while yet.

"He really wants a war?" I said.

"Oh, yes. Without a doubt. He wants one, but not a very big one. He just wants enough of one that when his troops put it down he gets the name of being a great Indian fighter."

"He must be crazy."

"No. He's a politician. He's running for Congress. And Governor Evans is running for the Senate. A little Indian war would suit both of them right now. It would help elect them."

"Don't they have any notion what they'd be starting?"

"Not in the least. Nor would they much care if they did. Twenty years of Indian war wouldn't bother them at all. In fact, it would help keep them in office. If they could save Colorado every election year they could stay in forever."

"If they don't take care," I said, "they're liable to start a real war, one that'll bring the Arapahoes and the Sioux, and maybe the Kiowas and Comanches into it."

"I think it's already started," my father said, "I think this is the beginning of it."

"What's the answer?"

"There isn't any. The west is opening and the Indians are a nuisance. It's that simple. It'll take a while, but they'll have to knuckle under in the end."

"Well," I said, "for our sake on the road I wish the government could get that treaty with the Cheyennes rati-fied and move them onto a reservation."

"It won't be ratified," my father said. "They didn't go about making that treaty in the right way. They didn't even know which chiefs to deal with. They don't know the setup, so they get a little bunch together, whoever happens to be hungry or needing guns and ammunition, and they draw up a treaty. The real chiefs weren't even there at Fort Lyon when that treaty was made in '61."

"But I thought William Bent was the one who drew up the treaty."

"Oh, he was back of the idea," my father said. "Yes. Bent can see what's going to happen to the Southern Cheyennes. He knows they've got to settle on a reservation and quit fighting and he wants them to do it and get it over with and save Cheyenne and white lives both. But not even Bent can get them to do something that goes against the grain that much. Some of them listen to him. Black Kettle, for one. And Lean Bear. They went to Washington, met Old Abe himself. They're willing to try. But they can only answer for their own bands. And they can't control the warrior societies even in their own bands. It just won't work till they're licked to their knees. And it's a pity."

"I hear George Bent has gone wild, too, now," I said. "Joined up with Charlie."

"Yes," my father said. "And one of the girls is living Indian, too. Julia, I think. The one that married a half-blood. Ed Guerrier."

"How many kids has he got?"

"Four by Owl Woman. Then she died and he took her sister as his wife, and Charlie is their boy. One of the girls married white. And the oldest boy, Robert, lives white, but he married Cheyenne. He and the old man work together." My father chuckled. "A man always looks after himself, don't he? Old man Bent has got the interests of the Cheyennes at heart and nobody would deny it. He works hard for them and tries to do the best he can for them. But he didn't neglect to get 640 acres of that Cheyenne restricted land for his boy, Robert."

"Well, Robert's a half-blood. Maybe he had a right to it."

"Not 640 acres," my father said.

"You think Charlie and George will have any real influence with the Cheyennes?"

"Well," he said, "I've heard that they feel bitter toward the old man over that treaty. Feel like he betrayed the Cheyennes. And they're young and hot-blooded. They'll throw their weight on the side of war, not much doubt about it. And their name is Bent. They'll be listened to, to some extent. But how much real influence they can have, I don't know. They'll have to prove up as warriors, like every other young man, before they'll have much weight in the councils. But if they do that, being half white, educated, knowing white men's ways, they can be a real threat."

That long road up the Platte was at the center of my

thoughts and I sighed. "I'd like it a lot better if they'd been turned like Robert."

"Yes," my father said. "Well, don't cross any bridges till you get there. They're just as apt to turn into lazy rum-pots as real leaders."

We watched the sun go down behind the mountains and throw a long sheet of fire and gold over the peaks. "That's the prettiest sight in the world," my father said, "and I can sit on this porch every evening and watch it. This is living again, boy. Real living."

We were quiet for a time, then he said, "Any news on Holladay's bid for the new mail contract?"

The old contract would expire on the first of July.

"Well," I said, "the talk around the office is that he's got a straw man to put in a low bid. His own bid is around $850,000, we hear."

My father laughed. "The straw man will get the contract, withdraw, and then Holladay will get it at his own bid. What are Wells, Fargo doing?"

"Oh, Holladay waited till his inside contacts could tell him what their bid was before he put his in. Then he just made it a little lower."

My father grinned. "Pays to have the President's ear and be kin to the Postmaster General, don't it?"

"It pays," I agreed.

"It's been cut and dried all along," my father said. "The bids are just a formality. Well, to know the right people is what makes the kettle boil."

A door slammed out back and Bucky came out into the side yard to gather the clothes off the line. I watched her, thinking with some surprise how much she had grown. She looked like a real little woman now, reaching up and taking down the clothes. She had begun to do her hair up. My sisters had persuaded her to cut enough of it so it could be handled, but it still made a thick, bright knot on the back of her head. Her dresses now were around her ankles, and it was a slim, mighty pretty ankle that showed when she raised her arms. She still had a small waist, but a real figure was forming. She was going to be deep-busted, like Emma, I thought, and maybe a little hippy when she'd finally filled out completely.

She turned and saw me and waved, and I thought how

pretty she was getting to be. Not as pretty as Bernie. She wasn't as soft looking and her features weren't as perfect as Bernie's. But she was a lot prettier than I'd ever believed she would be.

My father chuckled. "She don't look much like the scrawny little kid we brought into town with us last summer, does she?"

"That's the beautiful truth," I said. "I was just thinking she was growing up mighty fast and turning into somebody a lot handsomer than I ever believed she would. She's done real well this year, hasn't she?"

My father nodded. "Far as I know. She fitted right into the family. She wasn't much of a hand to help with the work at first, but she caught on pretty fast. Does as much as the other girls now, Mahaley says. But what they've all admired most in her is how smart and clever she is. Mahaley says she's the brightest kid she ever saw. Reads a lot, studies hard, learns everything she can and remembers it. She's kept Fanny and Nellie pushing hard to stay ahead of her."

"She was always bright," I said. "Never any doubt about that. But Emma had let her get out of hand a little. Got a little slack with her."

"You couldn't say that now," my father said. "How old is she?"

"You know," I said, "I have to count up every time." I counted again. "She's either fifteen or will be pretty soon."

"Humph," he said, "no wonder some of the boys are beginning to take notice."

"What boys?" I said. "The kids?"

"Not on your life," he said. "It's not been kids I've seen eyeing her downtown, or hanging around the house. I'd call 'em grown men. Of course, we've got a passel of girls in this house and they attract men like honey attracts flies. But Bucky comes in for her share of notice, I can tell you."

"Well," I said flatly, "she's too little for that kind of foolishness. Emma wouldn't like that a minute. I hope Mama is keeping her eye on her."

"Your mother," he said, "keeps her eye on all her girls and that includes Bucky as long as she lives in this house."

248

Bucky had collected two big baskets of clothes and I decided to go carry one in the house for her. She gave me a grin. "I wondered it you were just going to sit there and let me struggle with these."

"I wouldn't have thought it would be any struggle," I said, hoisting a basket, "for a girl that can break horses."

"Well, then," she said, "let's just say I wondered if you'd forgotten how to be a gentleman." She laughed. "I wanted you to finish talking and come listen to my new piece. I've learned a new one since you were here."

A piano had replaced Mama's old organ since they came to Denver, and Bucky, like Mama, could play by ear anything she heard. But she had been struggling all winter to learn to play properly by note. It hadn't taken too well. She was still inclined when she got balled up to fake it, and as far as I was concerned what she made up was a hell of a lot better to listen to than the notes she should have been playing. But she played me a prim, proper little piece and swung around on the stool. "That," she said, "is 'The Happy Farmer.' It is by R. Schumann. It is Opus 68, Number 10. It is written in one flat and it is played *allegretto animato*. I can't play anything written in more than one flat," she confessed, "or one sharp."

"You mean there's more?"

"Oh, good gracious, Starr, there's sometimes five or six."

"Flats *and* sharps?"

"One or the other, silly. You can't have them both at the same time." She swung back around and began romping all over the piano. Fingers twinkling, racing up and down, she played 'O Susannah' to a fare-you-well.

"Now," I said, "that is more my style. I like that kind of playing fine. Was that one flat or one sharp?"

"Lord, I don't know," she said, laughing.

Mama came to the door, beaming happily. "She's just like me. Don't know one note from the other hardly and can play anything and don't know how she does it."

"I call that being a good musician," I said. "Now, that's the way I blow my horn. I just keep blowing and messing around till it commences to sound like something."

Bucky whooped. "What your horn sounds like is a calf blatting for its mama."

"You've hurt my feelings," I said, "and I'm going home. I've been blowing Charge on that horn for five years and my *team* knows it's Charge, anyway."

"They'd get used to yodeling if they heard it long enough," she said. She walked me to the door.

"You doing all right?" I asked her.

"Yes," she said. "Fanny and Nellie say so, but . . ."

"But what?"

"Oh, I'm getting a little fiddlefooted. Now, you're not to think I don't like it here. I do. And I love all the Fowlers. But this time of year, I don't know . . . I'd just like to go home for a spell. Just a month or two. Couldn't I write Mama and ask if I could come home for a little while?"

"Well, she's your mama," I said. "You write to her every week, don't you? She said anything about you coming home?"

Bucky leaned her forehead against a porch post. "No. I guess it was understood I was to stay for a year."

I reached for a braid to yank and felt the miss of it in my hand. For as long as I'd known her, I'd pulled Bucky's braids. It seemed strange they were no longer down her back and handy. I patted her shoulder instead. "Try to make it the full year," I said. "If you don't dwell on it and just set your sights on September, the time will pass quick enough."

"All right." She raised her head. "It's best, I know. But I do get homesick. It's the time of year. I'd be outside at home, and there would be new calves and colts, and I could ride again. . . ."

"You can ride here. Papa's got horses."

"I didn't like to ask," she said. "The girls don't ride."

"They're town raised," I said. "I tell you. I'll bring you a horse of your own, if you'd rather. I'll find you one tomorrow and bring it over. And I'll come oftener myself and we'll go for some good rides. Would that help?"

She closed her eyes and drew a long breath. "I can't tell you how much it would help. Heavenly. Simply heavenly. That's what it will be."

I could have kicked myself. I should have known she'd get tired of being cooped up, studying all the time, learning to be a lady. She was Bucky Westmoreland, a Company brat, she'd been raised in big country, and I hoped some of that would never be educated out of her.

She suddenly went whirling round and round down the porch, her skirts flying. "A chestnut," she said, "a big, beautiful chestnut, with four white stockings and a blaze. Please, Starr? Please?"

"That's my own horse," I protested.

"And his name is Socks," she said, "and you can get another one. Please?"

"He'll be in the stable tomorrow," I promised, "but that's the best horse I ever rode and I'll never find another one like him."

She gave me a fierce hug and smothered me with quick little kisses. "That's why I want him," she said, "and he'll like me on his back a lot better than you. Thank you, thank you, thank you, and I love you a bushel and a peck and a hug around the neck!"

Nine years old, she used to say good night to everybody with that little rhyme. I tweaked her nose, spanked her, and left wondering what the hell had gotten into me to give up the finest saddle horse I'd ever owned.

Chapter 18

Bucky only had the joy of a few rides on Socks.

A series of Indian incidents was beginning to terrify the whole Territory. Young Lieutenant Eayre seemed to be running into horse- and ox-stealing Cheyennes all over Colorado. But he really put the fat in the fire when he went over into western Kansas on the trail of Black Kettle's band. He found them near Fort Larned. Black Kettle and Lean Bear, the leaders of this band, were great friends of old man Bent, and they had followed his advice and had long been trying to stay at peace with the whites. When they went to Washington, Old Abe had given them the usual medals and papers of commendation, which they held in very high regard. These things were very big medicine, in their eyes.

When Eayre's troops formed up and advanced on the camp, the warriors accepted the challenge and formed up themselves to meet them. Black Kettle and Lean Bear rode up and down the line and kept pleading, "Don't fight! Don't shoot! Let us talk to the white soldiers."

They put on their medals and got out their papers and they rode forward alone to talk to Eayre. They were met with a volley of fire and Lean Bear was killed. The warriors went crazy then and charged and drove the troops off the field. They killed two or three of them, and lost two more of their own men. And the damage was now irreparable and not even Black Kettle could hold them back.

They ravaged a ranch about thirty miles out from Denver, the Hungate ranch. They murdered Hungate and his wife and two children and mutilated them in the worst way. Governor Evans and the *Rocky Mountain News* whooped it up to the skies. The Governor had the bodies brought to Denver and placed on public display. The

252

Rocky Mountain News did its part and spread the panic rapidly. The Governor had all the women and children in Denver crowded into the second story of the Kountze bank building and called on all the men to gather up their weapons and stand guard to protect their families from massacre.

"Such idiocy," my father said, refusing to allow his wife and children to be crowded into such a situation, refusing also to haul out his own artillery and join the mob. "What the Governor had better do is fire his militia, start over with some sensible men and go out with some presents and try to make amends to old Black Kettle."

What gave everybody in Colorado the shakes the most, however, were the rumors that the Sioux and the Cheyennes were banding together to make all-out war. There was a big encampment, it was said, between the rivers and they were getting ready to strike. Every season there was a big encampment between the rivers, to hunt—mixed Sioux and Cheyennes—but this season, it was believed, was different. And where would they strike? Everybody was nervous and uneasy. There was a growing feeling, generated and nourished considerably by the newspapers, that big trouble was brewing in the Territory and that before summer was over it would break. It was like a storm cloud gathering. It would inevitably fill the sky and bust loose.

Then in July I had a letter from Ed. He wrote: "Spotted Tail's band of Brules and some Oglallas have been camped near Cottonwood. General Mitchell (General Robert B. Mitchell was head of the Department of Nebraska) has ordered all the Sioux to get out of the Platte valley. Old Spotted Tail told him the valley belonged to his people and they would come here to trade and hunt and cross north and south of the river whenever they liked.

"Gen. Mitchell bawled hell out of him and Old Spot bawled hell right back at him. It took them several days to cool down. Then Gen. Mitchell told Old Spot to get his chiefs together and bring them over to Cottonwood for a council. Which he did. But the general has got a bunch of Pawnees with him. There's about eighty of them and he's got them in uniform and on horses and is using them as cavalry.

"Well, them preachers and the peace party back east

have been crying for the government to make peace with the Indians. So the government thought it would commence with making peace between the Pawnees and the Sioux! Most fat-headed notion I ever heard. Gen. Mitchell was ordered to bring them together and talk. I don't have to tell you what happened between them everlasting foes of one another. The minute the Sioux seen them Pawnees, they got ready for a fight and commenced riding up and down in front of the Pawnees very fast, shouting and yelling for war, and making very insulting and obscene gestures, which nobody can beat the Sioux at doing. Gen. Mitchell had to unlimber his cannon and get between 'em to have enough peace to commence the talks.

"He finally got 'em to set down together and he made them a long harangue about living at peace with one another. They set there and glared at one another the whole time. Then a Sioux chief got up and said he didn't mind making peace with the Pawnees seeing as they were such a poor lot and couldn't the whole bunch of them do any great harm to the Sioux. He give a great catalogue of how many Pawnees his ancestors personally had killed.

"Then he set down and after about ten minutes of digesting this, a Pawnee chief got up and said he didn't mind making peace with the Sioux because every mother's son of them was a poor bastard and made like women and easy to lick with one hand tied behind you.

"They had at it backward and forward till they got worked up to fighting pitch again and lined up ready to charge. Gen. Mitchell got disgusted about then and give it up as a bad deal and told all of them to get the hell out of Camp Cottonwood and kill each other if they wanted to, but to leave white men alone.

"This was about as far as the preachers' peace party got. If they want peace so bad, you'd think they would try to settle the big war they've got going in the east, wouldn't you?

"Anyway, while I was over at Cottonwood trying to help make peace, some unpeaceful sonuvabitch drove off three of the stage horses and two of ours. There's so many redskins boiling around us this summer it could have been any of them. They done it quiet one night. The guard at the corral never heard a thing. I've reported it over at Camp Cottonwood but that will likely be the last of it. And I've reported it to the office in Denver about the stage stock. They can put in a claim with the government.

"Emma is upset about the Indian scares around Denver and she says tell you she'd like Bucky to come home. She figures things are in better hands along the Platte. She would write you herself but she don't feel very good these days. Her mother died, suddenly, in May and it's grieving Emma that she never did make that trip back home to see her. She was making plans to go this fall and then, according to her, *I* upset those plans. I don't know why a man gets all the blame for making a young one. It takes two. But after all this time and with Bucky nearly grown Emma's in the family way, and it'll be here in October, she says. She says tell you to put Bucky on the stage and the boys will look after her. Says don't argue about it, just do it *right now*.

"I'm sorry about the stock, but Brownie is as good a man as I am and if he couldn't help it, I couldn't have either."

Maybe. But I decided I'd better get out to the ranch and get the feel of things for myself.

There was always a great plenty of young drivers hanging around in Denver, waiting for a break, itching for a chance to drive even a relief run. So, without giving up my run, I asked for a relief immediately and two weeks off. I was too old a hand to be denied a reasonable favor. I would take Bucky home myself and have some time to look around.

I broke it to Bucky that her mother wanted her to come home. She shot straight up into the clouds with joy, but of course when she came down she lit into me. "You told them I wasn't happy here!"

"You ever know me to write a letter?"

"You wouldn't have to. You could send the word along by the boys."

"Well, I didn't." I must have looked hesitant, though. Bucky was quick. "Has something happened?"

"No," I said, "not really. You know about your grandmother, don't you?"

"Yes. Is Mama still grieving about her?"

"Some," I said. "And then she don't like all this Indian business around Denver and the Territory. Seems to think she'll feel better if you're back home till it's over."

My choice of words was bad. Bucky pounced. "Feel better? Mama's sick, isn't she? How bad sick is she?"

You didn't commonly talk about babies with a young lady . . . unborn babies, that is. It was a subject that was completely ignored, as if babies were picked out of the bushes. Women in the family way quit going about in public as soon as they started to show and they stayed more or less in hiding until the youngster was born. Then it was all right to be proud of this little evidence of all the hidden, and by inference shameful, physical details. Everybody loved a baby, but nice women pretended babies arrived immaculate.

This was Bucky, though. Young lady she might be, but she had been around calves and colts on the ranch enough to know at least some of the facts of life. I knew she would be in a swivet the whole 275 miles home if she wasn't calmed, and the best way to calm her was to tell her the truth. "Your mother is expecting a young one," I said, plainly and flatly. "In October."

Her eyes made round circles and both hands flew to her mouth. She couldn't say anything for a moment, then, as usual, a torrent poured out. "Oh, my goodness . . . well, I should say so . . . well, of course . . . oh, for heaven's sake . . . can you imagine . . . a baby . . . oh, good gracious, a baby! Why didn't she tell me sooner? Oh, Lord, she's been needing me all spring! Well, what are you *standing* there for? For heaven's sake, get busy! Do something. Right now!"

"What am I supposed to do?"

She was circling around and around her chair like a fluttery bird. She stopped suddenly, caught the back of the chair and leaned on it, then started laughing. Then the laughter turned to tears and she buried her face in her hands. I went to her and held her and patted her and smoothed her hair and made soothing noises. She leaned a moment, then caught her breath and pushed away. "I'm really happy. Happier than I can tell you. So happy I just had to cry."

"I know it," I said. "Women cry when they're sad and they cry when they're glad. They even cry when they're mad. Now, wipe your eyes and listen. You're the one that has to get busy. You have a trunk to pack and it has to be taken to the express office. You have books to pack and a lot of other odds and ends . . . all the clutter of stuff you've collected this year."

"And some laundry to do . . . and some ironing . . . and ten million things! When are we going?"

I couldn't resist teasing her. "We? How do you know I'm going? Your mother said just put you on the stage and head you in the right direction."

"But you *wouldn't!* Of course you're going. This is an emergency!"

"Not until October," I said.

"But you *are* going. Aren't you? Aren't you? Oh, *damn!* If you don't go, too . . ." She began hop-skipping around the chair again.

"Don't start cussing," I said, "and quit that ring-around-the-rosy business. I'm going. I'm going."

"You're going to be the death of me," she said, on a sigh, "with your teasing. Honestly. You're getting too old for that sort of thing, Starr." She sounded just like Emma.

"I'll try to remember that," I said.

"Besides," she added tartly, "you've been working out of Denver too long already. I'm not going to leave you alone to get into trouble." Her chin went up. "I know all about that woman at the Dutchman's."

"If you do," I said, "then you know she's not been there for six months."

"Where'd she go?" Quickly and suspiciously.

"Carson City," I said. "That far enough away to suit you?" I was astonished that she might actually have thought I had put the Pearl in a love nest some place in town.

The reddest blush I ever saw started at the base of Bucky's throat and slowly crept up into her face. But she kept her head up proud and ignored it. "San Francisco would have been better," she snapped.

I assumed a gruff, brusque manner. "Now, you get busy, young lady. If you have ten million things to do, you're wasting time. I want us to leave tomorrow."

"Oh, *yes!*"

A final problem loomed, over her horse. She wanted to take him, but I put my foot down. "I'll bring him later."

She wasn't happy about leaving him, but when my younger brother Pete promised to care for him as if he were his own, to ride him at least three times a week to keep him from getting fat and lazy, she could at least leave him with some peace of mind.

It was a rush but we left on schedule, Bucky riding in great state and fine clothes inside. That was for show and to uphold the honor and status of the family in Denver. It lasted to Pierson's when she mounted the box and wedged herself between me and the driver. "Now," she said, satisfied, "this is where I really belong."

At no stage were there many passengers. The Indian incidents had scared off a lot of travelers. We had four to Latham and out of Latham we had only two, both men. It made it convenient that night when Bucky grew so sleepy she was falling over to make her a bed inside. Next morning, however, as we pulled out for Valley station she was on the box again.

We changed drivers at Valley station and picked up Lon Huff, old Arkansaw, and we hadn't gone more than a mile till I knew he was a mighty sick man. Really sick, not just getting over a big drunk. He could soak up his portion of whisky, but it never affected him. What he had was the summer ague, malaria, which he'd picked up in Arkansas and which was a complaint that once you got it you more or less had it for life. It came and it went, but you could almost certainly count on one spell of it at least once a year. Lon was in the middle of such a spell and he had the three-day kind. You alternately chilled and burned up with fever, then you had an off day, then you had another day of chills and fever. It was his day to chill and he was shaking so hard he could barely hang onto the lines. "What are you punishing yourself for, with me along?" I said finally. "Get inside and wrap a buffalo robe around yourself. I'll drive for you."

"God," he said, "it'll save my life."

He got inside. Bucky spread out on the box, and then she begged to drive. If it had been my own run I would have let her, but on another man's run I didn't like to take chances. I said no, not this time. She wasn't downcast about it and chattered away a mile a minute, most of it going in one side of my head and right on out the other. You could do that with Bucky. As long as you said uh-huh from time to time, or nodded your head now and then, she was satisfied.

We clipped along to Dennison's and hitched in a new team, and moved right on out. It was hot now and the sun was like a brass reflector overhead. The heat wilted Bucky a little and her chatter ran down. She began to doze and nod a little. I felt sleepy myself and the heat waves shimmering over the big land were almost blinding.

It is thirteen miles from Dennison's to Spring Hill, the next station. We were two hours out, say eight miles, when all of a sudden, ahead of us and off to the right a little, a handful of Indians boiled up out of the sagebrush, whooping and shouting and coming angling over toward us. You aren't conscious of thinking at such a time. You size the situation up and as fast as your reflexes will act, you act. "Get down in the boot," I yelled at Bucky, who was uncoiling fast. "Get down in the boot, quick!" Then I commenced laying on the whip to make a run for it.

Bucky's reflexes were good, too, and she got down fast but not before she had sized things up also. "They're going to split you down the middle."

"You get down!"

The team bellied down and gave me all they had. The Cheyennes could split a dozen ways and my job was the same—to outrun them. I counted five, then, who split off the main bunch and angled across up ahead of us. It was the usual maneuver, to run you through a gauntlet. The team was fours and a good one. I didn't have any doubt we could outrun them, but it wasn't going to be very comfortable for a while. I kept laying on the whip.

The shooting was pretty fierce, but the men inside the coach were answering the fire now, and from the tail of one eye I saw one Indian go down. Then there was a loud report right under my nose and a cloud of smoke trailed up across my face and the smell of cordite was very strong. I cut a quick look and saw Bucky kneeling behind the mud-

259

guard with my shotgun resting on it. "You damned little fool," I yelled, "get down! The men'll take care of the shooting."

"I missed," she yelled mournfully, but she minded me and hunkered down.

Just as I saw she was safely down again, something like a cannonball hit my left arm and knocked me sideways, and the near reins went slack in my hand. I knew I was hit. I had that quick thought at once, I'm hit. But I wondered why my hand had no feeling in it and why I couldn't manage it. The reins were slipping and all my will couldn't hold them or bring that hand back up. It was exactly as if my left arm and hand were paralyzed. The hand kept dropping, lower and lower, the reins sliding through my fingers. But worse, I couldn't see very well. Things were growing hazy and dim. I made as strong an effort as I could to hang onto the lines, at least I thought I did. I was conscious of trying and trying also to clear my head.

Everything was one big noisy clamor—Indians whooping and riding round us, gunfire on all sides, smoke trails fogging, the horses thundering, the stage careening and rattling, dust smothering us. I kept trying to raise my left hand back up onto my knee, get the reins back where I could handle them. I had to. The near horses were already feeling the looseness and veering a little. The entire team would get out of control and off the road. The effort seemed endless, hours long, while the shooting scrape went on and on.

Next thing I knew Bucky was up on the seat beside me and reaching. "Give me the reins."

"If you'll just lift up my hand . . ."

"Give me the reins!"

I don't know whether I gave them to her or she took them, but in about ten seconds flat she had them, had her feet braced, was sitting on the edge of the seat and driving like hell. I felt a great relief immediately and absolutely no doubt she couldn't handle the team. There was a very solid feeling that Bucky could do it. I tried to make a joke. "It's a hell of a time for you to drive your first main line run." I had to shout it and I don't know whether she heard me, but she grinned.

I eased my left hand up on my knee and noticed that while it was as bloody as a fresh beefsteak, the blood wasn't pouring. So an artery hadn't been cut. It troubled me to see that Bucky's skirt was all over blood. But not for long. Blood will wash out.

For some reason, once my hand was rested my head began to clear. I suppose getting the hand up eased the flow of blood. For whatever reason I could see again and I could think. The team was still veering a little. "Get 'em back on the road," I said. I didn't have to tell her how.

She nodded and the team shortly began to answer to her near lines. Straightened out once more, I began to lay on the whip again. It had to be a long, all-out run. No slackening at all. "Don't tighten up on 'em," I said. "Let 'em feel the lines, keep their heads up, but don't tighten too much."

She nodded again, knowing exactly what I meant. Her bonnet had blown off right at the start and now all her hairpins had blown out and that blazing mop of red hair was streaming in the wind. If it was a prayer I didn't know it, but as a target she was the pip on the ace of spades, and inside myself I kept talking to something in a threatening sort of way—if she gets hit—if she gets hit, and my whip was cruel on the team.

It felt like an hour before we were through the gauntlet and had drawn a little ahead of the Indians. The men inside the coach were blazing away and one more Indian was hit. Old Arkansaw whooped and I figured it was his gun. It was a front shot and the Cheyenne threw up both arms and then it looked as if his horse just ran out from under him as he went over backward, arms, hands and legs flailing.

As if this were a signal the Indians hauled up and tailed off, but when I took a quick look up ahead the station was in sight, not more than a couple of miles away. It was that as much as the men killed that had made them quit. They wouldn't risk getting in too close to the station.

I turned for a look backward. They had scooped up the last man hit and were putting distance between us, going back the way they had come, as hard and as fast. They had chased us five miles, but it had seemed more like a hundred. I pivoted back. "All right," I said, "they've quit. Now, let's do some driving. No use killing this team. I'm going to begin giving them a little brake. You begin climbing. Just like it was a rig, now. Just a little at first."

Bucky nodded and set to work.

I was as proud of her as a mother hen. The kid had such good hands. "Steady now," I coached her, "a little more, then real steady."

It takes a while to pull in a team from a flat-out run. They can't shift fast and don't want to. They fought the lines some, but Bucky was braced good and her arms and her hands were strong. They came in, broke into a gallop, floundered a little, she didn't give them a bit of head room and they had to pull down, steady and steady and steady, until they finally hit the road gait again. I helped her along with the brake and some talk with the team.

A half mile this side of the station she had them in a nice trot, well in hand, going along as if nothing had ever happened. God, what a noble job she'd done. "Take 'em in this way," I said.

"You take care of that brake," she said, feeling her oats now, "and let me handle the lines."

We pulled up working together, me on the brake and talking, her on the reins. And we pulled up right in front of the door where we were supposed to. They had seen us skyhooting down the road and everybody in the station was collected out front to watch us come in, all their artillery out just in case we pulled any Indians with us. A tender sprang for the leaders' heads as we rolled up and the station agent was beside us as we came to a stop. He looked us over good and yanked an arrow out of the side of the coach. Then he looked up at Bucky and me sitting there on the box. "Well," he said, "I see we got a new driver."

"And a damned good one," I said.

"Ed Westmoreland's girl, ain't it?"

"Bucky," I said, "Bucky Westmoreland."

She was still sitting there, proud, the reins still threaded, her hair like an elegant, wind-tangled shawl about her face. One of the boys came up and she looked at me. I nodded and she looked down at the lines. She slowly gathered them, then with a final grace and observed courtesy, she

262

leaned slightly toward the hostler and threw the lines lightly into his hands. Her run was over.

"Take my whip," I told her, "while I get down."

The agent reached up to steady me. "Jesus, man," he said, "look at the size of that hole!"

I nursed the arm in my good hand. "Get her down."

He turned to help her, but she said, "Just a minute."

And my God, the kid was calmly coiling my whip. One side of her dress was smeared all over with blood and one sleeve was ripped and pulled loose. Her hair was hanging and blown. The dust was streaked in the sweat on her face and was slowly caking into mud. But without a shake and without any hurry she was attending to her last business, coiling her whip before she left the box.

I was so proud of her I could have busted, but I was suddenly very sick to my stomach and I suddenly had a very bad case of the shakes and just as suddenly everything went black again and for the first and only time in my life I fainted dead away. I could feel my knees buckling, my sense going, and I was full of shame for the weakness and helpless to help it. I ought to see to the passengers. I ought to make sure nobody else was hurt. I ought to turn this damn run back over to Arkansaw. I ought to . . .

I came to fighting my way up out of a smothering dark cloud into a red ball of pain and the feeling that I somehow had to fight that, too. "Don't hitch your shoulder around that way," somebody said, "you'll start the bleeding again."

I lay quiet and let things begin to sort themselves out. I began by opening my eyes a squint, just a squint to see where I was. In some sort of bunk in some kind of room. There was my whip on the wall, so it was a drivers' room. Then this must be a stage station . . . then like an explosion everything came back, I knew who I was and where I was and what had happened. And it was Bucky who had spoken to me. She was sitting beside me, watching me anxiously, her eyes red and swollen.

"You been crying?" I said.

"Who me?" She shook her head vigorously, then just as vigorously bobbed it up and down, yes. "I thought you were dead." Her chin started quivering. "You looked so white. And you just fell over . . . all of a sudden."

"You must not have been looking very close," I said. "I didn't fall over. Not me. The ground just heaved up while my back was turned and knocked me down."

Her chin stopped quivering and though her eyes were misty, she smiled. "You'd make a joke if you were dying, wouldn't you?"

"Not if I was dying," I said, "but to make a pretty girl smile, I would, any time. Help me sit up straighter."

She slid an arm under my shoulders and heaved and together we got me up with a couple of pillows behind me. I examined my bandaged arm. It was wrapped in so much white rag it looked like the hindquarter of an ox. "Who took care of this?" I said.

"Arkansaw. He got the bullet out and then washed it and then we bandaged it. I helped," she said.

"I thank you," I said, "but what the hell did you use for a bandage? A bedsheet?"

"That," she said huffily, "is my best white petticoat. Arkansaw said it would be a pity to tear it. Said we'd just use it all then I could wash it and get some good of it again."

"I thank you again," I said. "That makes real good sense. What you wearing for a petticoat right now?"

Her chin went up. "Ladies do have more than one, Starr."

"Excuse me." I quit teasing. "Arkansaw all right?"

"Oh, yes. Nobody was hurt but you. But you oughtta see the coach! It's got a dozen bullet holes in it and three or four arrows. Those men . . . the passengers, they looked it over real good and they said they didn't see how we got through without everyone being killed. They said they didn't understand how in the hell we got out of such a scrape."

"What'd you tell 'em?"

"Nothing. If they don't know it was because we had a damn good team and you and I were doing some damn good driving, they don't deserve to know."

"Bucky," I said, "those are my sentiments exactly. But you better let a man say 'em. You're going to forget and talk like that in front of your mother when we get home and your mouth is going to taste like lye soap for a week."

She giggled. "I know. But that was what Arkansaw said. Those were his exact words. I *did* do good, didn't I?"

"Nobody could have done better," I said, "nobody."

"Not even you?"

"Oh, Lord, much less me. Nobody. Not even . . . not even Arkansaw."

She stared. "Is *he* a better driver than you?"

"Didn't you know?"

"I don't believe it," she said. "You're the best driver on the line."

"You keep right on believing that," I said, "and then only me and God will know it ain't true."

Arkansaw came in and Bucky said she guessed she'd better wash up and put on some clean clothes.

"Hey," I called, as she was leaving, "when you get cleaned up, reckon you could find me something to eat? I'm as hungry as a stray dog."

Arkansaw told me I had a hole in my arm and some muscles torn, but the bone hadn't been hit and he had got the bullet out. "It's going to be sore as hell for a while," he said. "I had to gouge around in there a right smart to get the bullet out. It was lucky you was out like a light while it was going on. It ought to heal up pretty good, though. You being the nice clean-living lad you are." He grinned. "Besides, we poured coal oil in it."

"That's what I smell," I said.

"Yep. My ma used coal oil for everything. We even had to take the damned stuff with sugar when we had a cold in the head."

We talked, then, about the whole fracas. Where the Indians had come from, what their intentions had been, and so on. "Station keeper had a telegram a while ago," Arkansaw said. "They hit in three places up the line . . . all today. Pretty big band hit an emigrant train—killed a couple of folks. Another little bunch run off some horses from Gilman's ranch. And they give us a chase."

"All the same band, likely," I said, pondering it.

"Well, they were all Cheyennes," Arkansaw said.

"They're the ones Eayre has been chasing around here and there, in my opinion. And there'll be more of this before it's over."

"To my thinking, too," he said. "We better travel with pretty heavy artillery from now on."

We talked on. Then Bucky came in, so scrubbed up she was shining, her hair as neat as Bucky's hair could ever be and pinned up again, a spanking fresh striped percale dress on, bearing in her hands a tray with the most welcome sight on earth right then, a steaming cup of good, red coffee. "Look what the angels have sent," I told Arkansaw.

"I'd be willing to get shot myself," Arkansaw said, "if I thought they'd be half as good to me." Bucky grinned and Arkansaw unlimbered his long legs. "But it will be my luck to get shot tomorrow and instead of Bucky to do for me I'd draw that squaw of Raymond's down at Dennison's."

"You better go eat," Bucky said, "while it's hot and fit to eat."

"That I better," he agreed. "Well," he said to me, "it'll be a while before you have to worry about driving stage again. That arm is going to keep you laid up several weeks."

I swear it was the first time it had occurred to me. Never in my entire life had I been laid up a day, sick or hurt. I might not be the cleanest-living lad on earth but I was certainly one of the healthiest. I didn't know what it was to have my body tell me what I could or couldn't do, and I didn't relish the prospects now. I heaved up to protest it and my shoulder instantly reminded me it was true. I groaned. A one-handed stage driver was an impossibility. Like it or not, I was going to be on the shelf for a while.

Arkansaw grinned. "Nothing to do for a month but set around and draw your pay. I wish it was me."

"Which it would have been," I said, "except for my kind heart. Next time you can shake with your chills till you fall off the box."

"And much obliged," Arkansaw said.

"Pass the word back to Denver, will you?" I said.

"I'll do it," he said. "I'll say you'll be laid up three or four weeks." And he passed through the door curtains.

Bucky was all for feeding me every bite but I reminded her I still had one good arm, it could handle a fork, and I was not yet reduced to a bib and tucker.

"We'll go on home tomorrow," I said.

"If you don't have a fever," Bucky said.

"Fever or not," I said, "tomorrow."

I was grumpy over being laid up at all and determined to be where if I couldn't do any good for the Company I could at least do some good for myself . . . at the ranch.

Chapter 19

It was on the sixth of July that Bucky and I were chased into Spring Hill. The news went up and down the line like a prairie fire running before the wind and in no time flat Bucky was the most famous person in Colorado.

The *Rocky Mountain News* and the *Blackhawk Journal* both put her in headlines on the front page: "Heroine of the Overland! Mary Buchanan Westmoreland takes reins from wounded driver. With unsurpassed daring and courage, young girl outwits Indian attackers. Handling the reins like a veteran, 'Bucky' Westmoreland outruns Cheyennes and saves lives of passengers and wounded driver."

A lot of it was drivel, some of it was true, and Bucky deserved every word of honest praise. Having read about her, and having heard the drivers talking her up, the stage passengers asked to have her pointed out. The women gushed and oohed and ahhhhed, the men ogled and leered at her. It all went a little bit to Bucky's head.

"It says I was daring and courageous," she read.

"You were," I said, "but you got any ideas what else you could have been? Unless you wanted your scalp dangling from some buck's war lance."

"It says with coolness and firmness I took the lines from the wounded driver."

"You did," I said. "I don't know as I ever saw anybody take the lines more coolly and firmly. You just plain snatched 'em."

"It says I am the heroine of the Overland."

"You are," I said, "and I am making you a crown to wear right now. I've got three more stars to put in, then you can commence wearing it."

She threw the newspaper down. "Don't you admire these pieces about me in the papers, Starr?"

"I do," I said, "I just don't want you to commence believing them. You know damn good and well you didn't feel daring or courageous or cool and firm. You saw I'd been shot, you could drive, somebody had to drive, and you did it. There's been other women before you picked up the lines from their men. And there's been women taken over a gun with their man killed beside 'em. You can take as much credit as them. But what I give you the most credit for, the newspapers don't even mention. What I give you the most credit for is the damned fine way you drove. Running hard, you handled that team like a real reinsman. That's what I'm proudest of you about."

Her head dropped and when she looked up her eyes were shining. "You just put those last three stars in my crown," she said. She swooped quickly and kissed me. "I reckon I needed taking down a notch or two."

We didn't resume our journey the next day. I never felt less like moving than I did that morning and nobody had to talk me into waiting over a few days. I wouldn't have believed that one bullet hole in his arm could make a man feel so weak and sick, but it did and I was glad to lie very still and move that arm just as little as possible. In fact, I yelled good and loud if anybody so much as jostled the bed.

It was three days before I put my feet to the floor and one week to the day before I thought I could bear the bumping of the stage. I would have sent Bucky on, but Ed and Emma had heard the news and they telegraphed for me to keep her with me. They didn't want her to risk traveling alone. Lord knows I was in poor shape to take care of her in an emergency, but if I only had one good arm at least I still had my head and evidently they believed I could still use it.

It was quiet along the line, however, the week we were at Spring Hill. No more incidents anywhere. And except for a lot of pain that made me feel as wrung out as an old dishrag the trip to the ranch was the same old jog. I was glad to ride inside, though, and grateful for a whole seat to myself.

There was a joyful reunion when we got there. It had been almost a year since the Westmorelands had seen Bucky and both she and Emma cried and hung onto each other. "How you've grown! I can't get over it—how much you've grown! And how pretty you are! Oh, Bucky, Bucky!" This was Emma taking on, holding Bucky off to look at her, then grabbing her again and hugging her.

And Bucky crying and patting and hugging and saying, "Mama, Mama, I'm never going away from home again. Never, never, never!"

Ed's eyes got wet, too, and he put in a few pats and said, "Why, she's taller than Emma. Bucky, you never said you'd grown up so big."

"Well," she said, laughing and wiping her eyes, "*I* didn't know it. Starr, you didn't tell me."

I had found a chair before my knees buckled on me. "Well, great blowing blizzards," I said, "I didn't know it, either. Not all that much."

Emma wiped her eyes again. "That's because you saw her all the time. You don't notice the changes in people when you're with them all the time. But to us . . . my soul and body, Starr—she went away a little girl and she's come back a young lady. It's going to take some getting used to."

Bucky got her feet down to earth soonest and began bustling about. "Starr has to go to bed. He's tuckered out riding, with that arm."

Tuckered or not I wasn't having any more of the bed and said so. "Emma, if you can spare that rocking chair in your room and if Ed will bring it in here, I can make good use of it. Now, hush up," I told Bucky, who was beginning to bluster, "I've got to get back on my feet and in the bed is no way to do it."

The chair was brought, and a pillow, and a low stool for my feet. Then Bucky and Emma disappeared. Ed grinned. "Woman talk," he said. "They've got plenty of it to catch up on."

I said I thought Emma looked pretty well. Her face was a little thinner, maybe, but her color was good and she didn't appear to be heavy on her feet or awkward yet.

"No," Ed said, "she's not commenced showing much yet. She's about as quick and light on her feet as common."

"We've got to have some man talk," I said, "but first, there's a bottle of good bourbon in my satchel. Get it out,

270

will you, and pour me a good, big drink. I'm all-gone inside."

He poured my drink, and I nodded for him to pour himself one. When the whisky had put a little stiffening into me, I said, "Ed, I didn't see one Indian, not one, between here and Julesburg. Usually you'll see two or three little bands drifting along every day. But there wasn't a one. What's happened?"

"Well, now, it's a queer thing," he said, "but they've gone. Just plain vamoosed. There hasn't been a Indian in here to trade in over two weeks. Nearly three, I'd say. And the last ones that come in was that little bunch of old Slewfoot's."

Slewfoot was a chief, the head of a little band, maybe ten or twelve lodges, of Sioux. He was slightly lame in one leg, not bad enough to keep him from being active and quick, but when he walked the foot slung out a little. His name was Man-Lamed-by-a-Bear, but whites all called him Slewfoot. He had been trading with us regularly since we opened the place.

"He had some hides?" I said.

"Some. Not many."

"What'd he trade for?"

"Some sugar and flour, and a case of cough medicine."

We laughed. We stayed within the law and did not sell whisky to Indians. But we comforted the Indians by selling them gallons of cough syrup that was eighty percent alcohol. It took a lot of it to get roaring drunk, but it went a long way toward easing anybody's pangs. I'm not sure we didn't make more than we would have selling straight alcohol.

Ed told me about the horse stealing. "Not a sign, not a track. They rode 'em straight into the road from the corral and then drove 'em right on down the road. Couple of miles down, there was a place where they'd milled a big herd. Then they crossed the river with the whole herd and from there was a hundred different tracks heading north. They just fanned out, like wild turkeys. You couldn't have followed 'em all in ten years."

It was about what I had expected. "I don't understand why the dogs didn't set up a clamor."

271

"Why, they'd killed 'em. All three of 'em. Throats slit from one ear to the other." He added, "They'd takened a couple of good saddles, too. And bridles."

"Any of the stage harness?"

"No. That was all."

All our horses were good horses, fast and reliable. The Company kept anywhere from ten to twenty in the corral. I had thirty to forty in my herd most of the time. I hated to lose even one good horse, but I said, "We just as well forget it. I can't see that you or Brownie either was at fault. We were just lucky they didn't stampede the whole herd."

I pondered the disappearance of the Indians. All I could make of it was that with the Colorado militia hunting them down and shooting on sight, with General Mitchell unable to make a treaty at Camp Cottonwood, the little bands that usually drifted up and down the river had the wind up and for safety had gone into a big encampment between the rivers. Every hunting season the Sioux, Arapahoes and Cheyennes congregated in that section in these big encampments. I said I thought that might be the answer and Ed agreed. "Probably keeping pretty far south," he said, "down on the Smoky Hill some place."

"That would be safest," I said. "They mean to keep away from the troops along the stage line."

Ed had the place in good order. I never had any reason ever to fault him on that. Between him and Emma they kept everything clean and trim, paint where it needed it, fences mended, buildings in good repair, and Ed was as good a stock man as I ever saw.

After a few days at home my arm was so much better it gave me practically no more trouble. It was a little stiff and tender, but the constant pain stopped. Emma dressed it every day, slowly reducing the size of the bandage. "It's healing just fine," she said, "and from the inside out, which is good. It'll itch considerably and sometimes shoot a few pains through, but there's not a bit of gangrene in it. Nothing to worry about. Wear the sling another week, say, to keep from jolting it, but if I was you and could bear it, I'd slip it out every now and then and bend the arm up and down to keep the stiffness from setting too hard. It'll pull on that hole and hurt, but it will keep it from tightening up."

They had heard the story over and over, of course, of Bucky's drive and they were immensely proud of her, but Emma said it gave her the shakes yet to think about it. "It was just the Lord watching over her," she said. "Up there on that box, you shot, bullets whizzing all around, arrows flying. . . . When I think what could have happened to her. . . ."

"Don't think about it," I said. "It didn't happen and Bucky isn't liable to be riding the box of another stage for a while."

"That is the beautiful truth," she said firmly. "She's going to stay right here where I can keep my eye on her."

It was hotter than the hinges of hell, with that everlasting blowing wind out of the west feeling like a coal-fired furnace belching at us. Bucky said she bet if we had an egg we could fry it in the sand right outside the front door and it wouldn't take three minutes to do it. I wouldn't have bet with her. But no matter how hot it was outside, inside the dobe house it stayed pretty cool. Stage passengers coming in as wilted as scalded cornstalks always appreciated it. "It's like a cellar," they would say, "as cool as if you'd dug it under the ground."

That was my only objection to it. To be cool, you had to be almost airless. Except at night Emma kept the doors and windows closed the way she did in the winter. To me, the air grew stale and lifeless after a few hours. So in spite of the heat I usually spent most of my time outdoors.

There was plenty of passing on the road, the stages coming and going, and wagon trains of one sort or the other, but the Indians didn't come back. I rode horseback down to the Doc's one day, thinking maybe he would have some news through his Sioux wife. "All I know," he said, "is they're avoiding any chance of a brush with the troops. All of them, Sioux, Arapahoes, Cheyennes, are together down there between the rivers. Same as they are every year. Only difference is that the little bands that move around on their own are being careful right now."

"That's the way I figured it," I said. "The troops have given them the word with the bark on it. Whether they've been raiding or not, they're shooting targets till after the election. They're smart enough to know that. I thought maybe your wife might know a little more."

"My friend," the Doc said, "my wife is an Indian first and a wife second. What she knows about her people she doesn't tell—not even to me."

"Any of her family been visiting lately?"

"Not lately," he said. "They were around earlier in the summer. But like all the others, they've got the wind up now. She did tell me she didn't expect them to visit again until after the hunting was over and they started back to the mountains for the winter, I," he added, "would just as soon they passed us by. I had no idea how many relatives an Indian woman possessed until I married one. By my count there are fifty-four we must always be hospitable to."

"You're lucky," I said. "I know a Cheyenne trader had a whole band that stayed with him the biggest part of the time."

"I would head back to civilization," he said.

He looked at my wound and said it was healing well. He rebandaged it. "Lucky that bullet didn't smash into the bone. You could have ended your stage-driving days right quick if it had."

"When would you say I can go back to work?" I asked.

"If you want to be sure it don't ever give you any trouble," he said, "give it a couple more weeks. If you *have* to go back to work, you could do it in another week. It'll twinge on you and let you know it's there a month or so yet."

"I dislike to favor myself," I said.

"Besides which," he said, eyes twinkling, "you get tedious to yourself sitting around, don't you?"

"Tedious as hell," I admitted. "I believe I'll get on back to Denver and put in the rest of my waiting there. There's always something for a man off duty to do around the office there."

He nodded. "Here's a box of salve to rub on the edges of that hole and keep it from cracking open. It's nothing but grease with a little carbolic acid in it. Won't help, except the grease will keep the scab from drying up too fast."

274

I thanked him, tried to pay him which he wouldn't have, and rode back home. That night I told the family I thought I'd go back to Denver. Everything was in good shape and there was no use me staying on. The big shipment of winter goods we ordered every summer was already on its way. We'd had a telegram from Fort Kearney that the train expected to arrive about the middle of August. My plans never had included being here for its arrival, and I saw no reason to wait over for it. I had no good excuse for hanging around any longer.

Ed and Emma saw the sense of it, but Bucky was a little put out with me. She wanted me to bump the Cottonwood driver and stay on at the ranch. "Get that notion out of your head," I told her. "I don't ever intend to drive one of these outside runs again. Not unless I have to, for my own business. I've earned the right to the best runs on the line and that's where I intend to drive the rest of my life."

The training Bucky had received at my mother's, and probably equally as much another year of growing up and getting more sense, had been showing. Instead of hanging around the stables and corrals with the boys, she took hold of the work about the house with as much energy as Emma ever had. It was funny to watch her doing things the same way as Emma, but younger and quicker and sometimes improved a little from things she had learned in Denver. She had the wit not to compare and get Emma's dander up. She never said, "Mama, Miss Mahaley sprinkles a broom before she sweeps. It keeps down the dust." Instead, she said, "I wonder . . . what would you think, Mama? Would it help keep the dust down if I sprinkled the broom?"

"Why, yes," Emma said, "of course it would. I don't know why I never thought of that. You've got a good head on your shoulders, Bucky."

When she washed the windows she shined them with crumpled old newspapers. She didn't say my mother had taught her that trick. She said, "I was too lazy to hunt for a dry rag."

"Well, I never," Emma said. "Look how the glass sparkles. And not one bit of lint. When I think how hard put I've been to keep in rags . . . and always a pile of old newspapers laying around!"

I wouldn't have credited the kid with so much tact if I hadn't seen it with my own eyes. It was the surest sign, I thought, that she was really growing up. As far as the way she looked was concerned, she was still small. She was going to be short, like Emma. But, by George, she sure was getting a shape on her.

The day after she got home she had rummaged out some old dresses, faded prints and stripes, and let the seams out and the hems down. She looked like the old Bucky, except even with the seams let out she strained them. I liked them, but Emma said they were tacky and scolded her. Bucky said tacky or not they were more comfortable to work in. Neither could she be bothered doing her hair up now that she was at home. She let it hang in braids again. I liked that, too. I reached for one, now, to pull. "You hear me?"

"I heard you," she said, "you'll be sorry. Just wait and see. You'll be sorry."

"Just how will I be sorry? What are you going to do? Find a husband? Get married?"

"I might," she said. "I *am* growing up."

"Let me know when you finish," I said. "And let me know when you find a man. I'll dance at your wedding, and that's a promise."

"Oh, Starrrrrr!"

When the westbound pulled in the next day I was ready to leave. There had been admonitions from Emma. There had been dozens of messages to my mother and sisters from Bucky. There had been a long-suffering silence from me and a grin from Ed. And from Bucky and Emma there had also been, at the last minute, a gift—a linen shirt they had made. "Mama cut it out and did the heavy stitching," Bucky said, "but I did the tucking and made the buttonholes."

Emma caught my eye, so I examined them carefully. "I never saw a more beautiful shirt," I said, "or neater buttonholes. I didn't know you could do such fine work, Bucky."

"Your mother taught me," she said, flushing up. "You know what fine linen shirts your father always wears. She makes every one of them for him. The *littlest* stitches you ever saw. Mine aren't that tiny yet, but someday they will be." She looked at her mother and laughed. "You know how she made me learn?"

"I've been wondering," Emma said.

"She made me rip them out if the stitches were too long. I bet I ripped out a hundred seams before she was satisfied."

"Now, why didn't I think of that?" Emma said.

Bucky hugged her. "Oh, it wouldn't have worked with you. I'd just have said pooh and thrown the old shirt in the corner, *because* you'd have picked it up and done it for me. Starr's mother wouldn't."

"Now I know," Emma said, "I'll not do it any more."

I folded the shirt carefully and put it in my satchel, grateful that Emma's eyes had warned me. Bucky's buttonholes were perfect. They were even, the stitching was tiny, they had been carefully measured. Only one thing was wrong with them. They were on the ladies' side of the shirt.

A fairly new man named Newton was driving the run that day. He joined us at the family table for his meal and had begun eating before he said, "I was about to forget, Mrs. Westmoreland. Your sister is on the next stage behind."

"Bernie! You mean Bernie's coming?" Emma was so dumbfounded she nearly dropped the pot of coffee in her hand. "Here, Bucky, take this."

"Yes, ma'am," Newton said. "She was on *this* schedule to Fort Kearney. I guess the heat was bothering her because she laid over a day there. But the word's been passed along. She said tell you to be expecting her."

Emma sat down suddenly and her eyes filled. "Oh, I've been pleading with her to come back. Since Mama died. We've got nobody left but each other. We just as well be together. But she never gave the least hint she had it in mind. Why, I had a letter from her just three weeks ago. She didn't mention such a thing!" She tucked some hair that was straying up. "But she did say she had finished settling up everything. We decided to sell Mama's house and the things neither of us wanted. She packed some dishes and bed linens and things to send me, she said. Oh, I'm just rattling on, but I'm so astonished . . . and so glad! Oh, dear Lord, nobody was ever more welcome. I'll be so glad to see her! Bucky, imagine . . . Bernie will be here . . . why, tonight, won't she? The next stage, you said."

"Yes, ma'am," Newton said. "Little Taw will be bringing her tonight."

"Who needs her?" Bucky said tightly. "We were getting along just fine, Mama. . . ."

"Why, Bucky," Emma chided, "your own aunt. My sister. Of course, we need her. And she needs us. Why should she stay back there alone? This is her home, now. Here with her own people."

I had my own hollow feeling about the news, but I couldn't help noticing that the kid had gone so white the freckles on her face stood out sharply. "Well, I wish it wasn't her home," she said. "I don't like Bernie Buchanan and you may as well know it."

Emma stood up quickly. "That will do, Bucky. You're not to speak that way about your own aunt."

"My own aunt or not," Bucky said, "she's mean and spiteful and she's . . . she'll make trouble again. You wait and see. There'll be nothing but trouble here now. All over again. I don't see *why* she has to come dragging her tail out here again. She's a goody-goody and eastern and she don't like it out here, she said she didn't, so what good will it do for her to come?"

"Hush! Just hush your mouth this minute! I don't know what's got into you. Bernie isn't mean and spiteful and you know it. And if Starr isn't here . . ."

"Which I won't be," I said. And I never meant it more. The picture of Bernie had begun to fade and I didn't intend to have it come back into focus again, to start all the aching and yearning again. "I'm leaving right now."

"You aren't going to stay and see her?" Bucky said, amazed.

"No, ma'am," I said, "not on your life. Without giving offense to your mother, I don't ever intend to see Bernie again if I can help it."

Emma turned red. "I hate for you to feel that way, but I know . . ."

"That's the way it has to be. I've walked over those hot coals the last time I mean to."

Bucky was suddenly joyous. "Oh, glory, glory be! You've finally come to your senses!" And the way she always did when she was excited or almost unbearably happy she went whirling and flying around the room, in a long, loping waltz that ended with a graceful flourish and curtsey to me. "My knight! My wonderful, beautiful, shining knight!"

Emma said, "Bucky, you're being silly."

I gave the kid a hand up, and she flung her braids back. "Oh, I've got half a mind to go back to Denver with you. Mama won't need me now."

"You'll do no such thing," Emma said. "Now, behave yourself. Act your years. You're getting too big for this kind of nonsense."

"First I was too little, now I'm too big," the kid said. She followed me out to the stage. "As soon as we get this baby over with," she said, "I'll come back. You tell Miss Mahaley that, will you?"

It sounded all right to me and made a good bit of sense. There would be a considerable amount of geeing and hawing between her and Bernie, now that she was growing up. I didn't blame her for wanting to avoid it. And Emma had always been dotty about Bernie. In her eyes Bernie was never in the wrong. "They'll be glad to have you," I said to Bucky, "any time. You know that." I stowed my satchel. "But if I was you, I wouldn't quarrel with Bernie. It would just fret your mother. Ride along easy with her and don't hackle her. Then come on to Denver."

"Oh, I won't," the kid said. "I won't even be tempted to quarrel with her . . . now."

"Yes, you say that," I said, "then the first time there's a good opening, you'll jab at her."

"No, I won't. I told you. I don't *have* to now."

"You never did have to," I said, "but you did."

"Oh, you're so stupid. Starr, are you going to stay in Denver?"

"Thereabouts," I said. "There are only three men who can bump me now and they're pretty settled. I'll be around there."

She gave a big sigh. "Isn't life heavenly? Just simply heavenly?"

I said I hadn't noticed it, told her to be good and heaved

up inside the coach. Newton had brought an important lawyer in on the box and he could keep it. I took a corner of the back-facing seat, hoping I could make it stick. With only four passengers my chances were good. I needed the room for my arm.

We departed on schedule and I settled down to think. Not that it did much good. If Bernie was going to live with the Westmorelands now, I had only two alternatives. Time had run out for me and the Westmorelands, that much was sure. I couldn't own the ranch and never go back. I could let the Westmorelands go and put somebody else in to run the place. But they didn't deserve that. Their efforts had gone into the place as much as mine. It was their home and only a dirty rat would take it away from them.

I would have to sell the place. Sell it and have no further responsibility for it, no reason ever to see it again. My thought ran this out to all the possibilities. I could afford to make good terms for Ed. Price it so he could afford to buy it, and still lose nothing myself. If Ed didn't want it on any terms, my father would undoubtedly take it off my hands and keep Ed on.

We were moving along briskly and smoothly and the heat made me sleepy. Half dozing I reached the decision. It was what I must do. Sell the place to Ed. I would wait to broach it until after the new youngster arrived. Put nothing extra on them until then. Let them get settled down over that excitement. Then talk sensibly to Ed about it. Tell him it was becoming too much of a burden for me. Tell him I was more or less settled in Denver and wanted to stay that way. It was a nuisance, I would say, to come back to the ranch several times a year.

It was the ninth day of August. The youngster was due, Ed had said, the first week in October. Well, then, say by November, make one more trip and get it over.

There was a sense of peace as I stretched out on the seat to let full sleep take it altogether out of my mind. Yes. It was what I would do.

Then, as idly as a thought ever runs through the mind, unbidden, unwished, I could see Little Taw and the next stage behind coursing along. And riding inside it, looking as fresh and clean, as sweet and perfumed as a wild rose, was Bernie Buchanan. Such an agony of longing to see her, just see her, went through me that I groaned. I didn't know it until one of the passengers said, sympathetically, "Hurt your arm, mister?"

I said I had and turned on my side, away from the three of them.

Sleepiness had vanished, but I sweated through the decision to stick to my course. I *would* sell the place. I would *not* go back there. I would *not* see her again. One more time, to sell the place to Ed, then I was finished with it. And with Bernie Buchanan.

Chapter 20

We came into Latham late in the evening of the eleventh with the wind up. We should have met the eastbound stage between Fremont's Orchard and Eagle's Nest, but we didn't.

There was no telegraph at Eagle's Nest, it was only a swing station, and the boys there knew nothing except the stage hadn't arrived. It was four hours late. "They been chased," one of the tenders said, "just like you was, Starr. Four hours is just too damned late. It's the same as never."

We talked all around it between ourselves, the driver, the tenders and me. We all came out at the same place—we couldn't make anything else out of it. The stage had been attacked and nearer Latham than Eagle's Nest. "If he was just a few miles out," I said, "Rattlesnake would circle wide and make a run for it back to Latham. He's got the earth to turn in anywhere along there."

The other men agreed. "That's the way of it. That's what's happened. Bound to be."

"You going on?" a tender asked the driver.

I sympathized with his feelings. When the stage left he and the other tender would be alone here. Two men could have a bad time standing off a bunch of Indians. I kept my mouth shut. It wasn't my decision. Old Pap Russell was the driver. He looked a lot like an Indian himself, leathery, wrinkled, scrawny-necked. He spurted a stream of tobacco juice into a handy sagebrush. "Hell, yes, we're going on. Ain't you boys heard? Nothing stops the United States Mail."

The tender swore, colorfully and creatively. He used some words I had never heard before. "It ain't going to be very comfortable sitting out here in the middle of the sage-brush by ourselves," he concluded.

"Aw, you ain't got nothing to lose but your skulps," Pap said. "You're better off than I've been many a time. You got a station to fort up in. I've stood off a Injun attack with nothing but my mule to hide behind. Ain't nothing gonna happen, anyway. If they've run Rattlesnake back to Latham that'll do 'em for a week or two. They're done up around Cedar Canyon by now."

The passengers had heard enough to make them uneasy and they had formed their own huddle. They walked over to join us. "You boys know anything we ought to know," the man I'd taken to be a lawyer, but who turned out to be a judge, said.

"No, sir," Pap said, "not for sure. We've not met the eastbound. We just been trying to put a few pieces together. She's overdue better than four hours."

"You think there's been an Indian attack?"

"Well, could be. Yes, sir, it could be."

One of the passengers, a thin fellow with a squeaky voice, was pretty upset. "I think we should remain here. I don't think we should run the risk of an attack ourselves. We all have guns . . . we can hold off an attack if we're in the station. I'm not in favor of continuing on right now."

The judge spoke briskly. "I don't agree with that. I think we should proceed. You said you weren't sure what had caused the delay?"

Another passenger spoke up. "I'm in favor of going on. It may be nothing but a hotbox. We'd look pretty silly forting up here over a hotbox, wouldn't we?"

"But if it *is* Indians . . ." the squeaky passenger said.

"If it is," the judge said, "we'll soon find out. I hope it is your judgment that we should go ahead, Mr. Russell."

"Well, sir," Pap said, spitting again, "I hadn't give no thought to doing different. The Overland don't expect its stages to stop running except on Company orders."

"Good," the judge said. He swiveled about to climb back up on the box.

"Judge," Pap said, "if you don't mind, let Mr. Fowler up on the box now."

The passengers knew by now that I was a driver and how I got my wound. The judge nodded. "I shouldn't have had to be reminded. Two drivers are better than one.

Though I hope, sir," with a nod at me, "you don't have to sacrifice your other arm."

I said I hoped I didn't either.

The judge looked at his watch. "Aren't we late?"

Comfortably old Pap said, "About ten minutes. We'll make it up. All right. Board, gentlemen."

The squeaky passenger looked longingly at the walls of the station and I thought he might refuse to leave them, but he climbed into the coach.

Nothing would have surprised me that thirteen miles. We could have found the stage wrecked and bodies, dead and mutilated, tossed like haystraw about it. We could have been ambushed ourselves. Or we could have met the stage bowling along, nothing at all out of the ordinary wrong, just delayed for some perfectly good reason.

None of these things happened. We neither saw a wrecked stage, nor met a delayed one. Nor were we ambushed. We saw no Indians at all, in fact. But we did, twice, overtake wagons headed as fast and as hard as they could go for Latham. As we passed the first one we overtook we pulled up and asked for news. "Where are you going, friend?" old Pap said.

A rancher and his wife were on the wagon seat. She was holding a small baby. The back was loaded with kids and bedding and odds and ends. "Latham," the man said, "fast as we can get there."

"What's your hurry?"

"Ain't you heard? Indians. Raiding again. *Rocky Mountain News* says there's thousands of 'em. Says for all ranchers to get where it's safe. Says there's no time to lose. They've called out the militia again and we are asking for every man to volunteer to protect the territory. For a hundred days, it says. Enlist for a hundred days."

"Are you on your way to enlist?" I asked.

"Me? Hell, no! I'm on my way to Latham where it's safe."

"Where are they raiding?" I asked.

"Oh, they cut up and butchered an emigrant train. Right on down the South Platte there. Killed 'em all. A dozen of 'em, anyway. Just massacred 'em."

"When?" I said. "I've just come up the South Platte.

Me and these other passengers. We didn't pass any emigrant train butchered up."

"Yesterday," the man said. "It was yesterday. Around Valley station."

Pap looked at me.

I nodded. "Well, we did pass a small train along there yesterday. It had just pulled out of Dennison's."

"That was it," the rancher cried, excitedly. "That was it. The very one. It was between Dennison's and Valley station. And there was three wagon trains massacred down by Fort Kearney! Thirty-five miles east of Fort Kearney, the paper said."

"East!" I said. "Are you sure? East of Fort Kearney? On the Little Blue? That don't sound right at all."

"It was on the Little Blue," the man said. "All up and down the Little Blue, it said. Stage stations burned. Folks killed. Oh, they're on the warpath good. They're raiding everywhere."

"Mister," I said, "have you got that newspaper with you?"

The man looked at his wife. "You bring it, Hilda?"

She shook her head.

"We left in a hurry," he said. "Ain't you seen the paper yourselves?"

"The eastbound stage is held up," I said.

"My God!" he said, grabbing his whip, "it's been attacked, and us just setting here. They'll come boiling down this road any minute. I'm getting out of here!" He laid on the whip and his team took off.

We circled around them and left them behind.

Neither Pap nor I said anything for a while, but there was plenty to think about. I didn't like the sound of this dustup at all. The *News* could be depended on to blow up any incident along the South Platte or anywhere else in Colorado Territory—but down east of Kearney, on the Little Blue? If that was true, if there had been attacks that far east, it was serious. It meant a full-scale Indian war. It meant the whole road was in danger, every last mile of it. Pap finally said, "Looks like a real ruckus, don't it?"

"That's just what I was thinking," I said, "and don't like it. Let's move 'em out a little, Pap. We're just lallygagging along."

Pap cracked his whip and the team stretched out a little. "You got that place of yours on your mind," he said, "best I've heard it's as good as a fort. The boys tell me it could stand off the whole Sioux tribe."

"I hope it's not having to," I said.

"Aw, the *News* is as windy as a stale horse," he said. Then he added, "But I would give a purty to know where that dad-burned eastbound is at."

"If you'll stretch this team," I said, "we'll soon find out."

We did. It was sitting in Latham under orders to proceed no further, and Latham was working like a hive of bees when we arrived, because the stage from Salt Lake had just come in and the stage from Denver had come in, and the eastbound passengers from both stages were milling around wanting to know *why* all stages had been stopped at Latham.

McIlvain, the station agent, had his hands full. "All I can tell you," he was saying, "is that these are my orders. No stages will go east of here until further notice. Mr. Street, the General Agent, is at Fort Kearney. He has telegraphed us to stop all eastbound stages right here. And they will be stopped here and nothing will go east until he says so."

"Is anything coming west?" somebody asked.

"Not out of Atchison, no, sir. All Overland travel has been stopped for the time being. You people who just came in from Salt Lake, we'll try to take care of you here. You people from Denver had better go home.

"Yes, sir, the stages will continue to run west of here and to Denver. We don't know how long the situation may continue.

"Yes, ma'am, the Indians are raiding. That's what this is all about. It isn't safe for you to travel east right now.

"No, sir," to an important-looking gentleman, "I don't know when we can resume operations. The Sioux and Arapahoes and Cheyennes have something to say about that, it appears. There's a stack of newspapers over there on that bench, sir. Came in on the Denver stage just now. They can tell you as much as we know ourselves.

"Yes, sir, we will continue to operate between here and Denver on schedule. If any of you people want to go into

Denver and obtain better accommodations, the stages will be running. Adjustments can be made on your tickets. No, sir, we can't pay for your accommodations in Denver. We can take care of you here, but if you go to Denver it's to come out of your own pocket.

"Yes, ma'am, we will try to accommodate everybody who has to lay over here. No, ma'am, there are no private rooms. This is not a hotel. Yes, ma'am, there is plenty of food for the time being. Meals will be served regularly as long as it lasts. Supper is being served right now.

"Yes, sir, all of us who work here have guns and we have a few extra. The mail agent has gone to Laporte to get some extra ammunition. We think we can stand off an attack, if it comes. Captain LaBarge is organizing the men for a defense. No, sir, he is not a member of the militia. He's a Missouri riverboat captain. No, sir, the militia is not here. They have been notified. We hope all you gentlemen have guns of your own.

"Yes, ma'am, the telegraph to Denver and to the west is in order. I'm sorry, ma'am, you can't send a telegram to St. Louis. The line is out between here and Julesburg. The troops are working on repairing the break right now and we may recover the connection any minute.

"Sir, the line is cut between *here* and Julesburg. That's right. Denver is getting information through Fort Laramie. They are keeping us advised of the situation. No, sir, we don't intend to abandon this station. Our orders are to defend it."

It was worse than useless to bother Mac for a while. Besides I had learned what I most wanted to know. I couldn't telegraph Cottonwood for news of my place. Not just now.

It was natural that the passengers should be anxious and worried and bothered. For whatever reason, they had started east and were now held up in this inconvenient place for what promised to be an indefinite time. They wanted information. They were being bothersome. But say this for them. Mostly they were westerners, used to sudden and unexpected developments. Once they understood the situation they took it with pretty good grace. Nobody made any great trouble. Nobody panicked. They asked their questions, Mac gave them the best answers he had, and shortly they began to laugh and joke about the whole thing. Mac's own attitude was a help. He was as matter-of-fact as if he'd been taking care of the usual transfer of baggage, passengers and mail. He kept things pitched easy and quiet. Mrs. McIlvain was a big help with the women passengers. She was an absolutely unflusterable woman at all times, with a kind of dry, pithy way of saying things. She moved around among the passengers not exactly mothering them, but giving the impression that as long as the McIlvains were at Latham there would be no nonsense with Sioux, Arapahoes and Cheyennes. They wouldn't dare!

I picked up a copy of the *News* and went outside with it, unfolded it to the bold, black headlines: "900 Sioux, Arapahoes and Cheyennes raid Overland road from Liberty Farm to Julesburg!"

The Governor's proclamation was on the front page: "Patriotic citizens of Colorado:—I again appeal to you to organize for defense of your homes and families against the merciless savages . . . Any man who kills a hostile Indian is a patriot; but there are Indians who are friendly and to kill one of these will involve us in greater difficulty. . . ." I wondered how you could tell the difference, on sight, and who would bother to find out. The publisher of the paper had his own notions: "A few months of active extermination against the red devils will bring quiet and nothing else will."

The details in the paper were grim. Nine men had been killed when the emigrant train near Valley station had been butchered and plundered. Plum Creek station had been attacked and burned and eleven men were killed. Three wagon trains carrying goods for George Tritch of Denver had been attacked thirty-five miles east of Fort Kearney. Fourteen men had been killed, several women and children had been taken prisoner, and all the wagons had been plundered and burned.

The whole valley of the Little Blue had been raided. At Liberty Farm, the station was burned and it was believed everybody had been killed. It was not yet known how many persons were there. Up at the Narrows, above Liberty Farm, Joe Eubank's farm had been burned. Joe had been killed and Mrs. Eubank and their little girl had been captured. At Thirty-Two-Mile Creek the station was burned and six men had been killed. I thought of the Emerys and felt sad. The whole valley was burning, going up in smoke, for a hundred miles—stage stations, post offices, stores, farmhouses, everything along the road. And all just 170 miles west of Atchison.

I kept searching for incidents west of Fort Kearney. One man had been killed near Cottonwood Springs. Gilman's ranch had been raided and three men killed. Gilman's was between Midway and Cottonwood. But there seemed to be nothing between Cottonwood and Julesburg. Then, on the South Platte there were numerous incidents of stock being run off and there was the emigrant train butchered near Valley station. That appeared to be all at this end of the line.

I folded the paper, feeling a little reassured but not much. Cottonwood and Gilman's were mighty damned close to the ranch. There didn't seem to be much sense in the way the Indians were raiding. Only on the Little Blue had they shown any consistent plan. It was evident they had meant to wipe out that whole valley. It was by far the most thickly settled section on the line. Obviously the Indians had meant to show the whites they didn't want any more settlers. They hit that whole rich valley hard. They massacred the three wagon trains for supplies and it had been a rich haul. Mr. Tritch was a hardware merchant in Denver and the trains were loaded with lead, guns, ammunition and other hardware the Indians needed.

Then they hit hard at Liberty Farm stage station and Thirty-Two-Mile Creek. Both were busy and important stations with depots of supplies. What they were saying in the valley of the Little Blue was plain. Get out. Get off the land. Get your fences and your farmhouses and your stage stations out of this valley. Anybody could read the message along the Little Blue. But out along the Platte they had only swooped here and there. Not much sense of murdering one man near Cottonwood, three at Gilman's, and a dozen at Plum Creek. They weren't the same bunch, I told myself. That band on the Little Blue was under a warrior society and a chief who knew what he was doing and made his message clear. The raids along the Platte were spasms, just a fist of rage hitting here and there.

But a spasm was as likely to swoop down on the ranch as anywhere else. I thought of our thick dobe walls and took some comfort from the thought. If Ed took care, they ought to be all right. I wished I could hear from him. We took telegraph service so much for granted that it wasn't until it was cut off we realized how dead the quiet could be without it.

The hubbub inside the station had died down a little and most of the passengers were having their supper. McIlvain was stacking sacks of mail under the windows when I went in. I flicked the paper with a finger. "This is gospel, Mac?"

"Fowler!" he said. "Where'd you come from? I didn't see you."

"You were pretty busy," I said. "I came in with Pap."

"From your place, huh? How'd things look there?"

"Quiet when I left. But that was three days ago. God knows what's happened since." I held up the paper. "Is this straight stuff?"

"Far as we know," he said. "The fact is, the *News* can get more details than we can right now. Through the militia. The telegraph line is cut between here and Julesburg, but it's open to Fort Laramie and open from there to Cottonwood. They have to go all around the mulberry bush, but they can still get through to Fort Kearney. The military has preempted the line but they give the *News* the details. We wouldn't know nothing if it wasn't for that."

"Believe I'll see if I can get a message through to Cottonwood," I said.

Mac shook his head. "Not a bit of use trying. They won't take it. Mr. Street got through before the military took over, but since then nothing but the military uses the line. What good that'll do, I can't figure. God, Starr, did you know there's only 250 troops on the whole line? Including Fort Laramie and Kearney? Two hundred and fifty! There's a little detail at Julesburg, another one at Camp Cottonwood, another one up at Halleck, and what the hell can they do? The Company's been yelling its head off for two years for more troops along the line. Now maybe they'll believe us."

"They've got a pretty good use for troops in the east," I said.

"And we've got a pretty good use for 'em in the west,"

he said. "They want us to keep the stages running and the mail going through, they better give us a little help."

"Is Street coming on through or is he staying at Kearney?" I said.

"He's coming on through. *If* he can get through. And we've got seven stages on the road ahead of him. They'd all left Kearney ahead of the trouble. If *they* get through, they'll bring the best news you can get of your place."

I nodded. "Street was at Kearney, was he, when it began?"

"No. He was on his way from Atchison to Kearney. It was the damnedest thing. He come along right behind the raids. Liberty Farm was still burning when he got there. In fact, his stage was chased into Big Sandy. That was how close he come to being massacred himself. It's not true, what the paper says about the Emerys, though. They got away."

"That's good," I said. "I hated to think of them being murdered."

"But the station is a total loss. They burned it to the ground and run off all the stock. Didn't leave a building standing. Same at Thirty-Two-Mile Creek. All the hands at Thirty-Two-Mile killed. And up toward the Narrows at the Eubanks place. Killed Joe and all his hands and captured his woman and kid. They hit the Lone Tree station and run off the stock and burned everything. The boys there got away. But they sure messed up the line all along the whole valley."

"Everything is stopped?"

"Between here and Atchison. Not a thing rolling. Except those seven stages already on the road. When they get here, that closes down the Denver division of the Overland. Mail, passengers, express . . . everything stopped. Mr. Street said all the freight trains on the road were corraled up. Stopped. Not a damn thing is moving."

It was strange to think of it. Not a wheel on the long road turning. Nothing moving. Nothing rolling over that busy thoroughfare. It had never happened before and you couldn't have believed it ever would happen. But a bunch of Sioux and Arapahoes and Cheyennes had sure closed the road. For a while, anyhow.

"Well," I said, "if it lasts very long some people in

Colorado are going to get pretty hungry and prices will go so high only the millionaires can afford to eat. How are you fixed here?"

"I commenced laying in extra supplies two months ago. When the first troubles on the South Platte started," Mac said. "We can last as long as we need to, I believe."

I thought of my father. His freight trains were among those corraled up somewhere along the road. The supplies in his store in Denver wouldn't last long if he was swamped. But the day hadn't come when one of his sons had to worry about him. He would take care of his own and as many others as he felt any responsibility for.

I remember my own winter supplies for the ranch were also stalled on the road. But with no stage passengers or freighters to feed, Emma could make the reserves in the store last them out. "The Governor," I said, "had better order rationing pretty soon for the Territory. And he better get busy on some kind of a deal with Brigham Young. Utah food and grain are about all we're going to get for a while." I laughed. "This is going to be profitable for the Mormons."

"What ain't?" Mac said.

"Last time I bought Utah peaches," I said, "I paid two bits a piece for them."

"They're four bits now," he said, "and going higher. Any women at your place, Starr?"

"Four of them," I said. "Emma, Bucky, Emma's sister, and Bonnie Dickson."

Mac gazed somberly out the window. "Makes a difference, don't it?"

I agreed that it did.

Mac shook off his somberness. "Well, Emma Westmoreland is a sensible woman. Like mine. And like Lizzie and Maggie Trout. She'll keep a steady rein on the others. When did Bernie come back? Last I heard she had gone home."

"She was on the stage behind me. Due in the night of the ninth. I reckon she got there all right."

It was strange, but when I conjured up the picture of the ranch now, and the people there, Emma and Bucky were plain and clear, going about their affairs with remembered and familiar ways. But I could only see Bernie the way I had last seen her, sitting at the small table in Oliver Wiggins's dining room, tidy, fastidious, determined, saying good-bye. I couldn't bring her out of Oliver Wiggins's dining room back to the ranch at all.

I was uneasy but I wasn't in any great turmoil about the ranch. It was built for this kind of trouble and unless it was besieged by a whole tribe of Indians ought to come through all right. And of course I was anxious for direct news.

"How's your arm?" Mac said.

"All right," I said. "I can drive. I was heading for Denver to report in."

"Going on?"

"Not yet," I said. "Soon as those stages on the road come in, I will."

"Gonna wait for some news here, huh? There's four of them between here and your place," he reminded me. "Be the fifth one before you hear."

"Yes," I said, "I know. Day after tomorrow. Anything I can do while I'm waiting?"

"Why don't you take that extra coach out there and go over to Laporte and load it up with anything you can find? Get as much ammunition as you can, food, whisky, whatever you see that we could use."

As I went out to have a team hitched in, a squad of men was drilling in the courtyard. Captain LaBarge was marching them by fours up and down, backward and forward. Sweating like mules in the hot sun, they were striving to follow orders, forward march, about face, to the rear march, halt and present arms. Two or three of the men still wore their good black cloth coats, but mostly they were miners and ranchers, rough-dressed and a little seedy looking. There was nothing that leveled classes quicker, I thought, than an Indian scare. You might be wealthy enough to buy yourself a state legislature but you couldn't buy your scalp if a Cheyenne wanted it. A million dollars meant nothing to an Indian. Lawyers, bankers, businessmen, were marching in Captain LaBarge's squad alongside of miners, gamblers and ranchers and sweating just as much.

Captain LaBarge was on the verge of apoplexy, it was plain. Nature had given him a round, tubby figure and a ruddy face. By slow degrees the sun was parboiling him. But he was manfully taking every step the squad took and it was obvious if he was felled by a stroke he meant to die doing his duty. It was funny—but it was also commendable. Under no circumstances would these men ever make use of drill formation, but if, in whatever time he had, Captain LaBarge could teach them instantly to obey an order, it might save their lives and those of dozens of others. The discipline would be invaluable.

Another driver went with me to Laporte. It was thirty-five miles and we were there before daylight. We were back at Latham by six the next evening. We had been able to bring another keg of powder, half a dozen shotguns, some bacon, flour, rice and canned milk. Two of the stages on the road had arrived while we were gone, and another arrived shortly after we did. Everything was fine at my place when they'd come through, they said. Quiet. No Indians. And Mrs. Westmoreland's sister had got there all right.

I felt relieved, even though these stages had come through ahead of the raids. They had no firsthand knowledge of what might have happened since. But at least they ticked off a few more hours of peace and quiet at the ranch.

The station began to get crowded as the through coaches from Carson City and Placerville continued to come in each day and unloaded more and more passengers who had to lay over. The agent at Denver stopped eastbound loading there, but one stage a day came in to take passengers to the city. The schedule was shot to hell with nothing running between Latham and Atchison but it was maintained on the regular time to Salt Lake and Placerville. The mail from the west also piled up. We stacked it around the walls of the station until we had a fortress of mail sacks as high as the ceiling and four feet thick. "By God," McIlvain said, "not even a cannon ball could get through that!"

The fifth stage was a couple of hours late. It didn't get into Latham until about eight o'clock the evening of the thirteenth. This was the first stage that had come through Midway and Cottonwood and my place after the raiding began. The driver gave me the word as it had been passed along to him. All quiet at your place. Ed sent word he had everything in readiness. All stock was corraled in the stable yard. Guards were posted. Everybody was taking care. No Indians sighted yet. I felt an immense load lift from me. If Ed was ready and taking care, even if they got hit the place was pretty certain to be safe.

Next morning the sixth stage did not arrive. When the stage from Denver came in with the newspapers, we felt great anxiety for it. The raids had been resumed the day before all along the line. Raids had been made on the swing station at O'Fallon's Bluffs, the station there had been burned and all the stock run off. The two tenders had escaped. This was twelve miles this side of my place.

A raid had been made on Julesburg and an attempt had been made to burn the Company buildings. But the troops had chased the Indians off and the people had been able to put out most of the fires. The paper said there was a lot of damage to property, however. The stables had been badly burned, much stock had been lost and one stagecoach was burned.

All day we looked for the stage. It finally arrived eight hours late. Drivers were doubling and tripling all along the line, now, and teams were having to work long stretches without relays. The schedule was frazzled out.

I talked with the driver. "These people," he said, indicating the passengers, "saw Indians near your place. They saw what was left at O'Fallon's and the panic at Julesburg. And they were chased up the South Platte themselves, between Antelope and Spring Hill. Your place hadn't been hit, though."

I talked with a passenger. "The people all along the line are leaving the ranches and stations. Going to Julesburg. Going to Camp Cottonwood. Going to Kearney. Anywhere. They're just getting out. Leaving everything. Abandoning everything. Going where they think they'll be safe. We met dozens of wagons. We saw many places burning. We saw some of the stage stations burned to the ground. All the stock run off. Several times we had no relay teams. Had to proceed without a fresh team. At O'Fallon's Bluffs . . . and at Sand Hill. The men had either left or been killed. No stock there. No station. It looks mighty grave, sir, mighty grave. And mighty desolate."

"What was the situation at Fowler's . . . Fremont Springs? Just this side of Cottonwood?"

"My God, man, we've been through so much since we left Cottonwood . . . let me think. Fowler's . . . oh, that's a dinner stop. Yes. They hadn't been raided. We had a good meal there and washed up . . . that was the last decent meal we had . . . last place where things seemed normal. Though there was some excitement there, too. Some people from a ranch came in while we were there. They had the wind up and came into the station for protection."

"But the station had not been attacked."

"No, sir. It had not been. And the people there were ready for it. They believed they would be attacked and they had made ready."

Well. There it was. And it wasn't much to take comfort from. Even this news was two days old now and anything could have happened in two days. I wished to hell we could use the telegraph. I felt like a prisoner, roped and tied. I wanted to make a beeline for the ranch myself, but it was two hundred miles with hostile Indians milling around over every mile of it. Common sense told me I could never make it. All I could do was chafe at the bit and do what I could where I was. Until the last stage came in. If it did. Then I meant to head for Denver and by bribery or bodily assault get through by telegraph.

Everybody now believed the Indians were coming up the South Platte and that Latham would be the next big station attacked. They'd hit Julesburg, Latham was bound to be next. We posted guards at night and Captain LaBarge continued to drill his men, and McIlvain continued to lay up all the stores and provisions he could put his hands on. We ate pretty well and, though we were so crowded you couldn't take a step for people sleeping on the floor, nobody complained. In fact, it was right comforting to have such a big crowd all about.

Along with the tenders and other drivers I slept in the stables, and took my turn at guard. We had an Indian scare that night. I hadn't yet been called and was sleeping when a guard came tearing in, shaking like a leaf, and yelling, "They're coming! The Injuns are coming! They're crossing the river right now! Everybody turn out!"

Then he went skyhooting over the station to rouse them

over there. We turned out and listened and we could plainly hear a lot of splashing down at the ford. Captain LaBarge took charge. "All right, men. Everybody to their posts."

His few days of discipline paid off. Nobody panicked. The women were told to stay in the station. The men took up positions all around it. Extra skirmishers were detailed and went out along the boundaries. Then the Captain picked eight men as a detail to accompany him to do a little patrol duty. I was one of them.

It was a clear night, the stars as thick as mustard seed in the sky, but it was dark except for the starshine. We crept down toward the ford as quietly and stealthily as possible. "Don't fire until I give the word," the Captain whispered. "We'll take them by surprise."

Inch by inch we moved along, the sand muffling our advance. As we got closer to the river the sound of many animals crossing was clear and loud. I wondered at the carelessness of the Indians crossing at a regular ford, so near the station, and so noisily.

Then we saw some dark shadows coming up the bank and we flattened on one side of the road. "Mind, now," the Captain whispered again, "don't fire till I give the signal."

We waited. As usual at such times, my stomach was fluttering and feeling oily, my nose was itching, my throat was scratchy and dry. All at once one of the men let out his breath. "They're oxen," he said. "I just saw 'em plain . . . see, over there, clear of the bushes?"

We watched as they came on, slow and lumbering. They began to pass us. Cattle! Nothing but cattle! "Careful," the Captain warned, "it may be a trick. Indians may have driven them over. They may be right behind."

"No, sir," I said, standing up. "If they were driven these oxen would be stampeding. They're just moving along. Maybe they've been stolen from some ranch, but there's no Indians driving them now."

The men began to laugh and one of them said, "Well, by damn! Attacked by a drove of cattle. Now, if that ain't something. Well, if I can have my druthers, I'd ruther be attacked by cattle than a band of Injuns, any day. They sure can't stick you full of arrows."

It was a good joke and it eased the tension among the

people considerably. Everybody had a big laugh over our cattle attack and then settled down for the night in a good humor. That was the night somebody stole Frank Root's gun. He was standing guard about halfway down to the river and he got sleepy and crawled up into the crotch of a cottonwood tree and went to sleep. Slept right through the cattle attack. We thought it would be a good joke to take his gun.

Next morning at breakfast somebody asked him, casually, if there'd been any excitement during the night. Frank wasn't riding messenger any more. He was mail agent at Latham now, and he'd learned to give as good as he got. He came right back. "Why, didn't you hear all the shooting? I was totally surrounded by Indians, fought a battle all by myself and killed three of the savages single-handed."

He had bested us and his gun was restored promptly.

We waited all day for the last stage to come in, with the last passengers and mail from the east. When it arrived the long cord of the road, the stages and the mail, would be cut. The *News* said that morning that General Mitchell had set out from Fort Kearney with a sizable body of troops to punish the Indians. The route he was following, they said, was down the Republican. He wanted, they said, for the Indians between the rivers to feel a touch of grape and steel. We thought he would have done better to patrol the Platte . . . put some troops along the road, at the stations along the line, for the *News* also told us that the raids were continuing. They were sporadic, made by little bands here and there. But they were hitting in, doing their damage and getting away with it.

The *Rocky Mountain News* had learned, also, that westbound mail was piling up at Atchison, and that it would be returned east and sent by steamer around the Horn to California. Salt Lake and Denver mail from the east would eventually arrive from the west! Brought by stages from the coast and over the mountains. This was a fine howdy-do! The Indians had finally stopped the United States Mail across the plains.

The stage rolled in a little after sundown. The driver brought me no fresh news. "Your people are all right. Still sticking there at the ranch."

The passengers had a story of being chased into Cotton-wood by Indians dressed in the finery of plunder from wagon trains. "They had on women's bonnets and veils and silk shirts and shawls and men's boots and jackets, and they were in high spirits. Our driver said they were drunk. Said they weren't really trying to catch us. Just chasing us in good humor. If that represents their good humor, I don't want to see them in a bad humor. They filled the sides of that stage with so many arrows it looked like a porcupine when we got to Cottonwood."

It did look a little battle-scarred.

I took the next stage into Denver and arrived the morning of the seventeenth. When I walked into the station, one look at the agent's face told me there was bad news.

Chapter 21

He spread his hands, as if trying to ward off the bad news, or as if trying to smooth something out a little, the way we smoothed out a bolt of goods showing it in the store, or a newspaper that was badly wrinkled. "What is it?" I said.

"Ed telegraphed. From Cottonwood. The line's repaired. They've had some trouble."

"How much trouble? When?"

"Yesterday. Well, it was this way. He was taking all the womenfolks . . . there was some ranchers had brought their families over to the station . . . and Ed was taking all of 'em over to Cottonwood. Figured they'd all be safer over there where the troops was at. He had three wagons . . . and they got waylaid around Cold Springs. About half-way. . . ."

"Who was killed? How many?" I felt as heavy and stiff as if I had been turned to a pillar of salt. Even my tongue felt swollen and dry and stiff.

"Now, slow down, Starr. Wasn't nobody killed. Wasn't nobody hurt. Nobody at all. But they got the girls . . . the little Westmoreland girl and Emma's sister. . . ."

"They got the *girls!* They got the girls? How could they get the girls? Without anybody getting hurt? How? How? Didn't anybody fight?"

"Now, wait. . . . The girls were riding. Horseback. They weren't on the wagons. They were riding alongside. Ed said tell you it was old Slewfoot. That's how come him to be took in. They just cut the girls out like you would a horse out of a herd, he said. Whilst he was talking to old Slew-foot, he said."

"Whilst he was talking to old Slewfoot," I said. Then repeated it. "Whilst he was talking to old Slewfoot."

I don't know whether it is ever possible to describe the

way the mind works but I have a very clear memory of the way images, names, thoughts flashed through mine at that moment and the triggered feelings. First and instantly my mind went to Bernie and the image of her was called up and there was a feeling of shock and horror. But immediately, and beyond her and larger, was suddenly the name Bucky, and the dozens and dozens of remembered pictures of Bucky, happy, gay, sad, tearful, rambunctious, larky, sweet, impudent, gutsy, brave, honorable, lovely—and the feeling triggered was terror, sick, bone-weakening, stomach-squeezing terror, absolute and pure blood-draining fear for her, and with it the certainty and knowledge that this was what love was all about, all mixed up with life, tied to its dailyness, its littlenesses and its bignesses, inextricable from life, and that Bucky *was* my life and was even myself, was corded into me like the reins I held daily, the meals I ate daily, the sleep I slept daily, the air I breathed daily, and could no more be separated from me than those other essential things. And the terror and the wrenching life-loss sent me wild and frantic.

A crazy, blind, bloody rage made things go black for me. I shouted and pounded the wall. "Why did the fool leave the station? Why? Why? The station was solid! It was a fort! It couldn't be burned! It couldn't be taken! It had provisions! Why did he leave it? Why didn't he stick there! Why did he leave those walls? Why go to Cottonwood? What possessed him to expose them all . . . they'd all still be there . . . the girls wouldn't be . . . he took them to their death and doom. Why? Why? God! God! A fool would have had more sense!"

I know I was shouting. I know I was pounding the wall. I know I was pounding human flesh when the boys came crowding around and somebody shoved me into a chair and somebody else poured a slug of whisky down me, and somebody else said if I didn't shut up he was going to clout me. I know I was still shouting and pounding and struggling and crying, and then they were hustling me into another office and shutting doors and windows to keep the curious from seeing and hearing. And I kept on fighting and clawing loose from them, and broke up furniture and threw chairs out the windows and wrecked David Street's desk and acted, generally, as crazy and witless and lunatic as I really was, and no more cared or knew it or felt it, or felt anything but a wildness that had to break things and smash things and try to kill down the wildness in me. When you can't do anything else in the world, when you are totally helpless, absolutely and wholly helpless to change what is unbearably unacceptable, you can always go berserk. I did, until somebody, finally realizing I was beyond any hope of reason or control, hit me over the head with something solid enough to knock me out.

When I came to, I was on the sofa in my father's sitting room. He was at the door, saying as calm as Sunday morning, "Thank you, boys. We'll take care of him now. Thank you for bringing him here."

After the wild outburst I felt like a rag doll and only half-witted. Something had burst inside me as shattered as a china plate and I thought it would take the rest of my life to put it together again. Bucky in the hands of Indians. Bucky . . . Bucky . . . it was like dying to think of her, helpless and captured. Little spitfire, little hellcat . . . her and her damned old white rooster . . . and the big old calf-size pup she practiced her rope on . . . and her swagger and impudence . . . and the swoop of those crazy waltz-arounds when she was excited . . . and two big, thick braids of the blazingest red hair on earth . . . and mischief and guts and temper and good hands and wrists and steady on a hell-for-leather drive . . . and, oh God, such a skinful of love, and such fierce, hardsteel loyalty . . . and isn't life heavenly, Starr, isn't life just simply heavenly! You couldn't remember Bucky and think of her captured without wanting to stop the war, blow Charge all over the earth, let the sun and the moon and the stars quit shining till she was free again. It twisted my mind into insanity!

My father was standing over me. "Well, boy. They tell me you just about wrecked the Overland office."

"I went crazy."

He nodded. "A man can. I have. Great grief can do it."

"They got Bucky."

"They got Bucky," he said. Then he said it again, softly. "They got Bucky. I see. I see. Yes, the boys told me. We're going to get her back again."

302

"Don't tell me lies," I said. "I'm not a kid to be comforted. How are we going to get her back? How? The Sioux have got her. You hear! The Sioux! Governor Evans can't get her back. Colonel Chivington can't get her back. General Mitchell can't get her back. General Pope can't get her back. Old Abe himself can't get her back!"

"I know one man who can," he said quietly.

"You?"

"No. Not with the Sioux. Old Bent. William Bent."

I reared up, galvanized. The perspective of youth is so short, it has such a narrow range. It lacks the long years of experience, of knowing how, out of experience, to go about getting things done. My father, wise through his experience, had put his finger exactly on the best hope, perhaps the only hope, of getting the girls released, of even perhaps keeping them unharmed until they were released. "Will he do it?" I said. "You think he'll do it?"

"For an old compañero? I think so." He shifted his feet, which made him stand taller. "I tried to do him a favor once. At Taos."

I stared at him. This went back a long, long time.

He went on, softly. "When Charles was murdered, I was there. I did my best to get to him."

1846, I thought. When Kearny occupied Santa Fe and took over New Mexico. And appointed Charles Bent the first territorial governor. And he was murdered in the Indian uprising at Taos just a few months later. "I didn't know you were there," I said.

"William Bent knows it," my father said. "Now," he continued, "I want to telegraph Major Wynkoop at Fort Lyon. Find out if Bent is at his ranch on the Purgatoire."

"That will take hours," I groaned.

"Nevertheless, it may save days. We can't go riding off in all four directions at once. Put your own affairs in order and be ready to leave when I come back." He picked up his hat and swung on his heel.

I followed him out, shucking despair like an old skin. There was something to do. We could move. We could hope again.

But first I had to telegraph Cottonwood. I asked the operator if Ed was still there. He said he was. He had been with the troops fanning out in a search for the Indians who had taken the girls. They had just got back. No luck. They had lost the trail north of the river.

I said tell Ed to stay there until he heard from me. Tell him I was beginning the search through other channels. Tell him my father was working on it. Tell him I would keep in touch. Tell him it looked hopeful.

That done, my father came and said Bent was at his ranch and we rode out of Denver.

Chapter 22

He would let me go no farther than Fort Lyon, which was near the Big Timbers on the Upper Arkansas. It was Bent's second fort. He had blown up his old fort in rage at the price the government offered him for it. He would not sell at such a price, and he would not leave it standing to be confiscated. He built his second fort lower down the river. It was leased to the government.

It brought back memories, even to me. I hadn't been here since I was a boy, driving our light supply wagon in the trains on freight hauls to Santa Fe. The immense stand of cottonwoods which gave the place its name, Big Timbers, was being depleted. It was neither so dense nor so extensive as it used to be. In time, it would go altogether. Men would finally take the last trees down, for houses, for wagon tongues, for fuel.

We had an argument about whether I should go or stay. I was insistent upon going on out to the ranch on the Purgatoire. My father was just as insistent that I should stay at the fort. "But why? I'll keep out of it. I'll keep my mouth shut," I said.

He had been answering me rather absently, if he had a dozen things on his mind, the way he used to do when we boys were little and bothered him about something. He sighed. "I keep forgetting you don't know about these things. Bent is more Indian than he is white, after all these years among them. But he is white enough to be ashamed that two of his boys took part in those raids. As wild, as murdering, as red Indian as any Cheyenne, they plundered and raided and killed. George was seen wearing silk shirts made from goods plundered from George Trich's three wagon trains. You oughtn't to need to explain, Starr. Your presence will embarrass him. There you'll sit, my son, whom his sons have damaged."

"It wasn't them. . . ."

"Close enough," he said. "No, you stay here. And I mean that. Don't come prowling after me. Stay here at the fort and wait. I'll be as quick as I can."

I finally agreed. "All right. Unless you send for me, I don't budge."

He was only gone five days but it was a long slow time for me. Only a handful of troops were at the fort. Most of them were on scouting details. Major Wynkoop, the commandant, wasn't even there. He had taken a detail out to a Cheyenne camp. A wise man, commander of the First Colorado Veteran Cavalry, Major Wynkoop was working against almost impossible odds to come to some sort of arrangement with the Cheyennes. On one side were the hotheads and the *Rocky Mountain News* and the often irresponsible Colorado militia. On the other side was the rigid tribal and social structure of the Cheyennes, of all Indians for that matter. It was an almost impossible task to bring them to have any understanding of each other. What was accomplished with one element, the other immediately undid with some reckless act. While the old, wise chiefs counseled peace and sued for peace, the young Dog Soldiers and other warrior societies continued to raid. While Judge Armour and older and wiser heads in Colorado counseled patience, the militia chased down all Indians, indiscriminately, and shot on sight. There seemed no way to bring whites and Indians together for even a temporary peace. Neither side really wanted to heed any warnings.

There was nothing for me to do but sleep, read old magazines and newspapers, and walk and walk and walk, a thousand times back and forth across the courtyard. To be inactive when every nerve in the body is keyed up to action is torturing. I wanted to be riding . . . tracking down that little bunch of Sioux up north by now, probably in the Powder River country. I wanted physically, right now, without any more waiting, to go after the girls and take them away from the Indians.

I didn't do a lot of straight thinking. I couldn't make my mind stay with any line of thought very long. It kept going to Bucky—and to Bernie—in the hands of savages. Even if they weren't molested they would suffer . . . heat and pain and indignity and abuse, at least from the squaws. They would be used like slaves, made to fetch and carry, they would be harried by some old squaw or a whole bunch of squaws who on any whim could claw at them, take a stick to them, scold and harangue them, make them wait on them. The hardest work they could devise would fall to the lot of the two girls, and they would get the poorest food and the meanest places to sleep.

My mind held tightly to one thing my father had told me. "Don't think about it, Indians don't commonly rape white women."

"Why don't they?" I said. "They're men. Like us. And we do. No Indian woman is safe with a white man."

"Yes. Well, there's a difference." He was blunt telling me and he used the bluntest terms, but what it amounted to was that they were so constantly and adequately served by their own women they weren't starved as white men were by the restrictions of society. "And in that way," he said, "they're really more civilized than we are. But it isn't on their minds all the time. They begin early and often . . . a dozen times a day if they want it and forgotten till the next time. They aren't always hurting for it. But a constant and frequent need is only for the young men. Once a man becomes a warrior it is beneath his dignity to have it on his mind all the time. He has more important things than women to think about. Of course he has his wives and he is well taken care of. Three or four wives," he added dryly, "can really be more than one man can serve and keep happy." He laughed. "I have often wondered if some of the laziness of Indian men wasn't from overwork at night. Several women, jealous and wanting their turn and tormenting till they get it, can keep a man worn out. Even a stallion has limits.

"Then there is another thing. Indians feel superior to white people. To take a white woman is a little degrading."

"But that woman we saw that time . . . that wife of that emigrant they'd put on the prairie. . . ."

"Yes. That was done as a deliberate insult. To avenge an insult. It's always done for that reason. Those Indians had visited that camp the night before. They wanted a few presents. If the man had had any sense he would have given them a few and nothing would have happened. Or if he didn't want to give them anything, nothing still would have happened if he hadn't insulted the chief. He spit on him. So the woman . . . the man's wife . . . was purposely degraded."

"Tell me the truth," I said. "Do you believe, do you yourself personally believe the girls won't be molested that way?"

"I do personally believe they are safe that way. Nobody had insulted that little band of Sioux that took the girls. The way they were taken, deliberately without harm to anybody, I feel certain they have been taken for ransom. I believe that was the sole purpose of their capture. They are going to ask for presents, and probably pretty expensive ones, for the two girls. Now, that is the truth of what I believe. The girls won't have an easy time, but they won't be killed, and they won't be raped. They represent presents. They are currency in the Indians' pockets. Through William Bent, we can let it be known we are willing to pay. Now, you must prepare yourself for it to take time. We aren't going to get them back tomorrow, or next week, or even next month. They aren't going to let them go until they've made us anxious enough to pay anything they ask."

"That's right now," I said.

"Yes, but they don't know that."

"When?" I said.

He hesitated. "I would guess this winter. They'll fool around and fool around and some time during the winter when it's cold and game is scarce they'll suddenly decide to trade the girls for food and supplies."

"But, my God, it's just August!"

"Well, we'll see. Maybe Bent can arrange it sooner. But don't set your heart on it."

When he came back to Fort Lyon he was in good spirits. He and William Bent had had a good visit and Bent was eager to be as helpful as possible. He could have done more for us, and faster, if it had been Cheyennes who had taken the girls, but White Antelope's band of Cheyennes had been hospitable to this little band of Sioux and he would work through them. He had already sent a runner out to White Antelope to tell him to send runners north to the Sioux, who were to say the two white women they held belonged to friends of Little Hat—Bent's name given him by the Cheyennes—and that if they came to harm he would be very angry, and that Little Hat's friends were ready to buy the girls.

"Now it's in his hands," my father said. "This is all we can do for the time being. Bent is working with the major here to try to get the Cheyennes to make peace . . . to come in here to the fort for a council. He will talk further with White Antelope when he comes in. The only way Bent can really deal with these Sioux is through White Antelope."

"I hope he's still important enough," I said.

I understood well enough what my father meant and I knew it had to be accepted. We were fortunate to have this old tie with the one man who might still be powerful enough to bring some pressure to bear on the Sioux. But I was fretted just the same. I was young and impatient. I wanted things to move fast and right now. I didn't want to mess around until these Indians, in their own good time, decided they would give up the girls. I would have given ten years of my life to have Bucky back in my mother's parlor playing "The Happy Farmer" for me again. But if I was young and impatient, at least I had a grain of sense. Ten years of my life wouldn't bring Bucky back. Only my father and William Bent could do that. I had to possess myself of what patience I could and be as thankful as I could for these two wise men.

We went back to Denver. I telegraphed Ed that everything possible had been done and all we could do now was wait for results. The name William Bent would mean nothing to him, but I told him he was an old Indian trader who had great influence and could get the girls back sooner than anybody else. He said that would be a big relief to Emma and that Emma had said all along Starr could get the girls back if anybody could.

I asked if he wanted to stick with the station, or did he have some notion of quitting now. He said he would stick. Said he and the boys were going back pretty soon, but he was going to leave Emma in Cottonwood until the baby came. I said that sounded fine to me, but not to take any chances, and we signed off.

It was the first of September and I hadn't worked since

July, but the office knew all my troubles and the line was torn up anyway. We were still running to Latham, so I just reported in and took over my run to Fort Lupton again.

The first half of September continued to be full of uncertainty and uneasiness with a few sporadic raids here and there. The newspapers reported there wasn't a ranch along the Platte that hadn't been abandoned, that the stage station had also been abandoned, and that there was nothing but ruin and desolation for five hundred miles from Julesburg to Liberty Farm. This was not true. Many ranchers and farmers had certainly flocked to Kearney and Cottonwood and Julesburg, and certainly many stage stations had been burned or partially burned, and there was much loss of stock and equipment. But there were ranchers who never did leave their homes and successfully defended them, and most of the home stations along the line continued to be occupied, the Overland people stuck with them, they kept alert and ready to resume operations when the Company was ready.

The most devastated piece of the line was down the Little Blue, but even it was not ruined. Almost immediately the Company began rebuilding the stations and before the middle of September staging was resumed between Atchison and Fort Kearney. Liberty Farm, which was totally burned, was abandoned and a new station, called Pawnee Ranch, was built. The swing station at Lone Tree was abandoned and one was put in at Elm Creek. Thirty-Two-Mile Creek station was abandoned and one was put in at Muddy Creek. Summit swing station, that lonely place on the wasted divide, was abandoned, and sixes were put on for a straight, twenty-six-mile run from Muddy to Hook's, just east of Kearney.

On the western end of the division it was slower. We continued to have Indian scares. Once it was reported that a large band of Sioux and Cheyennes were approaching Latham. There were now seventy or eighty people crowded into the station at Latham. They prepared for a siege. But it didn't come. Instead, Godfrey's ranch, down between Bijou and Valley station, was attacked. Godfrey had built himself a good solid dobe house. He and his family stood the Indians off for four days, neither asking for any help

310

nor receiving any. He killed so many hostiles that his place became known as Fort Wicked.

Godfrey's successful defense of his place made me feel even more bitter that Ed Westmoreland had so foolishly abandoned the solid walls of our station. Alone and single-handed he could have withstood almost any kind of attack. And he hadn't been alone. He had had several men besides himself. They could have given a good accounting of themselves. But it did no good to keep gnawing on that knot. It would have to wait for more information.

I knew now that the worst mistake of my life had been to believe that Ed was beginning to have good judgment. The truth was I had believed what I wanted to believe about Ed. He was a good enough man and I told myself he was learning, because Ed made it possible for me to have things both ways. I liked having it that way and wouldn't face what I knew to be true—that a man doesn't learn to have good judgment. He's born with the knack for it or he doesn't ever have it. It isn't something that can be learned. If a man has it, all he does through his life is sharpen his use of it. If he hasn't got it, nothing that ever happens to him teaches him. He just blunders along.

It was a pretty grim time for me. I was always haunted by the picture of Bucky, and Bernie, in the hands of the Indians. I was sorry about Bernie, but it was Bucky who made thinking almost intolerable. She wasn't old enough to be wise. She was too much a spitfire to be tactful. She wouldn't knuckle under an inch and I was afraid she would bring down on her all the wrath and abuse those old squaws could think up for her.

I would be doing the most familiar, everyday things and suddenly they would seem odd. It didn't seem possible that nothing at all was changed. That things still looked the same and felt the same and worked the same. My pipe felt the same in my hands and smoked the same. I put on my boots every morning. I climbed to the box of the stage and I drove my run. The lines felt the same. The team worked the same. The road had not changed. With Bucky a prisoner of the Indians *something*, I thought, ought to show it, come apart, work differently. For the first time in my life I understood what people meant when somebody died and they said life must go on. It not only must, it did. And even I got hungry and ate, felt sleepy and slept, made talk with people and, what seemed the strangest to me, had a laugh or two every day. I was not profound enough to understand that only in this way was life bearable under some circumstances. I just thought it odd and strange.

I ran into Henry Carlyle one day and he gave me a good laugh. He was the manager of the Overland's freight operations. He was riding the stage out of Cottonwood, headed for Denver, when the troubles began. There were no passengers. Just him and the driver. "We'd got to that ranch near O'Fallon's Bluffs, just beyond your place. The boys water the teams there, remember. Well, when we come in sight of it, we saw a bunch of Indians boiling around. Not many, just a handful, but they were working like ants in an anthill. The driver was all for whipping up the team and making a run for it on past. But it was a hell of a long run to the next station. I said no, just drive up like usual and act like they're just the usual little band drifting around, peaceful and quiet.

"He said, hell, they'll kill us.

"I said, they're just as likely to let us pass. You go running by flat out and they'll chase us sure. Now, when you pull in, stay on the box and keep the team in hand. I'll get down with the bucket and water the team.

"Well, when we pulled in we saw what was making them so busy. They had found a keg of whisky and knocked in the head and they all had tin cups and were drinking it like water. They were drunk and whooping it up big, gulping it down a cupful at a time, spilling it all over themselves, falling down, rolling on the ground, hollering, hanging onto each other and laughing, and some of them were sprawled out dead to the world. In their condition, I had my doubts they would even notice us. One old boy was standing by the whisky barrel pouring the stuff over his head, so drunk that every time he dipped out another cup he fell over the barrel.

"They didn't pay any attention to us at all. Didn't even notice we'd arrived, until I finished watering the team. I had the empty bucket in my hand when one of the bastards finally noticed me and made a dash toward me. He was reeling all over the place and he fell against me and almost knocked me down. I didn't even think what I was doing. I just hefted that cedar bucket up and jammed it down on his head as hard as I could. And by God, I jammed it down so hard it stuck tight. I let go and he reeled back and commenced trying to claw it off.

"He was staggering around, blind as a bat, running into the well and the other Indians, falling down, crawling around. And you know what those damfool Indians did? They stood there and nearly bust a gut laughing at him and finally, when he was still crawling around, one of them got on him and rode him like a horse, and they rode him all around the yard, slapping his rump, humping him around.

"That's when I climbed the wheel and said, let's get the hell out of here before they come to their senses if they've got any. And we got the hell out of there and they never did even notice us. I tell you, a bunch of drunk Indians can sure create pandemonium."

When I had chuckled over the story I asked Carlyle if Ed had said anything to him about leaving the station and going to Cottonwood. He shook his head. "No. No, but now I think of it, it was on his mind, I guess. He did say if things got too bad they could always go to Cottonwood. He was nervous, Starr. Pretty strung up. Seemed like he needed somebody to tell him what to do."

"Which I had done," I said, "a hundred times. He knew what to do."

"Well, there was a lot of women there. There was the Sizemores, and all his own womenfolks. And his wife expecting. Ed is a good man. Everybody knows that. But I wouldn't say he had the most nerve of any man I ever saw. He is kind of come easy, go easy."

"Yes," I said, "he has to be jacked up all the time. He just is not a man who can live all stretched out. But I've got a man out there who can. Browning. He's an old bullwhacker. I'm going to put him in charge and get the Company to give Ed the station again."

Carlyle nodded. "Somebody will always be giving him orders that way. He won't ever have to decide anything for himself."

"I ought to have done it sooner," I said.

"Well," he said, "hindsight is always a lot better than foresight. If it wasn't, we wouldn't ever learn anything."

All during September, Major Wynkoop and William Bent were working to get Black Kettle and White Antelope and the other friendly chiefs to bring their people in to the fort and make peace. They finally got most of them into the neighborhood of the Big Timbers and late in September, Major Wynkoop brought Black Kettle and White Antelope into Denver for a conference with the Governor and Colonel Chivington.

The chiefs later said they believed their bands had been promised safety if they would stay in the vicinity of Fort Lyon. My father said that actually Colonel Chivington had promised nothing at all. But they parleyed around awhile and then the friendly Cheyenne chiefs went back to their villages.

My father and I talked with White Antelope while he was in Denver. We had our first word of the girls. In sign, White Antelope told us his runners had seen the girls. They were being well treated. He thought they would be returned.

"Where are they?" my father asked.

White Antelope couldn't say. Those people who had them were moving about. He believed they would send word when they wanted to sell the girls.

"When will that be?"

He couldn't say. Sometime. He believed it would be sometime.

Indians can drive you crazy with their vagueness. But my father felt encouraged and because he did, I did. I wired the news to Ed. The girls were well. They were being treated well. And the Sioux would send word when they were ready to talk.

I had word back that Ed was at the ranch again, and that Emma's baby had come and it was a boy. Well, I thought, maybe the new little fellow would keep them from brooding too much over the girls.

All during September, Ben Holladay had been raising hell in Washington trying to get more troops out west, and more forts built. He said, finally, he would not resume operations until better protection was provided for the mail. So a small fort was built at the mouth of Lodgepole Creek by Captain O'Brien of the Seventh Iowa Volunteers and garrisoned by him, and Camp Cottonwood was fortified and renamed Fort McPherson. Captain O'Brien's fort near Julesburg was called Camp Rankin for a while, then it became known as Fort Sedgwick. Finally enough troops were assigned to the road to put a squad at stations every twenty or thirty miles.

New stock was brought in, stations were reprovisioned, the new stations were built and the line was slowly put in shape to resume operations. On the twenty-third of September we had orders in Denver to begin staging again at eight o'clock the next morning. Only the mail would be carried until the big stacks accumulated, which amounted to tons, had been moved out. I drove the first stage carrying the eastbound mail out of Denver on September 24. It was a good feeling, knowing the Overland was rolling again.

Westbound stages began leaving Atchison a few days later, through to Denver. The first mail since August 15 arrived in Denver the morning of October 2. A big crowd met the stage and snatched at express and letters and newspapers, whooping and cheering and blowing whistles and beating drums. The daily mail was arriving again. The lifeline to the east had been restored.

It was not the end of Indian incidents by a long shot. The Sioux who were between the rivers with the Cheyennes were especially persistent in continuing to raid, and the young warrior societies of the Cheyennes followed their lead savagely. Even with troops riding escort with the stages there continued to be attacks. Stages were chased, up the South Platte, out of Plum Creek, out of Cottonwood, out of Valley station. No driver picking up his lines ever knew if he could make his stage without trouble. But they kept on driving and the wheels kept rolling.

Late in October, when the schedule was working on time and passenger travel was normal again, the Company made a change in its stations at the Denver end of the line. Latham and the crossing of the South Platte there, and the run across to Laporte, were abandoned. A new road to Denver was built, which left the South Platte at Bijou Creek and a new station was built there called Junction

City. The road angled directly to Denver on the new toll road, and for the first time Denver itself was on the main Overland line. All travel to the west coast now went through the city. It was a long haul all around Robin Hood's barn for through passengers, but Ben Holladay had to do something to pacify Denver.

When the changeover was made onto the new road I felt free to make a shift that had been prickling at me all fall. I felt duty bound to stick where I was through the first heavy schedules and through the changeover, but when things were normal again I could serve the Company as well one place as another. I wanted to get back out on the Platte. Not only did I need to see how things were going at the ranch, and make the changes I had in mind there, but something inside me kept itching me back up that way. I kept coming back to the one certain fact we had—the girls had been captured there.

Normally when white captives are released, or sold as the Indians put it, it was done at one of the military posts, through the government's channels. I didn't believe the Sioux would bring the girls back to the ranch. But Overland drivers had long known that every band of Indians of every tribe in the country knew every movement made on the stage line. They watched it like hawks. And they knew, at least by sight, every driver on the line. Even if they were up in the Powder River country, those Sioux would know very shortly I was working on the Platte again, staying at the ranch. It seemed reasonable to me they might decide to make their first move in that direction—send word to me. It might even expedite things. Putting myself in their shoes as much as I could, I thought they would probably pick Laramie for the parley. They might send word to William Bent, but I didn't believe they would take the girls as far south as Fort Lyon. There were too many troops in between.

I talked with my father about it and he thought it might be a wise move. It couldn't hurt, to say the least. "I'll be in Denver," he said, "and I can get down to Fort Lyon if that's the way they work it. If they pick Laramie, you'll be up on the Platte."

"We can keep in touch," I said, "by telegraph."

With this understanding, I made the change and once more took the stage from my ranch into Cottonwood. The driver I bumped was relieved to be done with the run. "I've not driven a mile," he said, "since we commenced operating again that I've not expected to get my hide full of arrows. It ain't pleasant. This whole stretch from Cottonwood to Julesburg just ain't healthy nowadays. I'd rather work out on Bitter Creek as on the Platte right now." And as best I remember that is where he did transfer.

To a traveler, the big dobe station looked solid and reassuring, and it was. We had built it to stand and it had stood. It was one story high in front, which housed the station, the store and the dining room, and a story and a half in the back, which housed the kitchen and bedrooms. We had left it the color of the mud we plastered the dobe with, and it had seasoned and bonded to a mellow pinkish tan. It looked as natural and as much a part of the country as the bluffs along the river.

But there were evidences, now, of the raids. The dobe was smoke-blacked around the doors and windows, the only wood to burn, and where hatchets and logs had battered the corners the fall rains had melted the dobes and they had sagged and drooped. Ed had put in new doors and windows which were still raw and unpainted.

Out back where the big log barn and stables had been was a makeshift shed. It could shelter the stage stock but that was about all. A new pole corral had been put up. Something permanent would have to be built. I had no stock of my own left. Not a head of cattle or horses. The Indians had taken everything. I didn't intend to put more stock on the place until things were considerably more settled than they were at the present. I couldn't afford to lose it all again.

Emma met me at the door. She was so thin she was almost gaunt and the bright hair was tarnished with a lot of gray. She looked ten or fifteen years older. "I've not had the heart," she said, "to make things pretty again."

"No," I said, "I wouldn't think so."

The windows were clean but they were bare. There were no bright curtains. The pot plants had long since died and been thrown away. Emma said the pots had been smashed.

The floors were scrubbed but they were bare, too. No pretty braided rugs lay about. I wondered if they had been burned or if they were on the floor of some Sioux lodge, or even being worn as a blanket.

The station and dining room looked much bigger because the furniture was so meager. Ed had salvaged the best parts of tables and chairs and repaired what he could. But boards on trestles made a cooking table in the kitchen and kegs of various kinds and sizes pieced out the chairs. The big kitchen range was still there and it still worked, but it was cracked and the legs were broken off and Ed had propped it up on chunks of wood. The pride of Emma's life, her big walnut bed and chest, were gone. They hadn't even found any pieces of it, she said. The Indians had hacked it up and burned it. Ed and Emma were sleeping in rough bunks for the time being.

I had a strange feeling that all this was right, that the color and the curtains and the plants and all the little softer things of civilization were well gone. The place now looked exactly like what it was, a stage station and a ranch way out on the Platte, rough, bare, meager . . . the necessities for sustaining life sufficing. Let it stay that way awhile, I thought. I felt an almost keen pleasure in seeing it stripped down to bareness and skimpiness, an almost savage satisfaction with it. It was the softnesses of the civilized that had been so treacherous, had so betrayed them. Everybody on the road had grown careless, had believed that because it was so traveled by white men it had become the white man's home. But you couldn't make a home on the Platte yet. The Indians had proved that. The best you could do was throw up an outpost, and those who occupied it had better know they had left softness behind, that their best defense was the unwistful acceptance of a harsh, ugly, barebone way of life. The time for the soft flesh was still a long way off.

And yet. . . "Come see my baby," Emma said, and here was the soft flesh, living and forever renewed. He was big and fat and healthy, as redheaded as Bucky, and he had the roundest, biggest blue eyes a baby ever had.

She wanted me to hold him but I wouldn't have touched him with a ten-foot pole. He looked far too tender and wobbly. "He's a wonder," I said. "Bucky will love him."

"Bucky . . ." Her face, which had been smiling at the baby, went sad. "Will she ever see him, Starr?"

"Sure she will. It just takes time. We'll have her back before long."

"You're not just saying that to keep my hope up?"

"Emma, I swear I believe it," and I meant it. "I swear it!"

She knew what we were doing to get the girls back, the way we were going about it. She had agreed it was the best we could do. She searched my face, now, and was better satisfied. "I believe you. If anybody can get them back, you will."

The place had always been busy and it still was, with stages arriving and departing, freighters coming and going, drivers, tenders, ranch hands at their usual duties. The missing element was the Indians drifting about and the way I felt just now I could do without them forever. The store was meagerly stocked for the convenience of freighters and stage passengers. All Indians were enemies now. It might be years before a peace was made that would drift them in small friendly bands up and down the river again. We never saw them any more. They stayed off the road except to swoop down occasionally on a wagon train, or once in a while to chase a stagecoach. There was no need for them to trade any more. They had all the supplies they needed from the plunder they took.

I picked up the lines for my first run to Cottonwood on the fifth day of November with more than driving on my mind. The incoming stage had brought a letter for me from my father. After some family news he wrote: "We had Wynkoop to dinner on Thursday last. He has been relieved of his command at Fort Lyon. The *Rocky Mountain News* reports Chivington as saying it was for conducting *unauthorized* peace talks with the Cheyennes and Arapahoes. Wynkoop says peace is not wanted at all. *All* peace talks are unauthorized.

"Wynkoop had been able to persuade most of the Arapahoes and Cheyennes to camp near the fort until peace talks could be held. He promised them their annuities and safety. The Arapahoes have been in the Big Timbers but since Wynkoop's recall all but Left Hand's band have gone hunting up the Republican. Left Hand has joined Black Kettle, White Antelope, Lone Bear and War Bonnet on Sand Creek.

"Wynkoop's successor at the fort is young Major Anthony. The Indians call him Red Eyes because of some kind of inflammation of the eyes with which he is afflicted. It also makes him very irritable and he hates all Indians anyway. The Indians are very uneasy over Wynkoop's removal. The chiefs have been to see Anthony, who was brusque with them and high-handed. He ordered them all to clear out of the area in the vicinity of the fort, and he stopped their rations.

"Wynkoop tells me that Bent had heard something about the girls. He had reason to believe they might be released at Fort Lyon shortly. But he now believes the band who have them are too frightened to come in, since Wynkoop's removal. This is a setback and I know you will be gravely disappointed. So am I. But we must consider it merely a delay. They evidently do intend to parley concerning the girls. A month or two of quiet would reassure them and they would feel safe in coming in. But only the Lord knows whether we'll have a month or two of quiet or not.

"Wynkoop doubts it and he says Bent is very uneasy. Of course, Bent's personal problems with the boys and Julia make him apprehensive. All three are with their mother's band on Sand Creek. John Smith, who used to trade for the Bents, is there now conducting business, and his boy, Jack, who has also gone wild, is with them. They are all a passel of young hotheads.

"The blunt truth is that the entire situation is very unsettled and one false move can begin the war again. If he can make it, Chivington will, and of course he knows from Wynkoop where these Indians are."

A hard, fine, driving snow was blowing and I was miserably uncomfortable driving that day. The only way I could face that biting wind and snow was to tie a bandanna over my face and bend my hat brim as low as it would go. The physical discomfort seemed part of the general anger and disappointment I felt.

I was more worried than I had been at any time since the girls were captured. It could be next spring, now, before the Sioux would release them. Even if things stayed quiet they were just notional enough to decide not to travel during the winter. A winter with the Indians for the girls? My face was numb with cold right now, and my eyes were stung with it, and even through my heavy overcoat the wind was making shivers of cold go chasing up and down my back. It was a grim reminder of what they would have to suffer. Indians did not winter well any more. For a good many years they had depended on their annuities and presents to tide them over. The girls would be ill-clad and probably ill-fed. I couldn't stand to think of Bucky cold and hungry.

I damned Chivington and his greed for glory. Why couldn't he have let Wynkoop alone? Wynkoop was making real headway toward persuading the Southern Cheyennes onto the reservations. Now all his work stood to be undone by one man wanting in the House of Representatives. Damn, I thought, and damn again.

Chapter 23

The blow fell at daybreak on the twenty-ninth of November when Chivington, with a strong force of men, attacked the Cheyennes and Left Hand's band of Arapahoes on Sand Creek.

I was at Cottonwood when the first news was flashed by the *Rocky Mountain News* over the telegraph on the seventh of December. "Great victory of Colorado troops under the personal command of Colonel John T. Chivington. Over 600 Indians killed. 130 lodges of Cheyennes destroyed. 500 ponies, mules and horses captured. Surprise attack at dawn on Nov. 29th results in the most successful battle yet fought with the hostiles. Colonel Chivington a hero in Denver."

He was not only a hero in Denver, he was a hero in the entire west—for a few weeks. The *Rocky Mountain News* proudly printed an interview with him when he returned and quoted the colonel's exact words: "Having ascertained that the hostile Indians had proceeded south from the Platte and were almost within striking distance of Fort Logan, I ordered Colonel George L. Shoup, Third Regiment Colorado Volunteer Cavalry, 100 days service, to proceed with the mounted men of his regiment in that direction. On Nov. 20th I left Denver, and at Booneville, Colorado Territory, on the 24th of Nov., joined and took command in person of the expedition, which had been increased by a battalion of First Cavalry of Colorado, consisting of detachments of Companies C, E, and H. I proceeded with the utmost caution down the Arkansas River, and on the morning of the 28th ultimo arrived at Fort Lyon, to the surprise of the garrison of that post. On the same evening I resumed my march, being joined by Major Scott J. Anthony, First Cavalry of Colorado, with 125 men

322

of said regiment, consisting of detachments of Companies D, G and K, with two howitzers. The command then proceeded in a northeasterly direction traveling all night, and at daylight of 29th November striking Sand Creek, about forty miles from Fort Lyon.

"Here was discovered an Indian village of 130 lodges, comprised of Black Kettle's band of Cheyennes and eight lodges of Arapahoes with Left Hand. My line of battle was formed with Lieutenant Wilson's battalion, First Regt. on the right; Colonel Shoup's (Third) regiment, numbering about 450 men, in the center; and Major Anthony's battalion, numbering 125 men, First Regiment, on the left. The attack was immediately made upon the Indians' camp by Lieutenant Wilson, who dashed forward, cutting the enemy off from the herd, and driving them out of their camp, which was subsequently destroyed. The Indians, numbering from 900 to 1000, though taken by surprise, speedily formed a line of battle across the creek, about three-fourths of a mile above the village, stubbornly contesting every inch of ground.

"The commands of Colonel Shoup and Major Anthony pressed rapidly forward and attacked the enemy sharply, and the engagement became general, we constantly driving the Indians, who fell back from one position to another, for five miles, and finally abandoned resistance and dispersed in all directions, and were pursued by my troops until nightfall.

"It may perhaps be unnecessary for me to state that *I captured no prisoners*. Between 500 and 600 Indians were left dead upon the ground; about 550 ponies, mules and horses were captured, and all their lodges were destroyed, the contents of which have served to supply the command with an abundance of trophies, comprising the paraphernalia of Indian warfare and life. My loss was eight killed on the field and forty wounded, of which two have since died. . . .

"Night coming on, the pursuit of the flying Indians was of necessity abandoned and my command encamped within sight of the field. On the first instant, having sent the wounded and dead to Fort Lyon, the first to be cared for, the last to be buried upon our own soil, I resumed the pursuit in the direction of Camp Wynkoop, on the Arkansas River, marching all night of the 3rd and 4th in hopes of overtaking a large encampment of Arapahoes and Cheyennes under Little Robe and Little Raven. But the enemy had been apprised of my advance, and on the morning of the 5th, at 3 o'clock, precipitately broke camp and fled.

"My stock was exhausted. For 100 miles the snow had been two feet deep, and for the previous days (excepting on Nov. 29th & 30th) the marches had been forced and incessant.

"Under these circumstances, and the fact of the time of the Third Regiment (100 days' service) being nearly out, I determined for the present to relinquish the pursuit. . . ."

This was Colonel Chivington's account.

My father wrote me on December 22: "You have doubtless read Chivington's story in the *News*. It is pure bombast. You know, of course, that the Cheyennes in that camp were mostly friendlies. Only one band of warriors was there. The rest were old men, women and children. There were over 500 women and children. Only 200 men.

"I have been to Bent's ranch and talked with him. This is what happened. He had been working tirelessly to bring the Indians into camp at the fort. He believed that after the Denver talks if they came in and laid down their arms, peace could be made and the Indians could be persuaded to accept life on the reservation. He was very near succeeding when Chivington suddenly recalled Wynkoop and sent young Anthony down to Fort Lyon. Chivington was afraid Wynkoop would parley with the Cheyennes. To give the devil his due, however, General Curtis at Leavenworth had said that he wanted no peace until the Indians had suffered more. Chivington was determined to make them suffer.

"Anthony went down with orders to make no peace. He was to disperse the Arapahoes, who had gathered at the Big Timbers. They were being fed army rations by the army, since they had turned in their arms and could not hunt for themselves. Anthony fed them for ten days, then gave them back their arms and told them to go hunt buffalo and feed themselves.

"All but Left Hand's band moved over onto the Republican to hunt. Left Hand took his band up to Sand Creek where the Cheyennes were camped. This was an old and favorite camping place of the Cheyennes because the water was good there and the hunting was pretty good.

"All the Indians were scared, now, and uneasy. Bent said there were several bands on Sand Creek . . . Black Kettle, Sand Hill, Yellow Wolf, White Antelope, War Bonnet and One Eye. No Dog Soldiers were there at all. Left Hand had ten lodges, about sixty people, with him.

"Almost all the hostiles were over on the Smoky Hill. These people on Sand Creek were upset and worried, especially after Left Hand came in and told how the Arapahoes had been given their arms and ordered away. They sent a delegation to Fort Lyon to parley with Anthony. He told them he had no authority to make peace and he advised them to return to their camp and said he would notify them when he received word to begin negotiations. They did so, and waited.

"In the meantime, Anthony wrote Chivington and gave him the location of the camp and said if he had the troops he would immediately attack.

"Chivington was up on the Bijou, with Colonel Shoup and the 100 dayers, about 750 men in all. Their 100 days were just about up. He led them south to Fort Lyon, and to keep his movements from being learned he stopped all travel on the Arkansas. Then he sent a detail of twenty dragoons across the river to Bent's ranch with orders that nobody could leave. The troops stayed to be certain the order was obeyed.

"Charlie Bent had been with the Cheyennes on Sand Creek all along, but George had been staying at the ranch with the old man. Julia Bent and her husband, Guettier, were also up at Sand Creek. Several days earlier George decided to join them. So all three of Bent's children with that wild turn were on Sand Creek. Bent said he watched the troops across the river from his ranch march out on the evening of the 28th. He figured they were heading for Sand Creek. He could do nothing but wish for death himself.

"Worst of all, probably, Robert Bent was at Fort Lyon. Old Jim Beckwourth, one of the biggest scamps who ever drew breath, was guiding for Chivington. You could always buy him for two bits. It was so cold and the snow was so deep that old Jim collapsed when they got to Fort

Lyon. And at the point of a gun Robert was compelled to serve as guide for the troops to Sand Creek. You can imagine how he felt. He knew Charlie and George and Julia were all there, and he would be the instrument of their death!

"He confessed to using a few ruses to mislead the troops, but none of them worked. At one point he led them through a shallow lake, just deep enough to get their ammunition wet if they didn't take care. They began to suspect Robert was not putting his whole heart into leading them, so Chivington rode up beside him and slapped his revolver and said, 'I haven't had an Indian to eat for a long time. If you fool with me and don't lead me to that camp, I'll have you for breakfast.'

"Just at daylight they reached the camp. One detachment of troops rode out to stampede the horse herd and the rest of the troops formed a line and unlimbered the howitzers. The Indians began milling about, the women and children screaming and dodging here and there. Bent says Black Kettle stood firm. In front of his lodge he raised the United States flag on a lodgepole, with a white flag under it. He kept telling the people not to be afraid, the soldiers had come to talk, as they had promised, and they would not shoot.

"Old Blackfoot John Smith, one of my old compañeros and a trader with the Cheyennes, was in camp and some of the women ran to him begging him to talk with the soldiers. He started out toward the line that was forming. About that time the troops had formed up and they began firing. It was withering, with grape and a cavalry charge that divided the camp in two.

"The flag was hot from Black Kettle's hand and he now shouted for the people to run, to get away. He took his old wife and fled with her up the creek bed, where the banks were steep and offered some protection. His wife was shot, and believing her dead he left her and went on to where a bunch of his people had dug caves and holes in the bank.

"What happened in that ravine and creek bed was pure murder. Robert Bent told his father he saw five squaws under the bank and when the troops came up to them they ran out and begged for mercy but the soldiers shot them all. He saw one squaw lying on a bank whose leg had been broken by a shell. He saw a soldier come along with drawn sabre and when she raised her arm to protect herself, the man struck with the sabre and broke her arm. Then she rolled over and raised her other arm and he broke it. Then he left without killing her. A little girl about six years old was sent out with a white flag. She was shot and killed. One squaw was cut open with an unborn child lying by her side. White Antelope, who had not wished to live when he realized the betrayal, bared his chest to the bullets and was killed. His privates were cut off. A 100 dayer made a tobacco pouch of the scrotum. Woman had their privates cut out, before they died. Little children were clubbed down and shot. Babies were pulled from the arms of their mothers and killed.

"Robert Bent saw these thing with his own eyes.

"George Bent was shot in the leg in the sand pits up the creek. He escaped by hiding in a hole until night. Charlie Bent was captured by Charley Autobeas's sons . . . you remember they are half-Mexican. They refused to turn him over to the troops for execution, and the next day set him free.

"Chivington had ordered that no prisoners would be taken. Blackfoot John Smith's half-breed son, Jack, was in the camp and he was captured by the 100 dayers. Old Blackfoot pled for his life—but the boy is a real renegade. He was in the bunch that butchered George Tritch's three wagon trains on the Little Blue and some of the survivors said he raped the white woman they took there. No trooper could be expected to show him mercy. He was shot.

"Chivington claims between five and six hundred Indians killed. William Bent says the best count he can get is 137 killed, more than 100 of them being women and children.

"Chivington did not, as he says he did, follow up the pursuit. He broke off the attack late in the afternoon. He knew the warrior societies and the Dog Soldiers were on the Smoky Hill, and some 800 Arapahoes were on the Republican. He had no stomach for a fight with warriors. He rested in camp for two days dividing up the plunder.

"But the whole city here has gone wild with joy. The war trophies have been exhibited at one of the theaters. They include many scalps. Privately, I am told the plunder was very good. The troop wagons came back loaded with fine buckskin clothing, buffalo robes, blankets and so forth. And every man of the 100 dayers is said to have received a horse.

"Be on your guard at the ranch and when you are driving. Bent tells me the war pipe has been sent to all the tribes, north and south. They will certainly smoke it. This attack will certainly set them all off. And God only knows, now, when we can recover the girls.

"The follies of men are beyond believing. Not in our lifetime will this score be settled. The children and the grandchildren of Sand Creek will still be avenging it thirty years from now. And ten times 137 white men and women and children will die because of Chivington's idiocy."

I had divided feelings when I finished reading my father's long letter. It was idiocy, certainly, to attack the friendlies' camp, to massacre women and children. And yet . . . and yet . . . the fact that only two hundred men were in that camp testified to how many were over on the Smoky Hill still plundering and raiding on the Platte.

If Indians could never believe white men, it was equally true that even the friendliest Indians could not be wholly believed. So little control did the band chiefs have over the warrior societies and Dog Soldiers that even at the moment the chiefs were parleying, raiding and burning and killing were going on at other places. And there were those, and they were not in the minority by any means, who honestly believed that the friendlies covered for the raids; that they kept the troops engaged and their attention occupied while the warriors killed and raided. How could you know? What could you believe?

The Bent boys were in that camp, and Jack Smith, renegades all. It was known now that not only had Jack Smith raped the woman captured with the wagons on the Little Blue, but he had passed her on the prairie. She had not died of it, but she had managed to find a rope and hang herself from a lodgepole later. The Indians didn't bother to cut her down and she was subsequently found. Why were these boys in that camp? Not for one minute did I believe they had been converted to peace.

The government policy, the policy of nearly all westerners, was becoming one of simple, plain extermination. Since you never knew what even the friendliest Indian was going to do, it was slowly becoming automatic to shoot any of them. The one you befriended, the one you trusted about your place, could the next time he came lead a raid that would burn your place, run off your stock, kill your wife and children and before you died make you wish you'd never been born. Even old William Bent, who had been more Cheyenne than white for forty years, to this day never allowed an Indian inside his stockade. Better than any other living white man he knew the Indian mind, and he did not trust them.

So . . . and if, like me, your own people were hurt by Indians, you felt some satisfaction that at least these many redskins no longer lived to touch another white woman, and if they were women, no longer lived to breed more redskins, and if they were children, no longer lived to grow up and breed and fight. There were those who exulted in the massacre of the Cheyenne women and children. It expiated, a little, for the hundreds of white women and children who had also been brutally murdered. It was callous. It was cruel and brutal. But if you lived in the west you did feel such things, because it was right under your nose, it was happening to your own people, and it touched a living nerve of your skin and the blood of your heart.

A hue and cry shortly went up in the east over Colonel Chivington's attack at Sand Creek. The truth could not be kept hidden. William Bent, Judge Armour and other men of integrity telegraphed the military authorities in Washington, then wrote the true details. A commission was sent to investigate. Black Kettle's old wife, who lived, bared the scars of nine wounds suffered after she fell near the sand pits. Others testified. The whole horror of the battle was headlined in the east. The only thing that saved Colonel Chivington from a court-martial was that he had been mustered out of the militia. He could not be touched. Instead of famous, as he had hoped to be, he became infamous. His name is forever linked with what has become known as the Sand Creek Massacre and he is credited with having begun a war with the Sioux and Cheyennes that lasted twenty years.

He was not elected to Congress, nor was Governor Evans elected to the Senate. And Colorado was not admitted to the Union for twelve long years.

None of this is very fair to Colonel Chivington. The blame should have fallen equally on General Curtis, head of the Department at Leavenworth, who gave the order that no peace was to be made until the Indians had suffered more, and on General Connor, head of the Colorado and Utah departments, who believed that the only good Indian was a dead Indian. But Colonel Chivington used a very bloody and suspect way of implementing the policy so that both the government and the army allowed him to become the scapegoat.

One thing has become very clear in the years since. It would have been far better if the Autobeas boys had allowed Charlie Bent to be executed by Colonel Chivington. He lived to become the scourge of the plains, his very name coming to mean betrayal, cruelty and fiendishness. After Sand Creek his hatred of whites was so insane that he lived only for torturing and killing them, and it included his own father whom he once tried to ambush and kill. The little boy, William Bent's youngest son, whom he named for his beloved brother, became the worst desperado the plains had ever seen—until he himself was killed violently.

But this was all in the future yet. At the time, the most important thing to us on the Overland was the war that erupted on the morning of January 7.

As nearly as it is possible for Indians to act in unity, they acted together on that day when around a thousand of them descended on Fort Sedgwick and Julesburg. There were Brule Sioux, Oglalla Sioux, Northern Cheyennes and Arapahoes, Southern Cheyennes and Arapahoes, Kiowas and Comanches.

Their strategy was to engage the troops at Fort Sedgwick, which was several hunderd yards up the river from Julesburg, at the mouth of Lodgepole Creek. They wanted to keep the soldiers holed up in the stockade so they could not bring their howitzers to the aid of Julesburg. Now, Indians rarely laid siege to a stockade, for they had early learned it was expensive and futile. They used a different tactic. They lured troops out by boiling around and making sideshow noises with a small detachment. They did that this morning.

One company of the Seventh Iowa was stationed at Fort

Sedgwick under Captain O'Brien, who had built the stockade the autumn before. At this time it was still a temporary, hastily built log and sod structure with a log and sod stockade wall around it. Just at daybreak, as the stockade was waking up and coming to life, a small body of Indians detached themselves from the main army hidden in the sandhills, and following up a gully near the stockade crept closer. A few men with outside duties emerged and went about their chores. The Indians rose out of the gully and with their usual hideous whooping and screeching fell on them. Captain O'Brien reacted according to plan and boiled out of the fort with thirty-seven of his men.

At that time the main Indian army charged out of the sandhills and Captain O'Brien was shortly fighting for his life and trying to get his men back inside the stockade. Half of his troops were killed before he got the rest to safety.

At about the same time the westbound stage came bowling down the road toward Julesburg. Little Taw was driving. He said he saw the Indians about the same time they saw him and he laid on the whip and made a run for the station. A big clutch of Indians left off chasing Captain O'Brien to chase the coach. But Little Taw made it, threw down his lines and put wings to his feet over to the stockade. He didn't have but one passenger, an army paymaster —and he said he left that gentleman to take care of himself —who promptly sprouted wings of his own and reached the fort just two long hops and a jump behind Little Taw. Behind them came the station agent and the storekeeper and hands.

For a while the Indians rode round and round the stockade yelling and shooting, but most of them soon turned off and went riding down on the stage station, the Company store and the rest of Julesburg. The troops stayed right where they were inside the stockade. There wasn't anything else very sensible to do with that many Indians fanning around outside. And they had a good view of what went on all day in Julesburg.

They said as soon as the plundering started the Indian women came down out of the sandhills, leading extra horses, and all day they worked loading horses and leading them out. They plundered the store and the Company warehouses. They loaded flour and bacon and sugar, bolts of goods, canned goods, equipment of all kinds onto the horses. They found the strongbox containing Company funds, but not knowing what greenbacks were they just scattered them to the winds. For weeks after the raid greenbacks were found all over the prairies.

The soldiers fired their howitzers at the Indians but afraid of damaging the buildings they did very little damage to the Indians. Late in the afternoon the Indians withdrew with their heavy loads of supplies, guns, ammunition, loot of every kind. Indians take a fancy to the oddest things. One warrior was seen with a sugar bowl tied to his belt. You wonder what happens to such objects. Did he ever learn it was a sugar bowl? Did he use it for a drinking cup, or maybe a chamber pot? Or did he grow tired of it and smash it or throw it away?

An officer stationed in Colorado had ordered a new uniform. It was in the stage station among the express packages. It never reached the major. George Bent appropriated it and was seen wearing it later that year in the battle at Powder River.

The Indians did not burn Julesburg that day. We learned later that the whole raid had been shrewdly planned and directed by old Spotted Tail and his Brule Sioux. They couldn't carry off all the supplies and stores in one day, so they left the warehouses and stores still full of many things unburned in order to return another day and get the rest. It was later, when they had plundered all they needed, that they burned the entire settlement to the ground.

The Overland tried to continue operations for a couple of weeks, but there were so many Indians and they did so much damage, especially immediately east and west of Julesburg, that around January 25 the Overland abandoned their efforts. The line was closed from Fort Kearney to Denver. Every station from Cottonwood to Junction, on the Bijou, was hit fiercely.

It had been simple for me to get the Company to put Ed in as station agent when I took over the Cottonwood run. The former agent was ready to leave the Platte. He had had enough of Indians and the Overland to do him the rest of his life, he said. Ed was agreeable to the shift. In fact, he wanted it. He said it was more his line of work. I put Browning over the ranch and store. Now, under Company orders, Ed and Emma came into Cottonwood and the station was closed. Brownie wouldn't leave the ranch. He said he and Dickson would hold the fort. They might be able to keep damage to the buildings to a minimum. Bonnie Dickson came into Cottonwood with Ed and Emma.

It was the summer of 1864 all over again except that it didn't last as long. The army acted promptly this time. On the seventh of February the first westbound stage left Atchison and it reached Cottonwood the night of the tenth. But the rumors from up the Platte were so wild that it couldn't proceed. Nobody knew when it could go on.

However, the next night, the eleventh, there was a telegram from General Dodge, at Leavenworth, to General Mitchell at Omaha. The telegram was posted in the station for all to read. It said:

"Brigadier General Mitchell, Omaha: I have just informed the Overland Mail Company that I am prepared to protect their mail through this department. See that the proper protection is given it from Fort Kearney west to insure its safety.

G. M. Dodge, Major General."

There was a lot of rejoicing. With troop protection we could begin to roll again. Preparations began to restock the line from Kearney to Bijou Creek, and on the morning of the sixteenth three Concord coaches rolled out of Cottonwood headed for Denver. One of them was loaded with nothing but mail. Bill Trotter drove it with sixes. I drove the second coach and Arkansaw held the reins on the third.

Because the line wasn't yet restocked, we had to carry not only all our own provisions but the hay and grain for the teams. And we had three plucky passengers. But we also had a detail of troops as escort.

There was never a more beautiful morning for a departure. It was cold but the sky was high and bright and it was a happy bunch that moved out, everybody singing, laughing, whistling, talking. Hell, I thought, you can't keep the Overland down. You can knock them down but you can't knock them out. Not with a bunch of men like these.

We spent the first night at my place and I was a little proud that it was fairly comfortable. We cooked our meal ourselves, of course, and then the boys and the troops and the passengers rolled up and slept on the floor in front of the fire. Brownie and Dickson had stood off several minor attacks with no great damage done. Brownie said, "Hell, Starr, you could hold off the whole kit and caboodle of 'em in this place. Ed just got the wind up last time. Emma and Bernie bothered him. Bernie kept wanting to get Emma, on account of the baby, some place safer. Said Ed would have it on his head if anything happened to Emma. He heard that for a solid week before he gave in. And Sizemore's woman was scared, too. All they could think of was getting where the troops were."

Ed had never said the women had badgered him. He had just said it seemed best to take them to Cottonwood. It would have been hard to hold out, with the women dinging at me constantly. I could see why he would feel that if anything happened to Emma he would everlastingly wish he had listened and taken her to a safer place.

Next morning we went on and began to pick up stages that had been stranded along the line. Drivers were riding with us who took over these stages. We made quite a caravan. There were enough of us that we felt reasonably safe and our spirits were up.

We reached Julesburg the morning of the nineteenth, in a howling, blowing blizzard. The place was devastated. Everything, the stage station, the stables, blacksmith shop, the warehouses, the hay and grain depots, the big store of Thompson & Chrisman, all were burned to the ground. Not a thing had been spared by old Spotted Tail. Nothing was left.

We were hungry men by that time, too. Our provisions had begun to run short. The division agent was with us, Reuben Thomas, so he went over to the fort and requisitioned some army rations. We got a hundred pounds of hardtack, some sides of bacon, some coffee and sugar. We only stayed in what was left of Julesburg long enough to load these supplies onto the stages, then we went on. It snowed and blew all day and we had the most miserable ride of the whole trip. But we kept plowing along and then corraled up near the old Buffalo Springs ranch, inside its deserted dobe walls.

We cooked our first meal of the day after making things secure for the night and ate flapjacks, hardtack, coffee and bacon for supper. No food ever tasted better.

Next day we passed by what was left of Kelly's station. There had been a fierce fight there only a few days earlier. Two dead and frozen Indians were still on the burned-out premises. The nearer we got to Denver the colder it got and the deeper the snow was. We had a miserable time the last hundred miles, but we made it and arrived on February 22.

I had several good visits with my parents while I was in Denver. My father and I talked about Bucky and Bernie. There had been no word of any kind. We hadn't expected any. We had no reason to expect any until things settled down again. The war had messed up everything. We had no idea where the little band of Sioux were. For all we knew they were down between the rivers joining in the raids. The girls might be no farther away than the Smoky Hill. On the other hand, they might well be as far north as the Powder River. William Bent seemed to know nothing of their whereabouts. We had brought the army into it, and all troops were on the alert for any sight of the girls. Other than that, it was a game of wait and see, which I was not constituted to enjoy, but which nevertheless I had to play.

The big news in the family was that my sister Fanny was going to be married shortly. She was marrying a young army officer who was stationed at Fort Halleck. He had been graduated from West Point the June before, had served briefly with Grant's troops in Virginia, then during our Indian troubles the fall before he had been transferred to western duty. Fanny had met him at a ball at the Governor's mansion in December.

His name was Sam Burke and he was one of the most junior second lieutenants in the west. The two had fallen starry-eyed in love almost at first sight. With old-fashioned courtesy Sam had insisted on asking for Fanny's hand and it was during that interview the family had learned, to their great excitement, that Sam was actually distantly related to my father. As my father tactfully inquired about his antecedents, Sam said his people live in Fort Smith, Arkansas, but that originally they had lived in the Indian Territory where his grandfather had been a trader with the Osage Indians. His grandfather, he said, had been Stephen Burke.

"You can imagine," my father told me, "how flabbergasted I felt. The boy's grandmother was my own Aunt Rebecca, and his grandfather and my Uncle Johnny Osage had been partners at Three Forks! I was never more mortified in my life! I ought to have kept up with the family better than that. Of course, I knew Aunt Becky had three or four boys, but Lord, once I left that country I didn't get back very often. I've still got a brother back there some place . . . Little Rock, last I heard. That's Tully. But Savanna and her family came to Santa Fe years ago, and Jeff and his family are there, too. What happened to Aunt Becky's boys, who they married, where they went, I never knew. But one of them, this boy's father, is in Fort Smith. An attorney there. A man ought to keep up with his people better than that, but somehow you don't."

"That makes him and Fanny kin, too," I said.

"Oh, a little. Not enough to worry about. He's a fine boy. I liked him before I knew about the relationship. I don't know that I would have picked an army man for one of my girls. It's not an easy life. She'll always live from pillar to post. But she's picked him and I'm willing to bet she can endure as much as he can. They'll draw these western posts most of their life, that's certain, but both of them have as good a background for it as young people could have. They have the west in their blood and bones."

I was happy for Fanny, but I could not stay for her wedding.

The first stage carrying passengers east out of Denver left on March 1 and we were in business again, though for some time, until the stations were rebuilt and restocked, we had to carry provisions for teams and passengers with us. We had no relays for the teams. It was a long hard drive for both men and teams from Denver to Cottonwood. We had troop escorts for all stages carrying passengers. I took out the second one to leave Denver at 10 A.M. on March 2.

By the time we reached Cottonwood shelters had been thrown up along the line, stock was being put back, and various ranches and stations were being reopened. The station at my ranch was opened on March 8 and when I came through it was good to see Ed and Emma there again, and the passengers had their first hot meal since leaving Denver.

Chapter 24

By the first of April, though there were still occasional raids, the Overland was running regularly. The biggest difference was the troops. General Dodge kept his word. The mail was being well protected. The bitter lesson had been learned that the Indians were a tough adversary, that they meant business, and that if the mail was to go through it must be strongly protected. Of course, it had helped for Ben Holladay to raise a lot of hell in Washington.

We had six companies of the First Nebraska Cavalry Veterans at Cottonwood. Fort Kearney was reinforced with another company from the First Nebraska. Plum Creek had a company from the same regiment. At Fort Laramie the old faithful outfit, the Eleventh Ohio, was stationed, with various of its companies garrisoning Fort Halleck and Camp Mitchell. They were also at Fremont's Orchard and a temporary camp known as Camp Collins.

The Colorado militia and the Seventh Iowa garrisoned the stations along the South Platte. The end of the war in the east made it possible for the army to send many regular troops who could now take up the war in the west.

I had brought the eastbound stage into Cottonwood the evening of April 4 and was laying over that night. After supper I was playing poker with a bunch of the boys when about ten o'clock the station agent came into the back room and said the telegraph operator had something for me. "Fort Halleck's on the wire," he said.

Fort Halleck . . . Sam Burke . . . Fanny? Then my heart jumped and began pounding. It was something about the girls. Bound to be. I was certain of it. The operator, a youngster named Ike Smith, nodded at me. "Your brother-in-law is on the wire. Got a message for you."

"Go ahead," I said.

The key chattered and young Ike's face became intent as he listened. It seemed to me to take a very long time. A smile broke over his face. "They've sent a message, Starr! The Indians have sent word. Your brother-in-law says they've had a message the Indians are willing to turn the girls loose. At Halleck. God, Starr, you're going to get 'em back!"

The boys in the poker game heard him shouting and they came clustering around. "All right," I said. My throat was so thick I had trouble speaking. "Give me some air and let me think." He waited. "Send this. Ask him if the Sioux are there now."

The kid sent. The reply chattered back. "He says no. He says the message was brought in by a rancher . . . he says the Sioux . . . he says one Indian . . . went to this ranch last night . . . said they were ready to trade for the women. Wait. Starr Fowler. Trade with Starr Fowler . . . at Halleck."

The boys had gotten very quiet. My mind was suddenly clear and asking questions. "What rancher?"

Sending by wire is pretty slow when you're on edge. There is the long keyed sending, the wait, the long chattering response, and sometimes the necessity to repeat. "He says Harker . . . near Rock Creek."

I had never heard of the man. But Rock Creek was near Fort Halleck. We had a stage station there. The boys and I looked at each other and all shook their heads. None of us had driven on that division for a long time. The man had settled there since any of us had been there. "Ask exactly what the message said."

There was the long wait, finally the reply. "The message said they were ready to talk about the release of the women . . . to Starr Fowler, is what he says, at Halleck. They . . . want . . . presents. . . ."

"They'll want the earth," I said, "and they're welcome to it. If it's not a hoax. I wish I knew that rancher. But it's the first word we've had. . . . I've got to do it. Ask him when? When do they want to talk?"

The key spoke, then it stuttered. "Now, he says. You are to come now. They will send word again."

"Does Sam know where the girls are?"

"He says no. He says they think at Fort Halleck they are

probably in the Medicine Bows. Major Norton will send a detail . . ."

"Tell him, no!" I cut in quickly. "Tell him . . . God, if the troops go out hunting for them they'll scare 'em off! Tell Sam not to let the troops get involved. Tell him I think troops will queer the deal. Say for him to tell the major I'm leaving immediately. Wait till I arrive before taking action."

The key chattered. Ike listened, then sent, then listened again. "He says he will tell the major . . . wait, there's more." He listened again, then gave a whoop. "It's no hoax, Starr. It's real. He says *Bucky says bring Socks!*"

Every driver in the room, every driver on the division, every tender in the vicinity, knew that Socks was the horse I had given Bucky in Denver. She had pounded into the ear of everybody passing within sound of her voice how superior he was to the horses they drove or tended. Socks was the most beautiful horse in the world. Socks could outrun anything on the line. Socks could outpull anything on the line. Socks was perfect . . . the one, the only perfect horse ever bred. And they could see for themselves when she brought him to the station.

The boys shouted and laughed and pounded each other and the station agent said, "God, she's been telling them damned Sioux all about Socks . . . riding around on their crowbait she's been bragging on her own horse all the time! The kid's game. Don't that sound just like her? Bring Socks! I'll bet she's been bossing the whole danged tribe around!"

I motioned to Ike to sign off and walked out, so blinded by tears it made no difference that the night was dark. I couldn't see anyway. She was all right. She was bound to be all right. She couldn't have thought of anything to tell us she was all right better than those two words, bring Socks. Still imperious, still impudent, still Bucky . . . unbroken, and it had to be, unharmed. Bring Socks.

I went out to the stables and shook and cried a little and blew my nose and remembered and laughed and went a little crazy . . . nobody but the horses to know. Then I grabbed the brushes and combed and brushed down every horse in the barn to work off my excitement. They didn't mind and it did me a lot of good.

Ed wanted to go with me. Emma wanted to go, at least as far as Denver. But the baby had a cold and he was cutting his first teeth and in the end she was afraid to risk the journey with him. "It's cruel," she said, wiping her eyes, "it's so cruel having to decide between them . . . to have to think of this one now. . . ."

"I'll bring them straight home," I promised. "It won't be much longer."

I persuaded Ed to stay on the job. He finally agreed. "You and your father are the best ones to take care of it. I don't know as I could do a thing, except ease my own mind," he said.

"I'll telegraph you at once," I said.

Three days later I was in Denver. I expected that my father would want to go on up to Halleck with me, but I found him laid up with a broken ankle. He had slipped at the head of the stairs and fallen. "And a wonder I didn't break my neck," he said. "I slid, bumped, rolled and tumbled down every damned one of those seventeen steps in the whole stairway."

"All because he wouldn't take time to light a lamp," my mother said.

"What was your hurry?" I said.

"Oh, somebody was pounding on the door," he said. "Mahaley usually has a night lamp burning in the hall up there, but it had gone out. I was hurrying. Pulling up my galluses. Missed the first step, then missed all the rest of them."

He was sorry he couldn't go with me. "You remember," he told me, "they've got you over the barrel. Pay whatever they ask and don't fool around about it. They'll want provisions, maybe some guns and ammunition, some whisky. Just make a requisition for whatever you need on the sutler's store. What's the size of the band?"

"There weren't more than a dozen who drifted around with old Slewfoot, but I expect they've rejoined the larger band by now."

"Yes," he said. "They'll want enough for the whole band."

"Whatever it takes," I said.

There wasn't any question about that. My father had not

needed to remind me. I didn't intend to dicker long. I just wanted to get the two girls back.

To be on the safe side, and in case the army balked at it, I bought a dozen guns and two kegs of powder and a couple of kegs of whisky. With two passengers, they rode inside the stage and arrived with me at Halleck three days later. I hired a man down at the Elephant Yard to ride Bucky's horse along behind, in easier stages.

I had telegraphed ahead and Sam Burke met me. He was about my own age, about my own height, his eyes level with mine and looking levelly into mine as he talked. He weighed more than I did, was built more husky. He was a fine-looking man in a rugged, solid, strong way. He had straw-colored hair and gray eyes. My father had told me that he looked a lot like his grandfather, Stephen Burke, who had been English.

Sam and Fanny lived in one fairly good-sized room in the officers' barracks. Fanny had done what all young army wives do immediately to their quarters—tried to make it a home. She had put down some rugs and put up some curtains and she had made a little kitchen in an alcove. She had a good meal ready and we ate and then talked. I was pleased to see that Sam was a pipe man, too.

He said there had been no further word. He answered all my questions. The rancher lived about five miles from the post and he had been there a couple of years. He had the reputation of being a good man. Hard-working, young, just him and his wife yet. He was no greenhorn. He traded some with the Indians, like nearly every other rancher in the country. Had a little stock of goods on his premises, which he traded for furs and hides, mostly with Utes and Cheyennes. He disposed of his furs to the sutler at Halleck. He was friendly with the troops but he and his wife didn't hang around the stockade, took no part in the social life of the post. He was well liked and he was considered reliable and honest. His name was Frank Harker.

He had no idea why he had been picked as a go-between, and there was no reason not to believe him. He said the Indian, just one Indian, had suddenly appeared, about dusk, that night, at the barn while he was feeding and shutting up the horses. Scared the daylights out of him. But the Indian made the peace sign, then gave the message, then left. The Indian had used sign in talking with Harker. Hadn't opened his mouth except to grunt.

Harker had been so astonished he hadn't thought to ask any questions. Just stood there and watched and then made the sign that he understood. He and his wife had stayed up all night, afraid of an attack. Next day they had driven over to the post with the message. The major had sent a detail out to the ranch with them when they went home to protect them in case there was trouble. They were still out there. But there had been nothing more. And no sign of Indians in the vicinity. "As far as we've been able to learn," Sam said, "they're all divided and shifted around now. The hostiles have gone up north on the Powder River. Colonel Collins had several brushes with them up around Mud Springs. They were the ones who were between the rivers all winter and gave you all that trouble along the Platte. Just between us, there's a rumor that General Connor expects to lead a big expedition up in that country and hunt them down."

I said it had better be a big one.

"It will be," Sam said. "I guess you know there have been some fifteen hundred so-called friendlies up around Laramie all winter. Mixed bunch of Sioux, Cheyennes and Arapahoes. They claim they took no part in the raids. Say they're all friendlies and want peace. There's considerable doubt about that among the old hands at Laramie, but the government has let them camp there and has fed them all winter."

"Which is exactly what they wanted," I said.

"Probably." He grinned. "General Dodge ordered a company of scouts to be organized from among them. The idea was to get a little good out of them, since we were feeding 'em."

I laughed. "He ought to know better."

"You ought to see them," Sam said. "I was up there not long ago on special duty and Colonel Moonlight reviewed them. They'd all been issued uniforms, but it was hard to tell it. Not more than half a dozen wore the full uniform. Some fancied the hat and that was all. Some liked the coats but not the pants." He puffed on his pipe. "I tell you, Starr, an army jacket don't look very impressive over a breechclout."

I chuckled. "About the only thing that goes well with a breechclout is a tomahawk."

"Yes. Well they were pretty ragtag and bobtailed."

"As soldiers they won't amount to much. As scouts, they'll warn the hostiles of every move the army makes," I said.

"Well, we're stuck with them. And that's the disposition of the tribes as far as we know. Of course, little bands are always moving around and raiding here and there. The band that has your girls can't be very far from here right now. Probably in the Medicine Bows, but they haven't been there long. We've had the usual details out all winter. There's been no sign of Indians in this immediate vicinity."

"I would guess," I said, "they've just come into the area. Probably only a few days before they got in touch with Harker."

Though it was idle to speculate where they had spent the winter, we did turn it over a few times, then gave it up. The only important thing now was that they had made their move. We had to wait until they followed up on it.

Later in the evening I paid my respects to the commandant. He told me that he and his men would cooperate in every way they could. "The release of your womenfolk comes first with us. We will agree to any terms you have to make . . . until we get those girls back. Then we intend to punish the rascals, hard and fast."

"Yes, sir," I said, "but for the time being all we can do is wait. When we know more, plans can be made."

We had one week of waiting. I expected it and was prepared for an even longer wait. There had to be time for the Indians to learn I was at Halleck and go through all the rigmarole of making a decision as to how to proceed. They made their next move on April 18, and they made it through the rancher, Frank Harker, again.

It was plain he didn't like being the intermediary and was puzzled a little as to why they had picked him. "You ever do any trading with the Sioux?" I said.

"Some," he said. "They get over in here sometimes."

344

"Likely," I said, "these people have traded with you a little. But my guess is they've picked you to talk with because you're close to the fort, but not too close. And there's enough broken ground around your place they can approach without being discovered. I'm sorry, Mr. Harker."

"Well, I want to do what's right," he said. "I'm willing to do what I can to get the women back. But I wish they hadn't picked on me. My woman is scared. And I'm scared, if I'm honest. Even with them soldiers at the ranch, I'm uneasy. They could turn on me when the troops leave and burn me out, easy."

I admitted they could, said again I was sorry he was involved, but I didn't know what we could do about it now. He told what had happened. He said six Indians had ridden down from the hills and fired their guns to get his attention. They had stopped well out from his place and waited. He and three or four troopers had ridden out, but the Indians had signed that the soldiers were to stay back. "I'm not above telling you, Mr. Fowler, that even with those soldiers covering me I was shaking all over to ride out and talk with them Indians."

"Did you recognize any of them?"

"Well, I thought one looked like a feller used to come in once in a while, but I couldn't be sure. He was a Cheyenne, if it was him. They was all wrapped plumb up to their eyes."

"All right," I said, "go on."

"Well, I rode on out and the same one that come to the barn, which never traded with me and I never seen before this commenced, come to meet me. He said what they wanted and what they'd do . . . and I wrote it down and this is the way it is. They want you to send a wagon out with . . ." he looked at a list he pulled out of his pocket, "they want three barrels of flour, one barrel of sugar, three sides of meat . . ."

"If you'll give me the list," I said, "the boys can be loading the wagon. One wagon, is that right?"

"That's what he said. One wagon. And when it gets to my place it's to be driven out to the foot of the hill there . . . the same one where I talked to them . . . and it's to be left there, hitched. Don't take the team out. Then they'll bring the women down and leave them and take the wagon."

345

Sam spoke up. "How do we know they'll keep their word? Bring the girls?"

"We don't," I said. "The whole thing may be a trick. They may not even have the girls. Or they may take the wagon and keep the girls. There's no way of knowing. But we have to try it. We have to do it the way they say."

"By God, if they don't bring the girls," Sam said, "they'll not get away. We'll be there, watching."

"No," Harker said, "they said they wouldn't bring the women if there was any soldiers. What they said was that one man was to drive the wagon out and leave it there. Just one. Then he was to go back to the ranch. And the soldiers out at the ranch have got to leave. They won't bring the women if the soldiers are there. They said they would know if you tried any tricks. They said there was a big bunch of them. Many, he said."

"They've got their gall," Sam said. "And they've sure got it worked out in detail."

"Never mind," I said, "that's the way we'll do it. I'm the man."

Though he didn't like it, the major agreed to pull his men in from the ranch and to bring Mrs. Harker with them. "Let me have Sam," I said, "in civilian clothes. Sam and I will handle it."

Harker was suddenly stubborn. "Count me in. They picked me to do the parleying, they got me in it and I'm staying in it. I've got two hired hands out there we can count on, too. They didn't say nothing about them leaving. Or me."

The plan agreed on finally was for Harker and his hands and Sam and me to make up the party. The major would have his men ready and waiting. The moment we had the girls safe, somebody would ride in to the fort and the troops would fan out. If it was a hoax, or if we had trouble, somebody would ride in and the troops would come fast to the rescue. "It's their deal till we get the girls," I said, and they agreed.

The list Harker had written down was faithfully followed. Three barrels of flour, one barrel of sugar, three sides of bacon, sixteen guns, three kegs of powder, one hundred butcher knives, ten wool blankets, six saddles and bridles, one tent tarpaulin, ten woolen shirts, three ladies' shawls, one bolt of muslin, one bolt of silk, and a multitude of small articles such as needles, salt, soda, raisins and various kinds of trinkets. At the very bottom of the list Harker had written, "horse socks." He must have wondered if he caught the right sign for that one.

"This bolt of silk," the sulter said, "I've only got one. It's China silk and it's red and black and green striped."

"The gaudier it is the better," I said. "Load it on."

"If I was to charge you Rocky Mountain prices for all this stuff," he chuckled, "this wagonload would put a hole in your pocket, Mr. Fowler."

He would make a nice profit anyhow, but he bought a lot of supplies through Fowler's in Denver, and Fowler's freighted most of the stuff he bought in the east. Even though he would make some adjustments, it was not a cheap ransom.

"There's no whisky on this list," I said to Harker when we had checked it all over again. "You forgot to put it down?"

He looked at the list. "I don't recollect of it being mentioned. I could have missed it, but I don't remember . . ."

"I'll put a keg on," I said. "They always want whisky."

"If they knock out a head straight off," the sutler said, "they'll soon be so drunk they'll be easy to catch."

I admitted I had thought of that myself.

We left the post about noon and were at Harker's ranch by two o'clock. The soldiers and Mrs. Harker left immediately for the post. Harker brought the two hands into the house and he and they and Sam disposed themselves with guns at the windows looking toward the foothills. Sam had a pair of binoculars. "I won't take my eyes off of you," he said.

Harker showed me the spot. "Out from the foot of that spur, about three hundred yards. The ground is broken between there and the hills, but they came that far out on the prairie. So you can drive the wagon just to the edge of the first gully."

It took longer than I would have thought to drive the wagon to the place. It was perhaps a mile from the ranch-house, out on the flats. But the wagon was heavily loaded and the sand was deep. I was conscious the whole time of eyes watching from the hills. It was perfect ground for cover, however, and I saw nothing to indicate the presence of even one Indian. Bucky's horse and one Harker loaned me were tied to the tail of the wagon. Bucky's would be left with the wagon.

It was a chilly day, overcast, with a cold wind blowing down from the mountains. It could start snowing any minute. But I was alternately cold and hot. I sweated, then grew cold. It was a slow, slow ride and felt endless to me.

I came up to the gully and pulled the wagon parallel to it, dropped the lines, got out and rolled the keg of whisky around to use as a makeshift hitching post, untied my horse, got on and put him into a long easy lope back to the ranch. I didn't once look back. It was done, as best we could do it. Now, we'd see whether it was a trick or not.

We watched through the glasses for a while, but it soon began to spit snow, which gradually thickened until finally we could see nothing out on the flats and had to give up the watching. It had been pretty late in the afternoon by the time I got the wagon out. Now night came on and we ate and sat around the fire, still keyed up and apprehensive, waiting, waiting, waiting.

"What do you think?" Sam said, finally.

"I think we've got some more waiting to do," I said. "They've got to haul the wagon off, and either drive it wherever they're going, or unload it onto pack horses. Then they'll give themselves a good long start ahead of the troops. Then they'll bring the girls in."

"How long?"

I shook my head. "Maybe another day or two. Enough time for the main body to get a good safe range from pursuit."

In the back of my mind was always the fear they wouldn't bring the girls in at all, now that they'd got the supplies. And I began to be haunted with the feeling that I'd been a fool to do it their way. I should have let the major throw out some troops. But it was too late, now.

We set up a guard and Harker took the first watch. Sam took the second and I was to take the last, but Sam didn't call me. When I awakened it was beginning to lighten and soon it would be daybreak. I grumbled a little because he had let me sleep, but it was a sign of my weariness and strain that I had slept so soundly once I had got off to sleep at all.

We began scanning from the windows long before it was light enough to see. There was only a skift of snow on the ground. The wind had risen during the night and the snow had stopped. Harker and his men went out to feed. Slowly the dark faded and the sky bleached and the distance we could see increased. Sam had the glasses at the right moment. "The wagon is gone," he said, and passed the binoculars to me.

It was gone. We scanned the whole arc of the foothills for any sign of it, or of the Indians. There was nothing. The flats were as empty as they had been when I drove the wagon out. "What now?" Sam said.

"We wait."

"God," he said, driving a fist into his hand, "I'm tired of this waiting. I want to be out there chasing those scoundrels!"

"So do I. Where?"

He shrugged. "You're right. We wait."

We waited three days. Then Harker came in from the barn, just after dark the evening of the third day. Believing it would be Harker they would approach again, we had made it easy for them to find him. None of us went around the barn, after the first day, but him and him alone. At daylight and again at dusk he made it a point to linger there. "Well," he said, "he's been. Same one. Said you was to come at sunup tomorrow. Same place."

"They'll bring the girls?"

"He didn't say. Said you was to come at sunup. Same place. That was all. He just sneaked in and sneaked right out again."

It was a temptation not to let Sam ride into the post and have the major fan some troops out into the foothills and set a trap for them in the morning. It would be easy to nab whoever brought the girls in. Sam urged it and I considered it. "No," I said finally, "it's too big a risk. One smell of troops and they'd break off everything. And it might be six months before they got this far again. No, as long as they've got the girls they're holding trumps. We've played the whole hand their way. Let's don't throw it away now."

I didn't sleep much that night and it was a long, long night. But it finally ended. We made coffee and Harker sent one of his men out to saddle a horse for me while I gulped down a scalding cup.

"I'm going with you," Sam said.

"No."

"You may be walking into a trap."

"I may be," I said. "We'll see."

He knew it had to be that way. "I'll be watching. If things go wrong . . ."

"If things go wrong," I said, "I'll expect you to begin moving. But wait for me to signal. Or if they seize me. But don't make a move too fast."

The horse Harker provided for me was a corky roan and he was feeling frolicky. He was eager to cut up his heels. I had to let him get some of it out of his system with a good run out on the flats before he settled down. This brought us to the rendezvous point too early, and he was still fidgety. I let him trot back and forth until he finally was willing to stand.

It wasn't long. In the west you learn to scan the horizon constantly and most often you'll catch a movement from the corner of your eyes. It happened that way now. I caught a movement up a draw between two spurs of the hills that fingered out onto the prairie. Two horses were stiff-legging it down the steep slope of the draw. Still pretty far away. Too far to tell anything about the riders except that they were blanketed against the cold. Two? Only two riders? Were they sending the girls down alone? No reason they shouldn't, I thought. No reason anybody should have to bring them. Just start them down the draw and tell them to keep going. I never took my eyes off them, watching them drop down the draw. I felt tight and dry inside.

And then a slight shift in direction faced the horses directly toward me and I saw that one of them had a blazed face. Socks! My heart lurched, seemed to stop beating for a moment, then began thumping. Many horses were blaze-faced, but as they came into a clear patch I caught a glimpse of the white stockings, then I was sure. It didn't mean Bucky was riding him, but it almost did. If they had let her send for the horse, they would let her ride him in.

Next I could tell that the rider on the blazed-face horse was smaller, sat shorter in the saddle than the other rider. The ground was less broken for a short piece and it seemed to me they approached more rapidly. A minute or two later there was no mistaking that the other rider, the taller, bigger one, was an Indian. His legs hung long and straight . . . no saddle, no stirrups. And the legs were too long to be a girl's.

Fear shook me and the bitterness rose inside me. One at a time, I thought. They were only going to turn one loose this time. They're keeping one for another wagonload of supplies. Well, I should have expected it. Why should they turn both of them loose when they could double the price by stretching it out? But which one? Which one were they turning loose now?

They dipped suddenly out of sight into a gully and were out of view for perhaps five minutes, then they rose up over the rim, nearer now. I could see that the taller figure was dark, but I couldn't make out which girl it was, Bucky or Bernie. She was too swaddled up.

Then all at once and swiftly, as if knowing she was close enough to be recognized, she threw the blanket back from her head and the sun blazed off red hair and my heart raced so hard I had to bend over to ease it, and open my mouth to breathe. My whole chest hurt with the hard pounding, but there was such a feeling of relief I felt as soft as a baby inside. All that went through my mind was thank God, thank God, thank God. Thank God they had picked Bucky to turn loose this time.

They came well out onto the flats now and the Indian picked up the pace a little, putting his horse to a trot. I waited, facing them. They could see me plainly, of course. Then Bucky raised her hand and waved it over her head. She turned toward the Indian, evidently speaking to him, then she dug her heels into the flanks of her horse and came racing toward me. I kicked the roan out to meet her.

She was laughing when we met and pulled up, her hair blown about her face. I jumped to the ground and held up my arms. She sat looking down at me, studying my face, her eyes soaking it up. They filled and spilled over. She gulped and flung her head up, brushed the tears away and laughed shakily. "You didn't blow me a Charge, Starr."

I could not speak. I could not say a word. I just held up my arms and she slid down into them.

Chapter 25

We had only a minute or two before the Indian trotted up.
Just long enough for me to feel, tight inside my arms, that
she wasn't thin. She felt round and filled out. Time enough
for me to say, quickly, "You all right?"

"All right," she said, "no harm. Not ever. None at all."

I held her so tight then that she gasped and I knew I had
hurt her. But it was the best moment of my life. No harm.
They hadn't touched her that way. For whatever reason,
they had let her alone, hadn't used her. I held her and
rocked her and felt blind and dizzy, then said the most
ridiculous thing a man could have said at such a moment. I
said, "You've grown."

"How do you know?" Her voice was muffled against my
coat.

"Your head comes just under my chin."

"How heavenly. I hope I never grow another inch."

I heard the horse trotting up. Keeping one arm around
Bucky, I swung about to face the Indian.

I wondered why I hadn't guessed. All this time, why
hadn't I guessed. It should have been so plain to me. He
should have been the first one I thought of. But too fooled
by the Sioux, I had never thought of him at all. He hadn't
once entered my mind. Gone, not seen for months, he had
ceased to exist for me. But he should have, and it had been
stupid of me to forget him. He sat there on his horse—it
was one of my own, actually, he was that arrogant—and
he looked down at me, his fine, handsome face proud and
still, his eyes as gray as cold steel.

"You are the one," I said.

"I am the one," he said, speaking English to me for the
first time.

"You. Not the Sioux."

"The Sioux captured them for me."

"Where is the other one?"

He jerked his head back toward the hills. "She is there."

"What's the delay? You want another wagonload of goods? It will take a little time. . . ."

He cut in and there was contempt on his face. "Do you think I stole them for ransom? Do you think I wanted the other one for ransom?"

And I should have known that, too. "You won't be able to keep her," I said. "You can't go far enough or hide long enough. We will find you and we will bring her back."

He shook his head. "She will not come. She does not want to come. She is my woman."

"You're lying."

He made no reply. He just sat there on his horse and looked at me. Then he pulled the horse's head around. I spoke again. "I'll cut your black heart out for this."

He made an obscene gesture, whooped, dug his heels in the horse's flanks and ran it hard all the way back to the gully. I watched him go. And I had no doubt whatever that he had spoken the truth. Bernie *was* his woman. She belonged to this half-breed, this Popo, and she did not want to come back. She had been soft on him from the first. He had fascinated her. And he was, my God, a handsome enough brute to make any woman soft on him.

She must have tried to put him out of her mind, I thought. Tried her best. She went home. But it didn't work and she had to come back. Did she knew he would steal her? Did they, maybe, plan it together? If she did, I thought, she didn't have the first idea what she was doing. She couldn't possibly. Nobody could know what living with Indians was like. As fastidious as Bernie was . . .

I turned to Bucky. She nodded. "It's true. They have been married since the week after we were captured." She took a quick, short breath and went on hurriedly. "They're very happy together, Starr. I think Bernie loves him as much . . ." she paused, then went on bravely, "as much as I love you. She's going to have a baby in June."

"So," I said, "so . . ."

I gathered her close and rocked her again and then kissed her and rockets exploded and I remembered, funny and strange, all the little smothery kisses she used to plant all over me and which had made me so impatient, and the dozen or so quick little pecks I had given her, and I wondered how love blind a man could be.

We held each other so long and so hard it was like a dream, and then, breaking apart, I caught her face and covered it with her own kind of quick, smothering kisses. "I love you. I love you. I love you."

And she swayed against me and clung. "I love you."

I forgot Sam was watching through the glasses, forgot time, forgot where we were, forgot Indians were watching from the hills. There was nothing in the world right now but Bucky Westmoreland and me, touching again, our lips, our bodies, and rockets of joy exploding.

How long I would have been out of my head, foolishly exposing us to danger, I have no idea, but I heard horses and became instantly alert. I swung about. Two riders coming out from the ranch. Sam and Harker, I guessed. And I laughed. "They've decided to bring us to our senses," I said. "We must go. We'll have all of our lives for this."

I kissed her once more and boosted her into the saddle and swung up on the roan. I rode close and we locked hands and went to meet the riders.

She wanted to know about her father and mother. I told her they were fine. "They would have come," I said, "but I was afraid Ed might queer things. And your mother couldn't come because of the baby. He's cutting teeth. She was afraid to risk a trip with him."

"He?" She was quick. "He? A boy?"

"And a big fine one. Seven months old, now."

"Seven months! Oh, my goodness, I've got to get home quick and see him. I've missed a lot of him already. What did they name him?"

"Edward Alexander."

Her hand flew to her mouth. "Oh, they did it! They did it! They gave him the name I suggested. For Papa and for Grandpa. Isn't it a nice name, though?" She squinched her eyes shut and I suspected tears, but she laughed. "I was scared to death they would name him Starr."

"What would have been wrong with that?"

"That name," she said firmly, "is for *my* baby."

Such talk is so sweet that you must prolong it, even to the point of foolishness. "The first one, or the tenth one?"

"All of them," she said. "Every one of them. Maybe a dozen more Starr Fowlers."

"How will you tell them apart? Tie strings on their fingers?"

"Silly. There'll be Ed Starr, and John Starr, and Joe Starr, and . . . and Bill Starr. . . ."

"All boys," I said. "Suppose they're not?"

She held up her hand and went on reciting. "Jane Starr, Mahaley Starr, Fanny Starr, Emma Starr. . . ."

"That's enough." I stopped her recitation with a quick hug and kiss. She was so young, so Bucky-young, and so dear. Nobody ever like her. Not ever born, nor ever would be.

We met Sam and Harker and went on to the ranch. There we heard her story. She took a cup of coffee and sat beside me on a low stool, keeping her head against my knee as she talked, keeping one hand locked in mine. We still had to touch. It wasn't enough to be in the same room, to look at each other. We had to touch, keep hands locked, keep on touching this flesh, this dear flesh.

The Sioux had captured them, yes. Old Slewfoot's band. He had ridden up to the wagons and held up his hand in the peace sign and Ed had hauled up to talk, and the band had swirled about and edged between her and Bernie and hidden them among them, and pushed them slowly away from the wagons, while old Slewfoot talked on and on. Then suddenly they had quirted the horses and run them away. And they had kept driving their horses, hard, for a long time.

But they had been with the Sioux only a week. Up on the White Earth Creek. Then Popo had come and taken them away. Ever since, they had been with his band of Utes, and finally among the Cheyennes. "Not very far from home sometimes," she said. "On Ash Creek, and over on Salt Creek, and on the Smoky Hill. Mostly between the rivers."

"Why didn't William Bent know that?" Sam said to me.

"Maybe he did," I said. "Nobody ever said where they were. All we were told was that his runners had seen them."

Bucky wanted to know about this and I told her. "We were trying to work through William Bent."

"Well," she said, "we wouldn't have known about the

runners, I guess. But sometimes we were with the band of the Bent brothers. I didn't know them, but the old woman I lived with told me who they were."

"If old man Bent knew where the girls were all the time," I said, "he had his reasons for not telling us. He wouldn't play us dirty. But I doubt he knew. If the Ute wanted it kept quiet, not even Bent's boys would have told him. Not till the right time."

"Well, the Bent boys were raiding all the time," Bucky said. "So was Popo. All the time. They took an awful lot of plunder."

"They did a good job of misleading us," I said, "going north first. For a long time I believed you were up on the Powder, with the Sioux up there."

"We have been south of the river since Popo came for us. Popo and the Bents are good friends. They are together a lot."

I watched as she talked. She had cut her hair shoulder length. It was still tangled from the wind. She was wearing a handsome buckskin dress and there were moccasins on her feet. The blanket she still kept wrapped around here was a good one, new and thick-napped, plundered no doubt from some wagon train of goods. She looked well and well fed. Her hands looked scratched and a little work-scarred. "They didn't abuse you at all?" I said.

"Oh, no," she said. "Even the Sioux were kind to us. We belonged to Popo. They stole us for him and they were just keeping us for him until he came."

"When did you learn Popo had planned it all?"

"That very first night. The same night we were captured. We were kept together in the lodge of an old woman. She told us. She said he would come soon for us . . . come get us."

"Did Bernie know it?"

"No. I'm sure she didn't. She was as scared as I was until she learned Popo was back of it. Well, you know how everybody feels about the Sioux. It's just death! I was terrified. But when I found out Popo had planned it I knew straight off he wanted Bernie. And I didn't believe he would be mean to me. He was always good to me, Starr. When he came to the store, he was nice. And he was kind when Julius Caesar died, remember?"

"Probably beginning to lay his plans right then," I said. "Go on. Suppose he hadn't wanted you at all? Suppose when he came for Bernie he'd left you with the Sioux? Didn't you think of that?"

"Well, I did. A little. We knew right away he hadn't meant for the Sioux to get me. He just wanted Bernie."

"He stole two horses," I said. "It looked as if he might have meant to steal two girls."

"He had seen Bernie ride both of those horses. He didn't know which one she liked best, so he just took both of them."

"Why did they take you, then?"

"They couldn't get us separated. When they began to edge in between us and the wagons and kept nudging us farther away, I reached over and caught Bernie's bridle and hung on, and they quit trying to get between us. They just took us both. But if Popo had left me with the Sioux, I was going to escape. Or something. And besides," she rubbed her face against my hand, "I knew you'd find me."

I turned her hand over and looked at the callouses in the palms. "I see they made you work."

"Oh, yes. All the women work. I didn't mind. I'd have lost my mind just sitting around. Especially after Bernie was with Popo. But I tell you one thing, Starr. I don't ever intend to scrape another damned buffalo hide as long as I live! That's what made those callouses. The men had been hunting and there was the biggest pile of hides you ever saw, and the stink, and the mess. And all the women having to work on them. No, sirree. Don't you ever bring me a buffalo hide to clean!"

Everybody laughed. "I think we'll leave cleaning buffalo hides to the squaws," I said. "Bernie work, too?"

"Oh, yes. Some. But Popo is awfully good to her. He had the most beautiful lodge ready for her, Starr. It was as big as Doc's. And the skins were so white and beautiful and painted so pretty. And he had our horses for her, Starr! Our own horses he had stolen, especially. And our saddles. Oh, he'd been thinking of everything for a long time."

"I was stupid," I said. "When those horses were stolen I should have known. I should have guessed why only two were taken, with saddles. Did Bernie . . . did he make her go in his lodge?"

"I don't know." She hesitated. "I wasn't there. You see, he had his sister take charge of me. But I don't think so. That's his mother's band with him. She's dead, but there are several sisters and brothers. But they're all full bloods. He's the only half-blood. He put me with one of his sisters. And I didn't see Bernie for about a week. And then we moved to another camp, and we were with the Cheyennes now. And I was worried about Bernie, and Popo's sister told me she was with Popo and they would come soon. And they did come in a day or two, and Bernie came where I was and told me she had married Popo and was very happy with him. And I asked her if she loved him, and she said she did and she wouldn't have married him if she didn't. She said she had loved him for a long, long time. So I don't think he *made* her. I think she wanted to marry him. And she told me that as soon as the raids stopped Popo would send me home."

"She didn't say she wouldn't be sent home with you?"

"She didn't have to. She didn't want to come home. He told you the truth, Starr. Nothing would make her leave him now. I've seen them together. Ever since then we were always in the same camp. They love each other. But when we moved down here in the Medicine Bows and it was time for me to leave, she came to see me again and she said then she was going to stay with him." She put her free hand over her mouth and giggled. "She was so big with that baby that she waddled like a duck. You wouldn't believe Bernie could get that big. There must be two babies."

Sam chuckled.

"Bucky . . . !"

"Oh, fiddlesticks. I wish we could say things plain out, like the Indians. They talk about anything."

"Yes," I said, "I imagine you've had quite an education."

"Well," she said, "Popo's sister is married, you know. And I was in the same lodge with . . ."

"For God's sake, Bucky!"

"I do believe you're blushing," she teased. "Well. Anyhow, Bernie told me then that since Popo couldn't be white, she was going to be Indian."

"That may get pretty old," I said. "It's not much of a bargain for a white woman."

"Oh, I told her that. I said she might get homesick and wish she was back. She said she wouldn't. Said she didn't have anything to be homesick for, now. She said what his life was, she wanted her life to be."

Sam exploded. "My God, how can she be such a fool? What does she think of all this raiding and killing and plundering?"

"She thinks the Indians are just getting back a little of what's been taken from them," Bucky said quickly. "I can tell you that because I heard her say so. She's on their side ... the Indians' side."

"He's a half-breed," I said to Sam, "and she's a half-missionary."

"Lord, what a combination. Wonder who'll finally convert who? What's she going to do when he takes two or three more wives?"

Bucky twisted around and looked up at me. "He won't do that, will he, Starr?"

"Well, he had one already," I said. "What did he do with her?"

Bucky shrugged. "I never saw her. I'd forgotten about her. Well," her head went up and down vigorously, "Bernie won't like that a bit, and I'll bet she won't let him."

Sam looked at me over her head and shot his eyebrows up.

"You still like Popo?" I said to Bucky.

"Not as much as I did," she said. "He didn't have any business stealing us. And I told him so."

"How else was he going to get Bernie?"

"Why, my goodness, Starr, he could have just marched right up and asked her to marry him. Like a white man. She would have."

"But he isn't a white man. That isn't the way Indians do it."

"He's half white."

"And raised wild. All his ways are Indian."

Sam motioned to me.

"Bucky," I said, "the commandant at Fort Halleck will want to ask you some questions. Would you mind?"

360

"What for?"

"He will have to send the troops out to try to find Bernie. He can't leave a white woman in captivity."

"Even if she doesn't want to come back?"

"Even then. She may have changed her mind. She must have a chance to come back."

She shook her head. "He'll be wasting his time. Nobody can find Popo if he doesn't want them to."

"Did he give any hint of where he was going from here?" Sam put in.

She looked pityingly at him. "He wouldn't be so stupid. He never told anybody, anytime, what the plans were . . . where we were going. He and the Bent brothers decided things. We just went when he said so. Sometimes the women recognized places and knew where we were going, but sometimes they wouldn't know till we got there. He's clever."

"They all are," I said, "but the major will have to try to find him."

At the fort, Fanny took Bucky in hand, weeping over her, laughing with her, hugging and patting her. While Bucky had a bath and Fanny found her some clothes, I went to send a telegram to Ed and Emma, and to my parents. I had trouble with the telegram to Ed and Emma. How could I tell her that Bernie hadn't been released? I finally said that we had Bucky back, that Bernie was safe and well, and that I would give them the details when we got home.

We went to the major's quarters and he questioned Bucky for an hour. As best she could remember, she told him every place they had camped. He wrote them down— Bunch Timbers, the Solomon, the Republican, the Three Buttes, Cherry Creek. "We were there," she said, "with a big, big encampment. Sioux and Arapahoes and Kiowas and Comanches and Cheyennes. That was when they all smoked the pipe and planned to attack Julesburg. And then all the warriors left and all the young women went along with extra horses. . . ."

"Did you go?" I asked.

"No. Popo made Bernie and me stay in the camp with the old people and children. But when they came back, they had the most plunder of all. I thought they must have taken everything that was in the stores. You never saw so much stuff. Some of it they didn't know what to do with. Some of the canned stuff. The Bent brothers were in that camp and the Indians would take the canned stuff over for them to tell what it was. Canned oysters and fruit and tomatoes, they never saw before. They feasted and feasted.

"And they wasted what they didn't like. Just poured it out. And they didn't know what to do with the bolts of silk. They made a game with them. They'd get on their horses and start unwinding it, letting it fly in the wind."

"Silk," I said remembering, "a bolt of silk was on Popo's list. That was for Bernie, wasn't it?"

"I don't know," she said.

But you could always tell when Bucky was lying. She couldn't look you straight in the eye and lie to save her life. She wouldn't look at me, now. She knows, I thought. But she's been told not to tell. Bernie must be missing her pretty silk dresses already, I thought.

The major pored over the names of the creeks and rivers Bucky had given him. "There is no doubt," he said, "this Ute has been on all the big raids. He's been in the right spot every time. Where Duke and his family were killed. At Julesburg. At Plum Creek. At Aylette's, where nine were killed. All women and children."

Bucky looked at me. I had to nod my head. He was as much a renegade as the Bents. He was as savage as they. He hated the whites as much, and with as much reason. He was a half-breed. He could never wholly have either world. He could never be a whole person.

The major struck the paper with his hand. "Very well. We will find him. He is dangerous and we will hunt him down until we find him. You've been most helpful, Miss Westmoreland. Thank you very much."

Bucky was subdued, thoughtful, a little sad looking as we told Fanny and Sam good-bye and boarded the stage to Denver. "I didn't know they had killed all those people, Starr. Of course, in a battle somebody always gets killed."

"These weren't battles," I said, "these were raids and people, women and children, were murdered."

She flashed back, "Like at Sand Creek. They will mourn for that a hundred years, Starr."

"You heard about it, then?"

"Oh, over and over. It's all they talked about and grieved about. It was horrible."

"It's all messed up," I said. "Put it out of your mind now. There is nothing you can do about it. We'll go straight through to the ranch and you'll soon be with your folks. Don't dwell on any of it any more. It's over. Don't keep harking back to it."

"I won't." She chirked up, then, but I had to keep working at it to keep her mind off the killings for several hours. Then she seemed, of a sudden, to get hold of herself and lay it aside, and the rest of the journey into Denver she was chatty and happy and eager again.

But she didn't want to lay over, not even twenty-four hours, in Denver. She wanted to get right on home, so we made the next stage with only twenty minutes between. "I'd love to see them," she said, "all of them, but Miss Mahaley will understand, won't she?"

"She will," I said. "They know you're safe. I telegraphed them. You can visit with them later. I'll just have one of the boys take a note out to the house. You want to write it?"

She busied herself with it, but not for long. "I just sent my love and said I would write."

I was sorry she had to see the evidences of the raids all along the line. She hadn't known how bad it was. In the Indian camp she had known the men went out and came back, loaded with plunder, but she had not realized how hard they were hitting the Overland. It made her sad when we went through Julesburg. "All gone," she said, "all of it. And we used to have such good times here. Remember the dances, Starr? We used to drive all that way and dance all night and drive all the way back . . . just to be together and enjoy ourselves. Why did they have to burn it? Why didn't they just take what they wanted? They didn't have to destroy it."

"That's exactly what they mean to do. Here and everywhere else," I said. "They mean to stop the Overland, Bucky. They mean to destroy the line. They mean to stop the white people, right here and now, from building and ranching and settling . . . from crossing the land, from

363

using the telegraph, the mail, the stages, the road. And they will raid and kill and burn and plunder and destroy everything. Nothing is safe, now. No home, no stage station, no ranch, no people."

She began to cry. "But he is good to Bernie, Starr. He *is*. And he was kind to me."

"Which didn't keep him from murdering nine women and children at Aylette's. He is a savage, a hostile, and he is an enemy to all white men."

She didn't have a handkerchief so I gave her my bandanna. She blew her nose and snuggled close. "I'm all mixed up."

"It'll take a while to get unmixed, I expect," I said. "But quit crying about it. Give yourself some time. When you get home it will all come straight."

She took a breath like a little shudder. "I don't want them to catch him . . . it would make Bernie so unhappy. . . ."

"Let that play itself out the way it will. You didn't give the major any clues."

"I told him everywhere . . ."

"You told him everywhere he'd been. You didn't say a damned word about where he might be."

"Are you going to hunt for him?" She swayed away from me and looked at me directly.

"No, by God," I said. "It's in the hands of the U. S. Cavalry now. He can have her, for all of me. But if it's any comfort to you, I don't think they'll ever catch him, either. Bernie will be living with him in a skin lodge a good many years yet. Then when he gets older and lazier and decides to go on some Cheyenne reservation, she will live among the other squaws and raise her little half-breeds to be tame Indians."

"Oh," Bucky said quickly, "he wouldn't go on a Cheyenne . . ."

"Reservation?" I said. "Don't you believe he won't. He'll be as quick as the rest of them, when they get ready."

"Well, maybe. Maybe."

The third day we got home and inside of a week things were so normal again it was hard to believe Bucky had ever been away. I was driving my run, laying over at the ranch every other night, and Bucky was picking up the routine of the station life again. There was one difference. Love. We made no bones about it and Ed and Emma had no objections. "But not till she's sixteen," Emma said. "Wait to be married until she's sixteen."

"Well," Bucky said. "I've been waiting for him since I was nine years old. I suppose I can wait nine more months."

Chapter 26

There was no letup in the raids all summer, but they got it on the Denver-Salt Lake Division now. The Indians between the rivers went north into the Powder River country and along the Platte we had only an occasional raid. Up the North Platte, however, along the telegraph line which still followed the old emigrant road, the telegraph stations were hit hard again and again, along the Sweetwater, at St. Mary's, at South Pass, and then they moved down and began to raid the stage line west of Fort Halleck, at Rocky Ridge, Sage Creek, across the Bitter Creek division. For a couple of weeks the line between Halleck and Salt Lake was closed. Bob Spotswood, the division agent, refused to open the line until more troops could escort the stages. "The mail," he said, "is United States Mail. We are only the carriers. Let U. S. troops protect the United States Mail adequately and Overland stages will carry it. We can't be soldiers and mail carriers, too."

But we could be, and we often were. Along the Platte we still had a stage chased into a station from time to time, and we still lost a driver now and then.

In June, Colonel Collins of the Eleventh Ohio, at Fort Laramie, decided the big encampment of friendlies at Laramie must be moved. It was believed they were spying for the hostiles up in the mountains who were hitting the line so hard on the Salt Lake Division. The Indians agreed to be moved to the site of old Julesburg and the removal was begun. But it turned out to be as so many of the old hands had feared. They were no more friendlies than the active hostiles. They managed to get word of the removal to the hostiles and when an attack against the huge column began, they slid away like eels and rejoined their own people in the attack. There was a bitter fight at Horse

Creek and the troops counted eight casualties before it was over.

Riding in an ambulance in the Eleventh Ohio's supply train was Joe Eubank's widow and her child. They had been released in May at Fort Laramie. Since August of the year before she had been compelled to serve a Cheyenne warrior, as his servant and as his wife. It was said one of the reasons for the attack on the column was because General Connor had ordered the men who brought her in to Laramie hung. And they had been hung, in chains.

I cannot vouch for this. I was not there. But we heard that in addition to the child who had been captured with her, and which she had protected with her life, she now had a tiny baby, her child by the Cheyenne warrior.

She went back to her own people in Kansas and in time she married again. In the same circumstances, some white women refuse to return, ashamed of their condition. Some killed themselves. Mrs. Eubank, who could not deny the conditions of her captivity because of the baby, and who would not leave it with the Indians, took up her life again with courage and resolution. She married a good man and had a large family. At this writing, she is an old woman, much esteemed and loved by the people of her community.

In July, the Platte Bridge telegraph station and garrison was attacked and Colonel Collins's young son, Lieutenant Caspar Collins, was killed. The new fort built there was named Fort Caspar in his honor and the city of Casper on that site today (though spelled differently) continues to honor him.

July and August were the worst months of the summer for raids on the Overland between Denver and Salt Lake. Seventy-five men, women and children were killed along the line during those two months. Others were killed between Julesburg and Denver along the South Platte. Farther east, we had only occasional raids. But it was a disastrous summer for the Overland.

We did begin to get more troops and they were mostly regulars now. In August the Sixth West Virginia arrived at Fort Laramie, and the Twenty-first New York encamped at old Julesburg. But not a day went by that we did not hear of a new attack somewhere along the line, more drivers and more station agents and their wives killed or wounded.

We got hit as far east as Fort Kearney often enough to keep us all on edge. "These little bands raiding us along the Platte," I said, "are Bent Cheyennes. George and Charlie are with them."

"You think Popo is with them, too, don't you?" Bucky said.

"Why wouldn't he be? These little raids are just enough to keep us harassed and annoyed and to keep them in supplies. Right now nobody is being killed."

"I don't believe he's here," she said.

"I do," I said.

She just shook her head. She was pretty taut these days. And Bernie must often have been on her mind, and on Emma's. There was nothing I could do to ease their anxiety. I had my hands full driving every day, never knowing when my stage might be attacked. The whole summer became a sort of long nightmare.

The day I was chased into the ranch station with the stage stuck so full of arrows it looked like a pincushion, however, Bucky spilled over. I myself was madder than a wet hen. "So Popo's not raiding the line," I said. "Well, those were Popo's Utes that chased me. I saw them and recognized them."

Hearing me come in like thunder, Bucky had run out to make sure I wasn't hurt. She was still clinging to me. "It couldn't be," she said, "it just couldn't be. He was going to take them down into the San Juans. They were all tired of the war and homesick and they wanted to go home to the mountains and make peace. And he was going to take them. And Bernie was going . . . that bolt of silk. She wasn't satisfied with being married the Indian way. He promised her they would go to Taos and be married by the priest. He said he knew one in Taos who would marry them. That silk was for her wedding dress."

I began laughing. "Did you see the silk?"

"No."

"It was red and black and green striped. A wedding dress made out of it would look like a circus tent. It was the kind of silk a dance-hall girl likes."

Bucky started crying. "Poor Bernie. Poor, poor Bernie."

I was still too mad to feel any sympathy. "Oh, quit bawling. She made her bed, she'll just have to lie in it."

"He just can't be up here," she said, but sniffing her tears up. "You didn't see *him*, did you?"

I admitted I hadn't. "No, he wasn't with them. But they were his boys. I'd seen that bunch too many times. I'd know them anywhere. And where those boys of his are, Popo is not far away. He's their chief."

"Something happened then," Bucky said. "He *promised* Bernie."

"Yes, something happened," I said. "If he ever meant to go back to the San Juans, the savage in him got the best of him. The Utes are peaceful. They've given up. He's not ready to, yet. I want you to quit feeling sorry for that bastard, hear?"

"Oh, I don't give a damn about Popo," she said. "If it wasn't for Bernie. But what will she *do?* What will happen to her if he's killed?"

"She should have thought of that before she threw in her lot with a murdering, raiding half-breed. She'll have to take whatever happens, now. And Bernie or no Bernie, if that damned half-breed chases my stage, I'm going to kill him. With pleasure. I got one of his boys today, and I'll get *him* if he turns up. My job is to get the mail and my passengers through. Bernie's half-breed isn't going to stop me."

I turned around and started pulling the arrows out of the coach. "You want me to let him make a pincushion of *me* with these things, too?"

She came to help pull them out. She stood with a couple of them in her hands, looking at the barbs. It didn't take much imagination to see how they would plunge and tear. She shuddered. "No. When it comes to my man or Bernie's man, you know whose side I'm on."

"I'd begun to wonder," I said.

She melted against me. "Never. Never. But it's because I love you so much that I know how she feels . . . and how she'll feel if he's killed. She'll just have to bear it if anything happens to him, as I'll have to bear it if anything happens to you. But don't you let it. Don't you let anything happen to you!" She gave me a hard, choking hug and a lot of her old smothery kisses. "Don't you let it."

There would never be a time in our lives when Bucky and I didn't occasionally storm at each other. Both of us were stormy people. But it was always like a rage in your own blood, we were so woven together. And in the end the temper that flared in one and spread to the other blew itself out in the long, common, imperishable bond between us.

It was one week later that I brought the westbound into the ranch and threw down the lines and walked into the station and Ed met me and said, "You'll have to double on to Alkali Lake."

"The hell I will," I said. "I don't feel like doubling today. What's the matter with Newton? Drunk?"

"He was helping on the barn. Fell off the roof and concussed himself. He's not very clear in the head yet."

I swore. Brownie and Dickson had begun building a new barn. Ed, the drivers, and anybody else around the station lent a hand when they had time. Newton had had an hour he felt like donating. If he had been drunk I would have roused him out, doused him with cold water till he could hold the lines and made him take his stage. But obviously, with a concussion, he was going to have to lie up awhile.

I climbed back up on the box and we departed. This was a twenty-five-mile stage through alkali dust and deep sand. It was a mean stage. I cussed Newton the first mile, cussed the team the next mile, cussed the Overland the third mile, but did what every good Overland driver did, drove the double. I had three passengers, all men, riding inside, and Pete Rogers, the messenger, on the box with me.

Five miles west of the ranch we approached O'Fallon's Bluffs and ran along the rim of the canyon a mile and a half before we angled down to cross it. This was not the Devil's Dive. That was farther on, and we had long since been going around that part of the canyon because it pinched out and it was possible to build a road around its head. Here at O'Fallon's Bluffs it was not possible. The canyon, at one of its deepest points, had to be crossed.

The road was steep but not straight down. It wound down the near side, then ran along the smooth bottom for the canyon for half a mile before it climbed out the other side. From the day the first stagecoach drove over this road the floor of that canyon was a place every driver liked to cover fast and put behind him. There were a dozen good places for an ambush in that half a mile. The walls of the canyon were red dobe dirt, riven apart and eroded by the long centuries of time. The dobe had bonded and hardened to the consistency of rock, and from time to time huge masses had fallen and piled and jumbled, jutting out like abutments into the canyon. Behind any one of them a good-sized band of Indians could lay in hiding.

We began the long angling descent about an hour and a quarter out of the ranch and I took it fast. We all did. We reached the bottom and swung slightly right and leveled out. The run along the floor of the canyon was not true straight. There were four slight swings, right and left around the jutting masses of dobe. Vision was good only from one swing to the next, perhaps two, three hundred yards.

I had the team in a very fast road gait, bowling along nicely, when we swung slight left around the first buttress. The messenger suddenly stiffened and swung up his gun. "God, Starr! Look!"

He fired almost instantly.

The road was blocked at the next abutment, where it narrowed and swung right, by a double line of Indians who were already potshotting at us. Beyond the line of warriors blocking the road, the canyon was boiling with women, children and old people scrambling to safety. They were clambering to get up into the pockets on the walls of the canyon, behind broken dobe masses, anywhere at all they could find cover. The women were screeching at children, and grabbing at them, and the old men were hurrying them along.

I knew instantly what had happened. Only the day before we had had a change in schedule. The Indians hadn't yet caught the change. We had come along earlier than they had expected the stage. They had been expecting to cross the canyon between stages. Warriors would not have risked their women and children and old people on the floor of this canyon if an ambush had been planned. We had just had the bad luck to come along too soon, when they least expected us. The warriors had thrown themselves hastily across the road when they heard us approaching.

The mind works so fast at such a time you don't really know how you arrive at a decision. Perhaps you don't. Perhaps you act automatically. I don't recall deciding to haul up and swing the stage across the road because there were too many Indians to run through, and if we made it through, the long climb out when they could be sure to overtake us. My foot simply went to the brake, hard, and I began hauling up. I could get only a quarter angle because of the narrowness of the road, but it was good enough. The passengers piled out on the back side. Pete and I spilled down and with all five of us shoving we overturned the stage. We had a snug little fort, now, with the canyon walls behind us and the overturned stage in front. Pete and the passengers found places and started pumping away at the Indians.

The team was fours, and already the off leader and wheeler, on the unprotected side, had been hit. I cut the orders out and led them behind a buttress. Then I ran back to join the men.

The canyon walls made the shots echo and reverberate, and magnified the sounds until you'd have believed cannon was firing down on the floor. It was loud and thundery, and the Indians were whooping and yelling and potshotting at us, arrows were zinging all around, their horses were plunging about, the women and children were screaming, and all together it sounded like hell had busted loose. Which it had.

One of the passengers, an old bullwhacker named Andy Lewis, was lying next to me. He said, "They're going to charge us. They're trying to form up."

"Lying the way we are," I said, raising my voice to be heard, "everybody pick him a man from left to right. If they charge, pick off the front ones first. Hold dead center on your man till they get halfway, then fire and make it good." It might have been my father, calmly instructing us boys. "Then begin picking off the next ones." The first, the second, the fourth time the wagon train had had to corral up and fight off Indians, he had said exactly the same thing. Hold dead center, wait, then make it good.

The Indians had milled around and got into a reasonable formation. One warrior, who seemed to be the leader, carried a big shield and was out in front exhorting, shaking his spear and shouting. They formed down the road behind him. "I'll take that leader," I said.

The passengers were cool. All of them were men who made this trip several times a year. This was not their first

Indian fight. And we had a good position. We had five guns, seven with my shotgun and Pete's, and enough ammunition if we didn't waste it. It might take several hours and we might have to repel several charges, but I didn't think so. This was no ambush. It surprised me they meant to make a charge. They could have held us up till their people got hidden, and held us up till night and they could get away, by taking cover and sniping at us. But it was a sizable band of warriors. The leader must have believed they could butcher us and take some loot—horses, express, guns, ammunition, clothing.

They came into the charge with all their usual whooping, screeching, noisy fanfare. To a man new in the west it would have been terrifying. It was meant to be. Their first strategy, always, was to unnerve. All our guns went silent as every man picked a warrior in the first line and held his fire.

They came on, fast, and as they reached the halfway point I suddenly knew who the leader was. And I was not surprised. As if I had known all along it would be Popo, there was time for only the quick surging thought that this was the place, the time, the meeting, that had to be. And he was not as clever as I had believed him. It was foolish of him to make this charge. How he must have hated whites, to want to charge and storm us, tromple us under his horse's feet into the ground.

I aimed at his chest. It made a broad target. I squeezed the trigger and saw the shot jolt home, then squeezed again. He began falling with the second shot, slowly at first, just a long sway to one side from which he could not recover. Then he went tumbling down and there was a wild melee as the riders behind tried to avoid trampling his body. We pumped lead into them relentlessly and the whole leading line of men went down. We began picking off others in the same measured way. They surged up and boiled around in front of the stage.

The place grew thick with smoke, and the screeches of the men, and the wild screams of the horses hit, bounced off the canyon walls and echoed back and forth in a queer, ghastly, broken way, and there was a strong, heavy smell of cordite and hot blood. The riderless horses were wild with the smell, milling about, trying to break free and get away.

One loses the sense of time. It seemed to go on for hours, but it was actually less than five full minutes before they broke and fled. One of the passengers, taking a last shot, said, "They'll be back. Soon as they form up again."

"I don't think so," I said. "This wasn't an ambush. Their leader stirred them up into this, and he's down. I think they'll hole up now and wait till night to get away. They've got their people with them."

"Let's go get the bastards!" Pete Rogers said.

"You lost your mind?" I said. "They'll be holed up in the pockets. They could pick us off one at a time."

"What are we gonna do? Sit here?"

"That's exactly what we're going to do. For the next hour or two, anyway. See if maybe they do decide to fight some more. I don't think they will, but they might."

"How many did we get?" somebody said.

"Eight," Pete said.

"How many was there to start with?"

"About forty," I said.

"Well, that's not a bad day's work," the passenger said. "What were they? Cheyennes?"

"Mostly," I said.

We checked around for injuries. One passenger had been nicked in the shoulder, but it was just a crease. We tore a shirt up and bandaged him. Another had a hole in his hat. That was all. Of course, we had lost two horses. The roof of the stage was riddled, but the mail and the passengers were safe and the stage would roll again.

An hour went by, then another, and shadows began to creep across the floor of the canyon. "Let's move," one of the passengers said.

"We'd better wait till dark," I said.

"Hell, I'm tired of waiting. Let's try it."

"Anybody want any souvenirs?" Pete Rogers said. "I'm going to get me that big fancy shield that chief was carrying."

"Pete!" I shouted, too late. He had already darted out.

There was one reverberating shot and Pete Rogers went down. He hadn't gotten more than halfway to the big fancy shield.

"The fool," Andy said, "the poor sonuvabitching fool. Well, now we know. Anybody else got any notions of going some place right now?"

Nobody had.

It wasn't long to wait, an hour, hour and a half maybe. It grew cold as the dark came on. One of the passengers had some food in his satchel and he rummaged it out and shared the bread and cheese around, and a nip from his bottle. We weren't uncomfortable.

When it was full dark, we made ready to leave. I had no intention of leaving the mail in the coach for the Indians to ransack when they came back for their dead. The men helped and we stuffed it in crevices and crannies in the canyon walls. Then we dragged Pete's body behind the stage. Andy said, "We gonna bury him here?"

I thought about it and said, "No. Let's take him back to the station with us. I don't like to leave him down in this hellhole."

"Where'd you put the horses?" Andy said. "I'll go get them."

I told him. The other two men drifted back up the road to help him. I was standing there thinking how unnecessary it had been for Pete to die. Foolishness. Plain foolishness. It was very still, now, in the canyon. As quiet as a tomb. But something had moved. Made a sound. I froze to listen, uncertain. I heard it plainly then, something between a moan and a groan. One of those dead Indians wasn't dead. To this day I don't know why I did it. It didn't make much sense. He would die before morning, why bother? But I moved toward the sound with some vague idea of putting him out of his misery. You do as much for a horse, or a dog.

It was dark under the cliffs but in the middle of the road the starshine was light enough for good vision. I kept to the overhang, in the dark, slipping along and listening closely to locate the sound when it came again. I heard it again, and stopped, and then a figure, a woman, crept out of the dark on the other side of the canyon and ran swiftly toward the dead warriors, making little moaning sounds as she ran. She darted from one dead warrior to another, until she reached Popo. Then she flung herself down onto her knees beside him and gathered his head in her arms. An

Indian woman would have wailed so loud the cliffs would have rung with the sounds. Bernie's grief was quiet. She rocked the head against her breast and sobbed, and tried to stifle the sobs.

I went to her. "Bernie."

She was on her feet instantly, backing away . . . backing away, her hands flying to her mouth and her breath coming in short, quick gasps.

"Bernie," I said again.

Her hands dropped. "I might have known it would be you."

"Yes."

She made a little hissing sound. "You killed him! You fired the shot!"

"Yes."

"Murderer! Murderer!" She went down on her knees beside him again, touching him here and there, on the face, on the hands, straightening his shirt, stooping and choking back her sobs. "You are the savage. You are the savage."

I stood there, and Bernie sobbed while her hands wandered.

"Come home, now," I said. "He is dead. Come back to your own people."

Her head went down on his chest. "His people are my people. I have his son. I will rear him to be a Ute."

It grated. "Then you better get him off this road or you won't rear him at all. And the day may come when you wish you hadn't reared him. You better pray he don't grow up like this one, and end the way he's done."

She shoved up and drew her head back, just like an Indian or a snake, and spat a full mouthful of spittle in my face. "You fool! You blind crazy fool! He was your brother! Your father was his father!" Then she ran, down the road, into the dark.

Chapter 27

I had not known it, I swear. Not once had such a thing entered my mind. Not once had I ever thought, he is half-Ute and my father had a Ute woman in his youth. Not once. Dozens of mountain men had had Ute women, and Cheyenne women, and Shoshoni women, and Crows and Sioux. And they had bred many half-breed sons. The mountains were full of their half-breed sons. Every band of Indians had a few. There was no reason at all why I should have wondered, or suspected, or questioned. I could have guessed that there might be some half-breed children of my father's in some Indian village in the mountains. But it would have been only a guess. He had never indicated there were, or that there weren't. Nor had any other man. No man had ever, in my hearing, joked my father about Indian bastards. No, I hadn't known.

But I swear also that I felt no surprise, or shock, or disbelief. As if I had known, all the time, in some secret corner of my being that no more than William Bent could he escape his debts, I simply felt that this, this too, was a necessity, had been fated and ordained, was meant to be.

Brothers, but never brothers, and brothers pitted against each other, and their fathers, the harvest of the careless seed so carelessly sown. Half this man's blood the same as mine, the other half wild and savage and desperate and hating and blood-lusting for his unobtainable heritage.

My father made it a necessity when he bred him onto the Ute woman, and I was the instrument of the necessity. Blind chance had thrown him onto the plains, had taken him out of the mountains, a renegade from his own people, and blind chance had thrown me into his path. The two chances had collided, and necessity had been served. That was how I felt, accepting, not blaming, and there was no guilt at all. I stood there beside his dead body and wiped the spittle from my face.

Nor did I blame Bernie. She was a misfit anywhere. She would be miserable anywhere, and she would be as well off nursing her hate with the Utes as with the whites.

The men came back with the horses and we tied Pete's body on one and went winding slowly up the road out of the canyon. At the top, I said maybe I ought to take the other horse and made a fast ride to the station. "Just mosey along the road," I said, "and I'll bring a wagon out for you."

"Mosey is exactly what I mean to do," one of the men said. "My feet are hurting me already."

As I rode alone to the ranch I determined what I must do. I must keep my mouth shut. I must say nothing to Bucky or the Westmorelands about Popo, or about the short meeting with Bernie. It would only cause them grief. Inside of an hour or two the bodies of the dead Indians would be gone. Their people would come for them. Nobody would ever know the identity of those killed. The news would go out that the stage had been waylaid at O'Fallon's Bluffs by a band of Cheyennes and that eight of them had been killed. That was all anybody needed to know.

My father would never know his son had been killed. Nobody in the west, nobody anywhere except among his mother's people, and maybe my father, knew he had a half-breed son. If my father knew he had a half-breed son, I did not for one minute believe he had kept in touch with him. He would have had the strength not to. I remembered his words those years before: "They are far better off left alone."

But the mother hadn't left it alone. Bucky had said she was dead. When had she told the boy, I wondered. And why? Had she so loved my father that she wanted the boy to know who he was? Or had she so hated him that she had spewed the hate in the boy? Or had she simply, indifferently, answered his pestering questions? It would never be known.

What wisdom I had, what kindness toward my father, must keep him from learning that the necessity fated in his young careless days had come round full circle. And I

378

never loved my father more than at that moment. I felt tender and soft and gentle and unblaming and loving toward him, and fiercely determined that he should not suffer one moment of the kind of anguish William Bent suffered.

But I tell you the simon-pure truth and one thing more. I felt suddenly old. Old and wise and shorn of innocence. As if I were the father and my father were the son. And I knew I would not ever again be a young green kid standing in awe of his father's wisdom, running to him for counsel and for help. I had my own wisdom now—less than the god who made man and when he made him made sin, but more compassionate, perhaps, and not requiring atonement, the age and the wisdom and the shorn innocence equal to their need.

Chapter 28

The year of 1866 brought several momentous events.

First, Bucky was sixteen in February. In May, we were married. In my father's house in Denver. Everybody was there. Ed and Emma came for it. My brothers and their wives were there. Fanny and Sam came. My best friends among the drivers came. And the house was full and crowded.

The day was beautiful, blue and gold and diamonds. The air was crackling, the sun was dazzling, the old snowtops on the mountains were brilliant. The minister of the Episcopal church married us in the parlor, which my mother and the girls had made beautiful with green plants, flowers and much beeswax and polish. I was scared and felt very solemn. Bucky was scared and said she felt very solemn too. But happy, she insisted. Never more happy.

I was happy, also, but all the spit and polish and ceremony and my stiff collar and the new black suit and my hair slicked down had me in a straightjacket. I would much rather have jumped over the broomstick, or bought Bucky with ten horses the way the Indians did.

Fanny played a wedding march on the piano, and as Bucky and I walked in to where the minister stood I thought my knees would buckle under me. We faced him and joined hands the way he had told us to do. He began the ritual. Sweat was trickling down my body under that hot black suit and tickling my ribs. The long intoned service of admonition and injunction went on and on.

Bucky was very lovely for our wedding. She wore white. I don't know what the material was—satin, I think. But she and the girls had worked on it for a month, making it all by hand, putting lace here and there, and little ruffles and tucks and beads and what not. I wasn't allowed to see it until the wedding day, but often there was a great scurrying when I came unexpectedly into the house to hide it out of my sight.

She came on to Denver shortly after her birthday to get ready for the wedding. I was busy building a house. We were going to live in Denver. I sold the ranch to Brownie and Dickson. It did not unsettle Ed and Emma. They worked for the Company and could stay or go as they and the Company pleased.

Both Bucky and I liked Denver and had no trouble deciding it was where we wanted to live. There was a vitality in Denver, a wicked, wealthy, wanton wine of life like no other place I ever knew. Until it was laid over with too much society and culture and civilization, it was a bold and exciting place to live. I meant to drive one of the runs into and out of the city for the rest of my time. As long as Ed and Emma stayed on the Platte we would have ties there, but as far as I was concerned, the Platte and the plains were part of the past. I had, myself, come home to the mountains.

I had two weeks off for a honeymoon, which we intended to spend at the log house my father had built on the ranch up in South Park. The Company sent us on our way in a special stage, which the boys plastered with big new-married signs. We had the usual buckets of rice and confetti showered on us and we jangled off with tin cans and old shoes tied to every wheel. It was quite a send-off and the street, for a block down from the house, was lined with people waving at us and calling to us and wishing us well.

The Company had given us a six-horse hitch, the beautiful matched team of creams. I was deliriously happy with Bucky inside the coach, but my fingers did itch to be holding the lines on the creams. Of course she knew it. And of course, one mile out of town, we put Bill Trotter inside and Bucky and I climbed to the box. This, now, was all I wanted of heaven.

When we came back to Denver two weeks later, the seed of our first child was already planted, a male seed who was to be our son, Ed Starr. He was the first of seven children. I had given no more thought to the sweet foolishness exchanged on the day Bucky came back from the Indians, but Bucky had evidently settled it in her mind many years before. Each child of ours has his own name, but he is also a Starr.

Except for the curtains, and two rugs which had not yet arrived, our house had been ready for us when we were married. While we were up in the Park, these things came and my mother and the girls hung the curtains and laid the carpets so that all was in order, clean and shining, and waiting for us.

It took a while for me to get housebroke, but it was accomplished in time. I was proud of Bucky, proud of our home and proud that the boys were always welcome there. Bucky never lost her fierce pride in stagefaring men, and she never quit being part of the brotherhood. She was my wife, but she was also Bucky Westmoreland who had lived on the Platte, who had been a Company brat, and who had driven a team being chased by the Indians. Women like Bucky don't need trappings. Their grace is an inner grace, lovely, easy and sturdy. I need never have feared it might be educated out of her.

There was a new excitement all that year of 1866, too. Once the Civil War was over the railroad west became a concern of primary interest and importance. For years the line of battle about it had been drawn in Congress, neither the north nor the south willing to give ground on it. But that was over now, and construction began. All year the Union Pacific was pushing farther and farther west, and by late summer the rails reached Fort Kearney and Fort Kearney became the eastern terminus of the mail and stage line.

From California the Central Pacific was pushing over the Sierras to meet the Union Pacific line. Progress over the Sierras was so slow, however, and there were so many problems of mountains and deep snows and canyons to overcome, that the prediction everywhere was that it would be at least ten years before the Central could complete its end of the line. The Overland had a long, long time yet to run, we told ourselves.

It was a stunning shock, therefore, when Ben Holladay suddenly and without fanfare sold out, lock, stock and barrel, to Wells, Fargo & Company in November. "Why's he selling now?" was the question.

"He's shorting himself of ten good years with the Overland."

"What's his game?"

"Is he hurting for money, or does he know something we don't know?"

I believed he did and I promptly bought some stock in the Union Pacific. Ben Holladay was very close to the Administration. If there was any inside knowledge he could work to his advantage, he would. And it would pay a shrewd man to take heed of it.

Wells, Fargo didn't. They gave Ben Holladay $300,000 in stock in the company and they paid him $1,500,000 in cold cash, plus the market value of all his stores of hay and grain, and the supplies in all the warehouses, his stables and stations. It was one of the biggest deals ever made in the west.

Wells, Fargo gambled that Central Pacific would take ten years to finish their end of the line. They believed they would have that long to operate the Overland. They didn't. The last rail was laid in less than two years and Wells, Fargo was left holding the bag.

On May 10, 1869, a golden spike was driven at Promontory Point, Utah, connecting the rails from east and west. My father thought the occasion was so important that he corralled all of us boys who had helped bullwhack the Fowler trains across the plains, Matt, Dave, Pete and me, and insisted that we go with him to see the meeting of the rails. Young people never have the sense of history that older people have, but we went, to please him.

We went to Promontory Point, a short distance west of Ogden, and we watched Leland Stanford, who had pushed the Central Pacific over the Sierras, and we watched General Grenville M. Dodge, who had pushed the Union Pacific across the plains, and all the other bigwigs invited to participate in the occasion, bearded and paunchy, pompous and fatuous in their high silk hats and Prince Albert coats. I gave them their due. Their power, their drive, eastern money and influence in Washington had accomplished it. But I mostly watched my father. He was sixty-five years old now. He was not bearded or paunchy, he was not pompous or fatuous and he did not wear a high silk hat or a Prince Albert coat. He was decent in his old shabby black and he was only a little heavier than my first memories of him. His face was more lined, but it was still weathered and brown and lean, a strong, fine, handsome face. He was the most distinguished gentleman present, and maybe the only one.

And more than anyone else there he had helped open the west. He had seen it all, helped bring most of it to pass. He had seen all the wheels roll west, from Bill Sublette's creaking old supply wagons, to the huge emigrant wagons, the immense freight wagons, the light elegant stagecoaches, and now the swift iron wheels of the railroad. Wheels west, he had seen them all, and without a backward, regretful look he welcomed these new swift wheels. "Now," he said exultantly, "now just watch the west grow!"

There would be staging for many years on the short lines connecting to the railroad, but the hammers that drove the golden spike at Promontory Point drove death into the heart of transcontinental staging. The long nineteen hundred miles of the road, on which the feet of fours and sixes had drummed for ten years, was now spanned by the black parallels of iron rails. An era, an age, was over.

But we had ten years of it, ten exciting, glorious years of fine horses, fast service, good coaches, and the best driving ever done anywhere in the world. I wouldn't have missed those ten years for all the money ever minted. I had them and I still have them, stored away.

Most of the boys continued to drive for Wells, Fargo when Ben Holladay sold out, at least for a while. I did. I drove for Wells, Fargo from the winter of 1866 to the spring of 1869, then I bought some of their surplus equipment and opened my own stage line to the mining centers up in the mountains.

But I tell you frankly, the years with Wells, Fargo were not as good as those I drove for the Overland. Many people liked the Wells, Fargo line best. They felt it was a vast improvement over the old Overland. The Company bought new coaches and new horses and the service was fast, regular, predictable and reliable. But it was like the staid old age of a once glamorous girl. The men who ran Wells,

Fargo were easterners and they ran the line efficiently and reliably, but most of the color was gone, the drama, the dash, the splendor. And I tell you another thing. The rogue, Ben Holladay, was gone.

And he was a rogue, make no mistake about it. But he was part of the west, raised up in its bigness, and through the Overland he helped create the west in his own image. Something went out of it with him and his flair and his elegance and his guts and his cool rascality. He was missed, and the line was as settled as an old gray mare.

Some of the boys continued driving even after the railroad was completed and Wells, Fargo discontinued the main line. They drifted up into Montana and the Dakotas, over into Nevada and Idaho and drove for the short lines.

Bill Trotter continued driving, and Charlie Haynes drove all over the west until he finally bought a hotel at Shoshone, Idaho. Then he bought one of the old Concords and for many years he drove tourists and travelers in it out to Shoshone Falls—twenty-six miles—to see that great curtain of water sheeting down into the canyon.

Lew Hill drove, in the mountains, to the day he died. John Gilmer bought much of the Wells, Fargo surplus stock in 1869 and with a partner began operating short lines into Montana and the Dakotas. His most famous line was between Cheyenne and Deadwood, South Dakota. The Deadwood line has gone down in history.

Jim Harvard's people finally caught up with him and hauled him back to the east. It was a sad day for those of us who loved him.

My old friend Bob Hodge did a peculiar and mysterious thing. When the Union Pacific Railroad reached Fort Kearney in 1865 and notice was posted at the Atchison office that it was to be closed and all the stages and stock moved out onto a branch line, Bob threw down the lines that day and walked away. Nobody ever saw him again and to this day nobody knows where he went or what happened to him. One day he drove, the next he had disappeared. I often think of him and wish I could find him.

Both Bob Spotswood and Billy McClelland bought some of the Wells, Fargo equipment and opened a line to the mines in Colorado. But Enoch Cummings, the Virginia gentleman, threw down his lines for good in 1867 and bought a farm in Kansas. He married his lovely girl at Guittard's and raised a big family of five boys and five girls. But driving was part of him all his life and he collected a fine lot of relics of the old days which he always enjoyed showing people who visited him. Among them was his whip. Surely he never picked it up that he didn't wish, a little, that he was holding it, with that light tilt and dash he brought to every minute he was handling the reins, over the backs of sixes again.

You might like to know that while Charlie Bent died a violent death on the plains while still young, George Bent lived to a ripe old age. He went on the reservation with the Southern Cheyennes in the Indian Territory. He was always a hard drinker and he gradually became a fat and lazy and inert old man. I understand he wanted to write his memoirs, but lacked the energy to do so.

You might also like to know what happened to William Russell. That is a sad story. He lost everything he had, and he finally lost even his good name through a scandalous involvement with the embezzlement of some Indian bonds in the Department of the Interior. A friendly clerk stole $800,000 worth for him. The War began about that time, however, and neither the clerk nor William Russell was ever tried. The government absorbed the loss. But Russell was ruined. He went to New York and for years tried to make a comeback. He never did. He was finally reduced to selling a liniment called Tic Sano from door to door to make a living. When he died there wasn't so much as a line about him in the newspapers. *Sic transit gloria.*

The summer of 1866, the first summer Bucky and I were married, I was compelled to tell her and Emma and Ed about Bernie. I didn't want to. I would much have preferred not to. But the troops had given up trying to find her and it fretted Emma so much that I decided she must know that all search was futile. Bernie had chosen an irreversible way.

Bucky had never believed Bernie would come back, but Emma always had. Emma held tight to the conviction that if the soldiers could only find her, and she could talk to her, she could persuade her. So when the troops finally reported they had no clue to her whereabouts, and that to find her would be impossible, that her return could only be through an act of God or the generosity of the Indians, I knew I must tell them. I told them about Popo, about Bernie and about seeing her, about her choice. I kept back only one thing—that Popo was my father's son.

Emma grieved over her, probably for the rest of her life. She never could understand how Bernie could have chosen the man, and as for her decision to stay with his people after he was killed, it made no sense to her at all. "She has become crazed," she said, "she has lost her reason."

Bucky had a much deeper understanding, but she thought it was silly of Bernie to stay with his people after Popo was killed. "What good will that do?" she said. "Why doesn't she bring that boy back and raise him up decent and respectable?"

Things were usually black or white to Bucky, simple, straightforward and plain. She was not aware, either, of the twisted, hating streak in Bernie.

I saw Bernie once more, about the middle seventies. I was down in the San Juans putting in a line of stations. With some friends I went hunting for a week. A little party of Utes rode past our camp one evening, just before sundown. There were three men, three women and a whole passel of youngsters.

One of the women was Bernie. I did not immediately recognize her. I was watching the man she was following. He was a full blood, very dark, squalid and squat, with coarse heavy features. He was big, the way a bear is big, all chest and shoulders and arms. The blank expressionless face most Indians cultivate made him look brutish and unintelligent. He grunted something at the woman and she rode up alongside him and took a parcel he handed her. As she dropped back behind him again, I recognized her.

She was an Indian. She was dirty and coarsened and slovenly looking. Her hair was hanging loose, long and uncombed, and it was as oily and stringy as the hair of the Ute women. None of them had saddles and her legs hung down straight, dangling, bare up to the knee because of the bunching of her skirt. They were crusted over with dirt.

She wore a faded calico skirt and a dark loose blouse. The skirt was full-gathered over an advanced pregnancy. A short ragged piece of old blanket was pulled around her shoulders. There was a cradleboard on her back and a small youngster which couldn't have been much more than a year old joggled in it. Riding in front of her, among bundles and parcels, was one that may have been two, two and a half, and behind her, clutching her waistband, was another, older but still chubby with baby fat.

There, I thought, not much more than a year apart, and another one well on the way. Every year, then. Every year another one. Was that what she had wanted? Dark nights in a skin lodge and a savage to serve her? Constantly used, constantly bearing. Insatiable, year in and year out? Was that what was twisted in Bernie Buchanan? All outwardly so fastidious, so silken soft, so untouchable. But some deep darkness within requiring the fastidiousness, the silken softness, the untouchableness to be unrecognized, to be savagely ripped away? And no man of her kind able, too put off by the lady, the silken softness, too gentle, too nice? Deeply needing to be compelled, roughly, regardless, savagely, ever and ever delighting, ceaselessly needing, ceaselessly eased. I looked at the man again, the big hulk of him, the dark squat of him, and I saw him with her, again and again and again, and I was sick . . . was sick.

The child in the cradleboard began to cry, and with the ease of long habit she swung it around in front of her, opened her blouse, and with no effort to cover the exposure, she gave it the full, still milk-swollen breast which, with little rest, would so soon feed the next one.

They passed on and she did not once glance my way.

They passed on, but a good way behind them came a dozen or more children old enough to ride alone. Among them, on a rattailed pony was the one I was looking for. Much lighter than the others, a golden boy, he was . . . how old was he now? Nine, ten? He was dirty and scrawny and ragged, but he sat his horse well, and his legs were long and straight, and there was Popo in the fineness of his features, and there was my father.

For one wild moment I wished he was mine. I wished I could take him home with me. He was a Fowler, and he had a right—but the moment passed. He rode on, out of sight. They are far better left alone.

A Ute was serving us as a guide and camp servant on this hunt. "Who was the man," I asked, "the one leading?"

"He is called Gish," the Ute said.

"That was his woman?"

"Yes. They are Cochetopa Utes."

So had been my father's Ute woman. So had been his son, Popo. So, now, was his grandson, whose name I did not know.

When I threw down the lines for the last time as a regular driver, in 1869, and went into operating stage lines of my own, I took my brother, Pete, into partnership with me. Our lines branched out like tentacles until they ran into nearly every major mining area in the mountains. We ran them ahead of the railroad and connecting to the railroads for twenty years. We ran them as long as it was profitable and practicable. Then we closed out and I am in banking and railroads now.

As long as I owned a mile of stage line, I continued to drive occasionally. When we closed out, I brought one of the Concords to my stables. It is kept shined and oiled, the sandboxes filled, ready to drive. I keep, too, one good team of sixes, of beautiful, matched horses. On fine Sundays it pleases Bucky and me to load the neighbors and friends and visitors into the stage and drive out to see the country.

They are times I love, when I climb up on the box and thread those six reins through my fingers, settle my whip and nod for the boys to let the leaders go. And it is still flags flying, bugles blowing and the silvery stars shattering when those six horses settle into their brisk, spanking road gait and the sounds I love most in the world, the chuckle of the sandboxes, the creak of the leathers, the jangle of the chains, and the drum of the horses' feet on the hard road, merge together in one swinging cadence and become again the old siren song of the road.

I have had a happy life and I have been greatly blessed, but the two great gifts of my life have been the two faces of love—Bucky, and the reins. They have been more than enough.

THE STIRRING, AUTHENTIC NOVELS
OF THE BOLDSPIRITED PIONEERS
WHO BRAVED THE SAVAGE ELE-
MENTS TO FIND A NEW LIFE IN A
VIRGIN WILDERNESS

by

JANICE HOLT GILES

From Hannah, the iron-willed frontier woman, through
four generations of Fowlers, their saga is as rich as
the vast untamed land they settled—Johnny Osage, who
was made an outcast for befriending the Indians;
Savanna, twice-widowed and alone in the wild; and Joe,
who roamed the Rockies in the great westward adventure of the age—their lives interwoven, their destinies
bound up with the relentless onward march of a nation.

JHG 11-80